A Swordmaster's Tale

Cover illustration by Yura's Arts
Twitter: @yura_s_arts
Cover formatting by Izzy T.
Twitter: @systmaticwzl
Additional Editing provided by Ottercorrect Literature Service
https://www.ottercorrect.com/
Formatted by Thurston Howl
Published by Armoured Fox Press
Alberta, Canada

Print ISBN: **978-1-7751514-3-2**
Printed in Canada
First Edition Trade Paperback 2021

A Swordmaster's Tale

Edited by Tarl Hoch

Contents

Master Featherwind

Frances Pauli

The gravel path crunched beneath his soft-soled boots. Spring birds twittered in newly sprouted treetops, and a lazy breeze brought the steadfast aroma of blossoms, grass, and fresh dung.

Arne held the edge of his cloak over his short muzzle, blotting out as much of the stench as possible. He marched with a purpose in his steps, past the thatch-roofed stable, a series of mud caked hovels, and one broken-down donkey cart whose donkey had no doubt abandoned it.

He lifted his green velvet hem above the ruts and hurried his pace. They said a great hero lived at the end of this humble road. A swordsman with no master. Arne purred and brushed one spotted paw over his ears. He'd heard the stories. His free paw fell to his hilt automatically.

He was no novice with a blade himself, and still, his skill had never quite been enough. He needed more if he meant to achieve great things.

Arne needed a teacher.

Beyond the shacks, sparse pastures lined the road. A sizable manor rose to the right, fronted by a churned plot where new vegetables fought for survival amid a viper's nest of weeds and grass. Arne paused at the break in the fence. He swished his spotted tail back and forth, just above the road, and confronted the rotund posterior of a servant bent over a row of carrots.

"You there." Arne crossed his arms over his chest. "You there, is this the home of Master Featherwind?"

A snort answered him. The servant's robes, coarse and

brown either from lack of dye or a surplus of filth, bobbed along the row as if Arne hadn't spoken.

"Excuse me. Hello?"

"Hello." The voice was as coarse as the pig's garment, with a natural grunting to each syllable. "Nice day for a stroll."

"Is this the home—"

"Master Featherwind lives here. Yes." The servant stood, regarded Arne over a blunt-ended snout, and gave a snort that could have been dismissive.

Arne stood taller, threw his cloak behind his shoulders, and did his best to strike an impressive pose. "I wish an audience with Master Featherwind."

"Hrmph." The pig snorted again, and then returned to his weeding. His trotters pinched great tufts of grass, ripping it out roots and all, and flinging the clumps over the fence in a rain of soil.

"I, er." Arne dodged a clod that sailed too near his boots. "I seek Master Featherwind as a potential student."

"The master is very particular about his pupils."

Arne snorted, and the pig narrowed his eyes.

"I assure you, I am already a blade master of some skill." Arne spoke each word with pride. His shoulders drifted back, and his chin lifted enough that he could gaze straight over the swine's head. "I ask only a chance to prove my worth."

"What for?" The pig gave up his weeding and stepped to the fence, leaning a round hip against the middle rail and causing the whole affair to wobble. "If you're so good already, why come looking for the master?"

"Any man can learn." Arne smiled and uncrossed his arms, placing a hand on each hip instead. "I wish to be the best, and Master Featherwind's students are nothing if not that."

"Why?"

"What?" Arne sagged this time. The conversation had wiggled past him somehow.

"Why be the best? You're looking for fame or gold, maybe. You hope to impress some rich man's daughter. Master Featherwind is too busy to train just anyone."

"Perhaps," Arne clenched his teeth, spoke through them, "Master Featherwind should be the one to decide."

The pig harrumphed and scratched his belly. "You haven't answered the question."

"Why do I want to be the best?" It should have been obvious. Who wouldn't want to be the best at what they did? "I come from a small village. My people suffer injustice under a rich man's rule. I would see them released from cruelty, sir. And I would fight with honor for their benefit."

"A very pretty answer." A new voice spoke, and Arne knew who owned it before he turned his back on the stupid pig. There was much authority in the tone, and a pride that no mud-dwelling servant could muster.

He looked to the manor door and found an elegant figure, a person of substance and money, standing at the entrance. More than fine clothes marked him the master of this place. The hawk stood with his shoulders fixed and his feathers perfectly groomed and gleaming where they showed beneath his slashed doublet. He made a visage of silk and gold, and around his hips hung a sword belt and sheath so ornate that Arne salivated at the sight of it.

Jewels all over him. A razor beak and talons like hooked daggers tapping at his hilt.

"Master Featherwind." Arne dropped to one knee and lowered his furry head toward the soil.

"Who has come to visit us today, Wesley?"

The pig's snort echoed through the morning air. "He's a blade *master*, Master. Says he wants teaching."

"Is that so?"

The hawk strode forward, and Arne held his submissive posture. His long tail whisked over the dust, and he lifted his eyes to watch the glorious approach. Everything he'd heard about Featherwind proved true upon meeting the swordsman. He looked as sharp as his blade, moved with grace and a hint of the speed that had made him legend. When he stood two sword lengths from Arne, he stilled his feet, tilted his head sharply to one side, and flicked a wingtip to indicate that he should rise.

"Forgive Wesley's demeanor," the noble bird said. "He is but a lowly pig, and quick to judge in my defense."

"It's fine." Arne stood tall and set his chin high. "I hope that you'll consider—"

"You wish to study with me." The bird nodded, his black beak flashing in the sunlight. "I shall need to see what you're made of first."

"Of course." Arne nodded. He'd been prepare for that. No teacher worth having would take on a student without first testing his skills.

"You're a cheetah, is that correct?" Featherwind's voice snapped like the hem of his cape.

"Yes, Master." Arne placed one paw on his hilt, but executed a courteous bow. "I am that."

"Are you fast?"

The bird's eyes flashed, and Arne felt the time had come to take a small risk. He'd made it past the robust sentry, and now he needed to impress Featherwind or be sent along his way again. He put a hint of dare into his voice. "Why not find out, Master?"

Featherwind threw back his head and laughed. His beak clattered with each guffaw, and the feathers along his fine neck fluffed, made him all the thicker and more golden. "Very well, young cheetah. We shall indeed find out. Wesley!"

"Yes, Master?" The pig shuffled to Featherwind's side, bringing a cloud of filth that took the shine from the swordmaster's boots.

"Bring that cart of melons, will you?"

"My supper, Master?" Wesley hunched his back sullenly, and the great hawk turned his eyes on his servant and fluffed his feathers like a prickly crown. "Of course, Master."

"Come into the yard." Featherwind ordered.

Arne hurried through the gap in the fence, certain that he'd just passed the next barrier on his path to great things. The pig, Wesley, waddled to a shed at the back of the garden plot and retrieved a wooden cart on two wheels. It overflowed with globe melons, large and small. If that bounty was meant for the servant's dinner, Arne now understood where the creature's girth arose.

When the cart reached Master Featherwind, he raised one wing into the air and the pig stopped, huffing, and leaned over his cargo.

"Now we shall see," the hawk said, "just how fast you are with that blade."

He reached into the cart and removed a sizable green melon. Wesley whimpered, grunted, and shifted from one foot to the other while his master hefted the fruit, as if testing its weight. Featherwind's tail spread like a fan. He tossed the melon into the air and caught it with one wing.

"Draw your blade."

No sooner than the words left his beak that the master lobbed the melon straight for Arne's head. In a surge of panic, he snatched at his hilt, slid his broadsword free, and managed to bat the fruit aside, clumsily, with the flat of the blade. It fell to the dust and smashed on impact through no skill of his.

"Well." Featherwind crossed his wings and tilted his head at a sharp angle. "That was fast, but not exactly elegant."

Arne lifted the point of his sword between them. He spread his stance and fixed his gaze on the hawk, waiting for the next move. No use explaining with words. Ready or not, it was time to prove his worth.

The second missile was half as big, orange, and ripe enough to explode when Arne's blade sliced through it. The pieces rained to the ground, and before the last one hit, another globe flew from the hawk's wing. Arne stepped into it, slicing downward and easily through the rind.

Beside Featherwind, Wesley cringed and shook his head.

The master threw two at once next, smaller orbs that arched through the air toward Arne's chest. He leapt backwards, sliced upward through one and around and back down to cleave the other a second before it hit the dirt. He ended on one knee with is blade out to the side.

"Master," the pig pleaded. "What am I to eat?"

Arne leaped to his feet.

"You shall dine on the ones he misses, of course."

Featherwind's eyes fixed on Arne, and he slid his lower beak to one side, mirth flashing through his expression. There was no mistaking the dare there.

Letting a melon or two pass him by would provide the servant's nightly meal, but it would also be held against him. If he meant to impress Featherwind, and he most certainly did, the pig would go hungry this evening.

He'd come too far to do anything less than his best now, in the face of the master's judgment. Featherwind threw another melon, and another. Arne struck blow after blow. He stepped and spun, and once, when the hawk threw three at once, he dove for the ground and managed to skewer two of the round fruits on the tip of his blade.

When the cart finally sat empty, not a single melon remained intact. Arne stood, breathing with his entire body and surrounded by a sea of fruity carnage. Wesley snorted pathetically and kicked at the cart's wheel, but Master Featherwind nodded approval.

"Show our guest to his room, Wesley." Featherwind spun on his heel, snapped his cape like a whip, and sauntered back into the manor without another word.

Arne's heart pounded from his exertion, but his thoughts soared behind the master. He'd passed the test. Not a single melon had survived, and now he'd been invited inside, given a room even.

"This way." The pig's voice was hard as the stones along the pathway. His back hunched again, and he trotted ahead as if he meant to lose Arne on the few steps between the yard and the front door.

He'd made no friend in the servant today, and once more Arne wondered if he couldn't have let just one or two melons survive the test. He shook the idea off quickly this time. Featherwind did not accept just any student.

He hustled in the pig's wake, up stone steps and through the grand, wooden entrance. Inside, the manor was warm and as rich as its owner. Carpeting lined the hallways, and the lights in the entrance hung from a high ceiling and dripped with crystals and golden flourishes. The banister railing gleamed in solid mahogany, and as they climbed the stairs, they passed many paintings in frames that could have fed a village for a month each.

Featherwind's servant might have scorned the pursuit of riches, but clearly his master did not share the sentiment.

On the second floor the hall was lined with simple wooden doors. Wesley led him to the last of these on the left hand side and waited for Arne to open it and enter the chamber beyond. The pig followed him inside and waited while the cheetah examined his room.

"It's amazing." Arne spoke without meaning to and cringed when Wesley snorted a response.

He stood in the center of the room gaping openly at the furnishings: a chest that looked to have survived a pirate ship, a bureau that had golden drawer pulls, brocade curtains, and a bed…a bed that dwarfed his entire room at home. Four pillars rose from its corners, and atop each a golden finial had been mounted.

The pig snorted again, then grunted and cleared his throat. "Dinner will be at seven in the dining room. That is, for those who will actually be getting dinner."

The tone wormed under Arne's pelt. He turned in time to catch the nasty look on the swine's face, but the servant shuffled toward the door just as quickly as he'd dropped his verbal barb.

"Wait." Arne's guilt swelled into a knot in his belly. "I am sorry, but…but what was I supposed to do?"

Wesley stilled his trotters and looked back over one broad shoulder. His ears flicked forward and back.

"You were the one who told me he wouldn't take just anyone. I had to impress—"

"My fault, then? I see."

"That's not what I meant."

Wesley turned away. He stepped to the door and then, lifting one leg into the air, released a soft fart before exiting. He shut the door softly as well, and it took six heartbeats for the stench to reach Arne's sensitive nose.

"Gawd." He gasped and flew to the window. "Oh lord."

A diet of melons had its side-effects. Arne threw the shutters open and sucked in a dozen fresh breaths. He leaned his head against the window frame and let the breeze clear the air in the room. Might have made an enemy of the pig. It would make things difficult.

Still, he stood in as lush a room as he'd ever imagined, ready to be trained by the greatest sword master who'd ever lifted a blade. He could handle the pig's annoying vengeance. Maybe he'd even find a way to make amends.

His paw drifted to the curtain pulls, satiny, and tipped with tassels bound in rings of gold. One claw hooked beneath the band and it slipped free. Arne held the gold up to the light and purred. To live like this. What animal would hesitate to endure any testing for a chance like that?

Arne rolled the golden ring over his claw, dangled it in the fading sunlight, and watched it flash.

His plate sat on a charger made of gold. The goblet behind it was crystal, etched with Master Featherwind's house crest and filled with the finest mead Arne had ever dared taste. The dining room had papered walls with raised floral patterns, a floor of hardwood polished to a sheen, and sconces set along its edges.

"Bring that platter closer, Wesley," Featherwind barked from the far end of the long table. His chair's high back had been carved with lion's and boar's heads. He'd piled his plate with fruit and tubers, and held a two-pronged fork in one wingtip, waving it to punctuate his words. "And our guest's glass is nearly empty."

"Of course, Master." The pig settled a tray of figs well within Featherwind's reach, and then plucked up a pitcher of mead and waddled back down the overlong table. He kept his head down, but Arne caught his eyes darting to the bounty overflowing the silver platters, the absolute excess of the meal Featherwind's cook had prepared. When he poured more mead into Arne's glass, his belly rumbled.

"Good lords, Wesley, was that you?" Featherwind set down

his own glass and narrowed his dark eyes.

"Pardon, Master."

Arne shifted in his seat. The pig's distress sat poorly in his own, very full stomach. Master Featherwind, however, found it nothing but amusing. His beak clattered again, and he tilted his head and moved one elbow just enough to knock his silverware clattering to the floor.

"Oops." His feathers fluffed merrily. "Wesley, I've dropped those."

"Yes, Master." The pig scrambled back, set the pitcher down, and bent to retrieve his master's silver.

"Turn the other way, Wesley," Featherwind croaked. "I've no desire to have your monumental arse pointing in my direction."

Wesley turned, still bent over and teetering with the maneuver. His robes caught about his trotters, and he staggered to the side, knocking the table softly.

"Tell me, Arne." Featherwind leaned forward on his elbows and fluffed the feathers around his beak. "Have you ever seen such a rotund creature?"

"I, er..." The twitchy feeling in Arne's stomach intensified. He shifted in his seat while an embarrassed heat spread over his face. The tip of his tail twitched irritably, and he used one foot to shove the recalcitrant limb out of sight beneath his chair. "Not really."

"I should think not."

Wesley stood, placed the silver on the side of the table, and shuffled backwards away from his master, keeping his posterior pointedly away from sight.

"Turn around, Wesley," Featherwind ordered and the pig complied, head hanging and shoulders even more hunched. "I dare say you could keep a small trunk atop that thing. Keep all your jewels and finery right at your back, eh?"

"Y-yes, Master. I suppose I could."

Featherwind's laughter rattled all the way to the ceiling, but it was the pig's expression that Arne fixed on. He kept his gaze away from his master, but Arne caught the shame burning in the beady eyes, the sparkle of unshed tears. His supper threatened to come back up at the sight of it, at the sound of the hawk's mirth that died just as suddenly as it began.

"Eh, Arne?" Featherwind's attention focused down the table, pinned Arne to his fancy chair as if the spread of rich food were an arrow between them. The scent of the man's excess skewered Arne, and he couldn't help but see the risk in voicing his opinion. This man, Featherwind, had a mean streak, master or not.

"Yes?" Arne swallowed dry air.

"You've gone broody." Master Featherwind's voice carried a steely warning. "Perhaps you don't find my humor amusing?"

Arne formed words in his mind and threw them away just as quickly. What good would it do to point out the man's failings? To defend the servant that obviously chose to endure such abuse? It would certainly lose him the opportunity to train here, and mean or not, Featherwind's skill was legendary. His students had futures.

"I was only thinking, Master." Arne rearranged his thoughts, scrambling for the correct reply. "You said a *small* trunk. I believe the chest in my room would fit."

Featherwind threw back his head, pointed his beak to the rafters, and let out a merry chortle. One wing pounded the tabletop, sending the silverware dancing to the hardwood again. Wesley cringed away from the table, but not before throwing Arne a look that chilled his blood.

His whiskers tightened, and his long tail slunk deeper underneath his chair. He hadn't meant it. Surely the pig knew his master well enough to see the hawk had given Arne no choice but to play along? Arne cleared his throat with a gulp of mead and forced himself not to look at Wesley again.

He picked up his silverware and examined it, as if there could be a spot anywhere on that gleaming metal. Real silver. He turned the fork over in the light from the sconces while the hawk's laughter continued to echo through the room. A person like Featherwind didn't deserve to live like this, but then, the world Arne knew often rewarded his like.

Justice rarely found a humble pig, a fat servant who took too much abuse and did nothing about it. If he defended Wesley, Featherwind's scorn would no doubt land on him as well.

He set the fork down on the very edge of the table, picked up the knife, and eyed the distorted reflection of his own, spotted face. Featherwind didn't deserve what he had, but if Arne meant to remedy the cruelties of the world, he'd do it *after* the hawk had taught him all he knew.

His elbow bumped the fork and it tumbled into the napkin in his lap. The pig waddled to the far end of the room, sniffling, and Arne sat perfectly still and said nothing.

"Lower your shoulders," Featherwind chanted his directions from his perch on a comfortably broad stump. "And widen your stance."

Arne obeyed, keeping his sword tip up and his eyes fixed on the practice dummy. He'd scored several deep cuts already and the wooden armor bore the scars of his blade.

"Any opponent worth fighting will be armored," Featherwind said. "Strike upwards. Get the blade underneath the breast plate."

The dummy dangled from a tree in the practice yard behind the manor. A rough rope looped over one branch and down into the trotters of a sweating Wesley. Each time Arne struck at the thing, the pig jerked the rope hard, making the dummy dance this way and that.

"Again," Featherwind commanded.

Arne feinted to the right. Wesley jerked the rope and the dummy swung back and forward. Arne stepped into the swing, thrusting upward with his blade and catching the wooden torso as it moved into him.

Wood met broadsword, and a long trench spawned along the dummy's length.

"Well done," the master praised him, and Arne's chest swelled.

He stood taller, flashed a triumphant expression at the pig who, unless he'd imagined it, had spent the morning farting every time the wind shifted in Arne's direction. The stench of the servant's flatulence had permeated his nostrils, and now he could smell little else.

"Use your tail more," Featherwind continued. He hadn't shown any sign *he'd* noticed Wesley's emissions. "You're off balance too often."

Arne lashed his tail to one side and shifted his legs. He bent his knees and tried his best to clamp his nostrils shut.

"No." Featherwind jumped from his stump, landing with his tail spread wide and his wings out to the sides. "There's only so much you can learn from a practice dummy. You need to spar to get this right."

Arne sucked in a breath. Sparring? Would he get to face the master already, after only a half day of forms and simple movements?

"Wesley!" Featherwind hollered, though the pig could easily hear their conversation. "Go find a weapon."

"Wesley?" Arne lowered his sword and gaped at the sword master. "But…"

"A swordsman can learn from any opponent," the hawk said. "You two carry on for the afternoon. I've things to attend to."

He moved toward the rear entrance of the manor, and Arne's chest tightened. The master meant for him to spar with Wesley, though had no intentions of even staying to watch. He'd been sure that his swordplay impressed the hawk, and yet he saw dismissal in the way the master moved now, lazily past the pig who clutched a long stick in his trotters and fixed Arne with a murderous glare.

A stick.

"Don't let me catch you going easy on him," the hawk called back.

"I won't." Arne and Wesley spoke at the same time, echoed each other perfectly. They both snorted, though Arne's carried far less distance.

"I believe he was speaking to me," he purred at the pig and lashed his tail. "Maybe you should find a real sword. I don't want to hurt you."

"Oh, I think we both know it's too late for that." Wesley grinned and waved his stick in a sloppy arc. He closed the distance between them at a trot, with the sad weapon held in front of his ample midsection.

The yard stretched from the manor to the woods, and a few trees like the one the dummy still dangled from dotted the flat area. The stump where the master had rested marked one side of their field, and the long grass that grew between the estate and the road marked the other. Sunlight dappled their arena, spotting the field to match Arne's pelt.

The pig slowed and circled, just out of Arne's reach. His stick wavered, as if the weight of it was too much for Wesley's short arms to bear.

"Listen," Arne spoke under his breath. "I'm serious. I think you should get a—"

Wesley lunged, swung the stick low to the ground. Arne remained on his feet only by scrambling backwards. The pig moved faster than he'd expected, and as he struck, he farted for good measure.

"I think your guts are toxic," Arne said. He lunged slowly, testing the pig's reach and reflexes.

Wesley parried three of his thrusts and then began to backpedal, as if tiring already. Arne pressed forward, seizing the advantage and driving the servant back and back into the shade of the tree.

Where his eyes failed him.

The shift from bright sunlight to deep shade dimmed the edges of Arne's vision. He blinked, sniffed the air, and found the stench of Wesley far too dense for comfort. He kept his sword up and caught the blur of something brown at his right. Spinning, Arne blinked again, adjusted to the dimness, and managed to parry the strike of Wesley's stick just at the last moment.

"Here, kitty kitty," Wesley grunted.

Arne slashed downward, stepped into it, and frowned in disbelief as the pig spun away from him. Fast, and lighter on his feet than anyone would ever guess. He snorted proudly, spun again just for show, and filled the afternoon with his gas.

With a growl brewing deep in his throat, Arne flexed his knees, lowered his body, and reached far out with his tail for balance. He lifted his weapon and fixed his eyes on his oddly agile sparring partner.

They circled beneath the tree, weapons ready. Arne faked a lunge, but Wesley spun to the side and swung his stick, forcing him away, keeping him on the defensive. The pig pressed him, moving his rough weapon as if it were the finest steel. Gracefully, with practiced skill.

Just watching that swing told Arne he'd been played. Wesley was a student of Featherwind's. He had to be, to move like that. The realization pushed at him. Here was another test, and if he couldn't best this rotund, stick-wielding swine, he knew he had no place in Master Featherwind's company.

But the swine had a grudge to bear, and with each blow Wesley sent in his direction, Arne felt his own folly echoed. He parried and kept his feet light, his tail stretched behind him. He looked for an opening, studied his opponent's movements, and found no flaws to exploit.

Wesley moved like a dancer. His trotters flicked across the ground as if he'd sworn off gravity completely. His stick seemed to fall from all sides at once, lightning fast and as accurate as an arrow. Arne caught each blow upon his own blade, but found himself defending only, driven by a foe with far more skill and grace.

Where the pig floated, Arne staggered. Wesley's stick drove their battle, back and back, until they stood in the bright light again. Arne's vision sharpened, but the pig did not stand still. He moved again, spun and danced, and pushed the battle back into the shade and out again just as quickly.

Arne stumbled, kept his sword moving by reflex alone.

Wesley clearly had the upper hand and no intentions of giving it back. Arne snarled his frustration and swiped and batted fiercely at the pig to no avail. They fought across the yard and back, in and out of the shadows that played hell with Arne's normally excellent vision.

As his muscles tired, the pig's seemed to rejuvenate. Where

Arne's steps dragged, Wesley leaped and fluttered like a giant, flatulent insect. His shoddy weapon knocked hard against Arne's sword, and with each blow, the pig drove home a deeper revelation.

Here was no student; Arne fought a master swordsman. He fought, and he knew he would lose even before the pig's footwork drove him into a stumble, before the stick lashed out, hooked his blade in a wicked turn, and ripped it from Arne's grip.

His sword flew toward the long grass, and Arne fell to his knees with the tip of Wesley's weapon inches from his throat.

"It's you." Arne gasped for air, breathed deep even though each inhale was laced with flatulence. "Isn't it?"

The pig grunted, but didn't confirm Arne's accusation. He didn't need to. Only one swordsman could move like that, could fight like a furious wind and never tire.

"The name?" Arne sat back on his heels and looked at Wesley through new eyes. "I thought the feathers…"

In answer, Master Featherwind let out the softest of farts.

"Then who is the hawk?"

"His butler." The false Featherwind reappeared, as if summoned. He strode from the manor with all his usual arrogance, but it seemed thin now, fraudulent. "I've brought his pack as you requested, Master."

The bird dipped into a bow, confirming all Arne's suspicions. He laid Arne's pack on the ground at Wesley's feet. He'd brought the green velvet cloak as well, folded neatly, and he set that beside the bag. Then he returned to his stump and perched atop it, watching with his head tilted to one side.

"Your time here is at an end," the pig said.

"Wait… I didn't… Why?" Arne stammered like a fool, knowing full well that nothing could save him. The pig was the master. They'd played him for a fool, and for no reason he could guess except their own amusement.

"Injustice, cruelty, and honor." Wesley chanted the words as if they meant anything.

"Give me another chance, please."

"That was your answer, if you remember." Wesley's face

softened. His beady eyes grew wider, and his snout un-crimped. "Your words. To battle injustice, defend from cruelty, fight with honor."

"It's true," Arne said. "It's all true."

"And yet when you witnessed injustice against me, when you might have spared me a melon or two, you did not."

"I believed I had no choice."

"You believed it was my own fault. And when I was cruelly mocked and shamed before you, you said not a word except to participate in my humiliation."

"I thought it was a test."

"And it was."

"I thought he wouldn't...that he might..."

"You thought," the pig's voice grew gentler, but somehow stung all the harder for it, "only of yourself."

Arne's head fell forward. His eyes marked the dust of the yard, pressed downward by his own folly. He'd seen each test the sword master had placed before him, and still he'd failed.

"And the last." Wesley squatted, bringing his snout near to Arne's muzzle. He lifted the leather pack in his trotters and hefted it. "Honor."

Arne cringed as the pig upended his bag. His face burned as the items tumbled to the dirt—a golden band, a silver fork, one of the finials from his four-poster bed.

"There is no honor in thievery," Wesley whispered. "No matter how one might justify it."

He *had* justified it, certainly, but he'd been wrong just the same. Arne's eyes watered, and he pressed them tight and nodded. He managed to choke out only two words. "I'll go."

"Yes." Master Featherwind was very particular about his pupils. "Just as soon as we've arranged for payment."

"Payment?" Arne's voice cracked.

"Certainly." The pig sword master stood and brushed the dust from his ratty hem. "You came to my gate seeking a teacher, and you've most certainly learned a lesson."

Arne stared at the ground, at the stolen gold, and the sharp trotters of Master Featherwind.

"You *have* learned a lesson, haven't you?"

"Yes." Arne nodded and reached for his pack. He replaced only the items that belonged to him, draped the strap over his shoulder, and then gathered his cloak and stood, holding the green velvet out before him.

Wesley smiled, and took the garment.

Arne looked back once, as he ducked through the fence and onto the road. The pig had unfolded the velvet and draped it over his shoulders, wore it over his stinking brown robes. The green fabric swirled around dusty trotters, shiny in the afternoon light.

It was the finest thing Arne had ever owned, but he hadn't deserved it.

Bridges

Tony Greyfox

The hissing was closer.

It slithered over the ground, pushed down by the grey mist that hung over the graveled terrain, and crept into the sharp, perked ears of the hunter.

He ignored it, as he had for the past three hours. His ears were good, but his nose was better, and he knew the source of the hiss was still a safe distance away.

And so he carried on, booted paws crunching softly with each slow step, mist swirling around his legs.

In the edge of his field of vision, the blue dot that indicated a waypoint appeared. He stopped, sniffed the air—still plenty of time—and mentally triggered the map. It bloomed in his sight, transparent but visible, a combination of terrain and satellite photos. Those pictures were probably years out of date, but they were better than nothing.

His target was ahead, still invisible through the mist, but less than a kilometre or so off. Coming in from above rather than by climbing the hill from the valley—where the roads were—was perhaps more prudence than truly necessary, he mused.

With a sweep of one furred finger, he dismissed the map. He wouldn't need it from here on out. The direction was fixed in his internal compass, and he knew it was a short walk to the house.

He shifted the scabbard hanging from his belt, sniffed the air again, and walked on.

The mansion loomed out of the mist. In its prime, it had been painted in green and brown to blend with the Pacific Northwest forests within which it nestled. Now the colours had greyed and dulled, much like the bare trees that jutted into the mist around it.

Nothing moved but the clouds.

He studied the structure. The overheads didn't show where the doors were, but a garage on the nearest end of the building seemed to be a good starting point to make his way in. He moved forward just as the wind swirled sluggishly across the grounds.

He froze. His nose tilted upward.

The wind stank, the smell of a creature that was already dead but didn't realize it. Somehow it had slipped up behind him, and there were more nearby. Belatedly, the implant beeped. The map came up in his vision, settled low to the left, and showed five red dots edging toward the blue that was him.

He reached down. Fingers brushed past the empty holster to curl around a cord-wrapped hilt. He breathed, rubbed his dark canine nose with one finger, and waited.

It didn't take long. The first of the creatures came out of the mists at a dead run, hissing, its grey-striped pelt practically dripping off its skeletal form. Its ancestors had likely been cats, his implant suggested, but radioactive and biological effects had mutated it. Now it was large, thin with hunger, and dying from whatever disease had found a home thanks to the mutation.

In a flash it was on him, angry yellow eyes narrowed with hate and hunger. The implant suggested several shots from his sidearm, with inert bullets, to deal with the cat. Instead he let his mind fill with the memories from far, far before. His fingers twitched slightly, the built-in training trying to assert itself, but he held for a long moment, and then struck.

The blade whispered out of the scabbard. A single cut, and the cat thumped messily to the ground in two chunks even before the echo of the hiss had trailed off. He returned to an open stance, bringing the blade around in both paws, watching the mist.

Two more appeared and lunged. He lopped off one head,

and carved the guts out of the second—which fell, yowling and gushing green and red from its diseased insides. The crunch of gravel behind him announced yet more, and he spun to meet them, taking a bare step back and slashing downward. The ambusher fell with its head split open.

His implant tracked two more of the cat-creatures as they circled him slowly, just out of reach of his blade. Tactically, he knew, he should wait and watch for them to make their move. Emotionally, he had things to do, and damn tactics.

He dashed forward, three steps and a quick slash that cut the legs off one cat that jumped in surprise at his sudden approach. A quick spin put him face to face with the last. It launched itself into a long pounce, screamed and died as his blade burst through its chest cavity. He dropped backwards and kicked it off the blade into the mists, then rolled back to his feet.

Barely even breathing hard, the coyote wiped his blade on a furred body, slid it back into its sheath, and hurried forward toward the garage.

It had been but weeks since his "birth", and he didn't want to waste any more time. The compulsion pulled him forward too hard to wait.

He had not awakened when the lights went on.

His eyes had opened. Multicoloured figures, diagrams, groups of numbers flickered through his vision, before settling. In his mind, an image had been projected: tall, broad-shouldered but lithe, a long and sharp muzzle paired with perked ears, all covered with tones of grey and beige fur. He was informed that his designation was DW-147—the 147th member of the Delta Whiskey battalion of the Western American Army.

There had been a whirring sound, and DW-147—alongside two dozen other bipedal coyotes, all naked but for their fur—stepped out into the light. A few curious glances passed back and forth between the soon-to-be soldiers. One or two seemed interested in exploring more, but an alert had buzzed in his mind—in all their minds—and the implant took over.

Three days of what the implant informed him was quality

control testing took place; he and the other coyotes had been presented with fatigues and basic equipment, then marched into a parade square and exercised to near failure. Or, in some cases, beyond failure. DW-147 watched impassively as, after a vigorous ten-mile run, human orderlies carried off three members of their two-dozen. Another had collapsed during weapons training, never to be seen again. Yet another had, during the evening meal period, picked up a chair and coolly crushed the skull of a white-clad server with all the emotion of swatting a fly. Six MPs had converged with tasers, and the coyote soldier was gone.

DW-147 was never sure if the sound he'd heard a few minutes later had been gunshots, and didn't care.

After three days, the implant—and the computer it was connected to—had apparently decided that DW-147 was of sufficient quality for inclusion in the ranks. It had dumped a vast amount of information into his mind, directed him to the proper barracks for his unit, and set itself to background operations.

His mind opened as it was released. He knew how to drive vehicles, from scooters to tanks. He knew how to build a weapon from scratch. He knew how to hide in the woods, survive long marches, find the enemy, destroy the opponent.

But, with the weight of the computer filling him with information removed from his brain, he also knew one other thing: he was not DW-147. He was Minamoto Yasu, and this was not his first time treading the world.

"There is a field behind you. It is empty. There is a river ahead of you. It is broad and swift. There is a bridge. It is narrow. And there is a rock before you. It shall not move."

"Then I shall move the rock, however I must."

Yasu knew it would come to this, though he had wished otherwise. The man before him, dressed simply in a kimono of brown and beige, stood with a hand on the hilt of his katana and a smile on his face.

He was a friend, nearly family, and Yasu could undoubtedly kill him where he stood.

"Daiki. I have been sent by the daimyo, you know this. It is my duty to bring your brother for judgment, and you must not stand in my way." Yasu stood his ground. "Move, and allow me to conduct my duty."

"The daimyo is wrong. Kuro had nothing to do with the supposed plot against him. Our family has shared evidence proving without a doubt that Kuro was not at this meeting they claim to have infiltrated." Daiki shifted his position, moving his weight to the other foot. Yasu knew that movement; it meant Daiki was preparing for an onslaught. "Because Kuro spoke ill of the disaster that overzealous tax collector brought to our family's farm, the daimyo wishes him silenced. You are honourable, Yasu. You must know this."

He did. But what he knew did not matter; his master had given him explicit instructions.

Yasu stepped forward. "Move aside, Daiki, or I will move you. Rocks may not wish to move, but they can be crushed if needed."

"Your pledge is stronger than your honour, eh, Minamoto Yasu?" Daiki smiled sadly. "I am sorry. My honour comes from my family, and I shall not abandon them. I shall not move."

Yasu's blade whistled from its sheath, only to clatter against his friend's own katana. Daiki was fast—faster than Yasu remembered him to be. This may, the samurai mused, be more difficult than he had expected.

A quick slash from the other man drove him back two steps. He countered with an attack of his own that sent Daiki onto the narrow wood deck of the bridge. His friend recovered quickly and blocked another strike, but his own riposte carved a line into the railing next to him and left his blade lodged for just an instant.

An instant was all Yasu needed.

Daiki slumped in a heap to the bridge deck, blood pooling on the wood. His katana clattered, slid off the wood, and splashed into the river.

Yasu watched his friend raise his head, and met the man's fading gaze evenly. "My duty is my honour," he said quietly, and stepped over Daiki.

He was three steps away when the blade burst from his chest.

It was the strangest feeling: a chill, surrounded by heat that began to spread through his body, followed by a growing numbness that left him on his knees within seconds.

Yasu touched the tip of the wakizashi jutting from just below his sternum. A weight collapsed onto his feet. He looked, still unbelieving, back at Daiki, who lay on his back, staring up.

"Duty is not life," Daiki whispered through bloody froth. "May you learn this before you find peace."

Yasu watched his friend fall away from him. Or was he the one falling? The thump of his head against the bridge confirmed the latter.

He sighed, and closed his eyes.

For being abandoned at least eight years, the house had stood up surprisingly well to the rain and mists, made heavier by the changing coastal climate—visually, at least. To Yasu's sensitive nose it stank of mold and damp, signs that the structure would, within a few years, give in to the weather and become nothing more than a heap of useless building materials unless someone maintained it.

That was unlikely though, considering how far within the erstwhile front lines it lay. The coast war was over, but few people had returned to the northwest after it stumbled to an unsteady halt.

Yasu paced slowly through the house, sniffing at the air, a handheld light filling the dark rooms with white light that contrasted harshly to the steady grey outside. His booted feet were quiet on the mildewed carpets; the house was disturbingly silent, sounds dimmed by the mists that curled through broken windows on one side. At least one blast had been close enough to shatter the glass there.

The owners of the home had rushed out, it appeared, and most everything had been left behind. Good. Yasu licked his whiskers, then paused to wonder why this body engaged in that automated action. The implant murmured something about sensory organs. Yasu shrugged and carried on, methodically searching the ground floor of the home.

His quarry had to be here someplace. The research he had done before leaving his barracks—when the computers had still spoken to him—had insisted the owner of this home was one of the biggest collectors of Japanese antiquities on the west coast. Plus, whatever was causing the compulsion that he followed had flared hard enough to give him a headache when he had first seen the place.

A wealth of antiques decorated a recreation room. Yasu walked around the sagging mahogany of a pool table, admiring woodcuts, tapestries, and a few other pieces of art. He thought he recognized one or two of the artists, in fact. But his target—whatever the strange pull in his back brain drew him towards—was not present.

Yasu made his way up a grand staircase to the second floor. It opened into an even larger room, one that was artfully arranged so the various furnishings allowed a view out the bay window over the mist-covered hills, or of the various antiquities displayed professionally in glass cases along the walls.

One case held a samurai's helmet from the 1700s, immaculately cared for. He considered trying it on for size, but remembered how foolish he had felt trying to put on a motorcycle helmet after forgetting about coyote ears and left the case closed. Next to it, a silk kimono in lovely shades of blue and silver, showing its age but still radiant. Another case held a tea set that sent Yasu's thoughts back to an afternoon in a garden with a lovely young woman who had been dead for centuries.

The fourth case caught his eye not for what it contained, but what it did not contain.

He stared through the glass at the empty space between two holders, just the right size for a katana. Set neatly in the empty space was a folded piece of paper.

Hinges squeaked with age. Yasu spread the paper with his dark-furred fingers and blunt claws; familiar symbols greeted his gaze as it unfolded.

His implant chirped in the part of his brain that it called home, and words popped up in green type across his vision. The translation was unnecessary; Yasu could have read the neatly-inked kanji half-blind, drunk, or in a snowstorm.

"If you seek the past, search out the present. My pasts are lain bare by the present. The cycle has brought me here, and when I meditate, I sense it has brought you. Join me."

There was a set of coordinates below. As Yasu traced the symbols, the implant did its work and mapped the location. Not far, but far enough.

He folded the note back up and tucked it into the combat vest under his stolen coat. The coyote drew the sword from his belt and ran a finger along the enameled scabbard. He had found it in a broken shopping mall not far from the edge of the western exclusion zone, and since the DNA coding that allowed DW-147 to use WAA weapons had been removed from the database after his unscheduled departure from barracks, he needed something to defend himself.

It was barely adequate; the weight was awful, the balance was off, and he wouldn't dare bend the blade more than a degree or so out of true for fear it would fold over. In a word, it was garbage. It fulfilled a need. It would not, however, do for anything more than that.

Besides, he was Minamoto Yasu, and if he were to face his past, he would face it with a blade that would honour both himself and the fates awaiting him.

Yasu consulted his implant, which thankfully seemed to carry all of the information he sought in its built-in memory— wherever the transmitter was installed within his body, it had been blocked by the thick layer of aluminum foil he had lined the combat vest with as a way to keep from being tracked, leaving him unable to access any remote information. The computer pondered a moment, then presented three results near his current position. He grunted and marked one, then left the house, headed for his motorcycle.

His past would have to wait.

The further north that Yasu rode into Oregon, the fewer signs of life he saw. He stuck to the network of back roads that spiderwebbed across the Cascades. While some hardy souls had begun to drift back into the southern parts of the exclusion zone, the mists were still too much of a reminder of the deadly gas clouds that had rolled in from the coast in the early years of the war, and most west coast residents stayed inland and south.

Further north, though, the mists were less a problem than the radiation. Yasu didn't mind; he had work to do, and didn't need to answer questions while he did it. DW-147's body was engineered to resist certain levels of radioactivity, and the drift maps he called up suggested that would be enough. Probably.

Along the way, he stopped twice to charge the bike's batteries at solar stations that still functioned, and left signs on the two others that didn't so anyone else in the zone might not waste their time. He ate tasteless field rations that the implant said would provide the prime blend of nutrients for healthy muscles and a sleek coat.

On the east side of the Cascades, the mists thinned as the desert began to take over. He ignored the heat as best he could and followed battered roads to a small town that had once been a refuge to many artists. Deserted but for occasional animals, Yasu hoped it still held the things he needed.

When he had navigated through the streets cluttered with tree limbs and junk to the address pulled from the map, he noticed the place looked reasonably untouched by the years. Yasu pulled his bike behind the modest house and parked it out of sight from the road. He scanned the area, saw nothing of concern, and approached the shop that took up much of the back yard—a metal building with a slanted tin roof and two small windows, topped by a large, round chimney pointing towards the misty sky.

He tried the door. It was, to his surprise, locked.

A firm kick didn't do the job—no wonder the building had gone untouched. While there certainly weren't many people in the area to ransack unattended properties, Yasu would have expected this one to be an early target for anyone leaving town.

The back door of the house opened to his boot, however, and a few moments' searching turned up the tools his implant told him were needed to force the lock. He also found a stock of food that seemed to still be safe to eat, and carried several cans back to the shop. They would be a good break from the ration bars.

Inside, the shop was dark and silent. Tools were neatly placed where they would best serve the craftsman, and at the bottom of that chimney was what he sought: a forge. Even better, there was a heap of coal nearby; had it been gas-fired, he would have needed to search out another option. Trust a backwoods artisan to prefer the old-fashioned methods, Yasu thought, opening cabinets until he found what he sought.

The artisan was well-stocked with steel for the forge. Yasu drew a flat, narrow sheet of metal from the cabinet and weighed it in one hand, then added another and hefted the pair. That was more like it. He'd need to cut the pieces apart to fit the forge and his needs, though.

None of the equipment, the supplies, or anything in this workshop was anything he could relate to directly—his own forge had been far different, and he'd never had bars of steel to work with—but the implant was happy to provide him with information on modern forging. Yasu trusted this body to manage the job.

He opened a can of beans and ate. It would be a long few days, and he—or rather DW-147—would need his strength.

Air quivered over the red-hot steel, and sparks fell as Yasu—his thin coyote tail tucked uncomfortably down the back of his pants to avoid any unfortunate fire incidents—set it on the anvil with care. He looked at the metal. It was ready.

Was he?

The samurai took a long, deep breath, focused his mind on the task, and hefted the hammer high.

CLANG

Piled together and wrapped with a piece of narrow metal to keep them from scattering, the chunks of steel sprayed red embers under the blow of the hammer.

CLANG

The metal distended, started to spread, to blend.

CLANG

Yasu watched the effect of each contact, judging the condition of the steel and adjusting the strength of each strike. It was remarkably familiar—far more than the world in which he found himself, more than the body in which he resided.

A few more blows, and he set the steel back into the forge's heat. It was already beginning to meld from the conglomeration of chunks into a whole; he would work it a little more until the individual pieces were indiscernible, then start the folds that would ensure a good blending.

The coyote—the swordsman—stared into the fire, the radiant orange shimmering around the darkness of the steel. Crafting had always been Yasu's escape from the pressures of his world and that of his master. He often worked with the younger men of the town to share his knowledge, but many jobs had been himself, the steel and the heat of the forge.

Yasu removed the steel and set it onto the anvil again, clamping the long tongs down in lieu of a helper. He took a long breath and started hammering again. Eyes focused on the glowing metal, he let his mind drift in the soothing beat of iron on steel.

Amid the heat and noise, the past arose around him.

"She's sinking for sure, Captain. They're putting out boats on the port side."

The language was not Japanese. Nor was it the English that DW-147 spoke. When the view changed—perhaps the viewer turned their head to sweep across a battered man-of-war some distance off and down to the cluster of officers on the deck—he saw men with olive complexions, a mixture of blue and brown coats over red shirts and white trousers, scurrying here and there. Not a few figures were lying silently on the deck of the pitching ship, some in puddles of blood, and there were chunks of decking and railings shattered here and there.

A shot rang out from above, and someone on the other ship screamed.

The viewer turned back, and Yasu saw that he stood on the stern of the vessel, leaning against the railing next to a small cannon mounted on a swivel, its muzzle still smoking gently. He watched through the viewer's—his?—eyes as a short stick with a swab was picked up and run down the barrel of the gun. A powder charge was inserted, a ball of wadding, and then a round ball.

There was still chatter occurring amidships, but the sailor who was Yasu ignored it. Instead, he lifted a spyglass to one eye and surveyed the other ship. Yasu registered that the two ships were near a shore of some kind, though he could make out nothing beyond that—land was some distance off. But land was not what the sailor—his name was Teodoro—was interested in.

He scanned the battered vessel across the way. A torn and battered ensign, white with a cross in one corner, still hung limply from the wrecked rigging. Nobody was rushing to strike it, Teodoro thought, and thus the enemy vessel had not surrendered. A shot and puff of smoke from the deck, followed by two shots from his own ship, suggested that some of them were still fighting.

Movement caught his attention. He turned the glass and saw a boat, crammed with sailors and a few officers, moving out from behind the other vessel's bow. It crept across, hidden by the vessel's bulk from most of their cannons and the snipers above. But he had a line on them.

As Yasu observed impassively from god knew how many years in the future, Teodoro laid the spyglass along the length of his swivel gun and turned the pair of them towards the small boat. He watched the men aboard shuffle around. Two of them held muskets—one was fiddling with his weapon frantically as the boat held steady, its prow turning towards the shore far beyond. He lined up the shot with care, centering the bore on the middle of the little boat.

On it, the sailor messing with his musket lifted the muzzle. Something was tied to it. Teodoro saw a white rag begin to rise at the end of the barrel. Their intention was obvious.

He paused a moment. They were the enemy. They had killed

many of his comrades. It was his duty to kill all the Englishmen he could.

Teodoro touched off the cannon.

It fired without the roar of the larger bore weapons and without much of the kick; it still jarred his shoulder, but his weight held it true.

The shot struck the English boat amidships and shattered it. Wood shards scattered—so did several men, an eruption of red rising with the passage of the three-inch ball. The boat came apart under the blast sending sailors into the water, where they paddled frantically amid the growing dark stain.

Heads turned along the length of the Spanish vessel, and a pair of officers ran to where Teodoro was coolly reloading his gun. "What was that?" one of them demanded.

Teodoro pointed to the scrambling Englishmen. Several had already disappeared beneath the waves. "They were running. Some of them were raising muskets."

The officers looked at one another, then back to where the English vessel was settling, its stern dipping low, obviously headed for the bottom of the ocean. He slapped Teodoro on the shoulder. "Nice shot. Watch for more."

Teodoro nodded as they walked away, and looked over the sea with his spyglass. A white rag floating on the waves amidst the English sailors caught his gaze. He stared at it a moment, then went back to work. It was his duty, after all.

The dream—memory? hallucination?—fell away, and left Yasu staring at a cooling block of steel and a forge beginning to lose its heat.

His tongue was lolling, his breath coming in quick pants; had he been human, he would have been pouring sweat, and not all from the heat and exertion of the work he was performing.

Yasu took more coal from the stockpile and set it into the forge, lost in thought. The occasional Buddhist monks and priests he had known all shared the concept of samsara, the cycle of life, death and rebirth that all men were destined to suffer until they were truly able to release themselves from need and want, and finally reach the heavenly promise of nirvana. When questioned on whether one would have recollections of the other lives they had lived on the six realms, they had spouted something about the soul being permanent, yet disconnected.

Perhaps, the swordsman thought as he fanned the coals to life, they had been wrong on that count. He certainly remembered the life of Minamoto Yasu, and the vision during his meditative bladesmithing had been vivid enough to touch. He thought back onto that memory, and realized there was more—foggy and dim, but there nonetheless. Yasu tried to focus on it, but the dull memories seemed to lead to the name of a place—Trafalgar—then were gone.

His implant provided a short history lesson. Yasu nodded and turned back to his work.

The steel sat on his anvil, the inner heat gone for the moment. The coyote turned it one way, then the other, staring at it in the light of the forge. How many times had he folded it? He had lost track in his meditative state.

From the color of the metal, though, it would do.

Yasu set it down. He used a saw to take the top off a can of beans, ate, and settled near enough to the forge to savor the heat. Then he checked the foil in his vest, wrapped himself in his coat and his tail, and slept.

Six hours was all Yasu let himself take before he was back to work on the forge. The steel looked good, but it still needed working, and while his craftsmanship was some of the finest in northern Japan, it also took time. The coyote picked up hammer and tongs, set the metal back into the forge, and waited for it to heat back up.

When the hammering began, he emptied his mind and the memories returned once again.

There were many of them. Yasu found himself reliving snippets of lives lived far and wide. Some were nebulous and vague, nothing but sensation and need, desire, pain, emptiness. Others were more organized.

The swordsman watched from the eyes of a thief who abandoned a friend while retrieving goods for his master, a teen boy enlisting in the army to escape marriage to a girl who carried his child, a soldier that lobbed a grenade into a bunker to kill two enemies, even though several civilians were inside as well.

Memories swirled, came faster, each highlighting a period in time, showing him bursts of time that he tried to focus on and remember, only for them to fade and be replaced by more.

There was a thread to the memories though, especially the more vivid ones. In each, his life was built around duty—duty to a lord, duty to a country—and in each, he followed that duty blindly toward disaster. Much like the first.

Yasu blinked his eyes open, ravenous and aching, and set the hammer down with memories echoing in his mind as they faded. He looked down at the anvil and the shining blade laying on it. He would polish it in the morning, and make the various finishing touches.

He ate a ration bar and fell asleep with confused memories of his past lives swirling together.

When the door rattled, Yasu found his body on its feet and moving before he was remotely conscious.

The coyote darted to a dark corner of the room where cabinets held various tools and materials while Yasu processed the situation. He found himself pressed into a narrow gap between the storage spaces, two heavy hammers clutched in either paw.

Metal rattled again, then the thud of something slamming against the door was followed by a clattering of lock parts skittering across the floor.

Yasu held his breath as the door swung open. In the dim light of the forge, three figures filed their way into the shop.

They were short and squat, and moved in oddly jerky motions. He asked his implant to provide a better look, and the processors behind his eyes switched to infrared. Two blinks later the room changed in appearance, the figures showing brighter. The forge was a blinding flare that the processor quickly blotted out.

In the new light he saw they were mice, wearing battered combat gear, each carrying a small machine pistol and various other pieces of gear. The implant immediately identified them as Asian Confederation engineered troops.

They were the result of a North Korean program to double its standing army by using cloning to uplift rodents, Yasu was informed. Dangerous in numbers, they had been useless in battle beyond heavy wave attacks. There had long been rumours of troops from the ill-fated invasion attempts still living rough in the Oregon mountains within the exclusion zones.

Yasu breathed a bit easier at that. These were hardly dangerous opponents, and in fact this trio seemed…off. They walked strangely, held themselves hunched over, and moved slower than one might expect. Perhaps they had been affected by the chemicals remaining after the mists, or were simply badly engineered.

The mouse-troops made their way to the forge, speaking a language that sounded vaguely familiar, quickly identified as Mandarin. Translated, they were doing what most any military troops spent their time doing—bitching, about being cold, about being hungry, about having to rebuild their shelter again. It seemed they had moved further east in their foraging efforts than ever before, and had stumbled into town.

One of them picked up the katana blade and studied it, then whistled to the others. Yasu watched, tensing again, as the trio looked over his tools and rifled through his pack.

When one reached up to touch something on the chipped helmet it wore, a blip appeared in the coyote's vision, with the caption, "Night vision goggles detected".

The trooper was swinging towards him when his arm came up, snapped forward, and flung the hammer. In his own infrared, he saw the mouse's mouth open in surprise just before several pounds of metal caught it squarely in the jaw, sending teeth spraying across the room. It dropped bonelessly; the other two stared, and DW-147 leapt into motion.

The other hammer flew out of his off-hand as the coyote darted back across the room. This one, though, clanged against a cabinet across the shop, drawing the troopers' attention. Both brought up their weapons and fired a panicky burst into the darkness, showering sparks as metal struck metal.

When they turned back around, the coyote was already there clutching a three-foot bar of metal, and Yasu was in control. The bar had none of the balance that he wanted, but he slipped into a stance and swung anyhow. The metal whistled around and caved in the side of the nearest mouse's helmet, sending it reeling. It dropped the gun, and Yasu kicked it clear, moving in on the third mouse. This one brought its weapon up and fired, but Yasu had already twisted to the side and brought the bar down with a stroke that broke both of the creature's forearms. It screamed, a high-pitched yowl that pinned DW-147's ears back against his skull.

He turned. The first mouse was moaning and holding its face in a huddle on the floor, but the second had drawn a long, nasty combat knife and was stalking toward him.

Yasu glanced at the anvil next to the forge. On it, the blade shone.

DW-147 started to reach, but Yasu held back.

He would not quench this blade in blood.

Instead, the coyote rolled to where his gear sat, and came up a moment later with the cheap shopping-mall katana. It slid from the scabbard and glistened in the light.

The mouse shouted something that his implant refused to translate, and lunged.

Yasu killed it with two strokes, removing its knife-hand and following with an uppercut blow that sent the creature to the floor with the sound of a sack of wet grain striking hard dirt.

A body hit him from behind. He grunted and lunged forward, twisting into a strike. The broken-armed mouse died with its throat gouting.

The coyote stood straight and turned to the third mouse. It stared at him, eyes wide.

He raised the blood-covered sword, pointed at the door.

A moment later, and there was nothing left but a trail of blood droplets out into the waning darkness and mist.

Yasu breathed once. Twice. A third time. Then he cleaned his blade on one of the bodies and slipped it back into its scabbard.

Time had run out. He turned to the katana blade on the anvil. If the mouse came back with friends, he didn't want to be here.

Yasu found the materials he needed—wood, cord, carving tools—and got to work.

Yasu had to abandon his bike at the edge of the Willamette. The database told him that all of the bridges north of Oregon City had been destroyed, and a day of backtracking had proven that many of them south of that point were also gone.

He crossed on the skeleton of a rail bridge parallel to the twisted ruin that had once carried Interstate 5 across at Wilsonville, and started to walk.

Most of the roads and many of the urban centres along the way had been battered by bombings and other actions, but time and the coastal rains had smoothed the way to some extent, even in a few years. Yasu made good time as he walked north and slightly west.

Downtown Portland was an area he knew to avoid; a pair of tactical nuclear warheads had been used early in the war to eliminate the network of bridges over the Willamette, and a third had taken down the spans across the Columbia into Washington. The prevailing winds had, by all indications, pushed radiation east and north; Yasu knew DW-147 could take a larger than average dose, but he attached an exposure meter that one of the mice had been carrying to his combat vest just to be on the safe side.

It chirped to itself as he walked. He noted absently that the pace of chirps had quickened the nearer he got to downtown.

Night fell twelve miles north of the river. Yasu took shelter in the shell of a warehouse store as a stiff breeze swirled the mists. In occasional pools of moonlight breaking through the clouds, he stared into the reflection of the coyote staring back from polished metal until he fell asleep.

Between Tigard and Beaverton, a ribbon of asphalt that had once carried thousands of cars a day lay empty and torn by earthquake and weather. It was still smoother than the ground around it, and Yasu made good time. He skirted south of the hill that his implant informed him had once been the home of the Oregon Zoo, but a more urgent tone to the radiation detector's alerts stopped him as he topped a rise.

Below, the shattered city spread out for miles; here and there structures remained, a silent rebuke to the blast waves that had radiated from the two craters, now filled with water. The hill he stood on had not been touched, and even the trees remained, yellowed and weak from lack of sunlight but still standing.

That boded well.

He turned around and circled the hill on its west face, through empty suburban streets and forgotten parks, following the marker blinking inside his eyes.

On the north side of the hill, Yasu descended through a grove of sad cedar trees to stare at a weathered sign leaning askance against a hardy maple that was still making a good attempt at life under the misty skies. The coyote took a moment to straighten the sign as best he could, then walked past into what the board announced as the Portland Japanese Garden.

Had the pull of compulsion not drawn him here already, Yasu would still have known he was in the right place.

His detector was chirping a worrisome warning, but the coyote continued on.

The gardens had suffered from the long years under filtered sunlight. There were no flowers to speak of, and the brushy plants were squat and sickly yellow. Still, there was a familiarity to the place that drew Yasu forward, deeper into the bounds.

There were buildings, most of them still standing—good Japanese workmanship, of course—but Yasu walked past them. He had a feeling he knew where the pull was leading him, and as a pond appeared ahead, the feeling was proven right.

It was a pond garden, surely a good one back in the day, before the war; now, its water was greenish and still, and the trees that had once arched over it drooped and fought to hold even a few leaves.

Yasu made his way along the pond's edge, the swishing of his tail brushing against the fabric of his combat pants deadening the breeze pushing through weakened foliage. On the breeze, a scent traveled—one that was animal, but not. His pace quickened.

His path led to a narrowing of the water, and there he found a bridge. And on the bridge Yasu found what he was seeking.

A tall, lanky figure was seated on the bridge. It—he drew long, slim ears upward attentively and turned toward the coyote, though he remained seated.

Yasu studied the rabbit. Much like the Asian labs had started their work with rats and mice, rabbits had been an early part of North American soldier development, but they had proven less useful as soldiers than other uplifted species. Instead, they had been used for logistics and other work behind the lines, and were still employed in some parts of the western military system.

This one was wearing the olive-drab work gear that most rabbits were issued, battered and aged. He looked thin, thinner than the images that Yasu's implant flashed up for him to compare to, and wobbled as he stood, drawing on the bridge railing for support.

"I knew you would make it." The voice was strange, high-pitched and occasionally stunted by the big front teeth, but the Japanese was perfect. "Something told me you would be here."

Yasu walked to the end of the bridge and stopped, his gaze locked on the rabbit in the middle of the wooden span.

"When my mind appeared in this—" the rabbit gestured at himself "—and I realized I was in some creature of the far future, I thought to myself that the gods would not amuse themselves by doing this to just me. No, I thought, to truly pull a prank of this magnitude, they needed something even bigger than simply dropping me into a giant rodent."

He gestured happily—almost manically—and Yasu for the first time saw the scabbard hanging from his hip. The rabbit took no notice, and leaned heavily on the railing.

"So, a coyote, eh? It suits you, old friend. You were always the hunter. I was the gardener. We made a good pair."

Yasu stepped onto the bridge, combat boots thumping on weathered wood.

"Daiki."

He paused, marveling at the strange voice, realizing it was the first time that he—that DW-147—had actually spoken.

"You do remember me. Hello, Yasu, old friend." The rabbit smiled. "You sound like you have been eating rocks, you know."

"I haven't had much to speak of."

The rabbit that was Daiki chuckled, then coughed, a rough, grating sound. "I am glad you got here in such a timely manner, old friend. A little while longer and we may have had to wait for the next time around to have this conversation."

Yasu stepped forward a few more feet. From there he could see the sores on Daiki's ears, raw spots of flesh on the forearms, fingers that seemed to flex poorly. He paused. "You are not designed for radiation, are you?"

"Not like your dog there, Yasu, no. Rabbits were for behind the lines, not on the front. We didn't need it." He coughed again, longer, and sighed. "Ah well. Let us take care of this."

Daiki took a position at the middle of the bridge and drew the katana, scabbard and all, from his belt. It was immediately familiar to the coyote.

The rabbit followed his gaze and nodded. "It is one of yours, isn't it? I knew it was when the pull drew me to that house. Those damn cats nearly got me, though—lucky I still had bullets for my gun." He drew the sword. It shimmered in the dim light as the rabbit drew himself painfully into a fighting stance. "There is a rock."

"No." Yasu shook his head. "I have not come through so many times on this world to fight you again."

"Oh come, Yasu, what other reason would we have to seek each other out again after so long? We—" He broke off coughing again, wiped a fleck of red off his lip. "Our fight was not honourable, and we do not know who was the better. The universe has brought us back together to end it on the proper note. You have even made yourself a new blade for the occasion, I see."

Yasu pulled the scabbard from his belt and drew forth the katana. It shone in the dim sun, and he stared at his reflection in the polished steel for a long moment. "No, Daiki. This blade is not mine."

"What?" He heard confusion in the rabbit's voice. "I don't—"

"The balance is all wrong for me. I prefer a slightly longer blade, and a different wrapping on the hilt." Yasu held it up. "Yet this was the blade I built while lost in meditation, in understanding, in the past. But it is not made for me."

"Why?"

The coyote reversed the blade, held the flat of it across his forearm, hilt towards the rabbit. "Because it is yours."

Daiki flinched back, stumbled, dropped Yasu's own katana to the wood of the bridge. "W-what…"

"When we last met—when I left to do what I thought was my duty—there was a sword on my work bench. It was for you. And then I left it unfinished and did my duty, and both of us died foolishly." Yasu met the rabbit's red-rimmed gaze. "It was dishonourable. This was what the gods, the universe, whoever is behind all of us wanted, to remember that honour is my true duty. I am completing my duty to you, my friend. Give me back my honour."

The rabbit slowly, painfully closed his fingers around the hilt and lifted the katana. He looked over the sword, traced a white-furred finger across where his name was stamped into the steel near the hilt. "It is…perfect. The weight. The feel in my hand. After all this time, it is perfect."

Yasu nodded. "I remembered much while working that steel. And realized much about how wrong I have been in my life. Lives."

"Thank you." Daiki straightened then coughed again, hard, and fell to a knee, still clutching the hilt of his katana. Yasu moved forward to support his friend. The rabbit wiped blood from his chin and panted. "It is a rather late delivery, though."

The coyote's laugh was a rasping thing that lasted only a moment. Yasu helped Daiki to rest against the bridge railing. "What can I do?"

"You have done the greatest thing you could already, Yasu: you have found yourself again." Daiki smiled a crimson smile and leaned back. "And you have found your honour. I've missed it, and you. Perhaps we will see one another again, hm?"

Yasu sat against the far railing. "Perhaps."

The rabbit closed his eyes, and then there were four figures where there had been one. Yasu was on his feet in an instant, his katana—truly his, every cord, every nick, every ounce of weight felt like home—clutched in his hand.

A shimmering glow surrounded the figures as they slowly separated from the form of the dying rabbit. They were nebulous, shining, weightless, but their gaze as it fell upon Yasu carried with it the weight of the world and thousands of years.

Yasu's implant ran through a half-dozen attempts to define what it was seeing before it gave up and flashed 'ERROR' in the corner of his vision. It didn't need to tell him anything, though. He knew what he was looking at.

The three devas knelt around Daiki. His eyes opened and he gazed in wonder at them. Two stroked his long ears gently, then supported his head. The third knelt before him. A soft smile spread across the nebulous face, and the rabbit smiled weakly back.

Then it reached out and touched him between the eyes, and in a whisper that echoed off the sickly trees, said, "Sleep."

Yasu watched as Daiki's eyes glazed and ears slumped down. The rabbit body relaxed and settled against the railing as life faded. He felt...sad? Relieved?

Nothing?

The devas rose and turned to Yasu. The one that had taken Daiki neared, cast a piercing gaze that burned through the coyote.

"You brought me—us—here."

They nodded agreement.

"Why?"

The central deva's formless face settled into a smile. "You were lost for a very long time, but ever closer to being found. We saw you both pass by, then again, and yet more; it was, we felt, the time for some small assistance."

Yasu pondered that, watched by the divine beings. He

tapped his—DW-147's—chest. "Were you responsible for this?"

"Your current incarnation was no doing of ours. Your emergence, your enlightenment, though—that made our intervention possible."

Yasu's ears perked forward at the word 'enlightenment', but he said nothing. Instead, he slowly ran his fingers along the back of the katana. It needed polishing. He slid it back into its scabbard, settled it on his belt, and turned to the watching devas. "And now?"

"Our business here is concluded, Minamoto Yasu. We return to our own places to continue watching man stumble through the turns of the world." The deva regarded him for a moment. "This life of yours is one of darkness and pain. If you wish—"

It raised one spectral hand, held it out to the coyote.

Yasu considered it, then raised his gaze to the indistinct face. "All lives but the last are darkness and pain. I accept that." He bowed to the three figures. "Thank you, but I will find my own way home."

He stepped forward. The devas parted, allowing him to kneel next to the limp form of the rabbit. Yasu closed the empty eyes, settled the body in a more comfortable position, and clasped one dead hand. Then he turned his back to his friend and the watching devas, and walked off the bridge.

It took two days for Yasu to make his way through the wreckage and remnants of war and civilization, but he eventually reached the shores of the Columbia. The radiation detector had settled into a steady hum early the second day, and the implant was nothing but a series of nonsense characters. He ignored them both.

In a forgotten outbuilding, the coyote found a boat. He cast a critical look at the dim sun showing through the clouds, set a small solar-powered motor into the boat, and dragged the whole works to the river. The effort had left him aching far more than it should have, and the tickle in his lungs suggested the coughing would start soon.

He ignored that as well.

It took effort that left him panting to row the boat into the middle of the broad channel. The sun was brighter there, enough to start the motor running weakly with occasional lapses, but well enough to push the boat downstream with the current, guided by one oar off the stern.

Yasu sat amidships and opened his mind once again. Lives drifted past like leaves on a breeze, leaving memories, loves, needs, hates. He absorbed them, welcomed them, learned from them, then dismissed each.

He barely noticed the night fall and day return. By the time a coughing fit lifted him from his meditation the river had spread wide before him, and the mists were tattered and weak.

Sunlight spread across the greenish water, unfiltered for the first time in his current memory. Above, a bridge sprawled across the river, one portion of the span twisted and black, but the majority still standing proudly.

Yasu savored the warmth and the light, and guided his boat the last miles, past the points and the bar and into the wide blue expanse of the Pacific Ocean.

He coughed again, spat blood overboard.

Slowly the coyote drew his oar aboard. He settled painfully on his knees and set his katana before him.

It had been a short life, and it was nearing its conclusion. He wondered at the deva's words from before.

Would this be the last?

The Winter Born

NightEyes DaySpring

Perched on top of the wall so no one could see him, the black wolf scanned for anyone in the street below. Once satisfied the road was deserted, Joren pushed himself over the wall. Catching the familiar handhold, he swung his legs over before he let go and dropped the ten feet to the street below. He landed gracefully, his feet hitting the ground silently as he dropped into a crouch.

Five years of living in Hofsfell had taught him to be weary, to watch the shadows. As he stood up, he let himself relax, his tail lazily uncurling. Tonight he did not have to be so cautious. If they caught him today, they could not punish any more than they already had.

Hopefully a good drink would take his mind off of his problems, or at least numb him enough so he didn't care. It had never been his idea to come to Hofsfell; it had been parents' idea, in order to protect him. Lately the city felt less like a sanctuary and more like a prison—andhe still had three more years of service to complete before he could return home. Additionally, the latest letter from home had deepened his already dark mood. His younger brother would be staying in Iznit and only going to Toreaken for training.

"You know, for someone who tries to keep a low profile when they sneak out, you always use the same part of the wall."

Shit! He spun toward the shadows, hand instinctively sliding down to his waist.

"Well, it's true," said the voice.

"You again? I thought we agreed to stay out of each other's business." Was the gray and tan wolf invisible? Could a mage even do that? He could not see his accuser, but he knew that voice well.

"I'm just amused you keep taking the same way out of the citadel. Doesn't anyone check to make sure you're all there at night?"

"I am allowed out you know," Joren replied, still glancing around for the mage.

"Not after dark when you are on restriction." The hooded figure stepped out from an alleyway.

Joren sighed. "What do I owe your presence to this time, Fargis?"

"Must I remind you? We have a deal."

Joren walked up to the mage. "You told me you could pull strings and would get me on that assignment. They assigned me back to guard duty. The deal is off as far as I am concerned."

Fargis was silent for a moment before he responded. "I did what I could."

"Did you now?" the black wolf asked. "I will not be accosted by you in a dark alleyway for stupid errands. Find someone else to go intimidate. Did you even try and help me?"

The mage huffed. "I passed it along."

Joren shook his head and turned to walk away. "I'll be down at my favorite tavern, drinking."

"If you didn't spend most of your time in the evening drunk, they would have given you that assignment," hissed the cloaked figure.

"Yeah, well the lasses like me just the same," Joren called.

"More like the lads!" exclaimed the other wolf.

He turned, looking back up the street. "Have you been following me now?" Joren asked Fargis, a growl under his words.

"Word gets around," said the mage smugly. "There's nothing wrong with your tastes either," he added.

"Word does not just get around. You are nosy. There's a reason no one will tell you what's in the royal armory."

The figure sighed. "It's of upmost importance to the college to find out if the High King has in his possession certain magical relics."

"Which are?"

"I can't tell you," said the mage.

"You don't even know. They just gave you some stupid mission to keep you busy, didn't they?"

Fargis grumbled. "It's not stupid. I am trying to help us both out you."

"Suit yourself," laughed Joren. "I'm going to go get drunk. If I am lucky, maybe I'll score some action, but tonight, I want to just get stupidly drunk. Then I'll come back here and see if I can get myself back over the wall without breaking my neck or having to bribe the night watchman."

"That is the dumbest thing you could do you know. You just got off of a disciplinary assignment to the dungeons."

Joren shrugged and turned to walk off. "You get used to the smell after a while."

The mage flicked his tail. "What is it that eats at you Joren?"

The black wolf paused, and turned around. "That is not your concern to worry about."

"I'm willing to listen if you want to tell me."

The black wolf huffed. "You really want to know? Come to the tavern and I'll tell you, but the first round is all on you."

"Is alcohol all that matters to you?"

The black wolf shrugged. "No one else is there for me."

The mage sighed. "Fine. I'll buy you a drink."

"Five years, and all they see fit to give me is guard duty around the city," Joren remarked, clutching a tankard of mead. Since Fargis paid for the first round, he started with the good stuff tonight. He stuck with the mead through the subsequent rounds. The mage sat across from him. They made small talk for a while, but the conversation was finally getting serious.

"It's not so bad here you know," offered the mage.

"The High King is going east in a few days, and I'm stuck here guarding the palace. I would like to finally get a chance to see a place that isn't Hofsfell."

The mage picked up a tankard of ale and sipped at it. "Guarding the place better than prison duty, isn't it?"

"I guess. I just want to do something useful. Here, I am useless. They won't give me anything important to do since my family lineage runs through Iznit's Westmoor."

"Your father is a Jarl in Iznit. You're in line to have your own hold someday. Isn't that something?"

"Yeah, and do you know why Father sent me here to train with the King's Guard?" Joren sneered. "To get me out of Iznit to avoid the bickering of the Westmoor wolf clans."

Fargis's ears flicked. "From what I hear of your father, Bertil is a fair man."

Joren chuckled. "My brother gets to stay in Iznit and train in the capital."

"Yeah, but Hofsfell is much bigger than Toreaken. I remember visiting Toreaken when I was young, before I came to the college. It still hasn't recovered from the last war."

Joren grumbled. "The wolf clans of the Westmoor are still the laughing stock of the empire. At least there I'd be closer to our homelands."

"It surprises me the High King doesn't pay Iznit a visit, but apparently High King Asger doesn't want to get involved in lupine politics. He's leaned on the king in Toreaken to square away the clans."

Joren took a gulp of mead and let the sweet taste swirl in his muzzle. "They want us to fight, I think. It keeps us occupied."

The mage shrugged. "You would know better than I. It's been years since I've been back home. My aunt doesn't write me much."

The black wolf sighed and finished off his tankard, putting it down. He fished out his purse. It felt light already, and he did not get his wages until next week. He turned it out and three coppers tumbled out.

"Can you spot me a few coin, Fargis? I'm a bit light right now."

"I need to hang onto what I have left. Didn't your father

send you something?"

"A little, but it was much smaller this time since he found out about my disciplinary actions. I already spent what he sent. I also had to pay Fjork back the money he lent me."

"What did he say?" asked the mage, concerned.

"Oh, that I'm his representative in Sendal, and I need to represent our holding well. He's also not pleased about my dalliances."

Fargis grinned. "Is he now?"

"Well, I don't have a pup to bring back, so on that, he's at least not too mortified."

"That's a unique way of thinking about it. It's getting late, so I need to turn in." Fargis yawned and stood up.

"You go ahead," suggested Joren.

"You aren't trying the wall again? I remember when you fell off it and sprained your tail."

"Oh piss off, Fargis. I know what I am doing," huffed Joren.

The morning light was bright and it hurt his head, but Joren was up on time and reported to Commander Bjorn. The bear looked at Joren and shook his head.

"You stink of mead," he remarked as he looked over Joren's orders.

"I was toasting last night down in the great hall to my friend Fjork's assignment with the guard escorting the High King to the east."

Bjorn sat back and gave him a look. Everyone knew the kitchen watered down the mead in the great hall for the soldiers. The only strong drink they served was a bitter dark ale. Only on holidays did they serve the good stuff.

"Toast a little less vigorously," the bear said finally. "And if I ever catch you sneaking out when on restriction, I will have no qualms sending you back to prison duty for a whole year."

"Yes, sir," said the wolf.

"I mean that. You spend your entire salary on mead, lads, and lasses. You're turning into the type of soldier I do not want. Just because you are winter-born does not mean you can't be a good soldier. At this rate, prison guard is all you'll be useful for."

Joren laid his ears back. "I'll try to do better."

"You'll do more than try. You're lucky I'm not going to be keeping an eye on you for the next week. I got orders this morning saying you are to report to the Mages' College."

"The Mages' College?" asked Joren.

"Yes. They're putting you on duty there."

"We guard the college now? I thought they had their own guards."

Bjorn shrugged. "I got fresh orders for you in this morning. They apparently need a few men to be at their disposal. Make sure you show up sober for duty. Go to the college at day mark, and someone will be expecting you."

"Yes, sir."

"Now get out of sight before I send them someone else."

Joren nodded and made his way back to his quarters. It had to be that damn mage Fargis who set him up on this.

The citadel of the High King sat on the tallest hill in Hofsfell. The streets of the city all led up toward the fortress and its imposing walls. The guard's barracks stood at the foot of the citadels near a gate in the outer ramparts. The outer ramparts consisted of a stone wall built around the main fortress a hundred years after the fortress had been completed to relieve overcrowding issues with the royal household. Since it did not form part of the original defenses of the citadel, its walls were lower, and in some parts, were barely taller than the houses on the other side.

The Mages' College stood on the second-highest hill in the city. At the top of the hill rose a tall stone keep, suitable for sky observations. Around it, a cluster of buildings stretched down the hill, surrounded by a simple stonewall. The buildings inside were three-storied halls and quads. Between the halls, gardens provided secluded spaces for the ongoing studies at the college.

At the gate, Joren found a mercenary with a bad disposition loitering in the shade of the wall. The red fox scowled at Joren before she waved him in with a grunt. "Go to the Arcanarium;

they'll be waiting for you there."

Finding the Arcanarium was harder than Joren expected it to be; he had to ask twice for directions. It turned out be one of the large quads in the back of the complex.

He asked a passing kobold carrying a stack of manuscripts if he might know who he should be looking for, but the kobold just shrugged before going on his way. Entering the building, he found it deserted. A staircase stood in the back of the room heading to the upper stories.

"Hello?" Joren called out. There was no response.

The wolf stood in the entrance perplexed, wondering who had summoned him. Turning to leave, he nearly bumped into Fargis as the other wolf entered through the front door.

"Ah, you're here. Good," said the mage, pulling back his hood to expose his face. His gray and tan fur gave him a regal look in the light coming in from the windows. White fur trimmed his throat. Joren would have found him attractive, if he didn't find him so frustrating to deal with.

"You summoned me?" asked Joren cautiously.

The mage nodded. "Come with me," he said, walking down a hallway off the entranceway. Halfway down the hall, he stopped at a door and opened it. He stepped inside, and waited for Joren to enter before closing the door behind them.

The room they entered contained a fireplace on one end and a set of benches at the other. The fireplace was cold and the room dimly lit, with only a few shafts of light peaking past the drawn shutters and penetrating the gloom. Fargis walked over to a table near the fireplace and produced a bottle from under his cloak. He set the vial down.

"Why did you call me here?" Joren asked.

"I need some help with an experiment."

The black wolf grumbled. "So that gives you the right to drag me down here? I should report you to my commander."

"You wouldn't do that," said the mage.

"Why not? Are you going to tell him how many times I've snuck out to that tavern when I'm on restriction? I'm sure your interest in the King's Armory is enough to at least keep me in the guard, even if I have to spend the next three years down in the dungeons. If this plot is as serious as I think it is, I can make sure you get fed you when I am on duty."

Fargis took a deep breath. "I just wanted you to show some damn discipline."

"By manipulating me?"

The other wolf lowered his ears. "I wasn't trying to manipulate you. Not at first."

Joren snorted.

"Seriously! By the stars, do you know how lonely it is being the only wolf from Iznit in the whole damn college? They call us winter-born because no one wants to associate with a wolf from Iznit. I am lucky Master Einar could look past my birth and see my talent."

The mage rung his hands. "Last night was kind of nice. I haven't seen my family in years; I spend the majority of my time studying and practicing. I get one night a week to myself. Apparently though, you're too blind to realize I've been trying to be your friend."

Joren chortled. "Friends don't threaten to blackmail each other. If you weren't such a pompous ass about being a mage when I first met you, I might have felt you were worth talking to."

"Why am I arguing with you? You'll go back to Iznit in a few years, and I'll still be here studying away."

"As if that is such a good deal. I get to be Father's shadow until he dies. Then I get to inherit all the problems of our little holding."

"At least you get to go home," grumbled the gray. "I know that Westmoor is a rough place, but I haven't been back north since I was twelve."

"I've been home only once."

Fargis shook his head. "Fine, fine, you've been home once."

Joren walked up to him. "Your problem is that you think the world owes you something."

"Like I need advice from you."

"If this is all, I can see myself out."

Fargis chuckled mirthlessly. "I'm sure you will, straight back to the tavern."

"I don't have a drinking problem!"

"No? You still smell like mead from last night. I paid for three rounds, and you bought more until you ran out of money."

"Why do you even care?" Joren huffed.

"I ask myself that often." Fargis reached down to pick up the potion bottle he set down earlier. "I thought when you opened up to me last night it wasn't just the mead talking, but I guess it was."

"Listen," growled Joren putting his nose a brush away from Fargis's and poking the other wolf in the chest. "Leave me alone."

"You can't threaten me," growled Fargis.

"Ha, why not? I'm sure there is some rule you've broken by summoning me here."

Fargis just rolled his eyes and shook his head. He turned to walk away, but Joren reached out and grabbed him by the wrist. The bottle slipped from Fargis's paw and fell. "Oh no," yelped the mage trying catch it.

The vial hit the floor and shattered. Glass flew everywhere and the blue liquid splattered across the floor and them.

Joren jumped back as the potion ignited when it came in contact with his fur. "Fire—"

"Wait," commanded Fargis. "By the stars!" he added as the fire started to spread onto Joren's paws as he slapped at the flames.

"What is this stuff?" yelled Joren in increasing panic, his eyes wide, ears back in shock.

"You are making it worse, just wait. It's an illusion I've been developing. Watch, it will burn off in a minute."

Joren didn't answer but held up his burning paw. Already the flames were dying down. He glared at Fargis. "Why is it staining my fur blue?"

"That is what I wanted to see about testing," remarked the mage.

They stood in the room nervously as the headmistress of the college considered them—a lynx with tawny, spotted fur that clung to her frame. She had looked over the orders Joren had with him and proceed to scowl at both of them. On one side of the room, in front of the large desk, sat Fargis's master Einar, an old stoat who had taught for the college for decades.

"Did you know about this, Einar?" she asked, gesturing to the two wolves. Their fur was still stained blue where the potion had splashed them.

"No," replied the stoat.

"You forged Einar's signature on this?" she asked Fargis, pointing to the orders Joren had been carrying that now sat on her desk.

"I was told I should—"

"Did you forge his signature?" she repeated.

Fargis lowered his ears. "Yes."

"I should have you expelled for that alone. The college does not need to antagonize the guard of the High King."

"Yes, Headmistress."

"And you," she said pointing at Joren. "How could you be so easily manipulated?"

Joren cleared his throat. "The orders were delivered to my commander this morning."

"Really," she looked at Fargis. "How did you manage that?" she asked Fargis icily.

"A small bribe, headmistress."

She leaned across her desk letting her fangs show. "Do you realize how much trouble you could have caused the college?"

Einar cleared his throat. "Freja."

She glanced at the stoat. "He's dangerous to the mission of the college."

"I believe what he needs is a sense of discipline and purpose, something I have not forced upon him. I have something I think would help."

She sat back. "What do you have in mind?" She grinned, showing her fangs. Fargis nervously shifted his weight from paw to paw.

"Fargis is a talented mage, but he is also a hands-on type of pupil. The college has definitely been confining for him. I think now would be a good time to have him test what he's learned, if he wishes to continue as my apprentice."

The lynx considered, tapping a claw against the desk. "What type of challenge?"

"As I understand it, the Kjord Hill's Barrow has had peculiar sightings at night. The inhabitants of the area have reported strange movements about the area. I think sending someone from the college would be prudent."

She looked at Fargis and then back to the stoat. "He doesn't stand a chance of clearing the complex on his own."

"I am hoping his friend might go with him."

"Me?" questioned Joren. "I have done nothing wrong."

Einar turned to him. "Meeting mages after curfew would be of interest to your commander. However, I think your sense of adventure would be reason enough to assist him. It's easy for me to arrange this for you since my name is already on the orders."

Joren squinted at the stoat. "How dangerous is this?"

"It is not without risks, but I do not think they are undue. You'll also have a couple days to prepare. The college will be grateful for your assistance."

Joren looked at the old stoat and the grinning lynx. "I'll need supplies."

"Of course," said the stoat. "Will this suffice, Headmistress?"

"I suppose," she said. "You will take care of the arrangements, Einar?"

"Of course."

"Good," she remarked, sliding the orders back across the desk toward him. She reached for a scroll sitting on the other side. "I like it when problems go away."

Einar got up, and the two wolves followed as Freja began reviewing the scroll. Once they were outside, he led them down the hall away from the office before he turned to them.

"I want you to know, Fargis, you will be my last apprentice. I have put a lot of my hope into you, so when I say I am disappointed by your conduct, I think you should know that comes from a lifetime of experience."

"Yes, Master," said the wolf, ears back.

"I apparently have given you too much free reign without teaching you the cautious restraint of influence."

"Master—"

Einar held up a paw. "I don't want to hear excuses or rationales. I've given you a path to follow. I expect you not to disappoint me. Do know though, if I ever see you doing something foolish like this again, I will have you kicked out of the college. There will not be another second chance."

Fargis gulped. "Yes, sir."

"Good," said Einar turned to walk down the hall. "Now come, both of you. Let me tell you about what I've set you up against."

The Kjord Hill's Barrow was an easy day's journey east from the city. It was located in a small, remote valley nestled in the foothills of Sendal. The area was heavily forested with only a small village surrounded by farms. There was no inn nearby, so they camped in the woods near the barrow.

Einar had told them the tomb in the barrow had been sealed, but probably was recently disturbed. He didn't know how big the area underneath would be, but that they should proceed with caution. After they inspected the tomb, they would reseal it and return.

As a precaution, they set up their camp a short distance away from the barrow, and Fargis and put wards up to keep any wandering spirits away. They concentrated on the various tasks of setting up their camp after they arrived. It wasn't until their first morning there that they went to inspect the barrow.

"How big do you think this thing is?" Joren asked as they stood outside. Carved standing stones stood before a small shrine at the entrance to the barrow. Behind the shrine, a passageway led down to the tomb itself. It showed signs of being recently excavated.

"I'm not sure," said Fargis. "The hill is pretty sizable."

"Yeah, but the tomb itself shouldn't be that big, right?"

"I want to say no. If it was just going in, putting an offering in the tomb, and coming back out, you wouldn't need to be here. Someone went through the effort to dig out the entranceway for a reason."

Joren got up and looked over the inscriptions. "The stones appear to be talking about a great battle that happened in the valley. For the fallen, this site was dedicated."

"This is where my lack of Sendal history comes into play. I don't know anything about this area. I have only vague knowledge about what predated the empire."

Joren traced a paw over the runes. "The stones feel weird to the touch, like they tingle."

"Weird?" Fargis came over and joined him, running the pads of his fingers across the inscription. "These stones have been enchanted."

"How do you know?" asked Joren.

"Whenever magic is used, it leaves a residue. That's why illusion magic doesn't work on the initiated. Magic-users can sense magic when it's being used, while most people can't. You obviously have some sensitivity to it." Fargis paused on one of the symbols. "I'm not sure how old this is, but it feels ancient."

"Well, I'm here to make sure you stay alive. What do we do?" asked the black wolf.

"We might as well have a peek at what's down in the tunnel."

Getting down proved to be tighter than they expected. Fargis conjured a ball of light to illuminate the way, but Joren carried torches as a backup. They had to stoop and crawl down the passageway until they reached an antechamber at the end of the tunnel where they could stand up. The walls were smooth, carved stone. There were more inscriptions here, wishing the dead safe passage to their afterlives.

"It looks like quite a broad group of people died here. There are references to both the Valhalla and Fólkvangr afterlives in these," remarked Fargis. He paused and traced over a part of a column where the text had been worn off. "Odd. Someone removed part of the blessing here."

"Die in battle, and go to Valhalla with your fallen pack-mates. That's what all the warriors back home wanted to do with their lives." The black wolf shook his head. "Can you light my torch, or do I need to get out the flint and steel?"

"Hold it up. Didn't you see me start the campfire last night?" asked Fargis.

The black wolf shook his head, and with a quick flick of his hand, Fargis shot out a small flame that caught on the end of the torch.

"Thanks."

"Don't mention it." Fargis looked around and settled his eyes on a doorway on the opposite wall to the entrance. "So, what do you think?" he asked, gesturing towards a heavy wooden door leading out of the antechamber. The door stood broken, the wood protruding from the frame.

"It looks like something wanting to get out, not someone trying to get in."

"Yeah, that's my feeling too, which makes no sense at all." Fargis sent the floating orb of light through the doorway. Beyond there was a stone corridor. "This tomb is much bigger than I expected."

Joren nodded and they stepped through the door in silence, heading down the gently sloping corridor. The tap of the staff Fargis carried echoed against the stone.

"Maybe you should just carry that," whispered the black wolf. "Why did you bring it anyway?"

"It gives me something to affix the light to. There's nothing special about it, but I have a few tricks up my sleeves that use it." The gray wolf paused. "I feel air movement."

"Yeah, I do too. We're underground though." Joren glanced back. "Do you sense any more magic?"

Fargis traced a paw across the stone wall. "Nothing distinct. Everything down here should be ancient, so some of the magic may have faded away. The whole place vibrates softly with energy." He took another step forward. "Something has to be producing the draft. Perhaps there is another way in."

Joren sniffed to scent the air. "We didn't see one on the

surface. All I can smell is the musky stench of decay."

They resumed walking down the tunnel until they came to a chamber cut into the rock. Here they found a series of shelves built into the rock walls. Each shelf held the remains of a warrior buried with their weapons and armor. The bodies came from every species in Sendal: foxes, wolves, lynxes, stoats, kobolds, badgers, and even a couple of reindeer. Some of the bodies were embalmed, while others had decayed to just bones. Two smaller rooms opened off the chamber, one on each side. Each held more internments.

They also found another passage, this one fairly short that led to a small shrine. The walls in here were smooth, and a stone altar had been placed in the center.

"Everything looks undisturbed," remarked Joren. A few offering bowls lined the wall and had been placed in front of the altar. If there hadn't been a thick layer of dust over everything, the shrine would look like it was still in use.

Fargis inspected the shrine. "It does, but there is definitely a strong concentration of energy in here." He looked up at Joren and frowned, his ear swiveling. "Did you hear something?"

Joren swiveled his ears. "Yeah. It sounds like it's coming from where we just were."

They exchanged glances with each other, a silent panic filling them. The sound of movement becoming clearer.

The mage took a step away from the entrance. "We aren't alone," he said, curling his tail under himself.

"Tell me something I don't know," said Joren.

"It's not just the sound, I can feel magic at work."

Joren walked to the entrance, torch in hand. "Fargis, I need you by the door. I don't want to be taken by surprise." He pulled his sword out of its scabbard.

"This isn't supposed to be happening. We're supposed to just come in here, make an offering, and reseal the tomb," mumbled the mage to himself, panic filling his voice.

Joren's eyes were focused on what was coming down the corridor. In the light of his torch, he could see movement. Decayed skeletal forms, with bits of petrified flash hanging on, marched down the hallway. The warriors housed within the tomb had come alive, and they were armed.

Thinking quickly, Joren tossed the torch down the corridor and pulled his shield off his back. He dropped into a fighting stance.

"Einar said there might be spirits. If we can hold the entrance, I think we stand a chance of walking out of here!" yelled Joren as a skeleton emerged from the corridor and took a swing at him with the rusted sword it carried. The sword slid across his shield as Joren swung back at the skeleton, taking off its arm.

"Yes, but not awoken dead like draugar," whispered the mage in panic.

"Fargis, now is not the time," grunted Joren trying to push the skeleton back down the hall into the skeleton behind it.

The mage wasn't focused on Joren; instead his eyes roamed over the shrine. "There has to be something pulling them here. Something powerful. I need time to think."

Joren growled low as a second skeleton slipped through the entranceway. "I can't hold them all back by myself." He managed to slice the first one's head off but another replaced it, this one carrying an axe. Now with two flanking him, he was forced back. "Fargis, you will get us both killed if you don't help me!" he howled with growing anger.

"The magic is old—"

"Fargis!" Joren sliced a skeleton in half as it thrust a spear at him, but he managed to dance around the thrust, the rusted point scraping across his chainmail hauberk.

"The whole place is enchanted." The mage blinked and stepped quickly away from the altar toward the door. With a flick of his outstretched hand, he shot fire past Joren, incinerating one of the skeletons attacking him. "We need to seal the door," yelled Fargis.

Joren deflected an axe blow with his shield. "How?"

Fargis shot another fireball out of his hand, striking another skeleton. "Just push them back."

Joren grunted and pushed a skeleton backwards as one took

a stab at him, striking the mail he was wearing. He spun and cut his attacker down. Together, they managed to push the others back into the corridor and Fargis held up his hands, staff in hand, and cast a wall of ice over the entrance.

"That should hold them back for a bit," said the gray and tan wolf.

Joren panted. "When I said I needed help, I needed you to come immediately, not wait around."

"Sorry, but the chamber—"

The black wolf growled. "Maybe my life isn't valuable to you, but I don't want to die down here. These things are trying to kill us."

"I—" Fargis laid his ears flat. "I'm sorry, and you're wounded." He gulped. "We need to hurry. I can't keep that barrier up forever."

Joren looked at the barrier and down to where a sword had sliced his side. The mail he was wearing had turned part of the blow, but he was still bleeding. "I'm all ears if you have some way to get us out of here."

"The entire complex is enchanted. The warriors out there were placed as guardians. There's got to be more to this place than a mere disused shrine."

"If we get out of this alive, I'm never doing this with you again," said Joren, sheathing his sword. He proceeded to pull off the cloak he was wearing and the damaged chainmail shirt.

Fargis sighed and walked back to the altar, then started looking over the inscriptions on it again. The altar sat in the middle of the room; runes had been carved into the polished stone.

"The shrine is dedicated to the eternal memory of the fallen warriors," said Fargis.

"I don't care," mumbled Joren. "I think that sword blade may have been coated with poison or cursed somehow. My head is starting to swim."

"Cursed?" Fargis abandoned inspecting the shrine. "What do you mean?"

"I feel light-headed," said Joren backing up until he bumped into the wall. Slowly he slid down until he reached a seated position.

Fargis leapt over and knelt before him. "Your eyes are dilated. I think it's some type of poison."

"Whatever it is, it's potent," mumbled the black wolf softly, blinking his eyes to try and focus on the gray.

"Joren," said Fargis, "I need your help."

"To do what? You can't maintain that barrier forever."

"I... I know there is a way out."

"Ha." whispered Joren weakly.

Fargis grabbed him. "You need to stay with me. We can get out of this together."

The other wolf didn't say anything. He just closed his eyes.

"Joren?" Fargis reached out and ran a paw across his muzzle. "You can't just die. Stay with me."

While his ears twitched, Joren didn't speak. Instead, his head rolled to the side. The poison was already working through his system.

Fargis kicked the shrine. "I need something I can use." His body sagged under the strain of continual effort. He'd only kept the barrier up for ten minutes, but already he knew he was running out of magical energy. The sounds of skeletal hands scrapping across the ice had stopped, but he knew they were still on the other side, waiting. Joren was breathing raggedly nearby.

The mage slumped down onto the ground and leaned his head against the cold stone of the shrine's wall. He'd just wanted to have a friend, to have someone who understood him. It wasn't just the fact they both came from Iznit that attracted Fargis; Joren's favoring of the lads over the lasses had been an added benefit. His selfishness, though, had brought them here, and it was about ready to doom them both.

"Stupid. I was just stupid," he said. His voice echoed around the smooth walls of the room. The room smelled of mold and dust, with a hint of loam.

His sniffed deeper to fix the scents in his mind. If he could smell soil, perhaps that was the source to the air current they'd felt nearby. He glanced around the smooth walls and floor, but they were unmarked. The ceiling, however, had a small channel cut into it. He got up to examine it. If he craned his neck right, he could see a faint bit of sky. His ears and tail drooped. The shaft was far too narrow for them to fit through.

He was destined to die here in this dank tomb now. He closed his eyes, feeling the drain of magic pulling out of his body. He extinguished the magical light, leaving the barrier up. In the darkness, he could hear Joren struggling to breathe.

"I'm sorry," he whispered in the darkness, tears coming to his eyes. "I wish I never got us into this mess."

Crying, he opened his eyes. The chamber was almost completely dark, but a small amount of light penetrated it; the torch was still burning on the other side of the ice barrier, casting shadows into the chamber. Fargis got up. They were supposed to pacify the tomb, but Einar never told him how.

If the guardians were protecting something, what was it? Draugar always desired to strike revenge on the living out of jealousy for the things they no longer had. If the spell that had been used to bind them here was designed to protect the shrine, they had grown to hunger for more.

Wiping his eyes, he knew what he must do. With great effort, he pulled Joren over to the altar and laid him on top. The black wolf didn't stir, and he felt cold to the touch. Once he'd gotten Joren up on the shrine, he took the warrior's sword. Taking a steadying breath, sword in one hand and staff in the other, he let the ice barrier fall.

They came in, carrying swords and axes. In the feeble light, it was hard to see them except as dark outlines. Fargis was grateful he couldn't make out the details of their decayed forms.

"As long as I breathe, you shall not reach this altar," proclaimed the mage.

They came directly at him. Focusing his mind, Fargis put magefire onto the sword. With the blade burning brightly he tried to drive them back, swinging the sword wildly, but for every one he managed to hack apart, another took its place. They flooded into the room, pinning him against the shrine. A couple of times he felt blades just barely miss him. With growing desperation, he growled low and struck the staff on the ground.

"I will not let Joren die for my own stupid selfishness!"

He pushed his dwindling magic into the staff, using it to concentrate his spell. Sparks of fire radiated out across the floor. His assailants were caught in the spell, but again, more replace those that fell. He pushed forward into the crowd, swinging the sword desperately.

Pain shot up his back as he was struck by a blade. Cursing, he swung wildly with the sword, fire flying through the room, but another blade danced out so close he felt it strike his whiskers. There were too many of them. With blood dripping down his back, he made it back to the altar where Joren lay. The black wolf lay with blood oozing form his side, and Fargis fell against the altar, depleted.

The walls of the shrine started to fade from his view. The wound in his back was burning. He could feel the beginning onset of the poison coursing inside of him, but in a moment of clarity, he realized the altar must be the source of their power. It hummed with hunger as he felt the draugar closing in.

With great effort he pushed the staff back against the shrine and channeled his life-force into a desperate spell. The stone rippled behind him and he felt the block of marble crack. Depleted, he slumped forward, knowing only darkness.

Joren woke up to pitch black nothingness. His body burned and he was weak. He managed to push himself to a sitting position. His side groaned in pain, and his ribs felt bruised. The stench in the air told him he was still somewhere in the tomb, but where? He could see nothing.

"Fargis?" he croaked through his parched throat. He felt around. He seemed to be on a slab of broken stone. He continued to feel around until he felt fur. Fargis's scent came to him as he traced the side of the wolf's face where he lay crumpled against the broken stone Joren lay on top of.

"Fargis?" he asked, shaking the wolf. When he didn't respond, Joren lowered himself so he could listen for signs of life. The mage was barely breathing.

Joren reached for the pouch at his side. He still had the flint and steel. Cautiously, he pulled his other torch off of his belt and put it down on the slab. Taking care not to drop anything, he pulled the flint out of his tinderbox. It took a couple strikes, whacking his paws twice against the stone, but he managed to light the torch. Grateful, he held it up and looked around.

He was still in the shrine, but he lay on top of the now-broken altar. The remains of the fallen warriors littered the floor of the shrine. Fargis was slumped against the altar, his staff clutched in his paws along with Joren's sword.

Gingerly, Joren got up from the altar. He felt exhausted and dizzy.

"What happened?" he whispered to the darkness. He swiveled his ears around trying to find some sound, but there was nothing. He crouched next to Fargis. The wolf had minor cuts along the side of his face, and his clothes were torn. A pool of dried blood lay behind the mage, and when Joren gently rolled Fargis over, he could see where a gash had been torn into his fur.

He grumbled. "I guess I have to carry you out by myself."

It took Joren over an hour to haul the comatose Fargis out of the tomb. With only a single torch left, he could only carry Fargis a short distance before he'd have to put him down and retrieve the torch to place it further down the hall. The climb back up was even more difficult as Joren had to drag the mage up slowly, careful not to try and reopen the wound in his own side. By the time they reached the surface, dawn was breaking.

After the climb, dragging Fargis back to the campsite was the easy part of the journey. He laid him on his sleeping roll and dressed both their wounds. Joren got some water into the other wolf before he ate a meal of dried meat. Exhausted, he passed out by the dead fire after pulling on a fresh shirt.

When he woke again, it was late afternoon, and the sound of Fargis thrashing on his bed roll woke him. Joren had to rush over and try to hold him still.

"Hey, hey," he grunted, holding onto Fargis. "It's a dream,

it's a dream—"

"Joren?" croaked the other wolf. "Joren, oh god, I'm so sorry, Joren. I should have helped you and now look where we are."

"We're outside the tomb," grunted the black wolf, trying to regain some balance.

"Wait, we are?" Fargis blinked and looked around, finally calming down. He tried to get up quickly, but cried out in pain. "Ow! Oh this hurts."

"You've got a deep cut in your back. I dressed the wound."

"It worked?" he said confused.

"What worked? I had to drag your unconscious butt out of the shrine."

"The altar, the altar was enchanted. I destroyed it! I had to lower the barrier, so they attacked. At the last possible minute, I could feel the stone humming as our lives were slipping way. I directed a bolt of magical energy into the altar. It must have worked!"

"I guess," said Joren, sitting back and letting Fargis talk.

"We should go back and figure out what enchantment is on it. There might be something to be learned from it."

Joren shook his head. "Look, I just hauled your lifeless body out of that hole. I am not going back in there."

"You dragged me all the way here?" stammered Fargis, taken back.

"What was I supposed to do, leave you down there?"

"No, no, it's just that makes me... Well, thank you."

"Makes you what?" questioned Joren, tilting his head.

"Well, grateful for one," he said with a slight blush.

"I'm supposed to make sure you come out of this alive. That's another reason I don't want to go back down there." Fargis propped himself up on his elbows while Joren talked. "We're lucky we're even alive and, hey—"

Fargis thumped his tail after giving Joren a quick peck on the check. "Thanks."

"You kissed me!" said the black wolf in shock.

Fargis chuckled. "I've known you long enough to know

that's what you're into, so thank you."

"Yes, but," he paused, "You. Kissed. Me," he said, putting emphasis on each word.

"Sorry, maybe that has the wrong social connotations."

The black wolf shook his head and got up. "You should eat something. You've been out for a while."

"Yeah," said Fargis, carefully getting up. "I don't feel too well. My magical energy is still drained."

Joren grunted and picked up an axe. He stalked off looking for firewood. Fargis waited until the black wolf had walked off before pulling off his ruined robes. They were torn in multiple places. He pulled out a fresh set of clothing from his pack and slipped it on. When he was done, he looked around to see if the black wolf had returned. He could hear him in the distance cutting something down.

"It's taken me years to get that kiss," he mumbled to himself as he searched through the food rations. "It totally wasn't worth it," he chuckled to himself. Still, his tail wagged as he started to get food ready to cook.

"You sent for me?" asked Joren after entering the study. He and Fargis had returned a few days ago from the barrow. When he'd gotten a note from Einar asking him to come to the Mages' College after his morning rounds, he'd been nervous. Still, he was relieved to see that this time it was Einar who summoned him.

"Yes," said the mage, who was digging through a stack of books. "Sit," he said, gesturing to a chair next to a small table. Einar's study was full of bookshelves containing volumes of books and scrolls. On one end he had a work table covered with odd trinkets, and on the other a set of chairs and a small table by the fireplace.

The stoat flipped through a book until he found what he was looking for and left it open on the table. He then came and sat down next to Joren. "Now, where are we?"

"You summoned me," remarked the wolf.

Einar chuckled. "That I did. Did you know I met your

grandfather, Goulon, once?"

"No," Joren remarked.

"I was of course much younger and traveling through Iznit. He was a brute of a wolf who proudly carried the scars of battles won. This was shortly after he had earned the nickname 'Stumptail', and he was happy to tell any who listened the story of how he lost half his tail. I understand he died of old age; not on the battlefield."

"He didn't make it to Valhalla like he wanted to," said Joren.

Einar shrugged. "He might not have sired your father if he'd succeeded. I don't know much about Lord Bertil, but people suggest he is of honor."

"I'm surprised you know anything about my clan. Few in Sendal care what happens over the border to us winter-born."

"They should," said Einar. "The fate of the Westmoor clans could be important to the fate of the empire. That's why I want to sponsor you."

"Sponsor me?" asked Joren.

"I gather your father sent you to Sendal to escape some of the petty infighting of the clans. The King's Guard is good for learning the ways of the sword, but if you hope to be a successful jarl like your father, you'll need to earn their respect. You'll also need to reach beyond the borders of the Westmoor. I can get you on a few diplomatic missions where you can get outside of Sendal to other parts of the empire. You'll get to see how the kingdom is ruled. While it won't always be hands-on, I think it will give you some insight into treaty politics. I'm sure a few weeks away from here would do you some good. Your father might even be proud of you."

"That is all well in good sir, but why help me?" asked Joren.

"That is indeed a good question. I know the future of the empire will depend on building up the connections within it. I'm old enough to remember the war that brought Iznit into the empire. I was a young neophyte, so I didn't see the wrong then. I later came to realize that what the mages did is an irreparable stain upon the college. I've sought in my later years to help fix that wrong. It's a big reason I didn't turn down the chance to take on a young winter-born wolf from Iznit as my apprentice."

"That is very noble of you."

"Perhaps." The stoat shrugged. "I have my reasons. I am one of the few mages left who still saw the carnage first-hand. I don't want that history to get lost. Magic may give us extra time, but even a mage doesn't live forever. On a practical note, I did send you along with Fargis on that quest. It was a test for the both of you."

"Did Fargis set you up to this?"

The stoat shook his head. "Not at all."

Joren regarded him. "Did you know what we were going up against in the barrow?"

"I knew there was some risk. It was more than I anticipated, however you both managed to handle it. I may be wise and old, but I don't know everything there is to know."

Joren pondered. "May I consider your proposition for a few days?"

"By all means," said Einar, reaching for a slip of paper he'd left on the table. "If you decide to take me up on it, take this over to the exchanger. It will get you listed for diplomatic service."

"Thank you, sir," said Joren. "May I ask, what do you plan to do with Fargis now?"

"I plan to keep a better eye on him. I have him preparing some potions for me right now."

Joren paused. "Is he doing okay? He seemed a little off when I pulled him out of the tomb."

"How so?" asked the stoat.

"Just a little overly ecstatic for someone who barely came out of there alive. The wound on his back ran deep."

The stoat chuckled. "Well, I am sure he was happy to survive, and the wound seems to be getting better. Let me get back to my work now, but I'll pass on that you asked about him."

"Thank you," responded Joren, getting up. He let himself out. His tail wagged as he carried the slip of paper down the hall. Diplomatic service? This could be the exciting change he kept longing for.

In the hallway he ran into Fargis who was carrying a potion.

"Joren?" he responded, confused upon seeing him in the hall.

"Oh hey. Einar had me come by. He says he can get posted for diplomatic service," said Joren, tail still wagging.

"Oh, that's great news." Fargis smiled.

"Yes!" Joren leaned in to give Fargis a quick peck on the cheek. "Thank you," he said, ears reddening before quickly retreating down the hall.

The mage watched the black wolf with the wagging tail stride down the hallway to the stairs as he carefully held onto the potion.

"Okay," he whispered to himself, "maybe it was all worth the effort." Grinning, he turned and continued walking back to see Master Einar.

To Catch the Lightning

Royce Day

"Don't hold that up to your muzzle," Becca advised. "We'll look like tourists." Feyd's ears flicked back in embarrassment, and he pulled the kerchief back down from his muzzle to rest loosely around his throat once again. Not that the vixen could blame the younger foxen male. Klippenhaffen was a typical Gerwart industrial port city: busy, crowded, and covered with a black cloak of coal dust from the nearby factories. The 'warties around her seemed to take no notice of it, but even Becca could barely keep herself from sneezing every five paces as they walked up the street towards the warehouse district.

Feyd shook his head, triangular ears flattening to his scalp. "How can they stand it here?" he asked. "You can't smell anything except the dust in your snout." The sandy-furred male was eight years younger than Becca's own thirty years, but despite his youth he'd proven a capable lieutenant in her command. Which was why she'd brought him along on this mission for their patron, Countess Longlake.

"It's Gerwart," Becca said, gesturing with her sword paw towards the factories belching dark clouds from their smokestacks on the edge of town. "They'll put up with anything so long as it's declared 'Progress'." She fought the urge to start rubbing at her own black and white fur, which would be soon black and grey if they stayed out in the open for more than the afternoon.

"They'll bury themselves in an early grave from breathing in this stuff," Feyd replied. After a moment he added, "I wish I had my sword."

"It would hardly fit with our current outfits," Becca noted. "Though I'll admit I'm feeling pretty naked myself." They were both dressed as Mother Country sailors, in tough canvas pants, heavy linen shirts, and kerchiefs at their necks, not the bright uniforms of Countess Longlake's personal guard. Swords would definitely be out of place, though Becca and Feyd both wore long utilitarian knives at their belts, and Becca held tight to a thick, wooden cane.

They dodged out of the street and onto the crowded sidewalk as an overloaded steam cart puffed down the road towards the docks, the brakeman cursing as it went down the steep slope. The crowd seemed to take little notice of it beyond stepping out of the way. Becca tried to imagine the carnage that would occur if the driver and brakeman lost control of the cart and it was allowed to barrel down the street unimpeded. A Mother Country countess would never allow something that dangerous, but would instead build a more expensive but safer funicular railway from the warehouse district to the wharves jutting out into the harbor. *Progress.*

They turned at an intersection at the top of the hill, following the line of bars, banks, outfitters, and other shops that catered to both the sailors that visited the city and the workers who tended the warehouses in this district. Becca reviewed the map of the town she'd memorized on the voyage from the Mother Country, counting storefronts until they reached a small tavern marked with a snarling grass chaser on its signboard. Stepping inside revealed a common room that was crowded with sailors and workers from several seafaring nations, the air smoky from the oil lamps on the walls. Beside her Feyd sneezed, and Becca felt her eyes begin to water.

"Where is he?" Feyd whispered desperately into her ear.

"Patience," Becca whispered back. She flagged down the bartender and purchased beers for them both. Grabbing the tankards, she guided Feyd casually toward the back of the room, as if looking for an empty table. Finally she found what she was looking for: a small table occupied by a single foxen male, with deep red fur and wearing a *pince nez* clipped to his muzzle, sitting alone and looking nervous.

"Mind if we sit here?" she asked in Gerwart.

"I am sorry, no, I am waiting for…for friends," he replied. His tail curled nervously around his knees, a leather satchel stuffed with papers resting in his lap. He was dressed in commoner garb, but his accent was obviously educated, and there were small white spots from chemical burns dotting the fur of his arms and paws, hinting at his true background.

"That would be us," Becca replied, sitting down and motioning for Feyd to do as well. "I am Swordmaster Beccalian Blacksailor, and this is my lieutenant, Feydian Cliptoe. We are agents for the Countess Longlake of the Mother Country Council of Countesses. You are Scholar Mond-Gaffer?"

"Yes," the male replied. His eyes darted up and down, examining their carefully common appearance. "You don't look like a swordmaster."

"If I did, I'd be standing out a lot more than you would want me to at the moment," Becca replied calmly. "I'm in disguise, the same as you. Were you followed at all?"

"I… I don't believe so," Mond-Gaffer said. "As far as the Science Ministry knows, I'm attending a conference in Eisenstadt. I even had one of my students purchase the train ticket for Klippenhaffen."

"So at least one person knows where you were really going?" Feyd asked in concern.

"No, no," Mond-Gaffer said quickly. "I told them it was for my aunt. I bought the ticket for Eisenstadt myself just before I got on the train to Kilppenhaffen."

Becca felt some of her concern ease. Despite his hesitant manner, Mond-Gaffer wasn't quite so starry-eyed as his name suggested. "That was well done, Scholar. Now we are all going to finish our beers, and then you're going to take a nice, relaxed walk with us down the docks to start a *lovely* sea voyage to the MC, understood?"

"Oh, no. Not yet!" Mond-Gaffer exclaimed. "We have to get

the prototype from the warehouse. We absolutely cannot leave without it."

"Prototype? What prototype?" Becca demanded.

"The prototype of the galvanic generator," he said. "I couldn't just leave it at the university; that would mean someone else could examine it and duplicate my work, even without my research notes." He patted the satchel protectively. "So I had it shipped here ahead for my arrival. I told the university chancellor I was sending it to the conference instead."

Beside her, Feyd's jaw dropped open. "So you had someone ship it all the way here, when it and you are expected in Eisenstadt?" He turned to Becca. "Swordmaster, the scholar here going missing might just be a case of him being a bit lost. *Both* of them being misplaced is going to set off somebody's alarm bells."

And there's going to be paperwork showing where it went. Mother Goddess bless us all, Becca thought in aggravation. "How *large* is this prototype, Scholar Mond-Gaffer?" She was hoping it was something the size of a trunk. Two sailors carrying a trunk down the street to the docks, with its owner following them, would hardly attract notice.

"Oh, not very large. Just the size of a pair of shipping flats," he replied affably.

Which would mean they'd need a steam cart to haul it back to the ship, she realized. "That's too big. We'll have to destroy it," Becca told him.

"Destroy it, are you mad? It is my life's work!" Mond-Gaffer exclaimed, his tail lashing in fury. "Oh, you are just like those idiots in the War Ministry, who only care about making bigger and better explosives. I thought the MC would be different!"

"Keep your damned voice down," Becca hissed. "All right, we'll figure something out. Just take us to it."

Scholar Mond-Gaffer nodded and stood up, almost losing his balance as the satchel's weighty contents made him lean to one side. Feyd stood and grabbed the scholar's arm to steady him, and together the three of them headed back out into the street and toward a nearby warehouse. By the time they reached it, the sky was turning a burnt orange color as the lowering sun's rays hit the perpetual smoke cloud hanging over the city.

"What did you put on the manifest when you had it shipped here?" Becca asked as they approached.

"Copper wiring, industrial magnets, lead plates, and sulphuric acid," Mond-Gaffer replied. "It is all correct. I just failed to mention what configuration they are in."

"Cute," Feyd muttered, while Becca wondered what such a bizarre combination of items could be used for.

"Feyd, find a steam cart we can use to haul Herr Scholar's prototype back to the ship," Becca ordered.

"Why do you think I can just conjure up a steam cart in the middle of an enemy city this late in the afternoon?" he asked.

"Because you are my lieutenant, and you'd rather die than fail me," Becca answered with a smile.

"This is true, swordmaster," he admitted sheepishly. He gave her a smart salute and turned smartly on one footpad, flagging down a nearby longshorefolk to get directions to the nearest livery rental.

After a brief negotiation with the warehouse clerk, involving a maddening delay while Mond-Gaffer dug through his satchel for the right paperwork, and they were brought before a large crate as tall as Becca, five arms long and half as wide.

"How much does this thing weigh?" Becca asked the scholar.

"The lead plates and the magnets are the heaviest components," he told her. "No more than seven-hundred pounds, I think."

Becca took a deep, calming breath and leaned on her cane. "Mother Goddess bless us all," she muttered.

An hour later, a deep puffing noise from outside the warehouse heralded the return of Feyd, hanging on the running board of a large cargo steam cart, complete with driver, brakeman, and engineer tending the puffing coal boiler mounted between the driver's cab and the cargo area. To Becca's suppressed horror they drove it straight inside, heedless of the burning coals being expelled towards the rafters. If it'd been an alcohol-fueled engine like a Mother Country design, she wouldn't have been as worried. This thing could set the whole warehouse on fire if a spark landed in the right spot. *Progress.*

After that it was just a matter of getting the pallet into the cargo bed, a task aided by a winch connected to the cart's steam engine, which hauled it aboard in less than ten minutes. Becca felt herself relax slightly. If they could get this blasted cart down the hill and through the town without running over anyone, all they'd have to do is load the pallet aboard the waiting ship and they could be on their merry way.

A commotion from the direction of the warehouse manager's office made Becca take firm hold of her cane and motion for Feyd to stay close to Mond-Gaffer's side. Four officers in the uniform of the local constabulary were approaching, the warehouse manager trailing behind worriedly.

"Scholar Mond-Gaffer?" the lead constable called out. "You and your companions are under arrest, at the order of the Ministry of State Security."

"Wha-wha-what?" Mond-Gaffer stuttered. "I-I have never heard of anything so... So outrageous! I am merely retrieving my prototype after it was accidentally shipped here instead of to the conference."

Becca tried not to applaud his quick thinking, even as she let her expression slacken from alarm to annoyance, suitable for a sailor finding herself stuck in an unexpected complication. "'ere now. We not with him," she said in Gerwart, making sure her accent was broken and barely understandable. "We were told to just bring his crate back to the ship."

"That will be sorted out by State Sec," the constable said firmly, letting his paw drop to the truncheon at his hip. "Now disarm yourselves and come with us."

"Becca?" Feyd asked urgently.

"Follow my lead," she advised in the Mother Tongue. Becca reached over with her left paw, awkwardly undoing the buckle of her knife sheath and letting it drop to the ground, and a moment later Feyd followed suit.

"Your cane as well, please," the constable ordered.

"All right, all right," Becca groused. She leaned over to set the cane on the ground, her paw reaching out to the side of the steam cart as if to steady herself. She felt a flash of heat on her paw pad, and she let out a loud cry as if burnt, swaying dangerously on her "good" leg. The second constable, Mother Goddess bless him, rushed forward as if to catch her.

Which was when Becca pressed a button on the handle of her cane, sending the heavy, spring loaded sheath directly into the second constable's leg, as the sword hidden inside it was revealed. She heard a sharp *crack* as the sheath hit, breaking the poor fellow's ankle and sending him tumbling to the ground.

"*Flats only!*" Becca shouted to Feyd, as he dove to the ground and rolled, coming back up to his feet with both of their knives unsheathed in his paws. She rushed forward, bringing up the sword toward the lead constable.

He waved his truncheon at her, the shorter club briefly parrying Becca's sword, until she pivoted the blade in her paw and flipped the truncheon free of his grip. She spun the blade, slashing the blunt edge towards the constable's head. Panicking, he tried to parry it with his forearm, and she heard a second nasty *crack* as it broke against her steel. As he doubled over in pain, clutching wounded arm, she brought the handle of the sword cane smartly down on the back of his head, knocking him to the floor unconscious.

She scanned the room for more opponents, to find that the third constable was unconscious but breathing, lying slumped against one of the wheels of the steam cart, while the fourth was disarmed and pinned against a pillar, with one of Feyd's knives at his throat.

Becca turned her attention to the crew of the steam cart, who exchanged brief looks with each other and then raised their arms in surrender.

Well this has gone completely to shit, she thought. She waggled her sword cane at the crew. "Thank you, could you all come down from the cart please? That's very good. Now if you could do me the great favor of picking up the constables and carrying them with you? That's it, excellent." With the crew's paws occupied and out of mischief carrying the unconscious constables, she started herding the group toward the warehouse supervisor's office. Speaking of which…

"Feyd, did you see which way the warehouse supervisor went?" she demanded, kneeling down to grab the cane's sheath and cover its blade.

"Sorry, no. He scarpered while I was dealing with my half of the constables," Feyd admitted apologetically.

"Which means we have two or three minutes at best before reinforcements arrive," she replied. "Help me secure our innocent bystanders and get ready to move."

Together they finished herding everyone into the supervisor's office, setting the locking bar in place. It wouldn't hold with a determined effort at ramming, but by the time the steam cart's crew got around to that, they'd be long gone.

Becca hopped up onto the driver's bench. "Feyd, do you know how to work the boiler?"

"I can," Mond-Gaffer spoke up unexpectedly. He'd been quiet ever since the fight had started, standing out of the way and clutching his precious satchel of papers. "I helped my father with the coal boilers at the factory he worked in."

"Get us going then," Becca ordered. "Feyd, open the doors."

Mond-Gaffer nodded, handing over his satchel to Becca to secure beside her on the bench. Feyd hurried over to the door and pushed them open, hopping onto the running board again as Mond-Gaffer opened valves and the steam cart rumbled forward onto the street.

Becca blew the whistle to get the crowd on the street out of the way as they headed toward the steep hill leading to the docks. She only glanced behind her once as she heard a loud whistle and saw a phalanx of at least a dozen uniformed constables rushing toward them from about three blocks back.

"More steam, Scholar!" she called out. He nodded and opened up a valve. The boiler's pistons chugged faster and the cart picked up speed, whistle blaring as they skidded around a corner and onto the main boulevard.

It was a straight, and very *steep* run to the docks, the early evening streets filled with males, vixens, and cubs. "*Brakes!*"

Becca shouted to Feyd as the steam cart rattled down the hill, the unsecured crate slamming into the front of the cargo bed. Feyd pulled back hard on the brake lever, and the steam cart's wheels shrieked as it skidded across the cobblestones, the crowd parting like a wave in front of them as Becca repeatedly sounded the whistle. The back end of the cart fishtailed and bounced over the edge of the sidewalk, smashing through a fruit seller's stall before she regained control and straightened out their plummet.

They slid another hundred arms and then the street finally began to flatten out. At Becca's order, Feyd managed to slow them down to a brisk walking pace, the hubs of the cart's wooden wheels smoking where the brake pads had dug in. "Well, at least we left pursuit behind," he said, laughing in the same barely constrained hysterical relief that Becca was feeling.

"I just hope no one stops us for that slide down the hill," she replied, guiding them toward the front gate of the docks.

"I do not believe we struck anyone on the way down, so they should not," Mond-Gaffer replied with a shrug. "It is not an uncommon occurrence in this city."

"I will take your word for it," Becca replied. *Progress.* She guided the steam cart through the dock gate, turning towards the pier where the *Windskimmer* was docked.

Windskimmer's captain, an aged vixen with gray speckles decorating her black fur, came down the ship's gangway toward them as the steam cart screeched to a halt. "Swordmaster, what's going on?" she demanded.

"There were complications," Becca said. "Please take this crate aboard and make ready to set sail. I think we have perhaps ten minutes before the local constabulary catches up with us. Scholar Mond-Gaffer, kindly follow the captain aboard and find a safe spot for yourself."

"Cold and *Dark*," the captain cursed. "Mr. Hotclaw, bring up the boilers to full steam!" She ran back up the gangway, continuing to shout orders. With shouts and curses the ship's crew made ready to cast off as team of sailors nimbly ran back down to the crate, the ship's cargo crane pivoting slowly to hang over it and allow them to attached cables to the four corners.

"Feyd, grab our proper blades and bring them back here," Becca ordered. As her lieutenant ran up onto the ship, she turned to the scholar. "Scholar Mond-Gaffer, you should get aboard," Becca told him.

"I will in one moment," the scholar replied, looking at her closely. "I first wish to ask a question of you."

"Fine. Ask your question, then *please* get aboard," Becca said with ill-concealed impatience.

"The constables who tried to stop us at the warehouse. When you attacked them, you ordered your companion to use the flats of his blades. Would it not have been more prudent to strike killing blows? Otherwise they might have overwhelmed you."

Becca looked back at him sharply. "Would you have preferred that?"

He shook his head. "They are my countrymen. I hold my nation's leaders in contempt—its people I have no argument with. Most simply wish to live their lives in peace."

"Then you answer your own question," Becca said. "Those constables were males and vixens coming to arrest, and I will admit to this, enemy spies acting against their nation. They have families who are expecting them to come home this evening. Better to use the flats of our blades than have some poor husband or wife have to answer the door and receive the news their spouse has been murdered."

Mond-Gaffer blinked in surprise. "Hmm. I have been told that Mother Country swordmasters are fearsome warriors, who cut down their enemies without pity."

"Warriors, certainly. If someone comes after me with lethal intent, I'll kill them without a qualm. Police officers armed with truncheons don't qualify," Becca replied without rancor.

Feyd returned, panting slightly. "Your sword," he said, bowing deeply, the naked blade resting on his upturned palms.

"Thank you, Feyd," she said, taking it up in her own palm. It was not a fancy thing. The pattern upon the blade resembled that of flowing water, but she knew that was an artifact of the manufacturing process, not artistic choice. The hilt was especially shaped to fit her palm, as with all swordmaster-quality weapons, but the design upon it was a simple cross-hatch pattern, just there to improve her grip. She gave it an experimental twirl between her fingers, the careful balance making it seem as light as air. "Do you see this, Scholar?" she asked.

"Yes," he replied. "It seems such a simple thing."

"It's a weapon. It is *only* a weapon. Feyd's knife can be used to cut meat, or a male's throat. The cane I carried before could ease an old vixen's gait, or bash someone's temple in. A sword, though…" She sheathed the blade through a ring hanging from her belt. "Has only one purpose: to kill. When I draw it with intent, it is because I wish another person dead. Someone as beloved in the eyes of the Mother Goddess as myself, perhaps more so."

Mond-Gaffer cocked his ears towards her in curiosity. "You sound as if you do not like your profession."

"I do not pretend it is anything but what it is: government-accepted murder," Becca replied. "I am Military Caste, Scholar. That means I was born to serve others, and that service requires that I be prepared to kill. But I take no pleasure in it, and will avoid it whenever possible. That is the only difference between myself and an armed thug." She gestured toward the ship. "Now would you *please* get aboard?"

"Yes, swordmaster." He turned and looked up the gangplank, as if pondering the wisdom of taking this last, irrevocable step, crossing into Mother Country territory and refuting his Gerwart citizenship. Then Mond-Gaffer gave a firm nod and headed up the gangway, his satchel of papers held tightly under his arm.

"You're in a philosophical mood," Feyd noted as the scholar was escorted into the forecastle. "The last time I heard that little speech was when you were training me."

"I get that way when I have to explain my job to idiots," Becca replied, grinning. Feyd grinned back, but then their attention was drawn to a growing commotion towards the main gate.

"Draw?" Feyd asked, as the *Windskimmer's* crew hurried to finish securing the cables around the precious crate.

"Hold," Becca ordered as an omnibus steamed up, screeching to a halt and disgorging a baker's dozen soldiers armed with rifles, in the black uniforms of Gerwart's dreaded Ministry of State Security. Becca and Feyd kept themselves between the soldiers and the steam cart, where the sailors had finally finished securing the last of the cables to the crate.

A black-furred vixen, an officer by the gold braid hanging from her right shoulder and a pepperbox pistol at her belt, shouted at them in the Mother Tongue. "Halt! You vill disarm yourselves und surrender, for aiding a traitor to ze Gerwart nation, Scholar Mond-Gaffer!"

"Draw?" Feyd asked again, his tone growing urgent.

"Hold," Becca repeated firmly. To the officer she stated, "There are no citizens of Gerwart aboard this ship; only beloved subjects of the Mother Country."

"Who are you to say zis?" the officer demanded.

"Swordmaster Beccalian Blacksailor," Becca answered in Gerwart. "Now allow us to leave peacefully, and you will not be harmed."

"I think you are overconfident." Despite the officer's words, some of her soldiers were looking at Becca and her lieutenant with a bit more respect, and perhaps a little fear.

There was a shout from the ship, and the crane began winching Mond-Gaffer's precious crate into the air, the sailors who'd attached the cables hanging onto them as they were carried along with it.

Becca grinned. "I think we just won."

"Stop them!" the officer shouted in Gerwart. "Take the ship!"

"Draw and roll!" Becca ordered. As one she and Feyd leaped forward, tucking and rolling as bullets from the soldiers' rifles whizzed above them. They came to their feet simultaneously and drew their swords, in the middle of the pack of black clad soldiers, too close to be shot at unless one of the State Security agents wanted to risk shooting their own comrades in the melee.

Becca's blade plunged into the belly of a soldier, then in one smooth motion she turned, her left elbow smashing a second soldier in the muzzle as she withdrew her blade and slashed the throat of a third. A shot rang out, deafening her briefly as a bullet nicked her ear, and she pivoted, striking the shooter in the face with the pommel of her blade. He staggered backwards, tumbling off the edge of the dock with a high-pitched scream.

"Wilhelm!" the officer shouted, drawing her pepperbox to raise it toward Becca, too far for the swordmaster to close the distance before the Gerwart could fire all four barrels. "Die, you murderous Mother Country lunatic!"

That was when Feyd's blade emerged from the officer's belly, as he rammed its tip into her back. He withdrew it, and she fell snout first to the ground.

"That's *skilled* murderous lunatic, thank you," he said.

Becca looked around. Five other soldiers lay on the ground, dead or sorely wounded. Add her total of four and the officer, and that left three very disconcerted but armed soldiers remaining, their rifles held with the muzzles pointed very carefully toward the ground.

"Rifles over the side of the dock please," Becca advised sweetly. They complied with gratifying speed. "Thank you," she said. "Feyd, off we go."

Feyd nodded and followed her up the gangway, leaving the soldiers behind. The moment they were on the deck of the *Windskimmer,* its whistle blew loudly, the great paddlewheels on the either side of the hull churning the water it headed out of the harbor, even as its crane finished lowering the crate into the cargo hold.

"Not bad," Feyd said, cleaning his sword with his neck kerchief as they both stood by the railing. "Poor fellows didn't really have a chance after we closed the dis—"

Becca head a loud series of pops, like a string of firecrackers going off. Something hit with a *spang* of metal on metal as her head snapped in the direction of the receding dock. In the last of the day's light she could see the State Security officer, pepperbox pistol in paw, snarling in triumph before she collapsed back into the pool of her own blood.

"*Cold and Dark*, Feyd!" she cursed, turning towards her lieutenant. "We should have checked to see if she was still..." She shut up abruptly, staring at the two bloody holes in Feyd's chest.

"Yes," Feyd answered distantly. "Yes, we should..."

Becca grabbed him as he collapsed, laying him down gently even as she screamed for the ship's surgeon.

Helpful paws carried him inside while she stood on the swaying deck as *Windskimmer* raced out of the harbor, Feyd's blood dripping from her paws. The surgeon would do their best, she was sure, but she knew her lieutenant had been dead before she laid him down on the deck.

Becca growled deep in her throat, ears flicked back, claws digging into her palm pads as they drew into fists. She shoved open the hatch leading down into the cargo hold. There she found Mond-Gaffer, still clutching his satchel, anxiously checking his oh so precious crate for damage.

The leather satchel dropped to the deck, papers spilling everywhere as Becca grabbed Mond-Gaffer by the shoulder and spun him around, pinning him against the crate with her claws at his throat.

"Bist du verrückt!" he choked, eyes bulging, toes scrabbling for purchase on the steel deck as Becca held him there. "What are you doing!"

"I just lost one of the best subordinates I've ever trained, Scholar, because you made us wait a bloody *hour* to retrieve that precious crate of yours. If we'd just left it behind we could have escorted you aboard the ship and sailed off, with Gerwart State Security none the wiser. What by the Mother Goddess' Cold and Dark hell is in that thing that's so damned important that it cost Feyd's *life*, and the lives of nine of your countrymen?"

She let go of him abruptly, and Mond-Gaffer dropped down to his knees, choking and gasping. When he'd regained his breath, he stood and said, "I am sorry. I am truly sorry, Swordmaster Blacksailor. I did not wish any of your people to be hurt."

The scholar retrieved a crowbar hanging from a tool rack by

the bulkhead and started trying to pry open the crate. After watching him struggle with it for a minute, Becca sighed and took it from his paws to peel back the wooden boards and reveal the prize within.

The side of the crate crashed to the deck, revealing a pile of equipment so random that Becca was hard pressed to identify it all. Most prominent was a crank, which was connected to a large iron drum by a heavy roller chain. From the center of the drum a pair of copper wires emerged, leading a series of lead containers the size of bread boxes, all wired together and stinking of sulphuric acid.

"What in the name of the Mother Goddess?" Becca asked, reaching out to touch one of the wires.

"Ach! Do not touch it!" Mond-Gaffer cried out, slapping her paw away from the contraption. At her annoyed growl, he explained, "It has been several days, but the batteries should still have a significant charge from the last test. You could have gotten a severe shock! Like being struck by lightning!"

"But what does all of this do?" Becca demanded.

"It is a galvanic generator," Mond-Gaffer explained. He opened the side of the drum, revealing several blocks of the copper wire attached to an axle, surrounded by several more blocks of dull gray metal mounted to the inside curve of the drum. "When the copper wires are turning, they are moving through the magnetic field created by the large magnets on the inner rim. Doing so generates an electrical charge, like the static you feel sometimes when your tail brushes against a rug, which travels through the wires to the batteries, those metal boxes, which store the charge."

"Lightning in a box?" Becca asked, eyebrow raised.

"That is an acceptable metaphor," Mond-Gaffer agreed.

"So, once you've generated and stored this lightning, what do you *do with it?*" she said sharply.

"The electricity, once it is stored, can be released again," the scholar explained eagerly. "Use a little bit of it, you can send signals along a wire. Wrap the wires into a coil, and the heat generated can be used to heat up a home in the winter, without the need for wood stoves, gas, or steam heating. Better still, you can turn a wheel with it!"

"Turn a wheel?"

"Yes, yes!" Mond-Gaffer exclaimed, growing more excited. "Wheels of a train, powered by electricity over wires, eliminating the need for big steam engines. It could even be used to turn the propellers of a ship like this one, directly, much more efficiently, without losing energy in the mechanical transfer from steam engine to piston to crank, and so on. Someday, when the battery storage becomes more efficient, it might even power carts for long distances, so they no longer need dangerous steam engines that might explode in the streets."

It was the *potential* of this new technology that was exciting Mond-Gaffer, and had also excited the Gerwart government ministries that had funded his research, Becca realized swiftly. What she was looking at right now was almost useless, just an expensive scientific toy. Whatever utility it might have in the future, she doubted she'd live to see it. But she suspected when that change came, it would affect the entire world.

"Swordmaster!" a voice called from the hatchway. Becca turned to see one of *Windskimmer's* crew, waving to her anxiously. "The captain requests you meet her on the bridge."

"What's the problem?" Becca called back.

"It looks like there's a ship approaching."

"Cold and *Dark*," Becca cursed. She waggled a fingerclaw at the scholar. "You stay here, and keep this generator safe."

"Yes, swordmaster," Mond-Gaffer replied as he kneeled down to start collecting his scattered papers.

Becca rushed up the ladder and to the bridge, where the captain waited for her.

"We've got a cutter coming from behind," she told Becca, handing over a pair of field glasses. Becca raised them to her eyes, spotting a small revenue cutter, probably powered by a steam turbine, chuffing its way toward *Windskimmer*. It was perhaps two miles behind them now in the dark, only visible due to the prodigious amount of sparks rising from its smokestack, hinting at how desperately it wanted to catch up to the larger vessel.

"I take it we can't outrun them?" Becca asked.

The older vixen nodded grimly. "*Windskimmer* is fast for a cargo ship, but only in comparison to similar vessels. That cutter has a smaller draft and a big engine for its size. They'll catch up, unless we get very lucky and can lose them in the darkness."

"If you can't, how long before they intercept us?"

"Perhaps forty-five minutes." The captain rubbed her muzzle. "I know what importance the Ministry of Intelligence placed on this mission, swordmaster, but my crew are sailors, not warriors. We deliberately didn't bring weapons along for this voyage, to avoid rousing suspicions if we were stopped for inspection. Do you think you can defend my ship if it's intercepted?"

Becca cocked her ears forward, looking at the captain carefully, "If I can't, what would your actions be?"

"Dump that blasted crate overboard, then do the same to that damned 'wartie scholar after we give him a lifejacket. If we're lucky, they'll be satisfied with that and end the chase."

"I doubt we'll be that lucky," Becca replied. She flexed her sword paw, the fur turning brown with Feyd's blood. "I will defend you with my life, if the Mother Goddess deems it necessary."

"I will pray to the Mother for your success then," the captain replied.

Becca returned to the cargo hold briefly to check on Mond-Gaffer. The scholar was sitting on an overturned bucket by his crate of equipment, forlornly looking through his papers as he stuffed them back into his satchel.

"Swordmaster Blacksailor," he greeted quietly. "What news do you bring?"

"We've got a Gerwart revenue cutter coming up from behind," Becca told him. "It'll intercept us in about thirty minutes. I have no doubt in my mind that its crew intends to board us."

"So," Mond-Gaffer said bleakly, "all of this effort, all of this blood, was for nothing."

"I will defend this ship, and you," Becca tried to reassure him.

"How many soldiers might be on that cutter, swordmaster?"

She shrugged. "Boat that size, perhaps ten."

"You and your lieutenant were able to take on that many on the dock, but you had the element of surprise," Mond-Gaffer said. "Now you intend to attack them by yourself, when they are prepared?"

"I know my duty," she replied evenly.

"Perhaps I should surrender myself to them. If the captain sets me in a lifeboat, perhaps picking me up will be enough for them," Mond-Gaffer said.

Becca winced, remembering the captain's similar suggestion of just dumping the scholar overboard. "We won't let it come to that." She gestured ironically to the generator in its crate. "Though it's a pity you can't use that to zap that cutter with a lightning bolt. That would certainly get them off our tail."

"Projected electricity without wires makes it nearly uncontrollable. It would indeed be like lightning. You wouldn't know where it would hit," Mond-Gaffer said. "You would have to be almost right on top of your opponent to…" His brow furrowed suddenly. Then his expression brightened into something hopeful. "Swordmaster, do you still have that sword-stick?"

"Yes," she replied. "Feyd… Feyd would have put it back in my cabin when he retrieved my true sword."

"Bring it to me, *schnell,* quickly!" he demanded.

Becca watched as the revenue cutter came up alongside *Windskimmer*, counting bodies. There were four unarmed foxen who were obviously sailors. Crowded along the cutter's port railing were a half-dozen constables in the uniform of the Klippenhaffen Port Authority, obviously drafted to help the four black-uniformed State Sec goons standing among them. Ten potential combatants in all, on a crowded deck, the four State Sec agents armed with pistols, not bulky rifles this time, and the constables with their truncheons. A workable problem, assuming she was able to keep her footing on the swaying deck. If she fell, Becca realized, they could just pile atop her until she was safely disabled, and then board *Windskimmer* at their leisure.

One of the State Sec agents raised a bullhorn to his muzzle and shouted in a heavy accent, "Mother Country vessel! You are illegally transporting a Gerwart citizen vanted for crimes against ze state! Ve vill board you, to impound your vessel und arrest you for aiding a fugitive, und suspicion of espionage."

Right on cue, the hatch opened and a sailor roughly shoved Mond-Gaffer out onto the deck, the scholar's paws bound behind his back, the captain following them both.

"You cannot do this!" the scholar shouted. "You promised me sanctuary!"

"This was a mistake from the start. You aren't worth the lives of my crew," the captain replied, loud enough for the cutter's crew to hear over the waves. She gestured to the State Sec agent. "Hold on! We'll lower him to you."

"We vill still haf to board you," the State Sec agent shouted as Mond-Gaffer began struggling wildly in the sailor's grip.

"No! I won't go back," he shouted, twisting free and falling against Becca.

Becca stumbled, letting out a loud cry as she fell backward over the railing, right down onto the crowd of 'warties. Then she let out another, very real cry of pain as she landed on two constables, the heavy metal battery hastily strapped to her lower back digging into her spine. Fortunately, she was able to roll to her feet, using the momentum of the battery to her advantage. One of the constables she'd landed on was unconscious, the second groaning and curled up into a fetal ball of pain.

That's two, she thought. She popped the release on the swordstick, sending the sheath flying into the chest of a State Sec agent, knocking them over the railing and into the water. *Three.*

"Stop her!" one of the remaining agents shouted. Then he took a step back as he saw the sparks running along the length of Becca's blade, the wires hastily wrapped with the shredded remains of a rubberized sea coat running from the blade to the battery.

She gripped the non-conducting wooden handle of the sword-stick tightly, her grip on the wet wooden deck steady thanks to the rubber foot-protectors Mond-Gaffer had insisted she wear, so she wouldn't be accidentally grounded and shock herself.

Becca swatted aside a constable who tried rush her, the 'wartie vixen suddenly dropping and convulsing as the flat of Becca's blade touched her sea-soaked uniform. *Four.* Then another agent raised his pistol and she dodged behind the cutter's wheelhouse, grabbing the edge of its roof with one paw and hauling herself up as the whole crowd tried to circle around and catch her. She slid along the wet roof, blade held high, and dropped behind them, stunning two more constables before they could turn and react. *Five. Six.* Then the fourth agent spotted her, and she ran him through with her blade, sparks arcing along the deep belly wound, filling the air with the smell of cauterized flesh. *Seven.* One constable left, and three of the State Sec agents.

A bullet zinged past her, and Becca turned and rolled again, slamming into the knees of an agent and sending him tumbling against one of his remaining comrades. She plunged the sword deep into their stacked bodies, then cursed as she tried to pull it free, the edge of the blade catching on a rib.

"*Halt!*" someone shouted, and Becca turned to see the remaining State Sec agent pointing a pistol right at her chest, the last constable standing slightly behind them.

Becca raised her paws, the damned wire running from the battery to her stuck sword leaving her effectively leashed and unable to dodge.

"You vill surrender yourself—you vill *all* surrender yourselves," the agent shouted up to the *Windskimmer's* crew. "You vill be returned to Gerwart to be questioned, tried, and *executed* as sp—"

The constable, who had been listening to this rant without noticeable emotion, raised his truncheon and brought it down smartly between the male's ears, dropping the agent to the deck, unconscious.

"Never liked those black-uniformed Security bastards," the constable said mildly in Gerwart as Becca succeeded in finally pulling her blade free.

"You won't get into trouble with your superiors over this?" she asked in the same language.

"It was a horrible massacre," the constable said without notable fear. "Sharpshooters on the enemy vessel gunned down all the State Sec agents before we could react. We were lucky to escape with our lives." He looked down at one his fellow officers who was rising to her feet shakily, along with the others. "Speaking of which, are my people going to be all right?"

"Shocked badly, perhaps some minor burns, but not quite dead," Becca replied.

The constable nodded in satisfaction. "Good," he said. "I knew it was going to be trouble when that State Sec officer started waving his credentials and demanded we come with them to chase you down."

The cutter's captain emerged from the wheelhouse, where she had stayed under cover with her small crew during the fight. "Is it over?" she asked.

"Looks that way," the constable replied laconically.

"Good. Help me roll these State Security idiots over the side. I don't like them bleeding all over my deck." The constable nodded, and started to heave the bodies of the agents over the side with the help of the cutter's crew.

"Keep at least one of their pistols," Becca advised, "so you can shoot some holes in the wheelhouse to show how the agents were gunned down."

The captain looked sour at the thought of her boat being so mutilated, but nodded in agreement. "And who are you?" she asked. "You're no sailor."

"Swordmaster Beccalian Blacksailor, at the service of the Mother Country Countesses," she said, giving the captain a little bow.

"A swordmaster?" the captain asked. "In this day and age?"

Becca smiled ironically, holding up her bloody, sparking blade in salute. "We keep up with the times."

After a minor argument, Becca succeeded in persuading the cutter's captain to douse her coal bunker with seawater, to provide a reasonable excuse as to why she didn't attempt to further pursuit. After that Becca yanked the wires leading from the battery to her sword blade loose, rendering it safe enough to sheath on her belt. Then she scrambled up a rope to the *Windskimmer's* deck, whereupon the cargo ship steamed into the dark night, to the safety of the open sea.

"Strange," Mond-Gaffer said to Becca as they leaned on the railing, while the ship's alcohol fueled steam engines kept its paddle wheels turning. "I had always been taught that the Mother Country, and its archaic swordmasters, was hopelessly backward. Yet you took to your electrified weapon as if it was completely natural."

Becca rubbed her aching lower back, where the edges of the heavy battery had dug in. "Not completely natural, but I understand your point," she replied. "Swordmasters are taught to adapt. If we're too rigid in our thinking, then we might not be able to cope when an enemy springs a surprise on us."

The scholar nodded. "My country, perhaps it is growing too rigid, as you say. I showed the government my galvanic generator, told them how it could be used to power trains, heat homes, transmit information. They said they wanted electrified fences and electrified floors for security, electrified chairs to torture and execute criminals." He shuddered, tail floofing out in suppressed fear. "It was then I knew that I had to leave. Gerwart has been changing, changing for years, growing more…more *hard*. I fear that a war may be coming. The people in Gerwart who might speak out against it are too fearful to raise their voices. They can only engage in small rebellions, like the constable on that revenue cutter, and hope the noses of State Security do not sniff in their direction."

"I hope there won't be a war," Becca told him. "I don't wish to kill any more of your people."

"Not my people now," Mond-Gaffer said sadly. He looked up at the stars, winking in the moonless night. "Sometimes I wonder if there are other foxen, or people like foxen, on other worlds, circling other suns, and if they have troubles the same as we."

"I was taught that the Mother Goddess tried many times before she was satisfied with the shape of the world, its plants, its animals, and finally the foxen. That's why we find the bones of creatures so different than what can be seen today, hidden in the rocks," Becca told him. "Perhaps she practiced on other worlds as well. Maybe she had more experience, and made them better than us."

"A terrifying thought," Mond-Gaffer said bleakly. "I would not care to be judged by such perfect people."

"Not perfect, just different," Becca said. "Like the MC and Gerwart are different."

"Not too different," Mond-Gaffer countered. "We both laugh, love, cry, and fear. Perhaps if we can both see that, it will be enough to keep those who speak of war at bay."

"We can only hope," Becca agreed.

Cat in a Doghouse

James Pratt

Alone in the dark. That was the circumstance in which Old Cat came upon the domicile. Dark was how he preferred it, alone more so. The Awakening had sharped minds, reshaped anatomies, and transformed forepaws into digits with miraculous capabilities, but spirits remained largely untouched. And so while much was different, much was also the same. In the days both old and new, felines were great at many things, but cooperation wasn't one of them. They weren't creatures of the pack; they didn't have to be. A cat needed no one other than itself. Except to mate-that was the only real exception. More or less. When the need was upon him, Old Cat took what he could get.

Mating aside, felines only came together in times of great need, like during the Canine Wars, and even then only when there was a chance of spoils. Old Cat was a veteran of those wars, maybe the last living veteran in the whole wide world, and had the scars in his tabby fur to prove it. Sometimes he thought about this, but never for very long. Cats weren't nostalgic. They kept few mementos and no records of their deeds. Dogs did; they kept records of everything. They emulated the ways of those who ruled before the Awakening. But not cats. Old Cat lost no sleep over the idea that the feline perspective of the wars would die with him.

The truth be told, Old Cat didn't lose much sleep over anything that didn't involve food or self-preservation. Or mating, though he didn't think about that one as much as he used to. He wasn't a youngster anymore. Most of the time he didn't think about much of anything. Like their feral ancestors, felines generally lived in the eternal now. Their thoughts never strayed more than a few hours in the past, because anything beyond that was irrelevant. As for the future, it hadn't happened yet, so it wasn't real. It was an idea, and ideas couldn't be eaten, humped, or toyed with. Why waste time on something like that?

Old Cat hadn't thought about the past in years, and that included the Canine Wars. It was the sight of the domicile, a canine domicile to be exact, that stirred up images long relegated to the dusty corners of his memory. The Canine Wars, or the Feline Wars as the dogs called them, had been a nasty business. Better at intuiting the use of Old World artifacts, the dogs had superior equipment, but the cats were craftier and quicker to adapt. In the end, things just sort of petered out. That didn't stop each side from claiming victory, of course, but only the canines took the time to record the particulars. Old Cat figured their version was almost certainly one-sided but, lacking both written records and the ability to read, couldn't verify that. Learning to read took discipline, and learning to write more so. Old Cat only had discipline for the hunt, and even the nature of that had changed over the years. Kittens hunted for play and young cats for the thrill of the chase. Old Cat only hunted when the discomfort in his belly overtook the ache in his joints.

Thinking about the Canine Wars reminded Old Cat that he hadn't seen a dog in many a moon. He would never admit it, even to himself, but canines fascinated him. After the fall of the Masters—the distant, two-legged gods of the Old World—canines were among the first beasts to *awaken* to themselves and become self-aware. Closest to the Masters, the canines tried to emulate them in every aspect. Realizing their nakedness, they clothed themselves as best they could. Discovering new sounds in their throats, they were the first to combine those sounds into words. Studying books and artifacts rummaged from the ruins of the Old World, they learned of hard and soft concepts like mathematics and metaphors. Other, more distant concepts, such as what lay beyond the blue dome of the sky, remained too big. Those concepts would have to wait for future generations to consider. Instead of disturbing the colossal hutches and warrens which the Masters had constructed with their own masterfully articulated forepaws that now served as their tombs, the canines used simple tools to construct dwelling places of their own. Felines, on the other hand, did what they wanted and moved on. Such was the way of cats.

Old Cat studied the canine domicile. Crafted with an emphasis on practicality over aesthetics, it was a domed adobe structure designed to resist the burning rains and howling winds which sometimes whipped across the land. This was important. Even on the best days when the wind was still and the sun shined its feeble best, a chill remained in the air. Secured in place by deep anchors, the structure was a far cry above the caves and thickets which did little to keep the cold from biting at Old Cat's bones. Having withstood countless storms, the domicile's scarred outer shell was a testament to its durability.

Old Cat was eager to find shelter, and not just to escape the cold. The fall of the Masters had done more than lay waste to the Old World and *awaken* some beasts. The strange and terrible energies their wars unleashed changed the world-weave of space and time, and the humblest of the world's creatures had felt this change in a most profound way. Reverting to prehistoric proportions, insects had become the undisputed apex predators of the New World. Some kept to the dead cities where they used vast networks of abandoned tunnels and the sagging husks of sky-scraping towers as burrows and hives. Others wandered the ruined lands, opportunistic killers bristling with natural weaponry and encased in shells that could turn away the sharpest claw.

Old Cat circled the structure a few times. Finding no evidence of habitation, he pushed open the unlatched door. The interior of the domicile was a single room, and the room was in shambles. Stools, shelves, and a table lay overturned on a carpet of debris. Sheets of water-stained parchment crackled under his feet like old, brittle leaves. At the center of the room was a fire-pit where tiny bones lay scattered among the ashes.

Old Cat laid down his belongings: an ancient machete reworked into a passable scimitar that he'd carried since the Canine Wars, a satchel in which he kept his meager supplies, and a tattered blanket he wore as a cloak, and went to work. First he placed the remains of a stool shattered beyond repair into the fire-pit, and used it as kindling for a fire. Then he sat for a few minutes, luxuriating in the warmth. After righting the furniture, Old Cat began rummaging through the mess. Finding an old broom, he swept most of the debris into the fire-pit. After that, he made a meal of the dried remains of a dead bird he'd found earlier that morning. An unawakened creature, it was small and had very little meat on its bones, but it was still better than nothing.

Safe and warm, Old Cat grew drowsy and his thoughts began to stray. That was when he did most of his thinking, when his mind freely drifted in the grey land between the waking world and sleep. He recalled one of the strangest ideas the canines resurrected from the Old World, which was the concept of divinity. It was the canines who declared the Masters to be fallen gods that would one day rise again and restore the world to its former glory. They even claimed they were made in the Masters' own image, and that all other awakened beasts were abominations. That was the reason for the Canine Wars, or so Old Cat had once been told by an Old Hound who, having grown weary of ancient feuds rendered meaningless by the relentless creep of time, bore felines nor more and no less ill-will than required by virtue of his species. Old Cat found the concept ludicrous. How could he not? What beasts were higher than felines? More importantly, it seemed to him that the biggest threat to the world was the Masters themselves. They were destroyed by a war they themselves started, not against another species, but against their own kind. Madness! Maybe that was the nature of gods: to create, destroy, and create again. Whatever the case, it sounded noisy, inefficient, and frankly quite silly. Old Cat didn't want anything to do with it.

The Old Hound who taught Old Cat about religion hadn't

been so bad as far as canines went. Old Cat tried and failed to remember his name. Unlike dogs, cats didn't abide by names. There were all sorts of ways for beasts to identify one another. Every beast was itself, nothing more and nothing less. What more distinction did it need? More importantly, no beast except Old Cat was Old Cat. No beast would ever be as fierce or clever as Old Cat. Everyone knew this, and anyone who didn't know this wasn't worth knowing. That's why it was more than enough for Old Cat to simply be Old Cat.

Old Cat considered all these things as he lay drifting off to sleep—the fall of the gods, the awakening of the beasts, and the folly of the canines were only some of the stories told around the neutral places where travelers gathered to barter for Old World artifacts, rented companionship, and dead flesh not yet grown too ripe to consume. There were tales of encounters with reaper-drones, metal-skinned automatons still fighting ancient wars on behalf of their long-dead creators. There were stories claiming that the fall of the Masters tore a hole through the world-weave, letting unspeakable things from other world-weaves slip through. And there were rumors claiming the Masters themselves lived on, hiding in deep warrens and waiting for the right time to return and reclaim their rightful place at the apex. Old Cat only shook his head at such tales. Why make up horrors when there were things lurking in the real world far worse than anything born of imagination?

Curled up before the fire, tucked beneath his blanket and sword within reach, Old Cat began to doze when a faint sound awakened him. Grumbling, he stretched and rose. He grabbed his sword and padded across the room, putting his ear to the door. Sure enough, something scratched at the other side. Soft yet insistent, it implied prey desperate for shelter, yet fearful of drawing its pursuer's attention.

Reinvigorated by food and fire, Old Cat gave in to curiosity and threw open the door. A red rooster and two chickens stood quivering outside. Shreds of his pre-awakened instincts kicked in, and Old Cat tensed to pounce. And though his mouth watered at the thought of fresh meat, Old Cat couldn't help but pause and scrutinize the odds of three delicious-looking creatures simply showing up at his front door. Maybe the canines were right after all. Maybe benign gods did exist, and Old Cat had done something to please them.

Reaching for the rooster, Old Cat froze. Strapped across the rooster's back was a parcel wrapped in a tattered blanket. The chickens likewise wore makeshift packs. Studying them more closely, Old Cat saw that the fear in their eyes was not the instinctive terror of simple beasts, but of creatures aware of their own mortality. They weren't mere animals. Self-aware fowl were exceedingly rare, but these creatures were surely awakened.

Old Cat had killed plenty of awakened beasts during and after the Canine Wars but only eaten a few, and even then only when he was exceedingly hungry. The word 'empathy' wasn't in Old Cat's vocabulary, but he understood the concept well enough, and damn that Old Hound for the knowledge. Comprehension of the *self* brought awareness of the *other*. The ability to think like one's enemies and anticipate their moves was of great strategic value. The ability to understand their pain was not. Whereas feral creatures fought for their lives because of instinct, awakened creatures fought to live because they feared death. Old Cat knew this. He also knew that because he didn't relish the thought of being eaten, other awakened creatures probably didn't either. Empathy, as it turned out, was a double-edged sword.

Old Cat's whiskers twitched in aggravation. He didn't understand why killing thinking creatures felt wrong, even though the Old Hound had tried to explain it to Old Cat's younger self:

"When you're able to know the heart of another beast, that beast becomes a part of you," the *Old Hound told him.*

"Is that good or bad?"

"That's for you to decide."

"Wouldn't eating it make it a part of me?"

The Old Hound howled. Startled, Young Cat took a step back before realizing the howl was laughter.

"What I mean is, killing it is like killing a part of yourself," the *Old*

Hound explained.

Young Cat considered that for a moment. "Everything dies eventually."
"Yes, but not everything understands death."

There were times when Old Cat almost thought he understood. A beast's dearest and most important possession was its own life. Take that away, and you'd take away everything the beast was and would ever be. Killing, therefore, wasn't to be taken lightly. That was the reason he once let a mouse go free after only a bit of good-natured fun. Old Cat could be kind when he wanted, even when it didn't serve his purpose. For some it was a way of life, but for him it was a luxury he doled out when feeling magnanimous. And a luxury it was in such a harsh world.

But Old Cat wasn't in a kind mood that night. He was in a hungry mood. The fact that his guests were chickens didn't help matters. Chickens tasted oh so good, and Old Cat hadn't had fresh meat in what felt like ages. Drooling, he reached for the rooster—

One of the chickens squawked in surprise as something grabbed her from behind and yanked her from sight. Shoving the rooster aside, Old Cat launched through the open doorway and into the night. Even as his eyes adjusted to the moonlight, Old Cat already knew the chicken was done for by the wet, tearing sounds coming from a nearby thicket. Creeping closer, he peered through the tall grass and saw a huge centipede tearing into the chicken amid a flurry of blood-stained feathers. Six times the length of Old Cat's own body and over twice as wide, the centipede's burnt-orange exoskeleton gleamed in the moonlight. Each of the centipede's countless legs terminated in a point sharp as the tip of a spear. Three pairs of legs pinned the chicken to the ground, while its mandibles went to work ripping and tearing at flesh and bone. Thick as Old Cat's forelimbs, the centipede's antennae lashed about as it feasted. For all his experiences with death, the sounds coming from the dying chicken made Old Cat's hackles rise.

A living armory wrapped in sturdy exo-plates, the centipede was a mighty hunter. The simplest course of action would be to return to the domicile and finish what he'd started with the rooster, but something had stoked the fires in Old Cat's belly. Maybe it was outrage at the sight of a potential meal denied. Maybe it was the drowsy musings that had drifted through his mind earlier that evening. Damn that Old Hound anyway for putting those ideas into his head. Yowling like he'd done as Young Cat in the heat of passion and battle, Old Cat raised his sword and charged. The centipede immediately paused in its grisly meal. Dirt and rock flew as the creature's legs churned, rushing to meet Old Cat's challenge. Barely dodging huge mandibles as he leapt over his opponent's lunge, Old Cat landed on the centipede's back and struck. Though he hacked with all his might, his sword couldn't penetrate the creature's exo-plates.

Rising up like a serpent, the centipede twisted and struck, but Old Cat dove aside and rolled to his feet. Charging in low, Old Cat intended to strike at the centipede's less protected underbelly, but it rushed in even lower. Slashing out as he sidestepped the centipede's charge, Old Cat managed to sever one of its antennae. As the centipede reared back, Old Cat pressed his advantage. He stepped in close, parrying and dodging its flashing mandibles, with the intention of sliding his sword between its overlapping plates. Moving with surprising speed, the centipede whipped its bulk about, slammed into Old Cat, and sent him flying.

Old Cat fell, face-down and swordless, and felt the earth tremble as the centipede reared over him. He only had time to roll over before it was on top of him. The thing's spikey legs dug into Old cat's flesh as it tried to pin him down. Furiously clawing at the centipede's underbelly with his hind-legs, Old Cat struggled to reach his sword. Adjusting so it could strike with its mandibles, the centipede gave Old Cat just enough space to free one of his forelimbs. As the centipede's head descended to deliver the death-blow, Old Cat struck. His extended claws raked across one of the centipede's eye-clusters. Goo dripping from its ruptured eyes, the centipede shuddered.

Momentarily forgotten, Old Cat rolled clear and scooped up his sword. The centipede shot forward, a living missile of primal instinct wrapped in a hard chitin shell. Old Cat planted himself and met its charge with a forward thrust of his sword. The blade slid between the centipede's mandibles and into its gullet. Old Cat gave the sword a twist and pulled it free. The centipede lashed out blindly then half-squirmed, half-tumbled away and began thrashing. Running up the prone centipede's underbelly, Old Cat ducked and weaved through its many legs, then leapt and delivered a reverse-grip blow to the narrow breach in the thing's carapace at the base of its wide, flat head. The sword bit deep. The centipede heaved, sending Old Cat flying once more. The thing continued to twitch, but it was only an autonomic reflex. The creature was dead.

Climbing to his feet, Old Cat surveyed the scene. The remaining chicken and rooster were nowhere in sight, and the door to the canine domicile was shut. Old Cat tried the door, but it wouldn't budge. Pounding at the door in what he knew was a pointless display of rage, Old Cat yowled his frustration at the moon, the stars, the Masters, the night sky, the spirit of the Old Hound, and anything else that be listening.

Stupid, heartless chickens, Old Cat silently fumed. How could they treat him this way after he saved them? Granted, the rooster had seen the look his eyes, but locking him out was a craven act nonetheless.

There was no time to brood; the centipede was only one of countless terrible things abroad in the land. Licking clean his sword, Old Cat pondered his next move. He spun at the sound of a door opening, and he saw his things laid out on the ground. As Old Cat turned back, the door shut, and the sound of the latch sliding back into place echoed in the gloom. After retrieving his things, Old Cat scavenged what meat and innards he could from the chicken's corpse and ate them raw. He savored the warm juices. There was something vital about fresh, raw meat. How was it that death tasted so much like life? Contemplating the absurdity of the turn of events, Old Cat suddenly understood why the Old Hound had laughed at his question all those years ago. Sometimes all a beast could do was shake his head and laugh.

Kharuk's Keeper

Kirisis Dhole

"Ralvo, please move. Baba would never forgive me if I allowed you to get hurt."

"He'll learn, Kima, " her mother said, her paws smoothing the corn out for *kwekwe*, the savory-sweet grain cakes their village was known for. "Leave him to his fun."

They chuckled as their rhythmic pounding echoed throughout the yard, ignored by the scuttling servants.

Ayoron, or the Harvest Festival, was the second-largest festival in their village, and Kima's family supplied all the kwekwe from their corn fields, so it was vital that it was pounded just right. That was proving difficult with sneaky rabbit kits around.

They were quiet as they molded it, separating some to be stuffed with sorghum paste and others in palm seed oil, but her mother smiled as she rolled.

"Pashoun has asked for you again."

"Yes, Mama."

"He's a good buck and has a lot of land. The baron has appointed him head grain collector, and I'm sure the ancestors will bless you both with many sons."

"Yes," Kima said, her ears lowered. "If that's what the ancestors wish of me."

"Why do you seem upset then?"

Her mother had stopped folding the kwekwe and placed a paw under her daughter's chin, lifting it.

"Because he is old and ugly, Mama, and I do not care for him." Kima turned away, her pink nose twitching. "Baba won't listen because he believes this to be a good match and wants to be rid of me quickly."

"Oh Kima, it's not that—"

"Then what is it, Mama? Baba won't heed my words and only thinks of the matchmaker's suggestion."

"I know Pashoun is old, but we wanted a good match for you."

"But I will be a third wife! Surely you could have found someone else—"

"Kima! You shame your father and mother with your disrespect. Your father has put a lot of thought into this, and we wanted to make sure that Djimon and then Ralvo will have good lands and can marry well. They must, so the ancestors will bless them will more sons to carry on our family name. Do you think I loved your father when I was presented to him on our wedding day?"

Kima looked away from her mother, her eyes watering. Marriages among the villagers were always for lands or fortune, never love. She was bound by duty.

"Onum wasn't my first choice for a husband, but with my father gone and my mother scrambling to feed us, she did what she had to. Without the guidance and thoughts of men like your father and my brother, we women would be lost, forced to work in a harsh world with no pity for females. Now, no more talk of this or you'll upset your father."

"Upset me how?"

Onum strode into the courtyard, a stack of papers under his arm, followed by Djimon, her brother.

"It is the Festival of Ayoron, and I am in great spirits. The ancestors couldn't have picked a more auspicious day for a harvest and coming together of great families."

The servants scurried to place jars of palm wine and cups before them, with Onum pouring a cup afterwards.

"I don't know why you insist on making *kwekwe* by yourself; we have plenty of servants who would see to that." He sniffed, placing the cup of icy palm wine under his nose. "Now, about tonight, I am sure that Pashoun will think you'll make a fine wife."

"She's a girl and couldn't fathom the hurdles we had to clear for this pairing," Djimon sneered, gulping down some wine.

"Onum," Akili chimed in, pouring her son another cup.. "I worry for her being away from us, especially since there's a rogue, possibly a demon, about."

"These are women's worries! That creature hasn't struck in weeks."

"But Onum—"

"Enough!" The elder rabbit slammed his cup down, spilling wine on the table. "There will be no worries tonight. I have made sure of it, and no amount of demon stories will sway me. Now, I will have no more of this fantasy talk ruining my good mood."

He clapped his paws together and waved for the servants to enter the courtyard. Several rabbits hopped in, carrying hefty platters of sautéed sweetgrass, steaming bowls of date stew, and more vegetables. The family chattered and ate, moving the conversation away from Kima's pending wedding. They were content to carry on, oblivious to their daughter, who sat with her head bowed, kneading her paws in her lap.

"May I be excused? My stomach troubles me," she mumbled, placing her pickled radishes down. Her father lifted a brow but dismissed her.

Kima bowed to her family and exited the room. Rather than run to the chamber pot, she padded to the family's shrine.

With her family's growing prosperity, the shrine had grown, but the heirloom—a gleaming katana—remained central to it. Legend said that the ancestor, Kharuk, protected the goddess Shimya while she fled a demon fox with that blade, and it had been divinely blessed by the goddess. Whether that was true, Kima didn't know, but being near the sword brought peace to her troubled mind.

Honored Ancestor, guide me during this strange time. Please grant me the courage to honor my family's wishes and be a good mother and wife—

Kima paused and looked, sensing someone watching her

from out of the corner of her eyes. She wheeled around to see Djimon eyeing her.

"Uh-yes, honored brother?"

"Oh nothing," he replied smoothly, hopping towards the shrine. Rather than give his own prayers, he towered over her kneeling form, his lips drawn into a thin line.

"Shouldn't you be resting?"

"Yes, Djimon. I only came to pray for healing from our ancestors," Kima said, clapping her paws to finish the prayer and standing in front of her brother. "They've always helped me whenever I've felt ill."

"You're too old to believe in fairy tales," he said, twitching his nose. "And the dead will do you no favors. They've left this world and don't care about your infirmities."

Kima flinched. Djimon had never found reverence of the ancestors helpful, but he'd never been this outwardly rude before. Since his return from the next town a few weeks ago, his derision of their beliefs had become abhorrent.

"That's not true," she shot back, feeling her paws clench in her robes. "The ancestors have always watched over and protected our family. We've blossomed because of their intervention. Kharuk risked their life for Shimya, and we are blessed for it!"

Djimon's eyes flashed, and he turned his ears sideways before pointing them straight out behind him. "Do you honestly believe that a demon fox was chased here from other lands and that a single ancestor of ours was able to defeat it with a rusty blade? You're foolish if you do."

Kima opened her mouth to protest him, but he held a paw up from underneath his linen robes, silencing her. "Do not argue, little sister. Go to bed and do not worry yourself about spirits or ancestors."

She bowed and padded past him to her room. As she turned the corner, she thought she saw him giving the sword a hungry glance, but he shook himself and headed back to be with the family.

The late autumn breeze whipped around Kima's ears, lifting them. She wanted to stop and enjoy it, but there were chores to be done.

The barn was alive with activity when she pushed the heavy door open. She watched as several chickens and a few cows shifted and bellowed at her, swishing their tails back and forth. Kima often had to stir them from their sleep to be milked, but they must have felt the festival's energy.

Having fed the hens, she spied a discarded rake. Heaving it in front of her, she imagined the dark wood to be the dusty hilt of Kharuk's sword. She traced her steps out in the hay, thrusting the rake, her steps dizzying in the early morning light. She believed herself to be a warrior is Kharuk's time, helping them defeat the demon fox.

With a final shout, she slashed in front of her, the imaginary creature evaporating with puffs of air.

Lolo, her cow, mooed expectantly at Kima, breaking the silence. Kima jumped and rushed to press her paws against the sides of the cow, hugging her tightly.

"Good morning! Didn't expect to see you awake so early, but it's nice to have the company. Let me prepare your—"

A crash from one of the back stalls made Kima yelp and press closer to the cow. Was it the demon her family had been speaking of?

"Come out from there!" she shouted to the darkness. Nothing responded.

"Come out or I'll-I'll—" Kima's voice escaped her. What would she do when whatever monster came charging at her?

A shuffling sound resonated from the darkness, and she could make out the steady panting of something.

The laborious breaths made her short fur stand on end, but she dug her heels into the ground. She clenched her paws around the rake, preparing for a fight. Just as she was about lose her resolve and run, a figure stepped into her lamp light.

The wrinkles on their wizened face made Kima recoil, but his smile made her lower the rake. He wore dusty linen robes, and thick tufts of fur grew out of his ears. He leaned on a mahogany cane, which he tucked against his side, knocking against brightly colored gourds, and cleared his throat.

"My apologies, young miss, but I've been traveling alone at night and, upon seeing your barn, I decided to use it as my shelter. Please forgive my intrusion," he said, bowing so that his long ears drooped on the ground. Kima backed away, but the intruder wiggled his ears and hoped forward.

"I don't want to startle you, but I would like to stay here through the winter, as I fear that I may be caught in the rains on the roads or by even bandits," he said, making Kima lower the rake.

"I could handle a couple of bandits, but any more than that and, well..." He made a slicing sound and drew a paw across his neck and winked at her.

"You can—you mean that you could fight off thieves and robbers?"

"Not as quickly as I could during my youth, but I can still give them a run for their kwekwe!" His laughter rang out in the barn, and Kima waved her paws to silence him.

"Shh, please! If my family finds you in here, they'll be upset," Kima whispered, placing the rake on the wall and twitching her ears. "But I do think we could reach an agreement. Do you think that you could show me how to defend myself from others, in exchange for hiding you here for the winter?"

The rabbit rubbed his long whiskers, weighing her offer, but then his face brightened, and he held out his cane to her.

"I think that would be most fortuitous, especially if that's how you hold your sword."

Kima pouted and raised the rake higher above her head. "I hold it just like Kharuk did."

Something flickered in his eyes, but he bowed low to her again, his whiskers still. "Well met then, Kima. I am Rashidi, and my apologies for interrupting your chores. I find your terms agreeable."

Kima lowered the rake and nodded at him, her bright eyes still on him. "I must attend to my chores, but I'll be back later with food."

"That would be fine. I only request that you come see me in the mornings for your training, when I am at my freshest. Now, to return to my nap."

Kima watched Rashidi bundle up in the hay of the last stall. She wanted to question the strange elder further, but the cattle calls pulled her away.

"Kima, hurry! We don't want to be late!"

She trudged along, counting the cobblestones in front of her. How many more steps did she have before she was forced to take the wizened, arthritic paws of Pashoun and hold her breath when he spoke to her?

She lifted her head, her brows furrowed, but she didn't recognize any of the cobblestone streets. Her servants were nowhere to be found either.

Where—Where am I? How did I get lost?

After stumbling around, she tried to retrace her steps, but succeeded in overturning a small shrine with her stubby tail. A red clay figure shattered on the ground while two foxes perched on the sides, their jeweled eyes following her every move.

Kima clapped her paws together, offering her apologies, and just as she was finishing, her servants found her and escorted her to the sprawling estate of Pashoun.

Truly, Pashoun had amassed great wealth, but as haggard, wizened paws beckoned to her, Kima couldn't help but shudder. Even as she bowed before him and his two wives, Kima found her thoughts darting to Rashidi and everything else she could be doing.

Speaking of the old one, he'd smiled and accepted the food gratefully, and left her alone. Then, when she thought he would retire, he'd cast off his bulky robes and began doing elaborate exercises with his cane without breaking a sweat.

He was patient and attentive to her, but what was he doing lurking around her father's barn and practicing moves like that?

"Did you hear me?"

Kima jumped, much to the amusement of Pashoun, who smiled, showing a row of blackened teeth.

"My apologies, Lord Pashoun. I was—" She stumbled to find the words, which prompted murmurs and tsking from Chief and Second Wives. Pashoun nodded and clapped at her, while she heard voices in the background.

"It seems that my charms have stolen her words! No matter though. What are you bringing me to increase my household and wealth?"

"I am able to cook and clean," she said, drawing snorts from the other two rabbits, "as well as recite the Twelve Laws of Virtue, sew, and—"

The voices grew louder, coming closer. If Pashoun noticed, he didn't show it.

"Well," he asked, drawing in closer to her, his pungent breath curling her whiskers, "what else can you do?"

"I can—"

"*Tch*! I don't think she'll make such a good wife, Honored Lord," Second Wife said, looking down her short muzzle at the younger rabbit. "What do you think, Chief Wife?"

"I agree," First Wife said, fanning herself. "What good is another wife if she can only do the bare minimum?"

Pashoun waved his wives away, chattering at them.

"I will decide that. I believe that she will make a good wife; she just needs time. But tell me, why should I accept your father's dowry and count you among my beloved wives?" His paws gripped hers, his long claws raking over her fur, sending waves of revulsion churning through her.

Kima tried to respond, but a servant saved her. Their eyes were wide and she hopped from paw to paw, trying to recite a message.

"Lord Pashoun, I-I—"

"Out with it, girl," he snarled.

"My apologies," the servant said, "but the message is for Kima. Your father wishes for you to come home immediately, but Djimon insists that it's nothing."

How dare he? she thought, her cheeks flushed with color. How were her brother's thoughts only on securing a marriage?

She bowed to the servant and turned to Pashoun, mumbling

out an apology. "Honorable Lord, I beg your forgiveness for leaving so suddenly, but I must go!"

Gathering up her long skirt, Kima raced after the servant. They traveled at top speed, the indignant cries of the wives and Pashoun fading quickly into the night. It didn't take them long to reach her family home and, in the dark, she could see a group of guards gathered near the woods. They held lanterns and other torches, forming a circle.

It took Kima a moment to push through the crowd, but in the middle, she saw her father kneeling near a large figure, with a stone-faced Djimon standing nearby.

"Baba, what's happened?" she asked, recoiling from the sight. There, sprawled in the tall, yellow grass, was Lolo. The cow's face was contorted into a grimace, the whites around her eyes showing and her tongue lolling out of her mouth. The lamplight illuminated the blood-sodden ground that surround her, the gaping wound in her side making Kima gag.

Her father pressed his long ears against his head. "Djimon and I agreed that it would be best to not allow you to see this. You're supposed to be at Lord Pashoun's home. This isn't fit for a young doe to see."

Kima shook her head, willing herself not to cry. "I don't care, Baba. What happened?"

"It appears that something led her from the pasture. There are tracks coming from the barn that way."

Kima felt her heart stop and she let out a small squeak, which her brother seemed not to notice, for he continued.

"The other animals are safe, as the tracks seemed to head back to the forest, and the door wasn't open, but it's still very strange."

"Indeed, Djimon. Why this butchery? I could have sold them the heifer if that was their intent. No need to cause such a panic," Onum added, scratching at his beard.

"True, Father. Do you think it could have been raiders?"

The conversation faded around her when she turned her eyes to the carcass of her favorite pet. Whatever had butchered the cow had done so with precision, taking only the liver.

While her father and brother conversed with the other men, Kima sank to her knees in front of Lolo, the blood soaking her robes, and gingerly closed the cow's eyes.

Lowering her head, she said a small prayer before she was ushered back into the house to clean up.

"I understand that holding a sword isn't your strong point, but you're making this way too easy for even an old rabbit such as myself."

Kima lowered her paws from her eyes to see Rashidi leaning on his walking stick, twirling her makeshift sword in his free paw. Straw from the barn floor floated down around her, covering her head.

"I'm sorry, Elder Rashidi, but the sword and your yell…" She splayed her ears but pursed her lips together. "You should have told me that you were going to attack like that!"

"Why? If robbers were to attack you, do you think they'd say, 'excuse us honored lady, but may we please steal your property'?"

Kima's cheeks burned, but she refused to give him the satisfaction of getting under her nerves again. She was beginning to reconsider their bargain. Everything about her form needed to be perfect, and she also needed to know when to use her sword and when to sheath it, according to his first principle: Earth. Inexplicably, she'd passed his test by throwing her rake at him and running away screaming when he charged. Knowing when to fight, he said, and when to run, was one of the most important skills to learn and may keep her alive someday.

"If you're finished with your indignation, would you like to learn about the next principle?"

"Yes…Elder," she added when he arched an eyebrow at her. Kima couldn't tell if he was trying to anger her, but she wouldn't break her resolve.

Rashidi twitched his head, and she scurried off to bring the wine gourd and two cups that she had brought to the barn for them to share. As she poured him a cup, he leaned in, his long ears draped over his shoulders, and sniffed the wine. When he seemed satisfied, he leaned back, stroking his whiskers.

"So," he began, "what do you know about balance? Order? Stability?"

Kima's ears perked up, and she remembered what she'd been taught as a kit. "I know that things must be balanced, and one yields to its other. Just as the night yields to the day, a wife to her husband, and—"

Rashidi waved a paw, cutting her off. "You're speaking of yielding, not balance. The moon is not a servant of the sun, nor is a wife a slave to her husband, no matter what they may be teaching you."

He jerked his head to the side, motioning towards the house before sipping at his wine. When he'd finished taking a sip, he placed the cup down. Using one of his claws, he stirred the wine, watching the liquid follow the direction of his finger. After a moment he lifted his paw out of the wine, watching as the liquid continued swirling in the direction he had established.

"Water, like all liquids, happily follows the direction of my claw, yielding to my power because I am more powerful than it in its current form. However, my finger will tire and the water will continue moving, until it over takes me."

"But Master, you could always pour the wine out," Kima said, her brows furrowed. "The wine won't overpower you."

"Yes, that's true for a cup of palm wine, but what about a river or a lake? Or even the sea? Can you pour those out?"

Kima opened her mouth to retort but closed it when she couldn't find a better answer. Rashidi chuckled and slurped down his wine.

"There's no shame in yielding to a force that is greater than yourself and allowing it to guide your movements, but balance is always better. For every force, there's an equally opposite force and they create balance."

"I'm not understanding, Master Rashidi," Kima said, breaking their gaze.

"I am saying that the second lesson for the element of Water deals with knowing when to yield to a greater force until you can overcome it. In the meantime, I will teach you how to use your opponent's force against them, until you can overcome them.

Now, let us begin."

Kima trained with Rashidi for the rest of the day, sparring with him and learning how to use his own energy against him. It was demanding, bitter work, complete with many raps on her back with his wooden cane, but when she trudged back to the main house, she couldn't help but stop by the ancestral shrine and gaze longingly at Kharuk's sword.

"Where have you been?"

Kima wheeled around to see Djimon standing in the doorway, his nose twitching.

"I-I was out at the barn, saying prayers for Lolo,"

"A stupid cow doesn't need prayers," he said. "She was valuable, but still property."

Djimon pushed past her, continuing his tirade. "Prayers are useless, if you ask me, but Baba says that I should indulge you, since your upcoming marriage to Pashoun is our greatest concern right now."

"I thought that he wanted to decide— I mean, I didn't know that Pashoun accepted the dowry," Kima said, lowering her head, fighting to hide the burning she felt in her cheek and the nausea that washed through her.

"Oh yes, he accepted, despite your impropriety. I was able to smooth things over with him."

"Baba didn't give you the—" Kima clasped her paws over her muzzle, startled that she'd spoken against her older brother. He appeared to be just as surprised because he raised his brows and stomped a paw at her. Kima shrank from Djimon's anger and knelt in front of him, begging for his mercy against her outburst.

"Forgive me, honored brother, I did not mean to speak out of turn."

"I would have never believed such impudence from you," he said, flicking his short tail, "but I will chalk it up to your impending nuptials. For now, you are to remain in your room, reciting your virtues and preparing. You will also stay out of the barn."

She pressed her ears against her head, but kept her head

bowed. "Yes, Brother."

"Good. I don't want any harm befalling you. Another cow was killed in the outer pasture, even though the guards kept watch all night. It isn't safe for a girl to wander the barn alone now."

Kima's mind flickered to Rashidi, but she didn't fight her brother. Tucking her paws inside of her linen dress, she nodded and turned to leave.

"I know it's difficult, Kima, but everything I'm doing is to keep you safe. You'll thank me someday."

Kima shuddered, his words making her short fur stand on end long after she'd left his presence.

Swish! Swish! Swish!

The short reed that mimicked her sword sliced through the cool air of the evening. The barn was mostly silent, the cattle and other creatures having been fed earlier and left to their own devices. True to her word she had stayed out of the barn, but she and Rashidi practiced their moves in the walkway, just outside the large barn.

Kima stomped her right paw and watched as her teacher darted in, his gleaming blade aimed at her stomach. She arched her back so that the "blade" didn't even touch her clothes and avoided the blow. As their eyes found each other's, she deftly swung the blade over his outstretched arm and grabbed his wrist in her paw. Clutching it, she moved the blade as if it were an extension of herself, making imaginary slices over his arm, and before he knew it, the short blade was pressed against his neck. Kima held his queued ears in her other paw and, with a smile, placed a quick peck on his fuzzy cheek.

"You move faster than anyone I've ever fought with," Rashidi said, nodding with a smile. "You seem to have taken quite well to the principle of Air."

"Well I have a great teacher, Rashidi." Kima grinned, releasing his ears to sheath her blade and bowing before her teacher. "I am honored."

Rashidi nodded and bowed at his student in return. "Bah to

these new traditions that call for girls and women to remain hidden and vulnerable. When I was just a kit, I remember my mother using her scythe to protect our home from raiders while father was away. They were in balance, though."

Kima nodded at her teacher. "Water. Yes, there must always be balance, but also the ability to adapt to a new situation."

"You've learned well. I have something for you," he said, hopping back into the hay before Kima could say something. Moments later, he shuffled back with a small box in his paws, which he held out to her.

"I think it's time for your fourth lesson. We can't begin it without these."

Kima took the box and unwrapped it, her beady eyes widening when she removed the lid. Nestled within a silk wrapping, was a short scythe. Grinning as she lifted it, she moved to hug him, but the footfalls of a servant sent Rashidi scurrying towards the nearest haystack. Kima had moments to fling her blade away from her before the door was shoved open, a guard standing there, their whiskers twitching with every short breath.

"Kima! I thought you were forbidden from leaving the main house without an escort. And near the barn?"

"I, well, I had come to see about the other cows. I wanted to bring them a special treat since they've been under such stress lately."

Her eyes darted to the nearest heifer who bellowed at her but returned to eating hay. The guard twitched his ears, but sighed and scratched his brow.

"Lady Kima, it isn't safe with some wild beast wandering around. It would be best if you kept to the house," he said, his eyes scanning the area, while he sniffed the air. "Your father would have my head if he knew—"

"That I was out without his knowing where I am," she finished for him. "Yes, I know."

The guard opened his muzzle but promptly closed it, tucking his paws into his robes and bowing before her. "By any measure, your father wishes for you to breakfast with him early this morning. He has much to discuss."

Kima tapped her foot, drawing a raised eyebrow from the guard, but her bow seemed to mollify him. He turned and exited the courtyard, his short tail bobbing behind him. Kima looked over towards the haystack, but the soft snores emanating from it told her that Rashidi would be unavailable for his advice. Sighing, she padded towards her father's study. He was seated at his desk, a tray of pickled vegetables, soup, dried sweetgrass, and kwekwe before him. He looked over his glasses and waved his daughter in.

"Come, I'll have one of the servants fetch us some wine."

Kima bowed before her father and sat, tucking her paws beneath her on a cushion, watching as he shuffled through scrolls.

"Kima, do you know what these are?" he asked, spreading several sheets before him and pursing his lips together.

"No, Baba," she replied, taking the wine jar from the servant and dutifully pouring a chilled cup for her father, and then herself.

"These are letters from Pashoun. He says that he is disappointed in your leaving him at the Harvest Festival, but that you will make a favorable wife, nonetheless. The preparations for your wedding will begin this evening, and we have decided that we will hold the wedding banquet in two days— Is there something wrong?"

Her father had looked up from his desk to see Kima's wide, round eyes, and hear the trembling of the cup in her delicate paw. He smiled, misreading her emotion, and pushed his glasses up farther on his snout.

"Ah, I understand that this is all overwhelming to you, but you'll appreciate my hard work. You'll be with a man of means who can provide and make sure that you have many soft dresses to wear. Even silk ones. That's what you want, yes?"

Kima lowered her head, fighting back the tears that threatened to free themselves from her the corners of her eyes. How could he do this to her now? She knew that it might come soon, but in her heart, she felt that her father would spare her. He couldn't force her to marry Pashoun, could he?

And there it was. For the first time in her young life, Kima felt the spark of defiance well up within her. She curled her paws up within her lap and whispered, "I don't want this."

Onum wrinkled his brows and pushed his long ears forward. "What's that?"

"I don't want to marry Pashoun."

"Excuse me?"

Kima chewed her lip, her will faltering in front of her father's stern gaze, but she continued. "I don't want to marry him."

"You would dishonor your family by refusing to marry?" He had stood to his paws, his long, dark robes swirling around him while his eyes blazed at her.

"Ungrateful because I don't want to be forced to be no more than a slave to a man who is three times my age?" Kima dared to lift her eyes to look at her father. They locked eyes for the briefest of moments before he pulled them away.

"Onum, come quickly!"

Kima and Onum looked up to see a servant with silky black fur bowing at the door. Her father waved at them to enter, the irritation radiating from his ashen fur.

"What is it?"

"It's Souko, sir. He-He's been, he has—"

"Out with it!" The elder rabbit jerked his head, glaring at the intruder.

"Miru has been attacked! His liver was taken," the servant panted, clutching a paw to his muzzle and trying not to vomit. "There was blood everywhere!"

"Impossible!" Onum snapped, stomping with both paws. "I sealed that door myself and left him in charge!"

"He seemed to have been running from something. We found him, just outside of the barn," the servant said, his fur flushing underneath with a green pallor that made even Kima gasp.

Onum stared for a moment, a scowl on his short muzzle, but snorted and headed towards the door. "Fetch my son and meet me in the barn!"

He started to turn, but Kima had run to stop him, her eyes

wide and searching her father's contorted face. "Baba, what's going on?"

"Nothing that women should concern themselves with. To your room, Kima!"

Her father pushed past her and headed out towards the large barn, his footsteps echoed by the servant. Kima stood there, eyes blazing in her father's wake.

I'm just as good as Djimon, she thought, wiping her misting eyes with a paw, *and I'm going to prove it!*

Kima hopped to the foyer of their home and put her shoes on, taking care so that her mother wouldn't hear her. She stuck an ear out the door, swiveling it in the evening air. Hearing no one, she slid the door open wider and slipped out. She hid in the shadows of the house as a line of bucks hopped past her, headed towards the barn.

"We must hurry, someone said they saw something in the barn!"

She clutched a paw to her muzzle to keep from squeaking. She had to warn Rashidi and recover her new blade. Pulling her robes tightly around her, she hopped towards the barn, keeping her body pressed to the shadows.

While normally cheery, the barn was an ominous figure at this time of night, lit only by bobbing of torch lights. The sharp, metallic tang of spilled blood permeated the air, raising every hair on her Kima's body. There were a few drops on the ground near her, which she kicked dirt over, the scent drawing bile to the back of her throat.

She could hear voices from inside, so she darted to a nearby haystack and burrowed into it, her ears pressed forward onto her head. A soft paw on her shoulder made her squeak out in terror.

"Shh," Rashidi murmured, pressing a claw to his short muzzle and pointing wordlessly towards the inner barn. Her father was pacing, his long, graying ears swiveling back and forth on his head, but Djimon had arrived.

"What took you so long?" Onum asked, stomping a paw on the hard-packed earth.

"I had to see to the servants before I came. What is the matter, Father?" Djimon wheezed.

"There's been another attack!"

"What?" Djimon asked, his eyes gleaming in the pallid lantern light.

"An attack, you fool. Whatever beast is sneaking past the guards is more intelligent than we thought. One more cow and we won't turn a profit at market this year!"

"Do you think that we are being cursed by a demon, or—"

"Nonsense," came the swift rebuke. "I don't believe in the superstitious ramblings of commoners or servants! Someone is plotting against me, but I will not yield! You will keep watch tonight and report to me in the morning."

Even from the haystack, Kima could hear her brother swallow hard before he answered their father. "Yes, Baba. I'll make sure they're fed, and then we'll keep watch and report to you in the morning."

There was shuffling as they left the barn, leaving Kima and Rashidi to deliberate.

"We've got to stop it!" Kima said, drawing her kaiken and preparing to leap from the haystack, but Rashidi's strong grip held her back.

"I know you're looking to prove yourself to your father, but this isn't the time!"

"Well," she said, snatching her arm away and glaring, "what do you suppose we do, sit here and wait until my family's ruined?"

The elder rabbit twitched his nose, his dark eyes burrowing into hers. Kima's ears lowered to her shoulders, and she could feel the color rising into her snowy cheeks. "My apologies, Master."

"If we run out now and effectively blow our hiding spot, we'll have to contend with not just an irate father, but also a house full of servants. I suggest we wait here," Rashidi said, his eyes now gleaming. "I'm certain that whatever is terrorizing your family will be back then."

Kima opened her muzzle to object, but realizing the truth in his words, sighed and sheathed her kaiken. "Until tonight then."

"Good, now rest," Rashidi said, leaning back into the hay

and crossing his large paws in front of him. "We'll need it for what's coming."

Kima awoke with a start, her nose trembling. She heard Rashidi's muffled snoring, making her look over to him. His cane rested on his belt, his movements causing it to tap gently against the orbs that he carried at his waist, but otherwise, all was quiet.

Peeping outside of the haystack, she saw one of the guards yawning, only to be swiftly rebuked by the head guard. Djimon rested beside another haystack, his whiskers twitching back and forth on his thin face. He kept looking over his shoulders at the slightest noise.

Things were okay, at least from Kima's vantage point, so she snuggled back into her spot and drew her blade. She inspected the scratching along the blade, admiring how they seemed to be ritualistically placed in an almost familiar pattern. She gingerly moved her paws, listening to how the metal seemed to hum in response to her touch. How Rashidi had come to possess such a blade shocked her. As she moved to touch the blade again, the sound of something heavy hitting the dirt floor made her freeze.

Peering outside of her retreat, she saw the guards fall, one by one to the ground, as if they had fallen asleep where they stood. Even the firelight seemed to be under the same lure, as their light seemed to fade and shadows began to loom.

They grew, feeding on themselves, and creeping along the barren floor. They covered the sleeping guards in darkness, obscuring them from view. Kima looked for Djimon, but he'd been swallowed by darkness as well.

The shadows swirled together until they formed a dark mass with gleaming red eyes and pointed ears. It sniffed the air, and its muzzle cracked open in a sinister grin. The creature turned, whisking its long, fluffy tail behind it, sniffing at the slumbering guards, acidic drool streaming from corners of its muzzle.

Demon!

Kima gasped, but Rashidi's paws were there, cutting the sound off. He pointed to ghostly fox-creature and held his other paw to his muzzle.

The ghost-fox bounded along, its translucent paws silent as it pranced through the dark, trailing an eerie *yip yip*. It gave Djimon a rap on his head, grinning when her older brother groaned in his sleep and turned over, the spell leaving him unaware. It repeated this dance until it stopped next to a guard.

Before Kima could make another sound, the spectral fox dug its muzzle into the abdomen of the guard. The guard, under the demon's spell, writhed and moaned in his sleep, but remained unconscious. Before it claimed the still-steaming prize of fresh liver, the guard had departed this world, agony splashed across his features. The demon then lifted the quivering mass of liver to its muzzle and began to feast, the sounds of chewing and slurping making Kima gag into her paws. The fox stopped its feast and looked up, its nose quivering in the air.

"I know you're out there," it said, licking its jowls and stepping away from the guard. "I can smell your fear, seasoning the air like a divine salt."

It sniffed and prowled forward. It neared the haystacks, shoving its paws into them. Beside Kima, Rashidi stiffened, his paw inching to his cane while his eyes followed the fox's movements. He nodded to Kima and scuttled out of the haystack, keeping his footfalls soft.

The spectral fox stalked through the haystacks, toppling them with swipes of its tail, taunting the pair.

"I hear the beating of little, rabbit hearts. Come out so that I may snack upon them."

Kima felt her breath catch in her chest as it prowled dangerously close to her haystack. She thought her heart would burst out of her chest when that semi-clear nose poked was thrust into that haystack, but something drew its attention.

"Looking for something?"

Rashidi stood before the creature, his wizened paws on his cane, his face stern. He looked frail, utterly dwarfed by the beast, but he didn't waver or run from it.

The demon turned on its paws and bared its teeth. "Well now, this is interesting. Usually when creatures look upon me, their hearts beat so fast, they often burst from fear. But you're so calm. Relaxed even."

It took a step closer and snapped its jaws at elderly rabbit, but Rashidi didn't flinch. The demon seemed to delight in his audacity, flicking its tail back in forth. "So very brave."

"You've tormented this family long enough. I will put your wretched spirit to rest and send you back to the Underworld!" Rashidi pulled at both ends of his cane, revealing a long, gleaming blade.

"A live one, aren't we?" the fox challenged, swaggering forward. "Here's to hoping that your liver is as tender as you are tough!"

The fox leapt at Rashidi, and Kima screamed and shut her eyes. There was no way the old rabbit could have dodged that attack from that. She braced for the sounds that never came.

When she dared to look, she saw the fox tossing its head, snarling and batting at the diminutive creature that dared to fight.

Rashidi moved with a speed that was impossible for his age, and yet the demon couldn't land a blow. Every snap of its massive jaws ended in a click of teeth on teeth, and then a frustrated growl as Rashidi landed another blow with his sword.

The fox staggered, pools of silvery blood welling up within its fur. From the tempo of its breaths, Kima could tell that it was becoming frustrated with the old master's skill.

They danced around each other, Rashidi slicing at the demon's body and the beast snapping at him. But Rashidi hesitated for just a moment and the fox turned, jaws open and viscous drool oozing from out of its mouth, and it caught one of the rabbit's ears, sending Rashidi tumbling towards Kima's haystack.

"Elder!" Kima screamed, and before she knew it, she had grabbed her blade and was racing towards them. Rashidi groaned with pain but swatted at Kima.

"Don't come any closer!"

"Oh, do come closer! Just a few more livers and I will be finally free!" the demon bellowed, pawing at the ground and flicking its tail behind it. "Cow liver is fine but adding more rabbit liver would be just what I needed."

Burning with the memory of Lolo's loss, Kima drew her scythe, ignoring Rashidi's warnings, and leapt at the creature, which batted at her like a cat does a mouse, sending her tumbling. Rolling into a haystack, she pulled herself to her paws and lifted her small blade in front of her.

"Y-You butchered Lolo and the guards!"

The fox gave a deep, sinister laugh and pawed at the ground, daring her to come closer. "And I would do it again if given the chance!"

The spectral fox leapt, and Kima clenched her paws around the blade, ready to take the beast's blow, but Rashidi was there, rolling her out of the way. They landed among another haystack, sending the flock of chickens scurrying away and blood spattering on Kima's clothes. The blade had hit home on the demon, but the monster grabbed the blade in its jaws and snapped it in half, sneering at her efforts.

"Is that all you've got?"

The demon prepared to charge, but the sound of many paws hitting the ground made it hesitate. It growled, its ear pressed against its head, and dissipated into mist, leaving Kima and Rashidi in the barn, surrounded by guards who being roused from their sleep with the spell broken.

Kima tried to run, but she was grabbed and held by a guard while Rashidi slipped away into the night, pursuing the monster. She struggled within their grasp, but they kicked her legs out from underneath her. By the time she realized what was happening, her father was in front of her, his face blotchy.

"Kima! What is the meaning of this? I thought I ordered you to your room!" he said, stamping his right paw.

"Baba, I heard screams and I saw a demon, Baba! A demon!" Kima shouted, struggling against her captor, but Djimon strode up, his eyes hard and flinty.

"She disobeyed you, Father. I too heard the shouts, but when I came, I saw her covered in blood and the dead guard."

Kima turned and glared at her brother, righteous anger brimming underneath her short fur. "You would lie to our father, Brother? You were sleeping the entire time!"

128

"Nonsense, Kima! I haven't the time to listen to your foolish stories about ghosts, ancestors, and demons. You would lie on your brother as well?"

"But Baba, I saw it with my own two eyes! The demon cast a spell! I can show you!" She grabbed his arm to tug him towards the inner chambers where her brother and other members of the family slept, but Onum pulled away, his eyes burning at her.

"Cease this senselessness, you witch!"

"Baba, I saw it with my own eyes!" Kima cried, her ears pushed forwards on her head.

"Silence! I have had enough of this from you! First you would lie on your brother and then you forget yourself? I knew I had spoiled you! You're a mad creature, a burden and a shame on this family's noble name, and I curse the day you drew breath! Leave this house before dusk or I shall have you thrown out myself!"

Kima sank to her knees, her face frozen in a horrified gasp as her father pushed rudely past her and traveled to the house. Djimon swallowed hard but nodded and followed their father back into the house, leaving Kima to weep in the dust.

Before the moon had completed its zenith across the evening sky, Kima had sought shelter in a hollowed tree, the rotting wood muffling her cries.

"Are you lost, miss?"

Kima stirred, wiping a grimy paw across her short muzzle. She winced when a ragged claw caught the unkempt fur on her cheek but shook herself into wakefulness.

The open stall that she'd been sleeping in for the past few weeks was beginning to brim with life, signaling that it was time for her to move out into the greater market as she usually did. She yawned and staggered to her feet, quickly pushing her ears back against her head to tidy up her appearance. She lifted her troubledeyes to gaze up at the stranger.

He had a friendly face, and his long, wiry ears were tied in a bun behind his head. He stretched out a paw to help her up off the ground.

"N-No, I'm not lost, sir," Kima said, bowing before the stranger. "I guess I slept a little longer than I intended to. Forgive my unkempt looks."

"No worries," he said, smiling again and, after hearing her stomach growling, reached into his basket and presented her with an apple. "I figure that you could use this far more than the temple monk could."

"Temple monk?" Kima asked, her mouth full of the delicious, sweet apple. "I thought most of the temples around here were abandoned or left to themselves?"

"Yes, but this one seems to have found favor with the gods, thus giving us all divine favor. Would you like for me to escort you there, so that you too may offer prayers?"

Kima chewed her lip but figuring that there might be more food there to feed her starving belly, she decided to follow him.

The stranger bowed, taking his leave of her, and headed into the temple. Kima hesitated, her paw lifted above the doorway. Her prayers had become distant since her banishment from her home. Even when she'd tried to shelter on Lord Pashoun's property, hiding in one of his shrines, he'd had her chased off, citing that she was a witch and he didn't want her curse to spread. Her prayers had gone unanswered then, so why would now be any different?

"Aren't you going to come in?"

Kima looked up to see a familiar face, but she recoiled when he came closer. The fur that sprouted from his ears was gone and his ruddy, brown fur was sleek and shiny. In fact, the only remnants of his previous appearance were his eyes, still kindly and somewhat mischievous.

"Elder Rashidi? But how"

He winked at her and beckoned her inside of the temple. Taking her inside of a room that was away from prying eyes, he presented her with a bowl of grains, stewed vegetables, and a warm broth. While she ate he inspected her, sniffing.

"You look a little worse for the wear." He sniffed, stuffing his paws back into his monk's robes.

"No thanks to you. You left when I needed you!" Kima

pressed her ears against her head and glared at him. "I've been banished for being a witch because of you!"

Rashidi lowered his head, sighing as he did. When Kima's glare didn't waver, he scratched the back of his head and held out his paws. "I know that you didn't want to hear this, but I didn't mean for that to happen. I'd been watching and listening for weeks and knew what was coming. I'd only so much time to find and train you. I tried tracking you, but your father was adamant about sealing his property off; I had to hope that you would follow one of the merchant paths. So I waited, and thank the gods that you're here."

Kima wanted to swat at him, but sighed, picking at the rest of her vegetables. "It doesn't matter now. I can't go home and I can't fight that beast. It's probably better if I stay here. Besides, who would believe that a demon is plaguing us? I don't even believe it."

Rashidi glared at her and lifted her head up. "I believe you, but there's little that I can do beyond giving you this."

He reached into his side robes and withdrew the three gourds that had remained at his side all this time. He rolled them in his paws until Kima could see that they were marked with various symbols and contained swirling green, blue, and red mists respectively.

"With these you can fight and restore your family, as long as you remember the principles that I've taught you. I can't leave the temple anymore, but trust in your training and when the time is right, you'll know how to use these."

"Why are you helping me?"

"Because of a promise and some heartfelt prayers I made a long time ago while I chased that monster around the world."

"So why can't you come back now?"

"Because I am bound to this temple," he said, looking away. "At least for now."

Kima wanted to question him further, but a merchant called him back into the temple. Tapping Kima lightly on the forehead, he bowed once more and retreated inside. For a time, Kima rolled the orbs within her paws before tucking them back into her tattered robes. As she was preparing to leave the temple, she saw the saw figures of the twin foxes within a shrine, but this time there was a rabbit between them, a blade held high as it prepared to attack.

Smiling to herself, Kima put her paws on the road and headed towards home.

Kima's eyes gleamed in the encroaching darkness as she stood before her natal home. Even though the building was still standing, it seemed that so much had changed in the weeks that she had been missing absent. There were no warm, flickering lights to light her path to the main room or even servants scurrying about, preparing the house for the evening. Instead, all that greeted her was eerie silence and a feeling of impending dread.

"Kima, is-is that you?"

The rabbit wheeled around, her paw slipping inside her linen dress and grasping an orb, but it was only Djimon, though not the same one she had left what felt like so long ago. His bright eyes had deep circles underneath them, giving him a haggard look.

"Djimon!" she cried, running into his arms and hugging him tightly. He seemed startled by her display of affection towards him, but once the initial shock wore off, he wrapped his arms around her, clinging to his sister as soft tears fell down his cheek. When they had finished their embrace, he welcomed her into the house. Kima hesitated, her paw hanging above the doorstep.

"Djimon, where are Mother, Ralvo, and Onum? We have to leave before it gets any darker."

Djimon shook his head and sighed, his ears dangling beside his shoulders. "Mother took sick last month. We learned that the creature only attacked at night, after it killed all the barn animals, so we thought it was safe to sleep during the day and remain sentry at night. But Mother…"

Djimon's shoulders slumped, and he took several deep breaths through his nose before he could continue. "The creature got her. Baba and I found her and buried her beneath the date palm tree that she loved so much. Father and Ralvo both fell ill shortly afterwards. Now come inside so you can rest, and we can be safe until morning."

Kima lowered her ears, but followed her brother inside the house, her paw resting inside her robe, clutching the orbs. Inside the house were several lamps, their lights dim because of the amount of oil needed to burn them but lacking the funds. As they passed by the family shrine, Kima noticed that the Sword of Kharuk was still within its case, though it seemed that something had disturbed the shrine.

Frowning, she hopped after her brother and headed to their father's office. As she waited for Djimon to return with soup, Kima noted how empty their home had become. There were no hurried steps of servants, no chattering of her mother as she oversaw dinner. Nothing but emptiness and dread remained.

"Disturbing, isn't it?"

Djimon placed a bowl of steaming soup and wine before her, nodding at her to eat. As she took a few spoonfuls of the steaming soup, Djimon relayed the rest of the story.

"The attacks hit father's interests hard, and since it was so sudden, many believed that we were cursed so they refused to work for us. I foraged the best way that I could."

Kima stiffened, the spoon halfway to her mouth before she tossed it back into the bowl. She needed to stop this immediately. "Djimon, hurry and grab what you can, we're leaving tonight."

"But what about the monster?"

"We'll have to fight it off somehow," she said, nodding and pushing away from the table. As she tried to stand, she noticed that Djimon wasn't moving, and the room began to spin.

"Djimon, something's wrong. I-I'm not feeling well..." she pawed at her eyes, fear filtering through her veins.

"Shh, little sister. Everything will be alright in the morning. I'll make sure that your family's memory lives on."

Djimon leaned against the doorpost of the room, his grin sinister in the lamplight.

"But how? What did you?" Kima collapsed on all fours, gasping as the edges as her vision began to fade.

"The soup, of course. It's always been the soup."

"But I—" Kima coughed and collapsed on the ground. "You were my brother…"

As the world faded around her, Djimon leaned down, his face becoming more angular and pointed. "Funny after all of this time, you still think I'm your brother…"

"The moon is almost at its zenith. Come now, I need you awake."

Kima groaned and opened her eyes. Djimon was crouched over a corpse, his gore-soaked muzzle chewing on something long and slimy.

"Djimon! What's going on?"

"Collecting my reward, and then some," he said, tearing off more flesh.

"After a thousand years, I'm can almost taste it. I have traveled the world, coming from lands afar to avenge my sister's death and claim what should now be mine. One more liver and then I will become a god!"

Djimon threw back his head and laughed, his body convulsing from the effort, as he grew larger and more cumbersome. With wicked glee he tore at his flesh, revealing the largest fox she had ever seen. His head pressed against the ceiling, but unlike the last time, the demon wasn't transparent. Its obsidian fur shone in the pale light as it stretched and preened in front of her.

"I admire your strength, Kima. My noxious poisons usually leave creatures unconscious for hours, but not you. You should consider it an honor that your liver is what will make me ascend to the heavens, not everyone is as fortuitous."

The demon dove back into its meal, jaws tearing into the soft flesh of his victim's abdomen. Kima swallowed the scream and bile that threatened to erupt from her mouth and staggered out of the room. She ran, looking over her shoulder, her nose twitching. The home she had loved so much had turned into a ghastly, twisted version of itself with shadows that stretched wretched claws at her. Unfamiliar with this place, her feet tripped over each other and she landed at the base of the shrine.

There was the Sword of Kharuk. Hearing the belching of the fox, she swallowed hard and snatched the sword from the shrine and hoisted it over her shoulder. Just as she was about to run, a roar shook the house, and Kima could see the shuddering of wood and clay as the creature crashed through a wall.

"Going somewhere?"

The demon laughed and shook itself, knocking over doors and collapsing rooms within the house. Covering her head with her arm, Kima dove through rooms with the monster on her heels. As she ran, she passed the rooms and, with a wave of revulsion, she saw the mummified corpse of her mother, curled around her younger brother.

She wanted to break down, but fear and adrenaline compelled her onward. The demon was also gaining on her, its long legs giving it more ground. Seeing an open window as her last resort, she dove through it, glass shards dazzling the nighttime sky around her.

Yelping as the sword smacked her in the back of the head, she pulled herself to her paws and, clutching the sword, she heard something jingle within her robes. Reaching in, she withdrew the green orb. Rolling it around in her paws, she looked at the window she'd just crashed through, and her ears picked up the sound of the demon crashing around. She hefted her arm back and threw the green orb at the window, just as the black muzzle pushed through.

The orb shattered, sending tendrils of thorny vines in its wake. They crept and curled around the muzzle and paws of the demon, sending drops of iron-gray blood splashing in its wake.

Kima choked out a grim laugh, but inexplicably, the fox pulled itself free from the tendrils, bleeding and patches of fur missing, but ready to battle.

"Kima, I will take great pleasure in hearing you scream while I gnaw on your liver!"

It came bounding forward, closing the distance that Kima had run in a matter of moments, but remembering the principle of Earth, she held her ground until the demon was nearly on top of her before she struck out with the sword.

The force of the blow sent the young rabbit rolling, her long ears trailing over her large paws, and she landed in a heap. When the bright lights stopped popping behind her eyes, she heard the thrashing and mangled growling of the monster. Her mood brightened when she saw the fox leaning to the side, a jagged cut running the length of one its limbs.

"Forget just your liver, your wretch! I will peel the flesh from your bones and leave your pelt for the crows!"

The demon charged at her, but Kima held onto the sword. Using the principle of Water, she adapted to the frenetic movements of the demon, dodging when the jaws came to close and thrusting with the sword when it dove away. They weaved this dance, the demon forcing Kima backwards into a tree.

Feeling the wood against her, she reached into her dress and withdrew the blue orb. Just as the demon's jaws opened to crush Kima, she tossed the blue orb into its mouth. The demon began choking as spouts of water rushed from its nostrils and jaws while the ground sunk underneath it.

As Kima scrambled out of the way, a bog erupted, dragging the creature down to the murky depths. Kima peered over the edge and, within a split second, she dove backwards, swinging the sword and catching the shrieking beast in its jaw.

Kima ducked and dodged, trying to flow with the beast's moves, but fatigue was beginning to wear her down. She held the blade up, but the fox's fangs met it, and the jolt sent Kima rolling once more, the red orb flying away as well. Scrambling, she tried to use the blade to block the fangs and claws that tore at her, but it was to no avail. After a misplaced swipe, the demon grabbed her in its jaws, shaking the rabbit. Kima had never experienced such pain in her life, but she managed to take her sword and slash it across the gleaming eyes, forcing the beast to drop her while it screamed out more curses.

Kima collapsed on the ground, feeling something go rolling near her. Opening an eye, she saw that it was the red orb, with a note attached to it. Propping herself up she palmed the orb, and felt her eyes widen as the fox took a running leap and sprang at her. Stuffing the note in her pockets, she flung the orb and braced herself for the impact.

Lifting an ear, Kima heard the mangled screams of the beast as the orb burst, sending flames flowing over the beast's face and muzzle. It crashed to the ground, writhing and cursing, but couldn't stop the spread of the flames. Just as quickly as it started, the flames died, leaving the charred skeleton of the beast. As Kima drew near, the wind stirred up, dislodging a single fly from the corpse and leaving her to face dawn alone.

As she took in the remnants of her home and the beast, she leaned against the sword, wondering what was left for her. Grimacing sharply, she felt something poking her side. Reaching into her pocket, she pulled out the note and as her eyes danced across the scrawled writing.

Kima, if you're reading this, it means that you conquered the kumiho. It is a beast from my home lands and though I was tasked with killing it, I had failed. But you triumphed over it! I'm not sure where your path goes from here, but if you are looking to complete your training and master the immortal blade of Kharuk, you know where to find me. —Rashidi

Swallowing, she tucked the note back into her dress and hefted her sword onto her shoulder. There were things in this world that she didn't understand, Rashidi being one of them, but perhaps on her way to mastering her family's heirloom, she could gain that understanding.

Smiling wistfully at what once was her home, she turned tail and began hopping towards the old temple.

Sunrise for the Shotelai

Allison Thai

Bruk could not tell if stares from the villagers fell more upon his missing right paw, or the shotel strapped across his back. He broke customs by eating a meal of thick red onion stew and flatbread with his left paw, but he could not help that. The village chief, Zere, knelt across from his guest and dipped his long neck.

"We are honored and blessed to have you here, Master Shotelai," the giraffe said. "Please, eat as much as you would like."

"I do not eat much." Bruk spent most of his days roaming the savannahs of Abyssinia, so feasting on large meals was a luxury he could not afford. He also had no time for idle pleasantries. The lion warrior lowered the flatbread in his paw. "Tell me more about the T'iniziza here. I received word of two wreaking havoc on your village. Two riding on a lioness and a cub."

"Yes, that's true." Talk of demons made the chief stir uneasily. "For all the kinds of animals populating Wide-Range, we have no shotelai among us. We welcome your service and protection. Without hesitation and with open arms, if I may add." Zere spread his arms. "How can we repay you, Master Shotelai?"

"I need no payment. Your hospitality is enough." Bruk rose to his feet. "Excuse me, but I need to get acquainted with my whereabouts. By sunset I will be patrolling the perimeter of your village."

"Oh, of course. Would you like to have someone be your escort?"

"No need. Thank you again." Bruk tugged at the tip of his mane in respect and left the chief's hut, covering ground in brisk strides. Villagers nearby bustled around him, weaving, preparing food, or sweeping outside of their huts, but he knew they had their eyes and ears on him since he had arrived this morning. Some toiled under the midday sun to repair homes missing thatched rooves. Others mourned over damaged crops. Such was the work of T'iniziza, evil spirits who always struck at night and left destruction in their wake.

Cloying incense came in a wave, stinging his nose, before he spotted a young cheetah rushing up to him. "Master Shotelai, I heard that you'll be walking around our village."

"It seems that you did not hear everything. I told your chief that I don't need an escort."

She frowned. "Anything's better than spouting useless old charms with the shaman. They don't do anything to ward off the T'iniziza from our village." She wrinkled her nose. "We just clog up the air with all that incense."

"I prefer to walk alone," he said, and she pouted.

"Doing anything alone is no fun." Not surprisingly, the young cheetah kept up with him on lean legs. Her footpaws were light and quick along the dirt. "Please, Master Shotelai, let me show you around. I was born here and have known this village all my life."

Bruk sighed. "Very well."

"My name is Saba. May I call you something else besides 'master shotelai'?"

"Bruk."

Her ears perked. "Very pleased to make your acquaintance, Bruk. Never until now did I think I would live to see a real shotelai, and a real shotel." Her wide eyes flashed to the curved blade glinting in the sun. "What a curve. If I hadn't known any better, I would have mistaken it for a sickle at harvest season. Can that sword really kill those demons?"

"They are not so much for killing, but to dismount or

disarm."

"I need to see you use it. Is that too much to ask, Master Shotelai—er, Bruk?"

The lion warrior fought back a twinge of irritation. "You will have to wait until nightfall. Didn't you say you wanted to show me around? Where do you pay respects to the dead?"

Saba lost some of the spring to her step. "Oh, well, right this way." Her ears drooped and her tail flagged. Bruk hoped that would sober her for at least a little while.

Saba led the shotelai through a trail where the grass thinned and rocks crunched under their paws, up to a small peak covered in ashes. Adding insult to injury, the T'iniziza liked to enslave the souls of those they had killed. Villages would burn their dead to keep their loved ones from torment by the demons.

"My mother was killed by the T'iniziza when they attacked two days ago." Saba swiped the back of her paw over her eyes. "I had her favorite horn bracelet burned with her, as she would have wanted."

He raised an eyebrow. "Horn bracelet?"

"My mother was a rhinoceros."

Bruk would have taken that for a bad joke had it not been for the tears wetting her fur.

"We're not related by blood, let alone species, but she protected me from those demons like any good mother would."

A long moment of silence enveloped them as they stood by the ashes.

"I still have a zebra for a father," she said. "He's nowhere as strong as my mother, with his weak legs and bad gait. I don't want to lose him or anyone else to more raids." She looked up to him. "You will help us, won't you?"

"Of course. That's my duty as a shotelai." He couldn't admit to Saba that he was only here for the T'iniziza seen on a lioness and a cub. Otherwise, wherever those demons went, he would follow. He was not here to stay. He owed his allegiance to no one and nowhere.

"Show me where the demons are most likely to attack," he said.

Saba led him back to the fields where farmers had grown their vegetables, which were now reduced to frayed stalks and leaves strewn about upturned dirt. Zere tried to console an elephant farmer sobbing over the rubble, his long neck bent low and his hoof patting the other's back.

The elephant smeared tears across his weathered face with his trunk. "I know I shouldn't be crying. Others lost their loved ones, while I only lost my crop." More tears sprang up. "But I can't help it. Four months of tilling the earth and tending to these lentils, gone in a single night... It hurts me to see this."

"There, there now," Zere murmured. "You have every right to be sad. You and your family have done nothing but work hard to provide food for the rest of us. Since sunrise you've been cleaning out here, and you must be very tired. See to your little ones and get some rest. My sons and I can clean up the rest of this mess. Whatever we can salvage will be stored to eat later."

"Th-thank you, Chief," the farmer said amid loud sniffles. His wife gently led him away, their backs bent and shoulders hunched from the unseen weight of their misfortune.

Zere turned to Bruk and Saba, who had kept their distance to avoid intruding on a sensitive conversation. "I see you have an escort after all," the chief remarked.

"She insisted on providing company."

Zere chuckled. "That's no surprise to me. Saba's enthusiasm in the right place knows no bounds." He returned to helping his son clear out the leaves and stalks.

Saba glanced at the elephant couple, and said in a soft voice, "Well, I don't need to say anything about the damage those demons have done here." She then led Bruk farther into the village, through a labyrinth formed by thatched huts. "The T'iniziza like to target the very young and elderly, the most vulnerable," she said. "We try to keep them in the center, surrounded by barricades and anyone able-bodied enough to fight." She then gestured to a large ring of dirt hemmed in by huts. "Here are the ritual grounds, where we used to hold all of our dances. We are a motley bunch, formed from the remains of other tribes raided by the T'iniziza. We bring with us many kinds of tribal dances." She scratched the back of her head, embarrassed. "I don't know the dance of my kind, sad to say, though I used to really enjoy the dance of the hyenas. Perhaps I'm biased, but I think my brother was the best dancer of them all." Her nose twitched and she glanced to her right. "Speaking of hyenas…"

One reclined in a wheelchair situated at the edge of the grounds. An embroidered shirt stretched tight over his chest, and its sleeves ended to reveal large, knotted arms not typical of his spindly-limbed kind. Saba made her way towards the hyena. "I figured you would be here, Meko."

He ran a paw through his stiff, messy mane. "Just thinking of my better days, before those demons shattered my legs."

Her face crumpled. "I'm so sorry they did this to you. I could have—"

"It's not your fault, Saba. Don't blame yourself. Besides, I don't have to worry about waiting to perform anymore. I'm a nervous wreck when I have to wait for my turn, you know." The young hyena looked up, taken aback by the sight. "And who is this?"

"Bruk, the shotelai who would help us. And Bruk, this is my brother, Mekonnen."

The young hyena bobbed his head. "So I thought I had heard from the villagers whispering around here. What an honor. You may call me Meko; everyone around here does."

"I'm sorry about your injuries," Bruk said. He held up the stump of his right arm. "You and I know well what those demons can do."

Meko kept his grin. "It has been a month since they crippled me. My legs don't hurt anymore." He returned his gaze to the ritual grounds, his broad shoulders slumping back against the wheelchair. "I do miss the dances, though. When can we be free to dance among here again? Can you imagine it, Master Shotelai? Every night filled with music and laughter, the beats of drums and feet around a huge bonfire?"

Bruk felt hard-pressed to see that. All he saw before him was a ring devoid of dancers, dirt too trampled and pocketed with holes for dancing. Unlit firewood jutted here and there from the ground.

Saba shook her head. "Since the T'iniziza came, no one dares to dance under the moon. It's just not safe. From our fields to our ritual grounds, those demons ruined every aspect of our village life."

"How have you been fighting back from their attacks?" Bruk asked. "Have you anything made of star-metal, to protect or arm yourselves against the T'iniziza?"

"We have very little," Meko replied. "Most of that goes into the barricades to keep the T'iniziza from reaching the young and elderly. Three or four of our spears have bits from the stars, as much as my claw, maybe." The hyena indicated with a pinched gesture to show just how little they had of the precious material. "Stars haven't fallen around this land in years. We don't have nearly as much as the metal in your shotel, of course."

Bruk nodded. "Keep up the defenses. I will do my best to put an end to their reign of terror and bloodshed tonight." He lifted his gaze to a sky painted in broad, warm strokes of fire's hues. "The sun is setting. You should be at home with your father, you two."

Saba frowned. "Already? I would like to see you fight."

He pinned the young cheetah with a stern gaze. "This is no time to revel in spectacles."

"But you said—"

"I made no such promises. Get inside, Saba. Now. You too, Mekonnen."

Her lips narrowed to a hard line, her tail tucked in, then she wheeled her adopted brother away. Bruk moved to the outskirts and trained his gaze on the red sun. As soon as it sank below the horizon, the demons would come. Villagers hastened to take shelter inside their huts. The chief and his sons made a patrol to ensure that everyone made it inside. Only the village's warriors remained, none of them shotelai, but wielding the spears Saba had mentioned. Looking at the small gathering, Bruk would not call them warriors—more like hunter-gatherers forced to do battle, with little experience in fighting demons and weariness from previous nights.

"We'll be scattered throughout Wide-Range," a gazelle with a clipped ear told him. "We have horns to call you if we ever spot them in our area."

Bruk nodded. As a shotelai he always carried a horn to signal his fellow swordsmen. That would be the most these villagers could do. He could not rely on them too much, and suspected that he would be on his own, trusted to take down the T'iniziza. Bruk stationed himself at the fields, his toes digging into the earth in anticipation. The full moon shined its face upon a village subdued and silenced in fear. Bruk heard only the sound of his own breath, then the rasp of steel as he unsheathed his shotel. Another moon gleamed, a crescent one, gripped tight within his left paw.

Bruk smelled the fog before he saw it, a fog brewing into dark, malevolent clouds. Two of them, as he expected. Rearing horns and red eyes took shape. The T'iniziza were named for resembling beetles, appearing as huge horned monsters towering over his head. Clutched within their long claw-like legs, wisps of a lioness and a young lion crouched on all fours, burdened by their cruel masters against their will. Rage welled within Bruk.

"Release my wife and son, you filth," he growled. "You've held them long enough."

The T'iniziza could not speak, but they waved their horns to taunt him. Bruk charged with a cry, steel blade meeting ghostly horn with a great clang. The lioness snapped her fangs at him and he sprang back. She did not mean to—the blasted demon dug its legs into her to force that move. A backhand swing parried the blow from behind, by the T'iniziza binding his cub. Their horns stabbed and lunged at him in a flurry, and with only one paw, he could barely keep up against their onslaught. Bruk ducked and rolled to slip out of close quarters, to give himself distance and time to breathe. If only he had both paws, or an opening to hook his shotel through their joints or bellies. To do that they would have to charge at him the way an angry rhinoceros would, then he could throw them off their mounts. But the demons were not dumb, and they gave him no chances.

Pleading, pained cries from his wife and son stabbed through his ears. Swipes of their paws swept him from under his feet. He landed on his back and thrust out the shotel to meet the demons' downward cuts. A T'iniziza's horn screamed along the edge of his sword to strike the guard, sending it spinning from his paw. Bruk rolled out of the way, then the T'iniziza turned and bolted for the huts nearby. He cursed and scrambled to his feet.

His horn! He forgot to signal the others. Not that it would do much to turn the tide of battle, anyway. Still he blew hard on it, then tossed it aside to retrieve his shotel. The village's warriors rushed in to intercept the demons, brandishing their spears and hollering war cries. The lioness and cub were forced to charge at full speed, but the warriors carried no shotels to counter the movement. The T'iniziza barreled through them, catching the shafts of spears within their horns. They knocked warriors aside like flies and sent them crashing into the huts. Bruk ran after them in hot pursuit. Despite the futility of the villagers' defense, they slowed down the demons enough for Bruk to catch up to them. No torches lit the way. Light from the full moon was enough for any villager to quail at the sight of these evil spirits. Bruk lashed out the shotel to snag a T'iniziza by the hindleg, not enough to dismount it, but he swung hard to send it colliding against its cohort. He tried not to cringe as his wife and son slammed against each other from the blow. He jumped ahead to bar their path.

"Eyes on me, you beasts," Bruk snarled.

The demons replied with hisses and horns clicking. He came between them and their prey. They were mad now, and they would charge. The two T'iniziza lowered their horns, forcing their mounts to crouch low on the ground. Then they sprang at him. Bruk tightened his grip around the shotel, readying for the sideways hook. At the moment their horns lunged just shy of his face, he twisted his hips and struck. The force of the charge jerked his wrist, but snapped the T'iniziza back and flying through the air. It landed on its shell with a screech. Pain flared up his left arm. He could not swing in time to strike at the other T'iniziza, who rammed into him. Its horn did not run through his chest, but the lioness's head digging into his gut still knocked the breath out of his body. His cub, suddenly freed of a rider, stirred and looked wildly around as if lost.

"Run!" Bruk shouted. "Leave this village."

Then like a shadow the T'iniziza swooped down upon the cub, who fell with a cry. The demon locked its legs around like hooks, ensnaring its victim in its grip once more. Bruk roared and swung his shotel at the T'iniziza who had kept him occupied. One shotelai was not enough. He could not free his wife and son fighting like this, but at least he could keep the T'iniziza from going after the villagers. So Bruk held his ground, deflecting blows and cutting off any attempts for them to run elsewhere. He did this until sunrise, when the full moon could no longer sustain the T'iniziza's spectral forms. Like fog thinning under the sun, the T'iniziza faded away, leaving Bruk to lean on his shotel to keep himself upright. He trembled from head to toe with exhaustion and anger.

A swirl of villagers' faces, many species blurred into one, filled his vision. He tried to wave them away, but he only had one paw. The shotel fell to the dirt and he quickly followed suit.

When he came to, he found himself shaded by a thatched roof and swaddled in blankets and dressings. Someone placed a damp cloth over his forehead. Bruk blinked many times until his vision sharpened.

"Saba?" he rasped.

She had bent over him and busied over his dressings, then she sat back and nodded. "I work with the shaman. I did mention that before, didn't I?"

Bruk tried to sit up, but she placed a paw over his chest. "Lie still. You may have lived, but the T'iniziza left behind plenty of wounds. Let them heal."

"They're only scratches."

"Scratches," she said with a snort. "Like the one that had split open to show your rib?" She patted his shoulder. "Don't worry. The shaman had that sealed last night. I can fix smaller cuts, but I haven't learned to do the big ones yet. You also sprained your left wrist, by the way. Don't wave it around. I keep wondering how it's not broken from that dismount you tried to pull off."

"What happened?" he demanded. "Did anyone get hurt? Did anyone…" He could not bring himself to say it.

She shook her head. "Thanks to you, no one perished last night." Her voice dipped to a whisper. "A spearman slammed into my house's walls and caved it in. I watched you fight. You held them back all alone, until sunrise… I had never seen anything like it."

Bruk bit back a growl. "Four nights of the full moon are now spent, but they were hungry for blood and I denied them that. Since they had claimed no lives, they will be back for more, on the next full moon."

Saba gasped and her ears perked. "Until then, you can train me. That's what I have been wanting to ask since you arrived. Please, teach me how to wield a shotel as you do."

Startled, he shook his maned head. "I won't."

"Why? Because I am female?"

"No, that's not why," he snapped back. "I have known many capable female shotelai, my wife once among them."

"Then why won't you teach me?"

Bruk thought of his wife and son, still bound to the demons. "I thought I was ready for the T'iniziza. I should have known what to do by now, and last night was my failure. I have no time to teach anyone, when I myself require more training. I must repay my debt to your village by fighting them next month."

"You fought well, Bruk, better than anyone I've seen, but you can't defeat the T'iniziza alone. I am not sure if you can even recover before the next full moon. You need help."

Bruk clenched his jaw. "No more about this, Saba. Leave me be and let me rest."

The young cheetah pursed her lips and furrowed her brow. "Maybe later you'll see sense, when you're not so much in pain." Saba left to treat the other wounded villagers.

Her eagerness reminded him too much of his cub, and that scared him. Villagers showered him with food, gifts, and wishes to get well soon, but Bruk sat in bed feeling like he had failed them. He had driven off the T'iniziza for now, yes, but they would be back. A shotelai's duty was not complete until those evil spirits were slain.

When Bruk was able to get out of bed on his own, Saba asked him about training her once more, and again he refused. Later that day, Meko wheeled himself through the door to greet the lion warrior.

Bruk raised an eyebrow. "Did Saba send you here to try convincing me?"

"I wanted to see how you were doing. She tells me that your cuts are healing well, but there will be scars."

"Nothing new. Scars are part of a shotelai's life." Some scars ran deeper than others.

Meko cracked a toothy grin. "You're probably annoyed with my sister. She means well, she always does. Our mother and father made her become a shaman's apprentice to keep her out of trouble, but at heart she is a fighter." He looked down at his paws. "She thinks that the T'iniziza killed her real parents, just as they had killed mine. That's the most common story you hear in this village. We had no kin to turn to, so we came together and called ourselves a family." The young hyena let out a reedy chuckle. "Some family we are. But I'm thankful for who I have, and Saba's grateful too. She wants to give back, and it's not through poultices and charms."

Bruk still had a nagging feeling that Meko had more to say. The hyena pivoted and rolled himself to the door.

"I would not try to butt heads with Saba," he called over his shoulder. "She can be very stubborn."

Days later, Bruk ignored the sting of his wounds and the throbbing of his wrist to perform his techniques slowly and deliberately. He practiced on the ritual grounds, smoothing the dirt with his feet as he worked through the stances. He felt eyes trained upon him, and he did not have to guess who that might be. Bruk could not focus now that he knew Saba had been watching. He lowered his shotel and uttered something between a growl and a sigh.

"No, I will not train you, if that's what you want to ask."

Saba crossed her arms over her chest. "You can't fight alone. You won't be so lucky next time." She kept her distance as Bruk continued his practice. "Where are the other shotelai, anyway? I heard there haven't been many lately, but more could come here to defend our village, can't they?"

"I came from a pride full of shotelai. My ancestors, after they learned to walk on two paws instead of four, forged the first blades from fallen stars." Bruk held aloft the shotel, and its edge seemed to cradle the sky. "We thought we were invincible. We kept to ourselves and shared our techniques with no one. The shotel was not just a blade of Abyssinia; it is a blade of lions." He shook his head. "Our arrogance became our undoing. Over the years, hundreds of other villages suffered attacks from the T'iniziza, losing lives without our aid. And upon hundreds of those souls, the demons descended upon my pride as an army." His gut twisted at the thought. "So much blood shed that day... I emerged from the carnage as the only survivor from my pride. It has been a year since my wife and son were killed. A year of these demons capering about and dragging along the tormented souls of my family. I have followed them through twelve villages, and I failed every one of them. They wanted to help, and they paid with their lives."

"You don't have feel guilty over something they chose," Saba said. "What *we* choose. And I choose to fight alongside you, if I get the proper training. Pride will be your undoing too, Bruk, if you don't let it go. Maybe it's time to share those secrets."

"It's not about pride."

"Then what? Why else would you be so reluctant to teach anyone?"

"My son was training to be a shotelai. Like that elephant farmer looking after his plants, I cared for him and cheered at his growth and nursed his wounds." Bruk shut his eyes and turned his back to her. "Now he's bones in the dirt, his soul bound by the demon that killed him. He's the cub you saw last night, the one I couldn't save. I do not have it in me to teach, Saba. Not anymore." He tried to keep his shoulders from trembling, but tears flowed freely down his muzzle.

The cheetah said nothing for a long time. Then she said, "I'm sorry, Bruk. I can't say that I exactly understand your pain, since I've never taught anyone how to use a sword, but everyone in this village is no stranger to loss. Maybe you already know that from Meko. I want to save my village, and that means saving your family too. I know you have no home to go back to, but as long as you're here, we are bound by a common enemy. By the desire to get rid of them." She did not step up to confront him, but moved away from the grounds. "Like I keep saying, Bruk, fighting alone won't kill the T'iniziza, or free your wife and son."

She left him alone to his thoughts, and he could not sleep that night. Throwing back the blankets, he stumbled outside to find a sky blinking with shooting stars. One of them flashed brighter than the rest, coming closer and closer, and he thought he was dreaming until villagers pointed and shouted. A great resounding boom shook the earth. Bruk gripped the door to keep from falling over. The next morning, curiosity overwhelmed him and he ventured outside the hut with the other villagers to investigate. On plains outside Wide-Range, something had punched a hole as wide as ten elephants through the ground. The chief climbed down to retrieve whatever sat in the center, but Bruk did not need to see it to know what awaited them.

"A fallen star," he breathed.

Sure enough, Zere held a chunk of black rock in his hooves. So did his sons.

"How many shotels could that make?" Saba exclaimed.

"Certainly more than one," Bruk replied. He shook his head in wonder. "A star does not fall by chance." He was bound to the village by more than his debt to it, then. Turning to Saba, he said, "I may have been able to resist your demands, but I can't ignore signs from the stars. My duty to this village is more than slaying the T'iniziza. I'll extend that duty to sharing my techniques."

She gasped. "You will train me, after all?"

He had to fight back a smile. "Don't get too excited. I have high standards and expect that they be met."

She puffed out her chest, but tried to hide it with a quick, deep bow. "I won't let you down, Master Shotelai, I promise."

Bruk disclosed instructions to blacksmiths on how to forge shotels from the fallen star. The ritual grounds grew populated once more when he commenced his shotelai training. Saba quivered with excitement when she received a brand new shotel. He gathered some villagers to don armor and imitate the T'iniziza, while others volunteered to act as the mounts. He would have Saba practice her maneuvers on them. To his dismay, her progress failed to match her initial enthusiasm.

Bruk sighed. "It's just as I thought, Saba. You may be quick enough to dodge blows, but you are not strong enough to dismount your opponent."

"I will try harder," she insisted.

"Don't try to do the impossible. You are not built to handle a shotel." He did not mean to dampen her spirits, but he did not want to see her get hurt either. "You struggle to dismount your fellow villagers, who have no ill will against you. How would you hold up against evil spirits bent on taking your life?"

Tears welled in her eyes. "I…I just want to help."

Meko, who always watched his adopted sister's sessions with Bruk, raised a paw. "I've seen how you make the villagers mimic the T'iniziza riders. My legs are no good, but my arms are very strong. I can ride on Saba, and while she makes the maneuvers on all fours, I have the strength needed to throw off those demons. Together, as a pair, Saba and I would be even against a T'iniziza rider."

Bruk considered this, and found himself impressed. "Very smart idea, Mekonnen. I have never seen this done in my years of fighting for my pride, but it might serve us well."

At first Saba looked dismayed that she would not be able to wield a shotel after all. Soon she found new drive and purpose in her role as half of a shotelai. Meko depended on her in their success with the techniques. Together they performed very well under Bruk's regimen. Meko and Saba managed to disarm and dismount most of their mock opponents. The pair thought and moved as one being, not like the T'iniziza and its victim, who moved as master and slave. Bruk felt confident that the teamwork would give his students the advantage, despite being pressed for time to assure victory on the next full moon.

On the night before, over stew and flatbread Bruk grew to be fond of, Saba could not stop shaking despite the fire almost licking at her fur.

"Nervous?" he asked.

"A little." She drew her knees up to her chest. "Meko and I have practiced a lot, but things don't always go according to plan."

"Battles are a messy affair. You have to be quick on your feet, and that's what you have shown me. I believe that you and your brother have what it takes to hold your own against a T'iniziza."

Meko grinned. "You think so?"

Bruk nodded, though he did not have the same confidence for himself. He would have to face his wife and son yet again, hear their cries and watch them suffer under their captors.

Saba had been eyeing the lion warrior from across the fire. "Bruk, you have been here for almost a month now. You're considered part of the village for staying this long."

He almost always never stayed somewhere for more than a week. One month certainly felt like a long time. He chuckled. "Is that so?"

"Your family is our family too," Meko said. "We will do our best to save them, because freeing them also means freeing our village."

When full moon came, Wide-Range Village descended into silence once more. This time more crescents gleamed below, ones formed by new shotels brandished alongside Bruk's. He took his stance behind Meko and Saba, the latter hiding under cloth that matched shades with surrounding grass and dirt.

Fog rolled in and the two T'iniziza heralded the village with terrible screeches. Meko and Saba held their ground, no longer paralyzed with fear as they had the month before.

"They go after weak prey," Bruk said to Meko. "You appear weak, so they will charge for you. Ready your stance."

The hyena nodded and complied, gripping the shotel so that the curve faced the sky. The T'iniziza atop the lioness gained on him fast, but the siblings were ready.

Meko signaled Saba with a shout and she darted to the side. He swung his shotel at a new angle, hooking it into a notch within the demon's underbelly, and wrenched hard. The T'iniziza flew off the lioness's back and sprawled onto the dirt. The other also charged at Bruk, who still wore dressings under his shirt to protect his wounds. Bruk bared his teeth and lunged forward with the same maneuver Meko performed, throwing his full weight rather than relying solely on the flick of his wrist. This took the demon by surprise and dismantled it from the cub, who skidded to a halt without his rider. Overthrown but not defeated, the T'iniziza sprang back hissing. Even without mounts to goad, they still proved to be foes who would not go down without a fight. Villagers ventured from their huts to usher in the souls of Bruk's wife and son to safety, out of reach from the enraged demons. Bruk, Meko, and Saba met their opponents with curved steel, baring the sharp inner edges for the killing blow. Every strike at their legs and horns chipped away at the armor.

"This is for my wife, my son, and my pride!" Bruk cried, accompanying each dedication with a savage cut through the demon's defenses.

"This is for our mother!" Meko shouted. "And my legs."

The T'iniziza reeled back from the onslaught, and caught up in the thrill of the fight, villagers cheered on their champions. Finally, piercing through armor and into the evil hearts of the demons, the shotels tasted victory. Saba shouted in triumph, and Meko shook from ear-tips to hips with jittery, high-pitched laughter.

"We did it? We did it!"

Bruk merely stood there panting, then he closed his eyes and let a wide smile grow on his muzzle. The lioness and her cub rose on two feet, trembling as if walking this way for the first time. Bruk held their paws to steady them. They smiled up at him and whispered, "Thank you." At this he fell to his knees and wept, with Meko and Saba touching his trembling shoulders.

"Thank you, thank you," his family also said to the young hyena and cheetah, before fading away to finally rest in peace.

The villagers celebrated their victory with dances. The bonfire roared high above the huts and the ground shook with the stamping of footpaws. These dances culminated in a ceremony to initiate Bruk into the village. Saba and Meko were among those who clapped the loudest.

"What are you going to do, Bruk, now that your wife and son are at rest?"

He had to think about that question. He had been so consumed with hunting down the T'iniziza for the past year. Now what?

Bruk considered his answer as he chewed at his favorite flatbread. "I think I will start a school for shotelai," he said. "Right here in this village. When we have enough swordsmen, we will travel far and wide to spread the art so it will never die, and T'iniziza will forever fear the taste of our steel."

The Night Wolf

Billy Leigh

"How would you describe the *Night Wolf?*"

I shifted uncomfortably under the mastiff's gaze.

"My name is Lieutenant Chow, and I am here to ask you some questions," the mastiff continued. He scrolled over a page on a holographic tablet clasped in his paw. "Name; Peter Beckett, age twenty-six, species dingo, Level Five civilian employee of the Asiana State Police. Charged with aiding Liberty Force. I've lost count of how many people I've interrogated in here and their backgrounds, but I've gotten the answers I want every time." The other canine gazed right into my eyes, and I felt sweat break out on my muzzle. The room was cold and sterile, with grey concrete walls and harsh bright lights set near the floor that cast irregular shadows everywhere.

"Well, he's not actually a wolf," I began as the mastiff's eyes bore into me. "And he's good with swords."

Lieutenant Chow leaned forwards until his nose was almost pressed into mine. I thought he was going to yell, but instead a sinister grin spread across a muzzle.

"Do you know the penalty for aiding Liberty Force in Asiana Four?" he asked. I already knew the answer: *death.* Lieutenant Chow seemed to read the thought in my head, and he smiled. "You have two choices: cooperate with me, or I shall name you as a collaborator with Liberty Force and you will be executed tomorrow morning."

The mastiff's gaze intensified.

I blinked nervously as Lieutenant Chow turned and reached for something on a table behind him. He placed the object in front of me, which was sealed in an airtight bag. I glanced down and recognised the blade inside.

"I think you know what this is?" The mastiff asked.

The sword was thin and curved with a red rubber handle. It looked graceful yet deadly, the sort that would be wielded by someone who would have to know how to use it.

"I do," I replied quietly.

"And this is the sword used by the Night Wolf, is it not?"

"It is."

The room fell silent apart from the faint hum of the air conditioning. The mastiff stood as still as a statue, but his expressionless gaze was starting to unnerve me.

"He's not a wolf, he's a brown and white Akita," I elaborated. "His real name is Dexter Rui."

"Good, now we are making progress. How did you come to know him?"

"He kidnapped me," I explained. "And forced me into his plan."

"And can you tell me more about what happened, how he kidnapped you, and how he coerced you into his plan?" Lieutenant Chow asked. "Providing he did coerce you, of course; if you went along willingly, you know the penalty."

I looked at the floor and sighed.

My meeting with the Night Wolf was a surreal tale.

A week ago I was working for the Asiana State Police—ASP for short—cataloguing crimes of the citizens of New Melbourne. I gazed at my monitor, watching as numbers spooled down the screen. My role was repetitive and tiring, but I guess I was fortunate to get a decent job. I gazed out of the window; it was lined with a sheen of tinted film that blackened the glass in both directions, but there was still a panoramic view over the skyscrapers of New Melbourne. Being a dingo, I was naturally inclined to an outdoor lifestyle. Being cooped up in an office was not my style.

"Psst, hey! What time are you leaving today?"

I turned to see Ben standing behind me. He was a red-tinged cattle dog who worked at the desk next to mine.

"Five," I replied, stretching out. It wasn't good to show that I looked too tired. Enthusiasm was key to the job.

"Ace, well, I guess we could head to the Paradise Bar after work."

The Paradise Bar was one of the few places in New Melbourne permitted to serve alcohol, and being a Level Five employee, I was allowed to drink. Anyone on an employee level below me couldn't. Alcohol, as my manager said, was a destructive influence.

"Yeah, that sounds like a plan," I replied, wagging my tail. I didn't usually go to the bar during the week, but after working all day, the prospect of a drink sounded good. I glanced at the clock on my monitor; just an hour to go. I continued typing away, hoping the time would pass by quickly.

The only colourful things to look at in the office were vivid hologram posters on the walls, declaring that we should look out for 'Undesirable Citizens'. They were mostly members of a group called Liberty Force, a banned organisation based mainly in the old Australian state. One such particular poster that was animated showed a shadowy canine called the Night Wolf. The Night Wolf clutched a sword and made slashing movements in the animation, as if he was about to stab the viewer. The caption, *Wanted. Dangerous Murderer connected to Liberty Force,* then appeared below. I shivered as I noticed the animation on a poster hanging on the opposite wall. Stories had spread about a wolf who carried swords and only came out at night to kill people.

I hoped I would never run into him.

The time to leave finally came, and I stood up. To get to the elevator I had to pass through a full-body scanner where a stern-looking rottweiler in a guard's uniform gestured for me to pass through. Everyone was scanned as they left the office to make sure they were not stealing electronic files. I shivered as I remembered when a co-worker of mine called Joshua had tried walking out of the office with classified records. The setter had stepped into the scanner and it had flashed red. Rather than surrender himself to the guards, he ran for the elevator and made it three steps before he was shot in the back of the head. I watched from my desk as they carried his body off before a group of canines in hazmat suits began cleaning the blood off the floor. I never knew whether Joshua had been trying to steal something or had panicked, but rumours were going around that our department wanted to get rid of him, and they had programmed the scanner to go red as an excuse to do this. I never paid attention to the rumours thinking they were silly, but as I stepped into the scanner I held my breath. Even though I hadn't stolen anything, I couldn't help but feel nervous. The scanner lit up with a green light, showing that I was clear to leave. I hurried towards the elevator with my tail wagging.

I can't wait to get away.

I reached the bank of elevators and pressed the button to call one. Behind me stood the flag of Asiana Four, showing a collection of red stars around a map of the Asiana state with the motto beneath it.

Diversity in Unity.
Peace through Justice.
Global not Isolated.

The elevator arrived, and I stepped inside. The doors slid shut and I was in the circular glass pod that sped down the side of the building. Outside, the skyscrapers stretched out into the horizon. Asiana Four covered what used to be Australia—where my ancestors were from—the Indonesian Islands, and much of what was Asia. Working in New Melbourne meant that a lot of the people in my office were either dingos or cattle dogs, although several felines and canines from the old Asian territories had moved into the office too. Asiana Four didn't have a government as such, but a single board of directors based in New Bangkok. I knew what governments were, since part of my job was reviewing and sometimes erasing old documents. The elevator rushed silently down, and the skyscrapers disappeared from view. The doors swished open and I walked out into the underground carpark. I'd left my car not too far from the doors. I jumped in, flashed my security pass to a calico by the barrier, and drove out onto the main road.

The Paradise Bar was located near what used to be the old docks of the city. The sea now lay beyond the concrete highways and skyscrapers, but the ramshackle old-style buildings that once lined the seafront still remained. The name of the bar itself was perhaps ironic as it was housed in a wooden building, and the lopsided sign above the door added to its character. It was one of the few places in New Melbourne that didn't feel cold and sterile, even if it took worn seats and the scent of spilt beer to achieve that. There was a pitbull doorman on duty and I flashed the band around my wrist, showing that I was permitted inside. The pitbull scanned it, fixed me a curt nod, and waved me in. Music hit my ears, something with a pounding beat from the Twentieth Century—the nineteen-eighties, perhaps? I glanced around to see Ben sitting in a booth. He raised a paw and waved.

"I see you made it," he said with a grin, gesturing to two pints of beer sitting on the table.

"I don't usually drink on a work night," I explained.

"Heh, you have to live a little," Ben chuckled, taking a gulp of beer and jigging around in his seat to the music. I took a sip of my beer and found it wonderfully refreshing after a day in the office.

I should do this more often.

"So what do you think?" Ben asked, gesturing at my beer glass. "It was a new kind they had out today."

"It's interesting," I admitted, taking another sip. Most of the beer was mass produced and crafted not to contain a certain percentage of alcohol, but this one tasted different, more potent somehow. "I like it," I added, wagging my tail.

"Fantastic. Now if you'll excuse me, I need to visit the bathroom." He used his paw to wipe beer suds from his muzzle. I sat back and nursed my drink. The place was half empty, but there were a couple of black hounds sitting at the bar, which was unusual. Most of the other canines that came in the bar were usually dingos, cattle dogs, or Alsatians. There was also a white and brown canine of some sort sitting towards the back. The light was too dim to see exactly what breed he was, but the way he sat at the back suggested that he didn't want anyone to pay attention to him.

Off-duty state police, perhaps?

I knew it wasn't wise to stare if the canine was an ASP officer, so I averted my gaze and kept drinking my beer until the glass was empty, hoping Ben would come back soon.

"Hey," the cattle dog called a second later, answering my prayers. "Listen, I got a call from my wife. I need to head back home—an emergency with a leaking pipe, apparently."

"Ah man, that's not good," I sighed as I got to my hind-paws.

"Tell me about it. We've called the municipal housing service what, like five times now?"

"Should I pay for the beer?"

"Don't worry, I sorted all that before you arrived," Ben explained as he hurried to the door with me in tow.

The distant scent of the sea hit my nostrils as we walked out of the door.

"Well, I enjoyed that. The beer was tasty," I remarked.

"Yeah, yeah I enjoyed that too. I gotta be off, see you tomorrow!" Ben said hurriedly. I turned to walk back to my car, but a paw clamped on my shoulder. I turned, expecting to see Ben, but my heart almost froze as I saw the hounds from the bar.

"I am arresting you for stealing classified documents from the Asiana State Police," the hound growled.

"Wait, what?" I managed to stammer as a van drew up. One of the hounds prodded me with a taser and my hind-paws buckled. I had no idea what was going on and I tried to wriggle free, but the hounds grabbed me by the scruff of the neck and threw me into the back of the van.

"I haven't done anything!" I tried to shout, but my voice came out as a slurred mess as a pair of handcuffs were tightened around my wrist. I heard a *thump* as Ben was thrown to the ground next to me before the van doors were slammed shut and we sped off with a squeal of tires. I tried glancing up, and could see the two hounds standing above us with guns in their holsters.

Their eyes were hidden behind dark glasses. I knew there was no way I could state my innocence; even if I could speak properly, no one would listen. I would be tried and most likely executed for something I hadn't done.

Would anyone miss me?

Both my parents were dead and I had no siblings. Ben was wriggling on the floor next to me, but I knew resisting was futile. One of the hounds reached down and pulled the fur between my ears.

"Any last words?" he asked mockingly. I opened my muzzle to reply, but a muffled shout came from somewhere, followed by a *bang*. The hounds stood up, but we were all thrown to one side as the van rocked violently. They fell to the floor and I tried to stand, but there was another *bang* and the world turned on its head.

The pain was instant. I was hurled into the side of the van as it turned on its side. I tried to stand up again as the hounds staggered to their hind-paws. My eyes widened as they drew their guns, but suddenly the doors at the back of the van were flung open and something was tossed inside. There was a deep *boom,* followed by a plume of smoke. Instantly I began coughing, and my eyes were burning. I could make out one of the hound stumbling about, firing his gun out of back door. This was followed by a second round of gunfire, and the hounds were blown backwards. I heard the sound of hind-paws storming into the back of the van.

"Which one is he?" I heard a voice ask.

"Here," a reply came. I turned, and could just about see two figures trying to help Ben up.

"Hurry, they've got backup coming," a third voice shouted. There was the sound of more gunfire, and the two helping Ben up cursed.

"We should not have tried rescuing him!" one exclaimed.

"Please," I coughed. "Help me too."

The figures both turned in my direction, and I could see through the haze that they were both canines of some sort. Outside the sound of gunfire was getting louder, and I could hear

ASP sirens getting closer.

"Help him, quick," one of the canines commanded. I watched as another of the canines ran over and began cutting through my handcuffs with a laser of some kind.

"Hurry, the reinforcements are coming," the other canine shouted, firing a round out of the open doors as the sirens grew louder. The smoke was starting to thin out, and I watched as Ben leapt to his hind-paws. My cuffs came off and I jumped up, but stumbled about as my eyes kept watering. The two canines had jumped from the back of the van, and I could see they were wearing masks over their faces. I stumbled out after them to see we were somewhere in the old part of the city, hemmed in by buildings which were crumbling slightly. Several ASP cruises were speeding down the narrow street, and both the masked canines were firing at them.

"Disperse!" one of the canines shouted to us. I stood, rooted to the spot in fear.

"Go!" the canine shouted again. I turned and tried running, stumbling past the upturned van and down the street.

My eyes were clearing, and I turned to see Ben running beside me.

"Look, over there!" the cattle dog shouted, grabbing my arm and pointing to a rusty fire escape. The ladder did not look sturdy.

"Are you sure?" I began, but a gunshot rang out from somewhere nearby, and I felt the bullet whip above my head. That changed my mind. I followed Ben as he ran to the ladder and began climbing. Grabbing the bottom rung, I began following him. Rust came off on my paws, but I didn't care. My instincts screamed at me to climb as fast as I could. Ben reached the top and turned to hold out his paw to me.

"Here," he called. I reached out, but the moment my paw met his, another shot rang out. An expression resembling a mixture of surprise and pain spread across Ben's face. I watched with horror as he pitched forward and fell off the roof.

"Ben!" I called, but it was of no use. Gritting my teeth, I scampered to the top of the fire escape and sprinted across the roof. It was flat and on the same level as the roofs of the neighbouring buildings. I glanced back and couldn't see anyone climbing up the ladder, but I kept running. In the distance the skyscrapers of the city rose up dauntingly, but I had no desire to stop and admire the view. Part of my mind was numb from losing my friend, but my instincts told me to keep running and try jumping to the neighbouring building. The roof was studded with rusting air vents and skylights, some of which were boarded up. I jumped over one skylight and dodged around a vent. Distracted by someone climbing up the ladder behind me, I turned and put my foot right onto a skylight. The weakened glass shattered instantly under my hind-paws, and I didn't have time to yell as I fell through it.

I hit the hard floor of the room below with a *thud* as broken glass fell around me. Panting, I tried getting up, but a wave of pain crashed through my body.

Have I broken my hind-paw?

I couldn't feel the lower part of my body, and if I had broken anything there was no way I could escape now. I glanced around frantically, searching for something I could use as a weapon. The room was empty, with bare concrete walls with two doors leading in. I grabbed a piece of broken glass in my paw. It was no match for a gun, but it felt mildly reassuring to hold it. Gritting my fangs, I began shuffling toward one of the doors, hoping it would lead to an exit of some kind.

If only I could just reach it.

The door suddenly crashed open and my blood turned to ice. An ASP hound walked into the room with his gun raised. The hound's eyes were hidden behind dark glances, but there was a satisfied grin on his face. I felt my vision growing hazy and dark, whether it was from the fall or the impending sense that I was about to die, I wasn't sure.

"Please, make it quick," I managed to say. The hound aimed his gun at my knee cap.

"Oh, I'm not going to kill you now, that'll happen after your trial," the hound replied with a grin. I let out a defeated sigh and felt my vision growing darker, but just as the light slipped away,

I noticed a figure clad in a black outfit jump through the broken skylight. He landed on the floor without a sound, and there was what looked like a sword clasped in his paws.

Another ASP officer?

It couldn't be. He wasn't dressed the same way, and I had never seen anyone carry such a sword before. The hound hadn't heard him, and was levelling the gun at my knee. The figure was creeping closer, and I could see his face was covered with a mask while a canine nose poked out of the middle. I could see the hound's face crease slightly into a frown as he noticed I was glancing over his shoulder. He turned and barely had time to open his muzzle as the figure swung gracefully with his sword, knocking the gun out of the hound's paw before running the blade through his chest. The figure effortlessly pulled the sword back out, and the hound crumpled to one side. My world was fading to black as the figure began advancing on me, but I managed to force the words out of my muzzle.

"Please, don't kill me."

The figure knelt before me and I blacked out.

I was first aware that I wasn't dead when I felt the dull pain in my hind-paw. I tried opening my eyes, and found I was laying on a low bed of some kind. *A futon,* I suddenly realised.

"You haven't broken anything," a deep, resonate voice called from somewhere. "You were in shock, it's why you blacked out."

I glanced around, trying to detect where the voice was coming from. I was lying in what looked like a small bedroom, but the walls were bare brick and the ceiling looked like it had been hewn from rock. I tried standing up, and made my way to the door which was constructed in the traditional Asian style of paper and wood. Gingerly I slid them fully open to find a large, almost cavernous room on the other side. My hind-paw felt a little sore, but I limped out of the bedroom to explore. The second room was like a museum; two glass cases stood opposite the door, which contained a variety of swords slotted into stands, each vicious yet elegant.

"Ninjato swords," the voice explained. "Small, but effective."

I turned to see a tall canine holding one of the swords. He was dressed in a tight black shirt, and I could see the outline of a slim but athletic build under the material. His fur was a luscious brown and white, and I thought at first he was a wolf, a breed I had never seen before. But as I got closer I realised he was an Akita, another breed I had rarely seen. The Akita's eyes were closed, but they fluttered open to reveal a pair of sharp blue eyes.

"Did you rest well?" he asked.

"I think so," I replied nervously. "Where am I?"

The Akita closed his eyes again, gracefully spun on his hind-paws, and used the sword to decapitate a wooden dummy. I winced, and began backing away.

"It's all right, I'm not going to hurt you. This is my home, fashioned out of a bunker from the Second World War. It's several feet beneath the ground," the Akita explained, opening his eyes again. I knew of the Second World War; it was a conflict that had happened over one-hundred years ago.

"The authorities don't know it's here; the city has since been built over it," the Akita continued. I nodded, but still felt nervous inside. I suddenly remembered running with Ben from the ASP. The Akita seemed to read my thoughts.

"Unfortunately, Ben is dead. I saw them take his body away." I was silent, not knowing what to say. "What's your name?"

"Peter. Peter Beckett," I explained.

"Let's go and have some tea, Peter. I'll tell you why you are here and who I am." The Akita gestured for me to follow.

I walked behind the other canine as he led me to another side room which contained a kitchen and a wooden table.

"Please, sit down," the Akita said. I sat as the Akita began preparing something on the stove. I suddenly realised where I had seen the Akita before: in the Paradise Bar.

"Who are you?" I asked. "You knew who my friend Ben was, and you were there when we went for drinks."

"I was. Ben worked for me, in fact, although we never met in person before then. I don't usually go to meet informants," the Akita explained. "Have you heard of Liberty Force?"

I knew of the name from the posters I had seen.

"Yes, it is a dangerous organisation that has carried out attacks against the Asiana state. Membership or association of it carries an instant death penalty." I repeated what I had been told.

"Depends on your perspective," the Akita replied. "My name is Dexter Rui; I'm also known as the Night Wolf."

The name sounded familiar, and I remembered seeing a warning message at work: *Wanted, the Night Wolf. Known murderer tied to the Liberty Force group*. The memory caused me to jump from my seat and start backing away.

"As I said, I promise I won't hurt you," Dexter explained without turning around.

"I recognise you now, you're a wanted man. You're dangerous," I replied, edging towards the kitchen entrance.

"Wanted, yes, dangerous only when I want to be." Dexter turned to face me. The expression on his face didn't seem at all dangerous—indeed the tone in his blue eyes seemed soft. "I only kill when I have to, or when my enemies deserve it."

I still felt uncomfortable.

"I'd like to go home," I said quietly.

"I'm afraid that's not possible right now," Dexter replied. "The ASP are probably monitoring your apartment." The Akita placed two cups of tea on the table. "Please, sit with me."

I sat opposite Dexter as he handed me one of the cups. I sniffed at the liquid, but couldn't smell anything sinister. I took a sip as Dexter did the same.

"So, are you going to keep me here?" I asked, not feeling sure how to approach the Akita.

"If you want to stay, you are welcome to," Dexter replied. "I don't often have company down here. In Liberty Force, we tend to live separately to minimise our chances of getting caught."

I suddenly felt curious as to why Liberty Force existed.

"Why are you trying to fight the state?" I asked. "I mean, Asiana Four provides for us, has brought us social progress. Former nations and species now live together peacefully." I stopped myself. Dexter listened as I spoke, and something close to a sad smile spread across his muzzle.

"You still think that after being thrown into a van and taken off to be killed?" he asked. "But yes, that's how Asiana Four appears on the surface. Ben thought the same, and then he worked as an informer to Liberty Force by smuggling documents for us, although paper documents so he could get them out of the scanner without them being seen. He managed to form a relationship with your boss, and she provided him with the documents, and he passed them onto us. Unfortunately she was caught, which meant he had someone following him to the bar. I assume the ASP thought you were working with Ben."

The Akita finished talking and sipped his tea. I couldn't help but feel bewildered. If Dexter was indeed the Night Wolf, he didn't behave as the posters depicted him. The Akita seemed to read my thoughts.

"I don't think the authorities did a very good job of depicting me. I'm taller in real life, and you don't stab with a ninjato."

"I see," I replied, still feeling unsure. "So, if I am to stay here, what shall I do?"

"You could work for us," Dexter offered. My eyes widened at the idea, and I wasn't sure what to say. "We need someone who knows the inside of the ASP. My commander would like that; I know he wants to meet you."

I opened my muzzle, but I wasn't sure what to say, so I gazed into my teacup.

We sat in silence as we continued to sip our tea. The Akita still seemed poised, and I wondered if he was some kind of former special forces operative that had defected to Liberty Force. I opened my mouth to ask, but Dexter spoke first.

"Do you have a mother and father, Peter?" he asked. I shook my head.

"No, they both died when I was young," I explained, wondering if Dexter believed I was concerned about them. "I have no real memories, just the odd flashback of me playing in their house. We lived on a ranch in the outback, and then I was taken in by the Asiana State and raised in a home."

Dexter nodded as I spoke.

"It was a similar story with my parents," he said softly. A melancholy tone spread across his blue eyes before he blinked it away. "You're welcome to join us, but you can sleep on it. Tomorrow I'll introduce you to my friends."

I wanted to ask the Akita more questions, but he gestured for me to follow him.

"I'm going to rest for a while; you happened to wake up at midnight," Dexter explained. "I don't know if you want to rest again, but it may help to normalize your sleep pattern. There is some food in the fridge if you get hungry." It was as if the Akita was speaking to me as a houseguest, and not a member of Liberty Force keeping me in his hideout.

I watched as he stepped through a set of sliding doors.

"I advise that you don't try to leave," Dexter said. "I'm afraid your face will be on the undesirable citizens list by now, or at least the ASP will be wanting to ask you a lot of questions."

"Okay," I replied. Dexter smiled before sliding the doors to his bedroom shut. I was now alone in the room of swords.

That was pretty trusting to leave me in here alone.

If I wanted to steal one and kill Dexter, I could have. I didn't want to, but I felt an urge to pick up one of the swords. The red-handled sword that Dexter had been using was on its stand.

A ninjato?

I was pretty sure that was what he'd called it. Glancing around in case Dexter was watching, I reached out and put my paw on the handle. The sword was surprisingly light as I picked it up, and the blade shone as I turned it over. I tried slashing with it, but I knew I must have looked silly. Instead I tried twirling it above my head in the same fashion that Dexter had when I'd seen him practice. The sword slipped from my paws and fell to the floor with a *crash*. The doors to Dexter's room slid open, and I splayed my ears like a cub who had been caught in the act of something naughty. The Akita stepped out dressed in something that looked like a bathrobe, but made of thinner material.

"Sorry," I said, holding up my paws. Dexter didn't look at all mad—there was something close to an amused smile on his muzzle.

"Interesting technique," he mused, before reaching down to pick up the sword. He glanced over at another wooden dummy before closing his eyes and striking gracefully at it, first effortlessly slicing through the dummy's arm before neatly removing its head, all in a blur.

"How did you learn all that?" I asked.

"By reading," Dexter explained coyly. The Akita gestured for me to follow him, and he led me to a wall at the far side lined with bookshelves. "I scavenged all of this when they were demolishing the New Melbourne museum and the library to make way for the State Centre for Information."

The Akita pulled a book off the shelf and handed it to me to. The front cover read *The History of the Shinobi by Professor Thomas Henderson,* and there was a drawing of a canine in a similar black outfit to what Dexter had worn. I flicked through the pages and looked at the drawings of the various weapons: swords, ninja stars, smoke bombs.

"I don't think they wanted people reading it and getting ideas," Dexter said with a wry chuckle.

"Could you show me how to use the sword?" I asked. "I mean, so I don't drop it."

"Very well," Dexter replied with a smile.

We walked back over to the rack, and Dexter picked up the sword again and showed it to me.

"Okay, Peter, your grip has to be firm, but not rigid. If you are rigid your whole body is tense, and you need to be able to move flexibly," Dexter explained. "You might want to step back."

I stepped back and watched as the Akita positioned the sword above his head.

"It's not just in the way you wield the sword, but how you move your whole body. Imagine you are dancing and the sword is your partner; it's a combined effort."

Dexter closed his eyes and moved with the sword toward a third wooden dummy, but he stopped short of decapitating it. He handed the sword to me.

"You try," he said, before standing back to watch. I held the sword above my head and tried focusing. I then moved forward as Dexter had done, but let out a yelp as I fell and the sword landed with a clatter beside me. Dexter let out a chuckle.

"It'll come with time, and you'll improve once your hind-paw is fully healed," the Akita said. "I had no idea how to use the Ninjato when I first picked it up. Now, try again."

I copied the same move, trying to decapitate the dummy, but I missed by several inches. I kept copying the move again and again before I finally scored a groove on the dummy's neck.

"Not bad," Dexter observed. I thought about Ben being shot and how he had fallen from the roof. A sudden flash of rage coursed through me and I stabbed at the dummy, causing the sword to get lodged in its chest. I tried pulling it out, but the blade was stuck.

"You can't let raw anger cloud your focus," Dexter said, reaching out to pull the sword free. "I suggest we rest for a little while. In the morning we're to meet some friends of mine, and then I'll show you how to use the sword again."

"Okay," I replied as Dexter made his way back to his room.

"Rest is very important; it'll help your hind-paw, and you never know when you'll need your energy." The Akita slid the doors shut.

I ambled back to my room, trying to take in everything that was happening. I had been rescued, but lost my best friend. Been taken to some kind of underground lair by a guy who was probably the most wanted canine in Asiana Four, but he seemed pretty harmless. I didn't feel particularly tired, but I tried lying down on the futon. Fleeting memories of my parents flashed through my mind—me playing in the backyard of the ranch house, the kitchen with a blue kettle on the stove, my mother calling me in for dinner. I tossed and turned, but I couldn't sleep. Instead, I retrieved *The History of the Shinobi* from the bookshelf. If I couldn't sleep, I decided I would read for a while. The pages of the book detailed the history of the ninjato sword. It was thought to have been developed in Feudal Japan, and was a common weapon of the shinobi. I flicked a few pages back to read more about the shinobi. A painting in the book detailed a canine that looked similar to Dexter, wearing the same black outfit. Shinobi, the book claimed, was another word for ninja, and they worked as secret operatives and guerrilla fighters. I carried the book back to my room and immersed myself in the information. It wasn't just skill as a swordsman that was required, but a shinobi also had to master the element of surprise and deceit, by either fooling his enemies through disguise or tricking them into thinking you were dead or harmless before you attacked.

An hour later there was a knock on the sliding partition. It slid open to reveal Dexter standing on the other side.

"We're to go and meet my friends," he explained. I nodded and got to my hind-paws, feeling apprehensive. Dexter gestured for me to follow him back into the main room. "I wanted to get changed after you woke up so I didn't startle you." I watched as Dexter went to his room, and I wondered what he meant. My question was answered a minute later as he emerged dressed in the black outfit with the mask that I had first seen him in. Two of his ninjato swords were strapped to his back, and I noticed he also had a pistol strapped to his thigh. The gun didn't look as elegant compared to the two swords, and Dexter seemed to read my thoughts.

"A precaution, but yes I prefer to use the ninjato. Guns are clumsy and can fail," he explained before gesturing for me to follow again. The Akita led me to a large, heavy-looking door at the side of the room. His muscles flexed under his outfit as he unbolted the locks and pulled down on a large handle. The door swung open to reveal what looked like a tunnel outside. I followed Dexter through the door.

"These are the subterranean tunnels under New Melbourne," he whispered as he closed the door. "Most are unused and they don't often flood around here, but we have to be quiet."

"Why?" I whispered back.

"The ASP send roving droids down here to look for Liberty Force operatives," he explained. "They can listen for sound. A little noise doesn't bother them as they think it's a rat, but if we make too much, they'll come after us."

I followed the Akita as he creeped through the tunnel. We

reached a spot where four tunnels met at a kind of crossroad, and he glanced around the corner. I held my breath as he nodded and gestured for me to follow.

He took one of the tunnels that seemed to slope upwards, and I wondered if we were heading to ground level. Dexter suddenly paused and sniffed the air.

"Get in here!" he whispered, pulling me into a pitch-black side tunnel. I was pushed against the wall as Dexter stood in front me. He pulled out one of the swords and put a finger to his muzzle. A second later I heard a faint whirring and clicking sound as something made its way down the tunnel. I held my breath as a white spider-shaped droid clicked past on four legs. Something that resembled a head sat on top of it, with two green eyes that I assumed were sensors of some sort. It paused briefly, shining its green eyes into the tunnel we were hiding in as if sensing we were nearby. I found myself quivering as Dexter gripped his sword, but the droid eventually swivelled its head and continued walking on. We waited in silence for a minute before Dexter glanced around the corner and gestured for me to follow.

The tunnel continued upwards until we reached a ladder.

"This opens out into the old quarter of New Melbourne," the Akita explained as he gestured for me to follow him. "The ASP patrol around here, but it's easier to pass by unnoticed."

I followed Dexter up the ladder and he reached a hatch. The Akita pushed it open and I shielded my eyes, expecting to see sunlight shining in, but it was still dark outside. Dexter sniffed the air before gesturing for me to follow him above ground. We were in a deserted side street surrounded by crumbling buildings that looked similar to the place where the ASP had chased Ben and I, but as I glanced down the alley, I could see a busy street with people of all breeds milling around. The faint scent of street food hit my nostrils too. The old quarter of New Melbourne was known to be a bustling but sleazy place, and it was somewhere I had yet to explore. Dexter led me across the alley to a door set in the wall. He knocked three times and waited. A small peephole slid open, and a pair of eyes peered back out.

"It's me, and I have a guest," Dexter whispered. The

peephole slid shut and the door opened. An Alsatian was standing on the other side, and he gestured for us to come in. I hurried in behind Dexter and the Alsatian sighed.

"Must you wear that in the street?" he asked, gesturing at Dexter's outfit.

"Yes," Dexter replied as the Alsatian led us along a corridor. The Akita removed his mask and I could see a grin on his muzzle.

"And this is the dingo we rescued from the ASP?" He sniffed at me suspiciously.

"His name is Peter Beckett, now take us to General Mason please," Dexter instructed. The Alsatian led us along the corridor and to what looked like a bare patch of wall. A rusty fire extinguisher was bolted to the wall, and the Alsatian tipped it to the right. I watched in amazement as a wall panel opened to reveal a flight of steps.

We made our way down with the Alsatian behind us. The staircase led into a larger room in which a doberman was seated behind a table, a female dingo sat beside him. She fixed me a smile as we walked in.

"My name is General Mason, I am the commander of Liberty Force," the doberman said in a gravelly voice as he got to his hind-paws. General Mason had a tall, muscular build, but I noticed he walked with a limp and a chunk of his left ear was missing. "It's a pleasure to finally meet you. I was sad we were unable to rescue Ben; he was a skilled informant.

"It's uh, good to meet you," I said nervously, extending my paw to General Mason. The doberman took it in a firm grip.

"This is Elizabeth," Mason added, gesturing to the dingo who smiled again. "She is also a former ASP worker, and is now a forger for us. We are trying to get more ASP personnel to defect to Liberty Force. Would you be interested in joining us?" Mason asked. I shifted uncomfortably; the doberman had phrased the question as if he was offering me to join a club rather than an organisation listed by the authorities as dangerous.

"You have doubts of working for us?" Mason asked.

"Yes," I admitted. "I don't know anything about you guys,

just that you are a dangerous organisation." Mason gestured to Dexter to walk over, and I watched nervously as they whispered to each other. Dexter nodded and fixed me a reassuring smile.

"I propose first that you watch Dexter go on a mission for us," Mason said. "Consider it a training exercise. It's a simple task of sabotaging an ASP transmitting station. I was originally going to send Elizabeth and Marcus on the mission." The doberman gestured to the dingo and Alsatian.

"And if I want to say no and leave?" I asked.

"You'd get caught pretty quickly. Your best option is to stay with Dexter, who can protect you." I weighed up the options. "Dexter will take you there. We are currently having papers forged and transport prepared so you can travel freely." I nodded, but inside I wasn't sure what to say. I still felt unsure about the whole thing.

"Do it for Ben and his family," Mason said. The image of Ben falling from the roof crept back into my mind, and I found myself growling. I opened my eyes to see Mason and Dexter looking at me with approving, but sad expressions.

"Okay, I'll do this," I replied. Mason smiled and took my paw again.

"We'll talk you through the mission," Mason said before gesturing to Elizabeth.

I watched as Elizabeth spread a blueprint over the table and began talking.

"The transmitter is protected by a wall. There is a hatch leading to the tunnels here, but it's alarmed," she explained, pointing at the print. "Your best bet is to use our disguises to access the service door in the wall." I listened to her speak before Dexter led me to a side room where we were alone.

"We can practice again while we wait," he explained, pulling both the swords out. He handed the one with the red grip to me. "Remember what I said about dancing."

I gripped the sword firmly, held it above my head, and copied Dexter's movements as he advanced forward. Dexter swung gracefully, and I could hear the blade sing through the air. I mimicked his moves, and found the sword felt more comfortable in my paw with no danger of it slipping from my grip.

"You're certainly learning this quickly," Dexter observed. There was a cough behind us, and we turned to see Marcus put his head around the door.

"Your car and ID are ready," he explained. "Elizabeth put them together. We also have a change of clothes for you both." The Alsatian handed us a bundle of matching blue clothes before setting a toolbox on the ground. "Be very careful with that; it contains the explosives to bring down the antenna."

"Thank you," Dexter replied, gesturing for me to follow.

A minute later we were walking back up to the sliding partition, dressed in our blue outfits.

"The car is sitting in the alleyway. Good luck," Marcus whispered as the panel slid open and we made our way into the corridor. Dexter was also dressed in a long coat, under which he had hidden the two sheaths containing his swords. I followed him out into the alleyway where a van was waiting with a *New Melbourne Municipal State Service* logo on the side.

"Not quite the car I was thinking of," I said. Dexter opened the door and passed me a cap with the same logo on it to me.

"It's not fast, but it gives us a more legitimate cover," he replied, slipping his cap on. I did the same before climbing into the passenger seat. Dexter fired up the engine and nosed the van out of the alleyway and into the bustling street. Species of all kinds walked close to the van as we ambled along. I glanced out of the window and saw street vendors selling various kinds of meat and vegetables. A couple of ASP hounds were standing by one vendor, looking over the street from behind dark glasses. I instinctively pulled my cap over my face.

"One area of shinobi study was the art of making oneself invisible, according to the book," Dexter said. "I find not drawing attention to yourself is a good way of being invisible— just relax and pretend they are no threat."

I sat back up as we continued driving. The crowds eventually thinned out, and we reached one of the main highways leading through the city.

"If we get caught, tell the ASP that I forced you into the

operation," Dexter said. "I threatened to kill you and you were not a willing participant."

"Okay," I replied, feeling nervous.

Dexter pulled off the highway, and I saw a checkpoint up ahead that consisted of booths and barriers. I knew you had to pass checkpoints to enter different city zones. Dexter drove up to a booth where a bored-looking tiger was seated behind the window. Dexter wound down the window and handed our IDs over.

"Take off your caps," the tiger said bluntly. We obliged, and I felt my heart pounding as the tiger looked at us and scanned our IDs.

Please don't recognise me as a wanted man.

"What takes you into the central city zone?" the tiger asked.

"Servicing a comms tower," Dexter replied. The tiger fixed us a hard, scrutinising gaze as he kept scanning our IDs. Outside a camera was tracking up and down the side of the van, and I wondered if it was scanning the inside too. I held my breath, but the tiger handed our IDs back and the barrier opened. Dexter put his hind-paw down and we drove off. We picked up speed, and the buildings around us suddenly became more modern and high-rise. The windows of the van were lit up by the garish neon lights and holographic advertisements on the sides of each building which cast out various Asian and English language messages.

Asiana Four—Global, not isolated.

Trans-Asiana Municipal Services—Delivering quality to citizens.

State Hygiene Services and CleanTech Inc.—Working together to make your house cleaner.

The various flashing lights were making my head spin, so I averted my gaze.

We eventually reached a gap in the skyscrapers where a communications antenna sat in-between the buildings. It was surrounded by a concrete security fence with a door cut into the side. Dexter parked the van outside the door.

"I don't normally handle these types of missions, but as General Mason said, this is a watch and learn scenario," he explained. Dexter opened the van door and I followed him outside. The door in the fence had a slot to swipe our IDs, and Dexter inserted his. We waited for a second until a light flashed green, and the door opened.

"I'm glad that worked," Dexter breathed as we made our way inside. The antenna was supported by four struts. I watched as Dexter set the toolbox down and shed his coat. He strapped the two ninjato swords to his back before opening the box. An array of tools were inside, and Dexter moved them out of the way before pulling out a set of explosives.

"Keep an eye on the door," Dexter said as he placed the explosives at the base of each strut. "We'll make our escape down there," he added, gesturing with his head at a hatch in the ground which I assumed led into the subterranean tunnels.

"Right, that's all of them set with the timer ready to go. Open the hatch; it'll trigger an alarm, but we'll be long gone," Dexter instructed. I reached down and began prying the hatch from the ground.

The door swung open, and I looked up to see the tiger surrounded by three ASP hounds.

"These two said they were here to service the antenna," he growled, "but when I checked, there were no services due this week."

The four of them raised their guns and aimed them at our heads. One of the hounds walked over and began frisking me.

"Get is his swords," he shouted to the tiger. Dexter raised his paws in surrender.

"Cover your eyes," he whispered. I raised my paws too, but used them to shield my face. Something slipped from Dexter's paw and hit the ground. There was a loud *bang*, followed by a plume of smoke. Quick as a flash, Dexter pulled a sword out and ran at the ASP officers who were stumbling about and coughing. The hound standing by me tried firing his gun, but Dexter knocked it from his paw before running the blade through his chest and withdrawing it. He delivered a kick to one of the other hounds before knocking the gun from his paw. I could hear ASP sirens in the distance, and the sound of a helicopter approaching.

"Get down the hatch!" Dexter called to me. I began to pry it off the ground, but the tiger began firing his gun in my direction. His eyesight was still clouded by the last of the smoke, but the bullets whipped all around me. The hatch swung open, but Dexter was still battling with the other two ASP officers. He knocked the gun from the tiger's paw before slicing into his arm. The sirens were getting closer, and I looked up to see an ASP helicopter hovering overheard.

"Dexter!" I called as the Akita took out the last hound. He sprinted over as I began climbing down the ladder. Dexter pulled the hatch shut and scrambled down after me.

"Run as fast as you can," Dexter ordered, and we began sprinting down the tunnel. The Akita pulled something out. "Manual detonator," he explained. Behind us, ASP officers had opened the hatch. Dexter pressed the detonator and there was a deafening *boom*. Dust fell from the roof of the tunnel, and I turned to see a fireball making its way toward us. Dexter grabbed my arm and pulled me into a side tunnel as the fireball shot past.

We stood, panting for a moment, before Dexter took my wrist and began leading me down the tunnel.

"You okay?" he whispered.

"I think so," I replied.

"I suggest we head back to my place and stay there for a while; the tunnels and streets are soon going to be crawling with ASP officers." The tunnel had an inch of water in it, which splashed under our hind-paws.

"The water can disguise our scent. The ASP use hounds, as they good at tracking. Here," Dexter said, handing me one of his swords. "Just in case you need it."

"Do you know the way back?" I asked. Dexter nodded.

"You come to know these tunnels pretty well after living down here for a while," he explained before suddenly going silent.

"What is it?" I whispered as Dexter put a finger to his muzzle. He led me into another side tunnel and pressed me against the wall. I listening out, and could hear something else splashing through the tunnel.

Another ASP officer?

My question was answered as I heard a sinister whirring and clicking sound. I remained as still as I could and held my breath. Sure enough, a spider-shaped ASP droid appeared a second later. I knew if I stayed still enough it wouldn't bother us, but as soon as it reached the tunnel entrance, its head turned in our direction and shone its green eyes right at me. I stayed as still as I could, waiting for the droid to walk off, but instead it charged right at me. My eyes widened with shock, but Dexter pushed me out of the way. Instinct kicked in, and I twirled as Dexter had shown me and swung with the ninjato. The blade connected with the droid's head and decapitated it. The head flew off while the body charged blindly down the tunnel, eventually crashing into one of the walls and falling on its side. Dexter walked over to examine the droid as its legs kicked in the air.

"That was an excellent move; you took its head clean off," he observed before taking my wrist and leading me on.

We kept moving through the tunnels as Dexter led the way.

"Why did it charge right at us?" I whispered. "I wasn't moving."

"I've never seen a droid act that way before; it was as if was actively looking for us," Dexter replied. The Akita's eyes suddenly widened as if he had thought of something. "Stop for a second." I stopped as Dexter placed his ninjato back in its sheath and began frisking me.

"As I suspected," he muttered as he pulled a small pod-shaped object that was stuck to my shirt.

"What is it?" I asked as Dexter tossed it in the water.

"Tracking device. The hound would have put it on you." He began walking again. "They've reprogrammed the droids to search for us."

We kept walking until the water in the tunnel stopped and the floor became dry. The tunnel opened up into the place where four tunnels converged as one, and I breathed a sigh of relief as I saw the door to Dexter's place. It blended into the tunnel wall, which made me feel safer. Dexter pulled down on the handle and the door swung open. I hurried inside as he closed it after us.

I walked to my futon and sat down, suddenly feeling exhausted.

"You did well today," Dexter said as he walked to the kitchen. "You would make a fine operative for Liberty Force."

"I'm not sure I want to do that again," I sighed. "Is there any way I can just disappear?"

Dexter thought for a moment.

"Sleep on it again," he eventually replied. "If you do not want to stay, we maintain a small island in the Pacific called Norfolk Island. The Asiana State abandoned it and we took over," Dexter explained. I nodded as the Akita spoke.

"It's just, well, I'm not a soldier or a fighter," I said. "Today was too intense for me."

"I didn't really have a choice; I wasn't a soldier or a fighter either."

"What did you do?" I asked. Dexter fixed me a wry grin.

"Museum curator," he explained. "As were my parents. My father was from the old Australian state, my mother Japanese, and they maintained an exhibition on the old cultures of each nation. The Asiana State closed the museum; I guess they thought it was too nostalgic. I salvaged all the weapons on display, which are now here."

"Oh," I replied, feeling rather surprised.

"As is the case with me, there is no return to your old life," Dexter added. I nodded, knowing I couldn't go back, not that I had much to go back to. Dexter opened the fridge and began preparing something on the counter. "I realised we hadn't eaten in a while." he said in a more cheerful tone.

"I don't think I've eaten anything since yesterday," I replied, and my stomach rumbled as if to confirm this. Dexter smiled as he retrieved something from the fridge and began preparing food on the counter. I explored the racks of swords and picked up the ninjato Dexter had given me. I repeated the same movements I had used to take out the droid.

"Are you sure you don't want to join?" Dexter called. "You make a fine swordsman."

I didn't answer, but kept practicing my moves for the next

ten minutes.

"The food is ready when you want it," Dexter said. I put the sword down and joined the Akita at the table.

Dexter had prepared rice with raw fish, and I knew it had a name: sushi. I remembered Ben talking about it once in the office.

"Go on, try some," Dexter encouraged, handing me a pair of chopsticks. I picked up some of the sushi but promptly dropped it, causing Dexter to chuckle. I picked it up again and managed to eat it.

"It's like using the ninjato," I said to myself. "It certainly comes with practice."

We ate until all the food was gone.

"That was really good! Where did you find all the ingredients, especially with you living down here?" I asked.

"I raided a supply of food going to an Asiana government building in New Melbourne." "I don't typically like to thieve, but I'd run out of food that day, and I wanted to make something I hadn't had in a long time."

The Akita stood and moved our plates out of the way.

"I say we keep up your practice with the ninjato until we hear a message from General Mason," he suggested. I hesitated, but nodded. Even if I didn't join Liberty Force, I wanted to master the weapon.

I followed Dexter back into the room with the sword racks.

"Okay, remember to copy my moves closely," Dexter instructed. "We're going to aim for that dummy again." He pointed at the wooden figure I had stabbed at earlier.

I raised the sword above my head and copied my moves from when I had taken out the droid. I severed the dummy's head clean off, and watched with satisfaction as it fell to the floor.

"Good!" Dexter nodded with approval. I grinned, but my satisfaction was short-lived. I noticed Dexter cock an ear in the direction of the door. I opened my mouth to ask what it was, but the Akita put a paw to his muzzle. I listened out. There was a faint *tap* sound, followed by a heavier *clunk*.

"Has General Mason come to see us?" I asked. Dexter shook his head.

"No, he never comes here. Someone is trying to pick the lock," he whispered. I gripped my sword and held it above my head. "Let me slow them down; you take the escape tunnel at the back," Dexter instructed.

"I want to fight," I replied, gripping the sword harder.

"I want you to find General Mason," Dexter cut in. "You're more useful to Liberty Force alive. I'll slow them down."

I thought the idea of running seemed cowardly, and I watched as Dexter moved closer to the door with his sword raised.

"The escape door is by the kitchen," he continued as the lock on the door kept clunking. Without a warning, there was a defining *bang* and the door was blown off its hinges. At least a dozen ASP hounds charged through. Dexter threw one of his smoke bombs, and the room was filled with the cloying gas. I coughed as I retreated backwards. I could make out the outline of Dexter battling with his sword, knocking the guns from the ASP officers' paws and running them through with his blade, but more and more of them were pouring through the broken door.

I turned and bolted toward the escape door, but a hound stood in my path with his gun raised. Copying Dexter's moves, I knocked the pistol from his paw and ran my blade into his chest. The hound let out a gasp and fell to one side. I tried lifting the sword out, but it was firmly embedded. The smoke was getting thicker, and I could see ASP officers wearing gas masks storming through the door. Dexter was still battling, his body almost a blur as his sword whirled above his head, striking down all the ASP hounds. Coughing, I reached for the small door cut into the wall by the kitchen and wrenched it open. There was a ladder on the other side, and I began climbing. I could hear the noise and confusion behind me and my blood turned to ice as I heard several gunshots. Gritting my teeth, I kept climbing. The ladder was in a pitch-black circular tunnel. I had no idea where it led, but I kept climbing upwards. Part of my mind cursed the fact that I was once again scampering up a ladder to escape, but the sound of gunfire below made me climb faster. The shots began to fade and my head banged against a metal surface. I cursed and almost fell back down the ladder, but I reached up and felt a hatch above me with a handle to open it. I pushed, and the hatch swung open. With pain still pulsing through my head, I hauled myself up and found I was standing in a narrow alleyway between two skyscrapers.

I turned and began running. I could see a busy street at the end, but I wasn't sure if running towards it was a good idea. I turned and tried running back towards the shadows, but a pair of headlights shone down the alleyway. An ASP van was driving at full speed towards me. I froze, wondering what to do. The van stopped right in front of me and the doors opened.

"Raise your paws!" One of the officers barked. I did as I was told and raised them. Behind me the hatch was flung open, and more officers climbed out of the escape tunnel. I felt my heart sink as I realised I was surrounded, and there was nothing I could do.

An hour later I was hauled into the interrogation room at the ASP headquarters and introduced to Lieutenant Chow, who ordered me to tell the story of how I met Dexter, but heeding Dexter's advice, I worded it as if he had forced me to help.

"I was told unless I went along with their plan, they would kill me," I explained.

"And this plan was to destroy the antenna?" Lieutenant Chow asked. I nodded.

"It seems strange that they would take you on that kind of mission," the mastiff mused as his eyes bore into me.

"It was as a kind of test," I replied, knowing I was half-telling the truth. "They wanted to show me what a mission looked like and see if I could do it."

"I see. Well, you are no longer at their mercy and savagery," Lieutenant Chow said, trying to muster a friendly tone.

The duel friendly-and-hostile interrogation, a common tactic, I thought to myself, but it was ironic given I was now at the mastiff's mercy.

"And this Night Wolf. Is he as feared as some make him out

to be?" Lieutenant Chow asked.

"How do you mean?" I replied. The mastiff reached to the table behind him and placed a book in front of me. I recognised it at as *The History of the Shinobi.*

"I find it amusing that this feared canine was seemingly inspired by an old library book," Lieutenant Chow said, and for the first time something close to a smile spread across his muzzle. I remained silent.

"What happened to Dexter?" I eventually asked.

"Dead, from what I heard," Lieutenant Chow explained. Inside I felt broken, but I knew I couldn't show it. Instead I kept my gaze fixed at the floor.

"I assume the Night Wolf was working for someone higher ranked?" The mastiff asked.

"Yes."

"What was their name and breed?"

I hesitated before answering.

"He was a doberman, but I didn't catch his name," I replied, trying to be careful with my answers.

"Where was he hiding?"

"I...I don't remember," I claimed. "They wouldn't let me see where I was going."

"Something tells me you know more than you are letting on," the mastiff said, his tone growing icier. "Where was he hiding?"

"I don't know," I stammered. "It was in an underground room somewhere, that's all I know."

Lieutenant Chow stood in silence for a moment. His face was expressionless and I couldn't tell what he was thinking.

"Very well, I'll hand you over to the interrogation team. They will know how to make you talk," he said. "I imagine they will start with the basics, but they have also been known to pull fur out too."

I winced, knowing the mastiff was trying to play mind games with me, but I remained quiet.

The door opened and two ASP hounds walked in.

"Take him down to the basement," Lieutenant Chow instructed. "He needs more pressure applied to get him to talk."

One of the hounds put a rough paw on my shoulder, and I was dragged upright. Feeling resigned to my fate, I allowed them to lead me from the room. Dexter was dead and there was nothing left for me. I could just reveal all the details to the interrogation team and hope they either spared me or offered a quick execution. The hounds frogmarched me into the corridor and towards an elevator. The door slid open, and I pushed inside before the hounds followed. The elevator was empty apart from a plump canine in a maintenance uniform, with his cap almost pulled over his face. One of the hounds shot the maintenance guy a look as if to say *don't talk to our prisoner.* I knew trying to talk to him was futile anyway; I doubted I was the only prisoner he had seen being taken to the basement. I looked down at the floor and closed my eyes, wondering what was waiting for me in the basement. I sensed some kind of movement behind me. I glanced up to see one of the hounds slumped on the floor, and another pinned against the wall. The maintenance guy was holding a blade, which he had run through the hound's chest. A ninjato blade. The maintenance guy pulled the blade out and removed his cap.

It was Dexter.

I opened my muzzle, but Dexter gestured for me to remain quiet.

"We don't have much time," he said. The Akita reached over and pressed a button to halt the elevator before unzipping his jacket to reveal another maintenance outfit and hat bundled underneath, which had caused the apparent plump bulge. I slipped them on. Dexter restarted the elevator and prompted it to stop on the floor below. The doors opened into an empty maintenance corridor, and Dexter began walking quickly with me behind him. I noticed there were security cameras dotted along the corridor.

"Keep your head down," Dexter whispered. We reached a door and Dexter swiped a security pass into a slot. The door opened to reveal an underground carpark, and there was a maintenance van parked nearby. Dexter opened the door and I scampered inside.

"We probably have three minutes max before they realise what has happened," Dexter said as he drove towards the exit of the carpark. There was a dhole guard sitting at the gate, and Dexter flashed his ID. The dhole scanned it before handing the card back to Dexter. The Akita drove the van out into street, and I could see the sun was now shining over the city. Dexter drove the van as fast as he could, weaving around the traffic

"I thought you were dead," I breathed.

"I managed the fight the ASP officers off, and dropped so many smoke bombs they got confused. I lay down and pretended to be dead, and they called in a disposal team to take care of my body. I waited until they'd put me in a bag before I leapt up and took them out. As the book said, a true shinobi either fools his enemies through disguise, or tricking them into thinking you are dead or harmless before you attack."

Dexter pulled off the road and down a side street.

"We must change cars; they'd have found out they've been tricked by now," he explained.

Dexter stopped the van, and I realised there was a car parked further down the street.

"I notified General Mason of my mission to get you, and he sent a car," Dexter explained as he climbed out and shed his blue jacket and cap before gesturing for me to do the same. We sprinted to the other car and climbed inside. Dexter fired up the engine and we sped back out onto the road.

"Where do we go now?" I asked. I noticed Dexter had placed his sword next to him, and the blade glinted in the sunlight.

"We can't go back to Liberty Force, as the authorities know your face and details now." He sighed. "General Mason has given you his blessing to head to Norfolk Island."

"That's what I'll do," I replied. "There's nothing here for me now."

Dexter nodded, and we began driving towards the edge of the city. The skyscrapers thinned out, and ahead I could see the ocean.

"Do you think we will make it?" I asked, glancing behind to see if any ASP cars were following us. The road seemed clear.

"We will," Dexter replied.

I glanced at the ocean in the distance and willed us on.

Fire and Ice

Thurston Howl

CW: This story is erotic horror and has gore and dubious consent.

Neither the steady dripping of a leak in the stone ceiling nor the scuttling of feral rats gnawing on bones in the corner wake you; it's the musk of acrid piss and stale earth that finally does the trick. You open your eyes, and pull your face out of the brown puddle that's collected in the center of the chamber. With a groan, you bring a paw to your face to wipe off some of the sludge that's stuck there, clumping your once shimmering grey fur together. As your eyes adjust to the dimly lit room, you remember what's brought you here. Siding with the artisans' camp, knowing it was illegal, landed you in front of the wicked tiger, Emperor Saldek. You had hoped and prayed for a quick death. You would bury both your sword—the infamous Eclipsyr—and your pen—the even lesser-known Bic, and your head would soon follow. But no, the tiger lord had grinned and sentenced you to the Labyrinth, the artificial dungeon beneath the tiger's palace, engineered to force its victims to choose their own fates in the dark.

You stand, your bones aching and creaking. The warp system was far from comfortable. Suddenly, a female's low, mechanical voice rings out above you, its coldness piercing your perception. "Hello, Combatant 0017940, welcome to the Labyrinth."

You growl back, "Where's Eclipsyr? I thought combatants were allowed their own weapons."

"Of course, Combatant 0017940. Proceed to the next room where you will find your allotted gear."

Clenching your fists till your claws pressed into your palms, barely drawing blood, you enter the next room. It is a smaller chamber than the one you started in, and there is a lone torch illuminating the sword on a stone altar. It's the sword you grew up with, passed down for generations. Your mother, a fighter herself, gave it to you when you were just ten years old, and it quickly adapted to your will. It took no time at all before you and it grew up to be a swordsmaster and masterblade pair. Even those in the emperor's service knew to fear the legacy of Eclipsyr.

You kneel in front of the blade, your tail wagging despite yourself, and you wrap a paw around its mechanical hilt. At your touch, the blade whirs to life, the chainfang buzzing around its edge menacingly. Your lips peel back in a smile. You know it's true that no one has ever survived the Emperor's Labyrinth. But you also know that most of the condemned wielded daggers, knives, and even pistols. The sword is outdated, yet Eclipsyr is legendary. After all, when you come from a family of assassins and writers—in today's time and age, is there really a difference?—a weapon like that sets you apart from the other criminals.

Standing again, you hold the buzzing sword over your head. "Alright, now what must I do?" you call to the robotic voice in the walls.

"Proceed to the next room, Combatant 0017940." You follow the voice's orders, and once you pass the next entryway, a metallic door slams shut behind you. Your ears flatten, but you do not jump. You know the stories of this place. There's not much that could surprise you too much. The next room is shaped like a circle. Despite the machinery that runs in the walls like mortar, the structure itself is stone. It's neither warm nor cold, but it is definitely humid; the moss-covered skeletons on one side of the room verify this. In front of you are two passageways, leading into the depths of the Labyrinth.

To ask what you are expected to do, continue to page 189.

"What must I do? Who do I gotta kill to get out of here?"

The voice seems to hesitate before continuing. "Combatant 0017940, there are two paths before you. Each leads to a different trial and your ultimate fate."

You take a few steps forward. Craning your head to your left, you sense a cool wind emerge from the tunnel. Your ears are able to pick up the sound of faint clicking in the background, and the clicking makes you shiver. When you squint your eyes, you think you can make out a blue glow in the depths, but you just can't be sure. All you know for sure is that the tunnel fills you with a sense of cold dread.

You look to your right. From this passage, you feel heat emanating. A red light reflects around a corner, but the stench of fire and brimstone halts your approach. You can barely make out the sound of a low growl, its tremors shaking the ground beneath your bare paws. The heat is almost arousing, but that excitement seems just as dangerous.

"Please choose," the voice in the walls commands.

To take the path to the left, go to page 190.

To take the path to the right, go to page 192.

With Eclipsyr in your paw, you proceed down the tunnel to your left. After the first corner you turn, you start to realize you weren't crazy. There are torches along the walls, but their flames are azure, flickering sapphires devoid of any warmth. With a grin, you grab one. *How kind of Emperor Stripey-ass to provide me a light, at least.* Your grin fades as you realize the flames themselves seem to be the source of the cold, their depths sucking out the heat from the air.

With each step, your breath mists thicker in front of your snout, and your ears flatten out of habit. *Damn this cold,* you think, not wanting to waste heat with talking aloud. The stone below your paws shifts gradually into snow and ice, and with each corner the snow seems to keep rising, getting up to your knees after ten minutes or so. Your teeth start chattering, and you sneeze despite yourself.

Look at me. A wolf getting frozen to death. What the hell…

Your ears perk up when you hear that clicking from before. You stop moving and power down Eclipsyr to focus. The clicking stops. Steadily, you inch forward until you're at the opening of a new room. The chamber is massive. If you didn't know better, you would think the tunnel had led you outside the Labyrinth, but you know that's not the case. The emperor has just too much money to spend on these things. He must have been able to create an artificial environment inside his Labyrinth. You've known this, so it should not surprise you, yet standing in a room the size of a disq-ball stadium filled with snow and ice formations with no exit in sight is...overwhelming.

The clicking resumes. It's louder and closer now. Quickly you duck down behind a mound of snow, dousing the torch in the snow. The clicking gets closer...closer...then it passes. You wait a few moments, paw tight around Eclipsyr, and then inch your way up the mound, looking over the top. Several yards away, you see it.

A giant spider, easily twice your height and twice that as long, is clicking its spindly legs against the ice as it walks. Its exoskeleton is black and shimmering, reflecting the light from the azure torches around the room off its surface; its head is covered with beady, lifeless eyes and prefaced with two curved jaws, shaped exactly like your own sharp fangs, but each is as long as your hindpaws, and you imagine the venom contained inside them.

You turn your head to look over your shoulder. The way out is still super close, and the tunnel is too small for the spider. You could easily walk out, no rush, and make it back to the central room if you so choose. But, on the other paw—*in* the other paw—Eclipsyr is thirsty for a fight, for *blood*.

To return to the central room, go to page 189.

To fight the giant spider, go to page 194.

Screw the cold. You move into the warmth of the tunnel on the right. You hold Eclipsyr in front of you, ready to strike whatever demon may be waiting around the corner. However, once you turn the first corner, you see there are just torches of blazing red light. Normally you would find this perfectly normal, but the light isn't natural. It's red like blood, not red like...fire. It's deeper. The heat emanating from it is intense, but still, knowing your vision in the dark is likely inferior to nocturnal creatures, you grab one of the torches and hold it in front of you, arm outstretched. The fur around your wrists singes in the face of the blaze, and the heat dries out your eyeballs. Still, you know it will do more good than harm. *Ever onward,* you think as you press on through the winding tunnels of the Labyrinth.

You focus on keeping your body as far from the torch-lined walls as possible, and you suddenly hate the fact you're a wolf. Species with less fur would be much better with this trial, but all the same, you know you cannot change your species on the fly like some morphs you know.

Finally, the tunnel opens up into a much larger chamber. The torches line these walls also, and you set yours on the ground, wary of your hindpaws. The chamber consists of several tall pillars stretching up toward a lofty ceiling, and multiple platforms hold doors and stairs that must lead further into the infernal maze. But, at least from a glance, this seems to be a central room for this section of the maze.

That's when you hear a roar.

Your first thought is that it's a lion; it has that depth. Your second thought is that, no, it has to be a devil; it has that sinister lilt to it. Your third thought is that you do not want to get caught by a monster with that kind of terrible bellow, and you twist around to hide behind one of the nearby pillars. You're suddenly close to a torch, and its heat begins to scorch your dirty-white chest fur. But still, a fiery haircut seems much more preferable than being mauled to death by some unknown beast.

The thing stomps toward you. Its stomps are metallic and feral. You hear it sniff the air, and your ears flatten. *It has to smell me,* you think, and you hold your breath. The beast doesn't move for a good thirty seconds. Finally, it stomps away. After a while you release your breath in relief, and gradually turn your head around the pillar.

The beast's back is to you, but your eyes still widen. It's a minotaur. You had heard legends of the minotaur being a prized possession of the emperor, but you didn't really believe it. Not until now. It stands at something close to eight or nine feet, and its naked body is muscular and fit. You can't see its face, but its sharp, black horns pierce the air above it and seem to twinkle threateningly in the torchlight. Your eyes trail down its form. A long bovine tail extends past its tight ass cheeks almost down to its hooves. Your eyes go back up and notice a thin corded belt around its sculpted hips, a sword without scabbard held there.

Then it starts to climb up a platform, grabbing on to the textured wall. You turn back to the exit. If you want to escape and try the other tunnel anyway, despite knowing it has its own dangers too, now would be the chance to do so. The hilt of Eclipsyr feels cool in your palm though, the one thing that reminds you of your ancestry. You are a swordsmaster. What should you do?

If you return to the central room, go to page 189.
If you decide to face the Minotaur, go to page 196.

Clenching your jaw, you grip your paw tightly around the warming hilt of Eclipsyr. You have to press forward. You launch yourself over the snow mound and allow your body to naturally slide down its side to the icy ground beneath. Before you have even slid halfway down, the spider hisses and turns toward you. Suddenly, its eyes don't look so lifeless. They're glowing red, a stark contrast to the white snow and its black body. It begins scuttling toward you, its legs slamming into the ice as it moves.

With a flick of the wrist, Eclipsyr hums to life, its fangsaw whirring, and you twirl the sword reflexively into a ready stance, high and pointing at your opponent. Before it has even reached you, the spider rears its tail end up, its spinnerets stabbing the air toward you, and tendrils of thick white webbing come rushing toward you. You take advantage of the ice and rush forward, sliding onto your back, the momentum carrying you closer toward the looming spider. You hold Eclipsyr ready to slide at the belly of the beast, but it is quicker, just barely, and a leg knocks you off course and into a snowbank.

Rather than crawling out and into the spider's jaws, you push Eclipsyr to full speed and break through the other side of the bank. The spider hears your bursting through and scuttles to the top of the mound, its hissing now at screeching levels, saliva dripping from its clicking fangs.

"Come at me, then!" you tease with a smirk.

It charges with a roar, and you grit your teeth as you realize it's coming too fast. Even if you killed it with one slash, it'd crush you under its weight. You jump to the side, out of the way, and the spider slides right through where you were, crashing into another snowbank itself. Running toward it, you raise Eclipsyr high for a death blow, but before you can, another blast of webbing hits your side, trapping the arm not holding Eclipsyr against your body and slamming you into the ground.

You curse as you crawl backward, trying to get to a mound so you can get your balance back, but the spider has already freed itself from the bank and is coming toward you. Except, now, it's different. It's not rushing toward you; its hiss is lower and not as threatening. Then you realize its slowness is no symptom of caution. It knows it's trapped you, and now it's just teasing you. You are about to be eaten by a spider bigger than you are.

Your back presses up against a snowbank. It's now or never.

Your eyes scan the spider for some weak point.

You can either go for the one of its legs, probably the closest part of it to you, or the head of the beast itself. Whatever you do will lead to the last few seconds for one of you.

If you stab at the spider's head, go to page 198.

If you slash at its closest leg, go to page 200.

Mustering up your courage, you come out from behind the pillar to face the lumbering minotaur. You hold Eclipsyr high and bring its intensity to a roar of its own. The Minotaur's head whips around as it rights itself on the platform. "Come and face me, monster!" you yell, commanding more confidence than you feel inside.

The minotaur stands to his full height and slowly puffs his chest out. You can see his muscles rippling as he inhales sharply. You swallow with a touch of nervousness. His chest is as sculpted as his back, and his hung cock and large balls dangle between his legs. His eyes, yellow and glowing, glare at you, while his nostrils puff smoke out over a golden ring. His virile strength seems even more dangerous than the flames adorning the walls. Tilting his head back, he releases another long bellow.

You run toward him, and he leaps from the platform to your level, raising his own sword at the same time. Your blades clash at the same time, sparks churning off the twin metals from the whirring fangsaw. You aim a blow at his leg, and he parries it, catching you off guard. You watch his tremendous sword come close to you, but you sidestep and dodge the swipe, hearing it crash into the stone floor. You grip Eclipsyr backhanded and slash toward his neck, but his elbow comes out and catches your chest, knocking you back.

Gasping for breath, you tumble against a pillar, gripping your sword tightly. The minotaur leaps toward you and raises his sword over his shoulder, ready to decapitate you. With a grunt you roll forward, under the swiping blow, between his thick legs, and stagger to a standing position behind him. By the time you've readied your weapon again, the minotaur is facing you and slashing at you relentlessly, his blade crashing into your over and over, the sparks flying through the room.

You manage to grip your sword with both hands, trying to just keep the Minotaur's blade from slicing you in half. Then, right when you've finally gotten your balance back, he punches at your with his free hand and catches you off guard. You fall back to the stone floor, Eclipsyr now out of your hands and between you and the approaching Minotaur. You manage to sit up on your hands, and the Minotaur's sword positions itself at your throat.

You look up into the amber eyes of the sneering guardian of the Labyrinth and realize not even your skills were good enough. The minotaur is going to rip you to shreds and then cook you over one of the fires of the room...or maybe do that in reverse order.

He pulls his arm back to gain momentum for the strike.

You hold your hands in front of your face and scream, "No, wait!"

You close your eyes for the impending blow...but nothing comes. You lower your hands and realize the minotaur is looking at you expectantly. "Well?" he growls.

He's capable of speech, you realize. You swallow and think of what you can possibly say to convince him not to kill you.

If you try to seduce the Minotaur, go to page 202.

If you try to intimidate the Minotaur, go to page 204.

With a yell, you kick off from the snow mound in an attempt to stab the monster between its many eyes. You're over its head. You feel as if time is slowing down as you drive Eclipsyr's blade downward, whizzing and thirsty to drench itself in the spider's blood. The blade's tip is mere inches from the shimmering carapace…

And then one of the spider's legs flicks toward you and impales your left shoulder, pinning you in the air and halting your momentum. As your mother once did, and her parents before, and all your ancestors, you howl. You howl in pain as the cold, pointed limb pushes through your shoulder until it's went through to your back, and then you howl some more. You drop Eclipsyr. It's not a moment of weakness. Some of the nerves connecting your brain to your paw have simply been disconnected.

You're flung to the frozen ground, and your head slams back against the ice. The spider leg is nailing you to the ground, and now the spider is approaching you, its salivating mouth hovering over your hindpaws. In futility, you raise your legs and begin kicking at the mouth. The fangs catch your paw by the ankle, piercing it from both sides, and you start to howl again. With your eyes closed, you don't notice the giant spider raising its spinnerets again, but you feel the sticky substance cover your whole body. You lose the ability to move any of your limbs. The spider leg frees itself from your shoulder, but the webbing is encasing you. One leg is in total pain from the spider bite, the other is cramped against the former, like they've been duct-taped together. Your arms are stuck to your sides, and next your head is covered.

You can barely feel the cold now. The webbing is almost like a blanket. You realize you're being dragged across the ice, but the venom is already working its way through your body. Your breathing slows down and deepens. You can't open your eyes as the webbing is keeping them shut, but your nose is free, just a little, enough to breathe. Your consciousness fades.

When you come to, you still feel drowsy, like someone just woke you up from a long nap that was meant to be much shorter. You can't open your eyes, and you still can't move. But your memory starts to remind you what happened. You sniff the air, and all you smell is death. Stale, cold death. You realize you must be in the spider's lair, and there are dozens of bodies around you, even though you can't see them. You can smell their intestines. Their bile. Their frozen innards. Your heart beat starts to increase.

Then, you hear the clicking. It sounds different than the movement of the spider's legs though. It's close, but it's less intentional...more...comfortable....

You're dimly aware of a pressure at your hip. That's where the clicking is coming from. The spider is there! You try to kick at it. Nothing happens. Literally, nothing. You frown under the webbing. You should at least be able to feel your injured foot...

Then, it sinks in. Your legs are gone. You're being eaten alive. The clicking continues.

END

The legs are closer. You decide to attack them.

With a quick dive, you slash at the first leg, and it's sawn off by your whirring sword.

The spider clearly was not expecting your recovery. It cringes back and screams. Its scream is high, and reverberates through the room. Without hesitating, you slash at the next leg, hewing it before the largest segment. Now the spider tilts a bit.

It strikes a leg out as if to stab you, but you're quicker. You're a swordsmaster, after all. You saw it off at the foot.

It turns as if to escape. It does not realize that all it's done is reveal its other legs to you. You rush forward and begin sawing off more of its appendages until it has three left and can no longer effectively walk. Its scream is pitifully high now, and a part of you worries that it might have children somewhere around who could hear the call. But you doubt it.

You continue your vivisection of the spider until its eight legs are twitching on the snow, several feet from the screaming body. Then you straddle the monster's head, spitting in one of its eyes before you start to cut its fangs off and then work on removing the head from the body.

Eventually it does stop screaming. When it does, you allow Eclipsyr, your sword and scalpel, to rest, and you lean back against abdomen of the spider. Despite the chilled air here, you're now burning up. "Well," you pant, "that was more of a work-out than I thought it would be." You laugh at your own petty joke. Leaning your head back against the slick exoskeleton, you consider taking a nap. Then you hear a scuttling sound again. "Hm?"

You lower your head and open your eyes to see what the sound was just as a sharp pain fills your lower right rib. "Ah, *fuck!*" you yell and looked down. One of the spider legs has entered your side. Except...it's the thick end, not the pointed end. "What?" you practically bark and grab at the leg, trying to remove it. But it's stuck, as if it somehow conjoined with you. At the very thought you wince, and the leg seems to cringe too. Even as your confusion increases, you feel two more sharp pains at your left, and you fall onto your right side. When you look at what caused it, you see there are two more spider legs now in your left side. "No!"

You look around and see the other spider legs are crawling toward you like petrified snakes. "No, stay away!" But you can't reach Eclipsyr. You dropped it after the first leg penetrated you.

The voice of the machine in the walls comes down from above you as the other legs start to enter your sides. "Combatant 0017940, congratulations on surviving the trial. Please note however, that each section of the Labyrinth must have a guardian and, as the new champion of the spider's lair, you must take on this role." As your lupine legs and arms are torn off by the spider limbs you barely control, you try to scream in protest at the machine, but the jaws that start boring themselves into your face make any intelligible words impossible.

You click your bloody jaws together and hiss in vain.

END

"Don't…" you start. "I could…um…" You blush, unsure of how to even begin this approach. You spread your legs and lean back. "I could serve you…sir," you say meekly.

The minotaur seems frozen by your words, and you feel your heartbeat pulsing in your ears, hoping he is convinced to let you live. He snorts, more smoke billowing from his nose. Finally, he lowers his head and stares directly at your groin. You turn away, uncomfortable at being sized up by this humongous beast. Finally, he smirks.

"You…you could serve…me."

It doesn't come off as a question, but you nod anyway. "Yes, sir," you say, not believing the submission in your voice.

"You would rather serve me…than die."

"Yes."

He smirks again. "Yes, *sir*," he corrects.

You swallow. "Yes, sir."

He steps toward you, and you're suddenly aware of his sheer masculinity, the musk of his sweat, the stench of never-washed fur, and the copper aroma of blood in the dark stains at his hooves. He bends over you, and suddenly he's wrapping his cord belt around your neck. He pulls it taut before making a couple of knots in the rope. You swallow against the collar and close your eyes, unable to meet his fiery gaze, his smoky breath filling your lungs.

Even as you wish he would stand up already, he grabs you sharply by the back of your neck and your mouth opens in a gasp. He leans forward and kisses you. His tongue is a mix of death and heat, but you meet his tongue with yours, even as it scalds the inside of your muzzle. He pulls back and stands finally. "Alright," he growls.

"Alright, sir?" you say meekly, wincing at the sting of stretching your burnt face.

"Yes. You will do nicely. I haven't had a bitch to use in a while. You'll do well, wolf."

"I—" you start, but your voice is choked off as your new master pulls on the leash. You start to resist, gripping at your new leash and trying to loosen it at least. But he yanks on it again.

"On all fours, bitch," he growls, and you dutifully follow behind, on all fours as your master likes.

Over time, your paw pads will callus and will get used to the heat. Your fur will get patchy in places, but you'll get used to that. There are some parts that don't heal. Your tongue becomes ash over time. Your eyes will boil out of your skull over time. But those holes, like your muzzle, get attention. Your master, after all, is loving and attentive. You get used to that too...but it takes a while.

END

"You... You're the guardian of the Labyrinth? Here I was expecting someone who knew how to at least hold a sword!" you bark, hoping you come off as way more confident than you actually are.

It works. He takes a step back and glares. "What did you say?"

You slowly stand. "You're nothing but a lonely cow. The only way you could beat me was through strength, not even skill. I'm clearly the better swordsman. Just because you can swing a sword around and knock people down just because you're bigger than others doesn't make you a warrior!"

He takes another step back. "I could kick your ass," he growls, "even without using my full strength."

"I'll take you up on that bet," you say as you reach down to pick up Eclipsyr. You brandish the sword in a fancy flourish. "One-handed then, brute!" you command.

The minotaur bellows as he obeys, and strikes out at you. You knew this pride was his downfall. With a nimble dodge, you do what he did to you and throw your full body weight against his sword arm. He drops the weapon and staggers backward. You lunge again, knocking him onto his back. Climbing over him, you slash and saw off one of his horns near the base. He howls in fear, hearing your buzzing blade so close to ears, and likely for the first time in the minotaur's life, he is probably wondering if he will survive this encounter.

This time, it was he who interrupts the fight. "Wait, please!"

Feeling a sense of owing the minotaur since he spared you when you called out, you pause. "What is it, beast?"

"Please, I'll serve you here. Do not kill me, wolf."

You stand, lowering the energy on your blade. "Serve me? I have no use for a minotaur out in the world. I just need to know the way out."

The minotaur sits up and rests an arm across his knees. He shakes his head. "I am sorry, swordmaster wolf, but there is no way out. I have scoured this Labyrinth from top to bottom, start to finish. There is no way out."

You clench your fists, and your tail twitches. "So, what?

You're offering to serve me for the rest of my life here in this miserable cave?"

The minotaur nods and, for a second, he looks almost cute. Sexy, but cute as a puppy. You find yourself smiling as you untie the Minotaur's belt and fashion it into a leash for him. "Alright, fine. On all fours, beast." He obeys yet growls, not used to this kind of submission. "You can serve me until I find a way out of here."

And the minotaur was true to his word. He became your best and only friend in the Labyrinth. His body stayed fit and strong, despite your forcing him into submission. But you? The years of searching for an escape kept working at your pelt till you were naked, your entire flesh burnt, and through it all, the minotaur served. He was the shoulder you cried on—although your tears boiled against your cheeks and created ravines that would scab red with time—the companion who warned you of traps—though not always in time; your claws have worn down from clawing for escape—and the body you took advantage of when you were feeling particularly lonely—at least until your sexual organs could no longer take the fire and are now a solid blackness between your legs. Still, in those moments of heat, your roars and your minotaur's roars filled the Labyrinth, an unintentional warning for future combatants to avoid the flaming maze.

END

Folly

J. Daniel Phillips

Forgive the folly, but never forget the face. Save for this crucial bit of wisdom, my father gave me next to nothing in life. What money he did earn, he drank away. A veteran of our war with Mexico, my father was a cruel creature. Aside from the bottle, he had an affinity for few things: pugilism, which he honed as a lad; bullshittery, which he perfected by the time he married my mother; and the blade.

You see, when the army landed in the gulf and pushed its way towards the capital, it had need of individuals with a very specific set of skills. While the musket tears armies to shreds, it has too many drawbacks. For one, it's loud and easily disabled. Plus, you have one shot and one shot only. If you miss, you'll regret ever pulling the trigger. Any idiot can work a rifle.

My father worked with two blades. One the length of his arm, a small sword he claimed to have forged himself, though I believe he stole it from a frigate floating in Boston Harbor. I know this because, aside from its eagle-headed pommel and its bright bronze handguard adorned with intricate, flowery, and expansive details, it featured a shallow yet prominent etching on each side of the blade which read *Mors Tyrannis*, Death to Tyrants. He couldn't even read English.

His other blade was a main-gauche, consisting of thick, cannon-grade steel with a swordbreaker cross guard and matching bell-style handguard, its blade was just a little over eight inches. My father preferred this to the sword, I've been told, as its short stature and razor-sharp edge allowed him to work in more confined spaces. He claimed to have won it in a card game in New Orleans before his deployment, despite its similarity to his small sword.

His brief moments of wisdom notwithstanding, my father was not a smart beast, though a clever one. Even for a coyote. His job was to slip behind enemy lines to disrupt and sabotage. Ideally, he was to detonate ammo dumps, clip telegraph wires, burn documents, and steal maps of troop movements. But they should have never given a beast like my father carte blanche to inflict his particular brand of cruelty with no repercussions.

It's why the blades of both weapons are blackened at every edge. I still keep both of them sharp, sharper than a cutthroat like my father ever could. But the blood? That stays on the blade. The blood always stays on the blade. I now believe that even if I wanted to wash away the filth, the memories of a hundred deaths, I wouldn't be unable to. Because even God can forgive the follies, but He never forgets the faces.

I've been living in Bakersfield for about three years now. Everyone knows me, at least by sight, despite the fact that I rarely make appearances in the town that has blossomed with the arrival of the railroad. It's difficult to miss a dog like me amongst all the cud-chewers. Even among other canines, I cannot be confused for another.

I only come down a few times a month to procure provisions, purchase raw materials, and handle my finances. My home is a few hours walk to the north, tucked in a fertile valley, the most beautiful in this part of the Dakota Territory. I have barns and warehouses there where I keep stores for the harsh winters, as well as to indulge in my hobbies. It also masks the true size of my house from a distance.

I often stay overnight when I do travel into town, as I want to limit the amount of time others are at my home. And while I do prefer to keep my life as private as possible, it's partly because I believe very few herbivores want to associate with me. Oh, sure, they force my kind to fight in their wars, often fresh off the boat and without a lick of English. But then they spit in our path once the dirty work is complete. Well, not my path. They wouldn't dare.

At the center of the town is a bar and hotel named the Six Swans. At four stories, it's the tallest building for a hundred miles in every direction. And with a dozen unique casks, it attracts every hopeful prospector, snake oil hawker, card and dice shark, and bloodied outlaw making his way between the Big Muddy and the Rockies. It's only gotten worse now that the railroad has come.

And with it has come the Union. To see a few bonded bounty hunters or the stray ranger come through wasn't not abnormal. But the gleaming steam engine with its sprawling body has spewed forth an unrelenting stream of blue-backed soldiers, black-suited federal officers, and worst of all, weathered marshalls with their wide-brimmed hats, long coats, and longer pistols. I try to avoid running into them at all costs, but these days it's becoming more difficult.

I watch them step off the first-class coach hitched to a train named 'The Spirit of Philadelphia'. She's a spritely silver engine. Brand new with a red tender, its moniker is emblazoned upon it in tight, opulent script. Three males—two in fresh, tailored black suits, one draped in a worn army long coat and a brown bowler—linger on the platform. They direct the unloading of their luggage, waving their fingers between the car and a waiting coach.

Or should I say, the two in black are. The third takes no interest in his immediate surroundings, preferring to survey the town, searching for something. When he turns in my direction, I conceal my head behind my black hat and wait. And wait. Because by the way his brow is set above his eyes, it indicates the kind of beast he is: severe, sober, and cruel. And I don't say that because he's a bighorn and I'm a coyote. Sometimes, you just know.

I figure that would be the end of it, but as they make their way up the street on foot, I peek from beneath the brim of my hat to study their approach. As they cross the square, the bighorn slows to a stop to have a chat with his compatriots who seem to have not been expecting any delay. A bull and mule, they merely nod their heads beneath their respective wide-brimmed hats after a moment and then continue onwards.

The ram checks his watch and then moseys towards the front door after allowing some boys from the general store pass by with crates in their hands. Then he opens the door to the hotel and enters. His hooves clack on the wooden floor and he pauses as the door whines shut behind him. I feel the hot rays of inquisitive eyes run me over before I hear hoof-falls.

Hoof-falls moving away from me. My hand grips the whiskey I suddenly remember I ordered with a vice grip, almost cracking the glass. Horace, the bartender, welcomes him with a smile and a 'what'll it be?' As this newcomer leans onto the empty bar, my eyes glide down his side. At his hips, hidden beneath his coat, hang a pair of revolvers—big ones, from the size of the bulges. Beast-stoppers, I'd guess.

But there's also another shape, hanging from the left side of his waist. It's long, curved, barely touching his coat. My jaw tightens as the image of a saber crosses my mind. That makes me bow my head and suck down half of my drink. He's a Marshall, alright, and an old-fashioned one to boot. I have an innate distrust in anyone wearing a badge these days. It's the reason I settled here, away from everyone else.

A part of me wishes I would've waited another week or two to buy provisions, fuel, clothes, and other supplies, and risked missing key items for the season. Anything to avoid seeing people like him and the idiots who blindly support them.

Without warning, something catches my cane and I swing the end upwards and into a gloved hand where it lands with a loud smack.

"Whoa there, friend, I don't mean any harm," a smooth voice announces with a chuckle.

I twist my head around and peek from under my hat, trying my best to conceal my left eye. The bighorn stands above me with a gentle smile and lying eyes. He reaches up to take his hat off as his right hand lets free my cane. I drop the tip back onto the floor and listen to my heart beat between my ears. My jaw is clenched as he helps himself to the seat across from me, directly next to the window.

"That's a hell of a quick reaction there," he tells me, his tone friendly and conversational. "I'd hate to have to draw against you."

My lips tighten and my eyes focus on the badge pinned to his vest. Then I look back to his mud-brown eyes and sniff. I finish the rest of my drink and furrow my brow, studying him. He's familiar.

"What do you want?" I ask, my hat still turned down.

"Just making conversation, fella," he says, sounding offended. "Horace says you fought in the war. I don't find many other veterans on this side of the Mississip'."

I grunt noncommittally and then peek over at the bar. Horace is wiping down the counter, speaking with the local sheriff—an old hare named Roscoe, and his sole deputy—his nephew Bobby. This is about how they spend most of their time in Bakersfield. They're good people. Horace among them and like his conversational partners, a bit old-fashioned. I wish he would've kept his big mouth shut for once. Then again, why would he think otherwise?

"Which side did you fight for?" he inquires.

"The Union," I admit honestly after a short pause.

He smiles, pleased by my answer. His expression communicates both gladness for familiarly and something else. The bighorn drapes his arm across the back of his chair and crosses his legs, kicking his coat back and revealing the handle of a thick saber, clothed in black leather and brightly polished brass. My eyes flick to it for just a moment before my tail curls behind me.

"As did I," he replies. "Army of the Potomac, Fifth Corp, First Division. I fought on every major battlefield from Gettysburg to Petersburg."

"Were you an officer?" I ask.

He just smirks and says, "Something like that, yeah."

My right hand tightens around the ball head of my cane and

I frown hard. Turning my head, I look out the window at the general store across the street. Now I'm definitely wishing I would have come later. Damn the weather, damn the risk. My associate seems to grow weary with my silence and leans across the table.

"How did you get that?" he asks.

Taken aback, I angle my head towards him to give a one-eyed stare. He smiles and places a limp finger onto his left cheek. With a subdued sigh, I turn my head so he can see my face full-on. My left eye is gone, or mostly gone. It's milky white and surrounded by scarring enough so that fur doesn't grow in some places. It's like rivers running to the sea in swirling pink, red, and black currents.

I choose not to wear an eyepatch as I yet can discern some things out of it. Shapes, color, light I still perceive, but not much beyond that. If I close my right eye, I'll be able to see the ram's shape and color, the movement of his arms and legs. But I wouldn't know who he was or the features on his face.

Another part of me wants people to see it, to see the damage inflicted upon me and know my pain. Most people wince at it, if they haven't already at speaking with a carnivore in the first place. It's also to remind myself of the things I've done and the places I've been. The hell I've seen. With a face like mine staring back in every mirror, it's hard to forget.

"Shell burst near me, took my eye, burned my face," I tell him, my voice barely above a whisper. "Petersburg."

The Marshall reclines into his chair with a knowing look on his face, but he doesn't appear to feel guilty for having asked. In fact, his interest has only been stoked. He twists his hand around so that his white gloves creak and moan. His hoof returns to the floor and he leans back in his chair. Suddenly he whips his hand up and snaps his fingers.

"Bartender, two whiskies!" he orders without taking his eyes from me. "What did you do during the war? You don't strike me as someone who would've fought in the infantry. You're too quick, too perceptive. Artillery, maybe? No, you don't have the build. We're you an officer, then?"

Our eyes connect and I feel my expression melt away.

"Something like that, yeah."

At first I expect him to snarl, but the bighorn just smiles and chuckles, amused by my quip. His left hand swings his coattail back to display his weaponry. He cocks his head to the right as I survey them.

"I bet by now you know what I am by how I'm dressed," he says cheerily. "And I don't mean a Marshall. The badge says as much. No, what I mean is that I'm a headhunter. They call me Hartwell, Jacob Hartwell."

"Then what are you doing here?" I ask without giving him the pleasure of a dramatic pause. "Not enough bastards roaming the deserts down in the Arizona Territory for you to hunt?"

The Marshall leans forward, tickled by my verbal jab.

"Killing from a distance isn't my style. I prefer to do it more," he says and grins, "intimately. So, you see, I'm up here looking for that special someone; a murderer who has slipped through the cracks of justice for the last time."

"Justice is blind. And whoever you're looking for isn't here. This is a peaceful place," I tell him.

My eyes flicker over to Roscoe and Bobby, who have ceased their conversation with Horace and have turned their attention to our conversation with only thinly veiled interest. I get a blink of approval from the graying hare. Hartwell nods his head and rises slowly to his hooves. He puts his palms down onto the table and leans towards me, pressing his muzzle uncomfortably close to mine.

"Oh, I know it is," he whispers firmly. "People can hide themselves, but not forever. They can ditch their clothes, change their name, even take their accent into a back alley and beat it to death. But they can't change who they are. And soon enough that little mask is gonna crack, and I'll be there to stick my sword down his throat and out his ass."

I avert my gaze and quickly close my overcoat, twisting my cane. He displays a disarming smile when I look back. Then he eases himself back down into his seat and crosses his legs once more. My heart climbs up into my throat and I'm deep in thought, watching this creature across the table from me silently gloat. Old memories float to the surface and I begin to suspect I know who he is.

I'm snapped out of my thoughts when two glasses thud onto the table and are swiftly filled with two fingers of expensive, East Coast whiskey. Hartwell snatches his up immediately while I refuse to touch mine. Reaching into my pocket, I fish a coin out and drop it onto the table. Then I creakily rise to my paws and press my hat down onto my head further.

"Thanks for the company," I tell him sourly and turn away.

I'm almost to the doorway leading into the hotel, just past the sheriff, when I hear the chair slide backwards. I steady myself on my cane and pause, my right hand twitching at my side. I turn my muzzle, expecting to see Hartwell's hands filled with his pistols. But he's merely pushed his chair back and holds one glass high in the air.

"I never did catch your name, coyote," he announces loudly, cheerily.

"St. Delaware," I tell him, "Richard St. Delaware. Good day."

As I cross the threshold into the hotel, I see him suck down both of his drinks in quick succession. Both my hands are shaking when I mount the first landing and collapse against the wall. Three years I've lived here. Three goddamned years people have let me be, without question and without harassment. At my hips, my sword and dagger tremble.

I left home at the age of sixteen. I believe it would be more accurate to say that I was forced out at the age of sixteen, and more accurately from place of living, not exactly 'home'. My upbringing was unhappy, one fraught with violence and poverty. But the way I left, I cannot be sure it improved my lot in life. My father had returned from whatever little shithole bar he dove into after working at the docks each day. He was drunk, but that wasn't abnormal. What was, though, was how much angrier he was.

My parents woke me up with their hollering, and I listened

in my room for a few minutes before he struck her. I didn't move because this was commonplace, but I cracked the door open all the same. The apartment we lived in wasn't big, but it was enough for me to sleep separate from them. And the best things we owned were hidden away with my father's old war trophies, including his sword set.

Father was cursing madly about money, my mother retaliating with our need to live being greater than his need to drink. I kneeled down and crawled towards where they slept because I could see his fists balling up. I was finally big enough to stand between the two, but with him as sloshed as he was, it would be like fighting three beasts. And the last time I did that, he thrashed me. I had considered retrieving his sword and threatening him, but I was just so scared.

He grabbed her and they screamed. He hit her repeatedly and threw her onto the ground when she struck him on the nose. That's when things changed. My father drew the dagger from his pocket. Knowing that it was now or never, I grabbed his arm to seize the weapon, but he knocked scrawny me down effortlessly. Then he whirled on me instead.

My mother grabbed him by both arms and he thrust her away, howling about how he was going to learn me some, at dagger point or with clenched fist. She struck the counter hard as he refocused on me. It became quieter as my father straddled me and threw the dagger up and over his head. Without thinking, I struck him in the gut and then dragged him onto the ground.

I punched him once in nose, stunning him, and then brought both hands, clenched together, down onto his wrist. The dagger skittered across the floor as he moaned, his drunken rage dissipated. I stood up and stumbled back off of him to get my mother out of there. It was only then when I had realized what had happened.

She had struck her head against the counter and passed on. I remember cradling her head and beginning to weep, but not much afterwards. I get flashes here and there, of getting my father's sword, of swinging it, and so much screaming. Afterwards I found that I was forever on my own, thrust onto the streets, terrified and inexperienced. My father taught me some swordplay out of either pity or desire to have a punching bag, but that got me nowhere.

It only got me nicked.

I'm not sure if I'm grateful that it wasn't for murder. No, I got nabbed for robbery. I was trying to hold up a little store in Charlestown with the only thing I had: my father's sword set. It was stupid, but I was so hungry. I was so scared that I didn't see when the shopkeeper pulled a pistol from under the counter. He shot me through the side before I could even react. I fled, and they gave chase, the shopkeeper and two of his boys. Luckily I managed to dodge his remaining shots by putting buildings, doors, even other people between him and me.

I slid beneath tables and crashed through stalls just to keep out of his reach or that of his assistants. And after several solid minutes of running, I lost them. Unfortunately, with all the activity and urgency, I had forgotten about the wound I had received. When I checked it, my clothes were drenched with my own blood. I had lost so much blood that when I was finally free, the only thing I was still capable of doing was lying down and subsequently passing out.

I woke up in jail not far outside of Boston. The male who found me was a distinguished and chiseled jaguar named Andrew Ring who wore a blue uniform with military stripes and bright eyes. He told me he watched the whole incident with great interest, particularly my flight to freedom. He said he was impressed, that he had taken a shine to me and told me that two things could happen now. If I pled innocent and lost, I would be conscripted into the Union Army and forced into an infantry unit where I'd likely perish. If I pled guilty, he would speak in my defense and I would be conscripted into the Union Army— except that he would choose where I went.

I took his offer. And all these years later, I'm unsure whether I regret it. Ring was a spy, or something like it, as he had an odd distaste for that word. Too simple, was how he described it. He said he recognized my sword and main-gauche, and wanted to see if I could use them. Ring was obviously blue blood, a difficult thing to attain for a carnivore. He was classically educated and classically trained. His own rapier was custom made and deadly in his claws. It was with that with which he intended to instruct me.

On my first bout with him, he beat the ever-loving shit out of me, which angered me. And the second time too. And the third, and fourth, and fifth, and so on, but I never gave up, no matter how angry I became. I spent the next few months somewhere outside Cambridge, sparring with the jaguar. It consisted of long, hot days of running and jumping; of climbing walls and dodging thrown objects; of hiding and diving and ducking; and of sneaking, surveying, and surprising. Of course, it also included making my sword a true extension of my own arm.

In the end, it focused me and tempered my emotions, as the European techniques that I was taught required poise and stoicism. I soon learned how to turn even the strongest cuts away, to anticipate his attacks, how to parry his thrusts and return them. I was no acrobat, but after four months, he said I was prepared, but not ready, for what was to come. I had also become that much calmer and self-controlled, maybe even happy for the first time in my life.

Ring treated me like his own son. He took me into his home, he clothed and fed me. He even managed to tolerate my anger and frustration with stride and took pleasure in soothing me and teaching me. It was in his care that I learned to read and write, to understand basic math, natural philosophy, and conversation. It was here where I found some semblance of belonging, of home.

It was about that time that I asked Ring why he wanted me, what he wanted me to do. I asked him what it was that he did. He told me he was a *sicario*, an assassin and, yes, a spy. And I was to be his apprentice. I had the perfect build, grace, strength, and ability to learn. He intended to travel with the Union Army south to combat the Confederacy from inside, but couldn't do it alone. He said beasts like him weren't made, they were born and molded.

That's where I came in. With a partner like me, maybe even successor, he could complete his work. At first I was excited, to be escaping my hellhole home. But that was before our sabotage at Gettysburg, our assassinations in Richmond, and our attempts to break the siege at Petersburg. Once it was all said and done, it only made me angrier, and made the drink all the more attractive.

I wake with a start as something creaks outside. The room is dark and quiet. Lamplight pours in from the windows peering down onto the street. From far below I can hear the roar of laughter, conversation, and bawdy music. It must be nearing midnight. Floorboards whine as someone rounds the top of the stairs. I've been here enough to memorize all the sounds this place emanates. And that is of someone trying not to be discovered.

Softly, I lift my covers and place my paws down onto the floor as my ears perk. I hear another creak, this time up the hallway. After standing, I turn and replace my covers after gently repositioning my pillows into the place I was once lying. Then I walk slowly to the corner where I hang my coat on a rack and retrieve my sword and main-gauche. Finally I turn, raising the sword and brandishing the parrying dagger in anticipation.

The doorknob turns and the door clunks to and fro almost silently. A key is then clunkily inserted into the other side and is turned with a distinct *click*. The door handle spins freely, and the door is cautiously pushed inwards. A shadow spreads over the floor, cast by the oil lamps across the hall, shapeless and featureless.

The shadow raises a gun and cocks the hammer. It is thrust into the doorway, and aimed directly at the bed where my pillow decoy has been placed. Taking a deep breath, I wait. And I'm not disappointed. In quick succession, the revolver fires three shots which pierce the bed to an explosion of feathers and fabric.

Wordlessly, I pounce forward and thrust the end of the sword through the back of my would-be assassin's hand. He brays and drops the pistol to the floor as the sword pierces his hand and delves into the door. I brandish the parrying dagger, displaying the intent to open his throat. The assailant wrenches the sword from the door and stumbles backwards into the hallway, blood dripping.

The mule looks up as I step into the doorframe, both weapons hanging at my side. He takes several hesitant steps towards the stairs, his eyes focused on me, on the wild coyote with the swords. His breath is shallow and ragged. His eyes are wide and wild and his expression one of true horror.

"You shouldn't have done that," I tell him firmly. "You shouldn't have missed. Tell Hartwell I'm not who he's looking for. That beast is dead!"

"We knew you were him. This isn't over," the mule chokes and takes two more steps up the hallway, almost pulling a sconce onto the floor. "You can't outrun the fire."

"Go," I tell him. When he doesn't immediately retreat, I yell, "*Go!*"

He takes one more step and throws daggers with his eyes. I whip both my sword and dagger up and leap forward aggressively. The mule promptly turns and runs to the stairs, tripping over his hooves as he rounds the bannister. As the sound of his hooves on oaken floors recedes into silence, I observe the trail of blood he's left behind. How apt.

I scoop up the revolver as I return to my room, and study the brand new gash in the door, splattered with fresh blood. Running a finger over it, I listen to the silence that wafts up from below. Not the kind of silence that is merely that—silence. It's more like the silence that occurs when you find a loved one has died or when bad news is delivered. It's not lack of noise, it's something else entirely.

After a few seconds, voices chitter when nothing new comes. I sigh, knowing that the officer is correct. I can't outrun this. Not anymore. I close the door behind me and return my weapons to their scabbards. Then I pop open the chamber of the revolver and remove the cylinder. Snapping the action from the receiver, I dump the cylinder onto the floor and go to the window.

Once it's open, I toss the other pieces into the darkness where they smack into the dirt and skitter across the square. Some folks watch me from the boardwalk across the street as they stumble home from a night of forgetting. I shut the windowpane and return to my bed, freshly filled with hot lead. I sit down on it anyways.

While I run a few fingers over the burned holes, I sigh and trace the cracks in my own face. They burn, even today, after three whole years. And while I should feel terrified and confused, I don't. In fact, I feel a bit of relief that the inevitable has finally arrived. Knowing that they won't be back tonight, I lie down, sending another handful of feathers soaring into the air. Before long, I'm asleep again.

Ring was taken from me at Petersburg. I was nineteen and he had been the only friend I had ever known. It was the delusional kind of attachment when one has no one else in their life. It's strong, but also obsessive. For me, though, it filled some sort of need I didn't understand. I looked upon Ring as the only father figure in my life. Because for three years, he was my father. And I was willing to forget my real one, if but for a time.

We were there to break the stalemate and force a swifter end to the war. It was Ring's belief that we had already shaved off several years by destroying intelligence and maps at Gettysburg, sabotaging communications all across Virginia, and disposing of five high-ranking officers in the Army of Northern Virginia.

But Petersburg was a hellhole through and through. I had never seen an army dig into the ground like they did, throwing volleys of fire at one another to no avail. With orders from above, our mission was simple and straightforward: end the siege. Methods be damned. Targets included artillery, ammo dumps, infantry captains, and communications officers.

We crept through the darkness, dressed as a Confederate captain and his lieutenant, and entered Petersburg from the north. We kept to the shadows and moved only when necessary. Our uniforms would cover us from a distance, but the moment they realized we were carnivores, we would be exposed. Luck was with us that night. We made it all the way into the battlements opposite the river before things went awry.

We were planting kegs of powder around a gigantic gun

nicknamed 'The Queen' when a pair of engineers stumbled onto us. Our cover was blown immediately, and we hid in the bunker taking fire as the entire encamped city awoke around us. Once they closed in, Ring turned rifles and pistols away as they discharged, cut fingers from hands, noses from faces, and tails from bodies. A wounded soldier takes two or three from the battlefield, Ring always said.

Even with his valiant efforts, and my covering of his flank, we lost more ground each minute. It was a lost cause. He pushed me back down a trench leading away from the river, and I consented without hesitation. At the mouth of the trench, two soldiers rushed in and randomly aimed their rifles. Spinning under the shot of one, I grabbed the muzzle of the other with the tip of my sword and turned it to his compatriot just as the hammer struck.

I then sucker-punched the horrified soldier and leapt over both as Ring rushed up from behind. Beyond was a street, and we instantly knew we couldn't escape back into the city. Lights were sparking everywhere, and footsteps echoed from every alley, door, and window. Ring grabbed me and swung me about, commanding me, "Run for the river, this whole thing's burned!"

We both sprinted around the earthen works surrounding the entrenchments, sometimes ducking as soldiers climbed over them and took potshots at our heads. Miraculously, Ring was able to keep us alive, even hitting a sharpshooter with a rock. As we peaked the hill, Ring lit a cigar and threw it back up over the embankment. Down below a line of trenches awaited us, fire raining down from every direction. Ring grabbed my shoulders and threw me forward, over the steep embankment. After I dove down into the trench, Ring fell in behind me.

I recovered quickly and turned to run, but suddenly realized that he wasn't making any indication of following. He wasn't moving at all. I stopped and grabbed his shoulder and shook him. My fingers came back wet and sticky, and I touched his back to find blood pooling. I remember gasping and feeling my whole body go cold. I didn't want to believe it had happened.

A ball had found him, hit him directly in the spine, and he

was gone before I even knew it. No dramatic fading out, no screams for help. Just dead. And me all alone. I remember pulling at his coat and desperately trying to drag him up the trench wall and into the river, but I was too weak. When I managed to crawl up into the mud myself, Ring's plan went into motion.

The cache we packed took light and exploded, ripping apart the hill and launching shrapnel, dirt, and bodies into the air. The shockwave hit me like a ton of bricks and threw me into the Appomattox River. However long later, I woke up on the shore next to a river running red with the blood of our victims. Ring was gone, and I had nothing save my skills to show for it. After I stumbled back to Union lines, I discovered I no longer existed and never had. Ring's body was forfeit, and I was to be jailed until someone decided my fate.

I wasted no time cutting my way out and vanishing into the darkness. The siege ended a few weeks later. And four weeks after that, Abraham Lincoln was assassinated in a theater. The clock began to run backwards, not only for the nation, but for me as well. The funny part is that I don't remember if I cried or not for Ring. All I remember is hatred and anger. It was nonsensical resentment at being abandoned by a dead person, and rage at the world for having taken him and erased him.

However, I still had my blades. I felt skilled enough that I could enter and exit Buckingham Palace without being seen. I could murder the president of the union if I so desired, and never have suspicion cast upon me. And if the world was going to take everything from me, I was going to take everything from it, by sword and fire.

Morning comes without incident. Everything is calm and quiet, like that moment before a storm. I dress and brush my hastily-washed fur in the mirror behind the warped vanity. I intend on collecting my order slip, loading up a wagon, hiring a few hands, and making my way back out to the house, all in the vain hope that I could avoid the hellish hurricane bearing down on me.

My cane fits my palm perfectly, and I use it to guide myself down the steps. Even though my remaining eye is unaffected by my blindness, I always fear what lurks on my periphery, unseen. And so it was that when I descended the main staircase into the hotel lobby with my suitcase, my coat and hat, my sword set, and the piece of that jackass's gun, that I found the trap had already been sprung.

Hartwell had collected Roscoe and his nephew, plus every able-bodied cud-chewing officer he could find, which consists of only three stagecoach guards who laze near the windows. A few gawkers hang outside the windows to get a good look at the show being performed inside. He sits in the center of the wide doorway leading into the bar, in a lone chair situated several paces beyond the frame. His legs are crossed and his eyes are bright, watching me with a mixture of delight and sick pleasure.

"Ah, Mr. St. Delaware," he says, and then chuckles, "it's rude to lie to others. It's also rude to try to kill my agents, Thomas."

His two thugs appear from behind the counter with firearms at the ready: a long, large-gauge shotgun and a repeater. From out of the corner of my eye, I watch the mule dig the shotgun into the small of my back and smile as if this were some kind of surprise. I drop my suitcase and withdraw my hands from my pocket, still holding my cane firmly.

"Hold your arms up, dumbass," the mule orders, "before my fingers get itchy."

He then swivels around my form, his shotgun balanced in one hand, and begins to undo my belt.

"You've assaulted an officer of the law, Mr. Booker, and for that you shall do time in a federal pen," the Marshall states with confidence. "Assuming I don't lose track of you somewhere on the route to Chicago or you find your way into the hands of a hanging judge I know down in Kansas City, should I be so inclined."

"You think I assaulted *him*?" I growl.

The mule yanks at my hip, and then shies away when I snarl at him. My belt and blades clatter to the floor and the bull retrieves them from the other side. The rifle is rested lazily on his shoulder as he walks my tools over to this thief, this rustler, this outlaw with a badge. Hartwell rises to his hooves and nods, a smile on his face.

"It's not difficult to imagine when he came back to me soaked in his own blood," he informs me. "Despite my desire to hang you here, Sheriff Roscoe has kindly negotiated your extradition back on the Philadelphia instead. He agreed with me that you matched the description of a notorious train robber and murderer by the name of Thomas Booker. But he wasn't sure— the eye, you see, which is why I sent Hobbs here to come fetch you for questioning. Once you confirmed my suspicions by stabbing, robbing, and intimidating him with his own firearm, well, you sort of forced his hand. I told him. Beasts like you, they don't ever actually change."

Roscoe, who stands next to the bar with his hands resting at his side, tightens his lips and nods his head. His eyes meet mine, but they're glazed over, disinterested in the proceedings. I've known him for years now. I've helped the town in tough times before the railroad came. And this is how they repay me? Bobby sits bolt upright on a stool next to his uncle, a shaky hand resting on his pistol, his eyes warily watching the Marshall. I think they're as afraid of him as they are of me.

"Your boy there drew his pistol and shot into my bed, believing the pillows I had stacked there to be me," I tell him, I tell Roscoe. "You sent an assassin to kill a beast in his sleep. I defended myself, disarmed him, and graciously let him *live*."

Roscoe's eyes flutter up to me, his eyelids narrowing. Then his head swivels over to Hartwell and he steps away from the bar.

"Is that true?" he asks, his voice wavering. "Is that why we heard gunfire upstairs last night?"

Hartwell turns to him with a charismatic smile and clasps his hands together.

"I assure you, Sheriff, I hold my agents to a higher standard. Such an underhanded action is highly unlikely," he says with a shake of his head in an attempt to allay his compatriot's concerns. "Now, please, allow us to depart. We'll be on the train and out of your fur within the hour."

"I have his gun, that is true," I admit, my eyes pinned on

Roscoe. "But I dismembered it once I had possession of it and disposed of half of it out the window. You'll find that I still have the cylinder with three spent casings inside. You'll find their tips in the floor of my room, beneath the bed."

Hartwell's eyes swivel in their sockets, and he turns to me with his brow high on his forehead. This is an unexpected development, it seems. Roscoe concurs, looking at me expectantly. I turn my nose down and look at my left pocket. I tap the bulge with the tip of my cane and then look to the sheriff pleadingly.

"You'll have to retrieve it. I don't see too well out of that eye," I say with an air of helplessness.

Roscoe goes to comply, but Hartwell bars him and crossly looks to Mr. Hobbs.

"Fetch whatever it is he's hiding in his pockets," he commands. "Turn them out for good measure, too."

Hobbs chuckles, and then grabs the back of my jacket before pulling at it and almost unbalancing me. The shotgun is dug squarely into my spine above my tail, and I whine at the pain that shoots through my face from the sudden movement. Hobbs's free hand rifles through my pocket and grasps at the only item inside, his pistol's cylinder.

When it appears, Hartwell's face goes slack. Hobbs studies it then walks to his commander, the shotgun still pointed in my general direction. When he gets close enough he offers it to Hartwell, but Roscoe intercepts it and looks it over. Hartwell appears unpleased, but allows the old hare to inspect it.

"He isn't lying," Roscoe says with a nod. "This changes things."

"This changes nothing," Hartwell declares severely. "We're taking him into custody. He has still assaulted an officer, and must pay for his crimes, present *and* past."

Roscoe shakes his head and then turns towards his nephew.

"Self-defense is not a crime. I'll have to wire Yankton to see what they propose," Roscoe says with certainty, his ears erect. "We have a jail here if that would make you feel more comfortable. For the meantime, just relax. He's not going anywhere."

"Oh, to hell with this," Hartwell hisses.

In one smooth motion, Hartwell unholsters a pistol and whips Roscoe across the back of the head before turning the business end towards his nephew. The poor boy throws his hands and starts to cower. Roscoe slumps to the ground like a sack of potatoes and groans. The cylinder rolls across the floor where it comes to a spinning stop against the edge of a rug.

"Stay down, old hare," Hartwell commands. "We're taking this bastard into custody, and I will see him swing at the end of a goddamn polearm if I have to do it from a water tower myself. Hobbs, Barnes, you two idiots grab him and get him onto the train. We have his swords, he's defenseless."

The officers turn with glee in their eyes. Alternatively, the hired hands are not thrilled with this development. Despite their shock, though, they do nothing to stop it. The crowd outside stares in with terror and then disperses, their eyes alternating between fleeing and gawking. My blood goes cold as I see a trickle of blood leak from Roscoe's ear, and give Bobby my apologies. Despite my own displeasure, I shake my head sternly when he desperately eyes his gun.

Bobby just bows his head and cries silently. Meanwhile, Hobbs and Barnes snatch my arms and twist them around my back. Shackles are produced and screwed into place. Hartwell approaches, and then snatches the end of my chin with his hand, yanking it so I stare into his maddened gaze. He smiles and turns his head.

"Do you recognize me now, asshole?"

Without Ring or the military pay, I found myself hungry, tired, and alone. Desperate and starving, I robbed a merchant going west and found myself along the Mississippi. The money I took from him ran out, and I couldn't justify robbing another poor traveler. I set my sights on someone who could shrug off a huge loss, something like a riverboat queen.

It turned out my skills had been honed to perfection for such a situation. I was able to sneak about a riverboat transporting plantation profits north from New Orleans. I had to deal with only one armed guard, who woke up the next morning not knowing what happened. I walked away with two-thousand in gold, bills, and some assorted jewelry. Getting in and out was easy. What was difficult was fencing the jewels afterwards.

Regrettably, that went about as well as could be expected. In St. Louis, a fat pig with three enforcers tried to shake me down. I was an emaciated twenty-year-old with a very nice set of stolen swords who had stumbled into extreme wealth. And I was alone. Like so many before them, they drew pistols on me only to find that this was as effective as pissing on a forest fire.

I made the first thug shoot his own leg, before turning on another before he could brandish his firearm. I sliced off each one of the buttons on his vest with fine turns of my wrist, tore open his shirt with the tip of my sword, and then sliced his chest for him to hold as he screamed and collapsed. The third managed to unsheathe a thick bowie knife with a spiked handguard and take a slash at me while I was distracted.

He slashed high and low, using his towering equine frame to overpower me and stay out of my reach. But every time he backed me into a corner, I would slip through his legs or under an arm. Finally he figured out my pattern and threw a bicep up, caught me by the chin, busted open my mouth, and put me in the dirt like a cheap rug. He jumped on me and brought his bowie knife down in a wide arc.

Unfortunately for him, he didn't understand what kind of dagger my main-gauche was. His blade slipped right into the catch near my handle and I twisted it hard to the right, using his own momentum against him. The knife cracked at the cross guard and broke every bone in his hand when he couldn't free it from the guard in time.

While he was writhing on the ground, I sliced open his unbroken hand for good measure and then kicked him unconscious. Only the fence remained. The swine graciously became very cooperative. He didn't consider trying to pull the scattergun he had hidden beneath his shop's counter. I made a very pretty penny off of that deal, but had decided that dealing with fences was too risky. I was going to stick to bills, coins, and bonds only.

That didn't leave many options. The first was trying to hit a bank itself. And while I was arrogant and confident, I wasn't stupid. Firearms had gotten much more intricate and useful since the war ended. Crank guns, pistols with metal-cased bullets, pump rifles, and breech-action shotguns sprang up everywhere. And the Union Army started playing guard dog for their favorite sons.

The second option was to keep hitting riverboats and hope I didn't drown one day or get caught in a gator's jaws. No thanks. The last option was the railroad. Train robberies were common, but they're generally undertaken in a particular style. It involved either stopping the train by force, or hopping aboard it somewhere along the line. But it always involved robbing it in broad daylight. It was noisy, cumbersome, and above all, dangerous and stupid. Loud and dumb can only get you killed.

I could and would do better than that. My first heist was a Topeka-to-Denver route with a car carrying crisp, untouched bills from the mint in Philadelphia to San Francisco. I had eaten well and dressed well since my river raid. Plus, nobody knew my face. So I bought a ticket and bided my time. When it finally came, as the sun fell and darkness reigned, I drew my blades and went to work.

I disarmed and incapacitated the first soldier before he could scream. Then I used his keys to unlock the door. When the door to the armored car was cracked open, I clambered onto the roof and snuck to the rear door with the keys. When I opened it, all of the guards were focused on the suddenly-ajar door on the other side. After cutting a candle's wick, the one closest one didn't know what hit him.

As he tumbled to the ground with a new scar, though, his shotgun discharged and blew a hole in the side of the metal carriage. The second guard, a tall giraffe, swung around with a pistol and fired at random. I dove behind the safe against the wall, and then hefted a bag of coins at him. I followed right after, slashing at the bag so it burst on impact, cut open his arm so he'd release the gun, and then struck him with a haymaker.

When he was prone, I punched him with the handle of my sword and he went limp. The last guard, terrified by the shadowy menace that had dispatched with all three of his associates without being touched, turned his rifle towards me. I extinguished the lantern with a swipe of my sword, and he fired into darkness. With each spent round, I would dance about while confusing him with a swing of the sword and a sudden, random movement. When I finally reached him, he was pulling the trigger and racking that rifle without any more bullets coming out. I smiled and cut open his arms. He stumbled back, and I grabbed him and threw him over the railing. He disappeared into the darkness.

My robberies went on like that. Daring nighttime infiltrations, the body count growing over time, and I never left anything behind. No money, no calling card, no evidence, nothing. If I left anyone conscious or alive, the only tale they told was of a ghostly swordsmith with magical powers or demon's blood. They were only half right. Of course, this wouldn't last. Because I got greedy; because I got stupid.

Over the years, my heists grew greater and grander. I was a folk hero to the poor farmers and prospectors who blamed the bank and the army for stealing their livelihoods. They liked to call me the Night Blade, or the Shadow. I always loved collecting wanted posters with those names emblazoned on them. But to the Pinkertons, U.S. Army, U.S. Marshalls, and other bringers of law, I was their prime target. I was their nightmare, as I had killed some and humiliated the rest. This went on for years. Sometimes I would go months without hitting a train or a coach.

When I had money, I would gamble, smoke, screw whores, and lavish it on everyone around me. And drink. So much drink. It got me into innumerable fist fights that always ended with my swords and a dead body. It made me an outcast in every town I entered. It angered every lawbeast I ran into, who dogged me day and night while I drank and whored away their fortunes. I was uncatchable, invulnerable. At least I thought I was. After enough time, I would invariably wake up hungover in an alleyway, flat broke, and the cycle would repeat.

Restlessness and boredom pervaded me and I sought the 'big one,' the heist that would make me legend. And just a little over three years ago, after seven years of starving, scraping, scuffling, slaughtering, stealing, squandering, and stewing, I found it. Her name was the *California Flyer*. She was a bullion train going express from Chicago to Denver, and then on to San Francisco. I would be set for life.

I waited high in the Rockies for her to layover before crossing the mountains. I kidnapped one of the guards and hid him away before donning his uniform. The Union Army always allowed carnivores into their ranks, and there were enough on that train that I blended in immediately.

I took a spot at the very rear of the train, where I assumed the vault would be stored and guarded. When the train started moving, that's when I sensed that something was wrong. The rear door opened under its own weight to reveal an empty car. After I crept to the imposingly large safe at the very center, I twisted the lock open to find it barren. The carriage door was pulled shut behind me and the train came to screeching halt.

Voices echoed outside before panels were stripped from over empty windows. Outside, the soldiers amassed with their rifles shouldered. Under orders from the officer leading the assault, they opened fire. I dove into the safe and reeled my legs and tail in as volley after volley ricocheted through the carriage. For the first time since I was a boy, since my mom and dad died, I was scared. I no longer knew why I was there, why I was doing anything. After the fire ended, I knew they would charge in.

Tears staining my face, I crawled on my belly towards the door and waited. If I was going to die, I was going to die fighting. The first soldier had his arm clipped short and his throat opened as he charged inwards, bayonet fixed. The next wasn't so stupid, and swung blindly around the corner. When I ducked under the gun, I stabbed him in the stomach and thrust him back down the ladder.

A gun fired from across the carriage and perforated my ears with shrapnel. I tripped backwards as another private entered from behind. Backing away from thrust after thrust of bayonet, I desperately fought to keep the safe between me and the pistoleer who'd materialized behind and almost opened a window in my skull. We danced around the car, the pistoleer emptying his Peacemakers and forcing a brief retreat, the private trying desperately to aim at me. Finally when the soldier drew back his hammer, I closed the gap, pointed the gun away and made him shoot his own commander. I then stabbed him.

One last fool dove in behind, and I dropped and hid behind the safe before he fired his rifle. I then rushed him and swung high. He intercepted with his rifle and rocked backwards as I slashed at his stomach. He stabbed multiple times with that bayonet, but I was always able to redirect. Finally he made his mistake, rearing the rifle up to bring it down like a club. After parrying, I forced it down with my swords crossed and then opened his throat, as if with scissors.

Shaken, I collapsed against the safe and peered at my own hands, covered in blood that would never come out. Something moved ahead of me and I gazed down the row of empty cars, their doors open, as a soldier pulled a sheet from over something that shined. He stuck a box in the top and turned the barrels in my direction. A Gatling gun. I dropped behind the only available cover as the crank was turned and it opened fire.

The heavy rounds tore through the edges of the safe and shredded the car. For what felt like hours, the gun crushed me into that safe like molten steel into a mold. Then, as quickly as it started, it ended. That's when I heard hoofsteps approaching. I peeked over the top just quickly enough to see something thrown into the carriage from the hand of a beast with large horns.

The stick of dynamite arced in the air, and I watched it approach in dumbstruck awe. It landed in the corner and spun towards me. The figure then laughed as I desperately bolted for the back door. Had I started earlier, I would've made it. Instead, the dynamite exploded and I couldn't see or feel anything on my left side as I was catapulted through the door.

I escaped by falling into the winter snow. Somehow I

recovered, and delved deep enough into the surrounding wood and snowfall where nobody would come searching. They would assume I was dead. *I* believed I was. Somehow I was offered a third chance. I tearfully took it. With a stash of money I had hidden away and the desire to disappear, I made my way to civilization. After receiving medical care at the hands of selfless people, I paid them handsomely and then vanished, hoping to begin life anew. It seems that he didn't think I was dead after all. He was just biding his time, waiting for me to resurface.

He must've gotten bored of waiting.

Hartwell, the figure from the train, leads me by the neck and thrusts me into a coach at the center of the train. Once I'm aboard, he doesn't gloat or revel in my capture. In fact, he sneers at me with deep-seated disgust. Then he dumps me into a seat, orders his hired guns to keep me there, and spits onto the floor before retiring to his first-class coach at the front. The train will be going back to Chicago with only us on board, by orders of the United States government.

Smoke and steam bellows from the engine ahead and the train rocks backwards. A raccoon sits in front of me, his arm draped over the back of the seat. He's armed with one pistol and seems disinterested in me. A horse lounges in the bench across the aisle, his shotgun propped against his shoulder. His eyes are hidden behind his hat.

Finally, a stoat stands at the back of the train, leaning against the wall and chewing on something stuck between his teeth. Effectively unsupervised, I withdraw a piece of metal from inside my coat. Hartwell should have known I would prepare for this situation. Although, how could someone prepare for someone like me? Shoot them and hope they die the first time.

It slips into the shackles, and with my wrists strained, I begin to turn over the lock. The train is accelerating. We'll be away from the town within moments, outside of earshot. My plan since being cuffed was to beat my guards unconscious and run. But after seeing Hartwell strike Roscoe, I realized he wouldn't stop. He's been following me for three years; he won't be deterred by yet another escape. I lived peacefully in Bakersfield all that time. I can't bring this trouble back on them.

No, I'm thinking this has to end here. I knew this day would come, though never when. I had merely feared that I would be left unarmed and would be forced to take another life. My cane was left with me, which offers me many options, despite not having my swords. Hartwell retained them, probably as hunting trophies.

The silhouette of the town recedes into the gray-green outline of the plains after only a few minutes. Smoke billows into the golden dawn, a black snake dissipating into the sky. After I've determined enough time has elapsed, I clench my jaw and relax back into my seat. Finally, I take a cleansing breath.

"How much did he pay you?" I ask quietly as my fingers work.

"Shut up," the raccoon spits without turning his head.

The horse glances up and rolls his eyes.

"Twenty dollars," I ask, "forty? That's not much to guard a beast like me. He robbed you."

"Shut *up!*" the raccoon hisses, and turns to me with a growl.

"Calm down, Jeb, Jesus Christ," the stoat admonishes from the back.

"Oh, it was even less," I mock. "How unfortunate. He stuck you with the short end of the stick, and *I'm* the thief?"

"I said shut up!" he hollers.

He stands up in his seat and rears back to hit me. The horse leans forward to stop him, but it's too late. The raccoon thrusts his body over the back of the seat and brings his fist down. To his surprise, my hands break through the manacles to catch his arm and guide it past my head. I twist it and lay a punch onto his temple. His eyes go hazy.

"What the hell?" the horse screams, and fumbles his shotgun.

Before the horse can correct himself, I seize one of the raccoon's arms as his limp form falls onto me, and catapult him across the aisle into the horse's lap. Snatching up my cane with my right hand, I spring forward and smash the silver ball directly on his head. His entire body drops like a ragdoll, sliding down onto the floor between the seats with his raccoon buddy atop him.

"Shit, shit, shit, shit, *shit*!" the stoat screams.

He almost drops his pistol as he yanks it from its holster, swinging it up just in time to blow three holes in the back of the seat I dive behind. The stoat's breath is ragged and shaky. He wasn't expecting to actually have to do anything, I believe. His coat jangles as he steps forward tentatively. Knowing I can't leap at him, I perch my hat atop of my cane and inch it towards the seat's legs.

The stoat holds his breath as my hat floats into the aisle. Then he manually cocks the hammer and fires his last remaining shells at the floor, where they blow my hat apart and reveal nothing else. Vaulting the seat, I close the gap as the frightened stoat tries to shoot his empty gun at me. I knock it from his grip with the edge of my cane and he takes a swing at me with his other hand.

Ducking down, I punch him square in the gut and ram him back into the wall. He lifts his arms and brings his elbows down into my back with enough force that I have to take a knee. Pain spreads throughout my face as my old wound asserts itself. After the stoat strikes me again, I toss him to the side and then grab my cane.

I twist the top off and reveal the blade within. Pricking it against his nose, I gasp for breath and look into tired, scared eyes. It's a look I know all too well. My hand wavers and I lower the blade.

"Go home," I tell him. "Forget this happened. Keep your money and tell no one."

I then lift the scabbard above my head and nail him behind the ears. His body relaxes and his mouth drops open. Winded, I stumble back into the seat behind me, gasping for air and shaking from the tip of my tail to my ears. My entire face hurts from the excitement, and my heart cannot keep up with my mind. My cane-sword rattles and my vision darkens as I stare at it.

I didn't want to have to do this again, but I have to. Loud

cries are coming from behind me. The two officers that arrived with Hartwell will descend upon me soon, probably better armed and, more importantly, alert. If I'm going to be able to escape this, I need to incapacitate them. And in order to do that, I need my swords.

As the sound of beating hooves becomes audible, I climb to my paws and rush to the door at the front of the carriage. I whip it open and dive into the next car, which is empty. Only one car remains between me and the tender. I open the door between the cars and step across. Upon opening the last barrier, blade at the ready, I discover the car dark and empty.

My swords are leaned against the back of a plush seat just a few feet inside. Carefully, I cross the threshold and approach them. I'm extending my arms to retrieve them when Hartwell materializes, one of his pistols, a heavy Schofield, in his hand. A bullet grazes my leg, and another deafens me as it burrows into the wooden wall behind me. A third clips my shoulder as I dive behind the upholstered seat.

He empties the gun into the seat, missing me by a length. Sheathing my cane-sword, I retrieve both of my blades from their scabbards. Next, I slide my back up against the seat and wait, panting and huffing, my heart beating in my ringing ears. Silence reigns, and I know that Hartwell will either be reloading, or drawing his other pistol.

"I knew you didn't change, you sick bastard!" Hartwell cries out. "I'm only glad I didn't have to walk to your house. How does it feel to be you again?"

"I just wanted to be left alone!" I answer. "I know what I did! The beast you met in Bakersfield is the one I am! The other one is long dead!"

"That beast is not dead!" he insists, hissing through his teeth. "You may have fooled those rubes, you may even have convinced yourself, but when push comes to shove, you're the same cruel bastard as the one I hunted down in Colorado! You are a liar, a thief, and a murder, Thomas Booker, and I will see you dead!"

He fires two rounds above my head for effect, and I flinch

as splinters rain down on me. The door leading into the car slides open, and the mule appears. He thrusts a pocket pistol at me with a self-satisfied grin on his face. Without hesitation, I launch myself onto him and shove the pistol over my shoulder.

Two bullets drill through the wall and window past my ear, a third into the ceiling as I bend his arm back. Hartwell fires two rounds around us in an attempt to hit me, but without endangering his agent, to my luck. As the mule screams, seizing his broken arm, I punch him with the handguard of my sword and he collapses.

I catch his revolver with my blade through the trigger guard as it tumbles from his hand, and whirl it towards Hartwell like a shot-put. It whips past Hartwell's head as he rolls to avoid it. Suddenly, the bull rushes into the car with his rifle. I aim it away with the broadside of my main-gauche so he fires a round into empty space. I then hastily cut shallow gashes along his arm, but his grip remains fixed.

He lays into me with his shoulder and knocks me to the ground. Rattled, Hartwell recovers and fires haphazardly, sending four rounds through the floor around my body. Rolling over onto my back, I sit up and slash open the bull's shins. He trips back and tumbles, his rifle tossed absentmindedly. As it strikes the ground, it discharges, sending a bullet past my head and nearly hitting Hartwell.

The bull howls in pain and writhes about, allowing me the opportunity to climb atop him and knock him unconscious with the pommel. Gasping for breath, I stand, straddling his head, and turn. Hartwell rises from behind an empty seat and aims two pistols in my direction. But he hesitates. His chest is rising and falling, his teeth clenched in rage. His eyes, though, swirl with uncertainty and fear.

"Please, stop this," I plead, exasperated, my head throbbing. "You've lost. Your rage will consume you if you don't forgive yourself and move on."

"I've done nothing wrong!" he spits.

"You got your men killed and you blame yourself," I declare with a shake of the head. "But killing me will not bring them back, nor will it bring them justice. That beast is gone. I own who I was and I will never be able to repay this world for the things I stole from it. But violence only begets more violence."

He doesn't answer. Instead, his lips close and his eyes narrow. Before the hammers can draw back on his pistols, I turn and dash for the door. A bullet tears through the wooden wall as I leap his deputy into the next carriage. Another whizzes by and explodes the back of a bench as I near the rear. From behind Hartwell rages, bleating over the thunderous echo of hooves on wood.

Another bullet tears past my chest as I throw shut the door into the final coach. Crossing it, I tear open the rear entrance and hop the gap to the caboose. I twist its handle, to no avail. I try kicking it down, but it stands resolute. Hartwell throws the door open behind me and I abandon that route.

Turning, I jump back to the coach and climb up the ladder leading to the roof. When I mount it, I turn and leap onto the caboose. Hartwell appears and fires as I'm midair, missing me, but piercing my coat. I land with a roll, recover, and rush to the edge. Looking down, I see there's nowhere else to go but down.

"Booker!"

I whip my head around as Hartwell stands, pistols akimbo, on the roof across from me. He extends the guns and pulls the trigger. Nothing happens. He examines them with frustration and then tosses them aside. He delves into his coat and withdraws his saber, polished and recently sharpened. I walk to the center of the caboose and ready myself. Hartwell steps back and takes a running leap across the gap.

He doesn't mince words after landing, and immediately slashes at me from over his right shoulder, screaming. I parry, and then thrust with my small sword. He steps to the left and catches my wrist with the reverse edge, drawing blood. Surprised, I twirl around and swing both sword and dagger, but he knocks them away and punches me straight in the neck.

I howl as horrendous pain spreads over my face, blinding me. Stumbling backwards, I try to keep him within view of my right eye, knowing that if he literally blindsides me, I'll be hacked to bits. Limping to the side, I draw sharp, shallow, uncontrolled breaths and regain my footing. He offers no quarter and charges. The sword comes across from his left and I deflect it downwards.

Hartwell pirouettes in an attempt to bifurcate me. Ducking down, I slide under his sword and watch as he stumbles forward, dragged by his momentum, towards the edge. Not thinking, I turn and snatch the back of his coat before he can tumble off. Dragging him back, I throw him onto the roof. His eyes look up to me with surprise mixed with burning hatred.

My gesture, though, is not enough. Hartwell slashes upwards and catches the front of my chest, ripping open my clothes and sending fur and skin flying. I yelp and watch as blood soaks my shirt crimson. In my confusion, Hartwell swipes at my legs, and I react quickly enough that he merely slices open my pants. After springing to his hooves, he charges madly, swinging a flurry of slashes, slices, and stabs that I parry effortlessly, accomplishing nothing but exhausting him and pushing me back.

His fury comes to a head when we run out of dueling space at the end of the car he intends to drive me off of. He brings his saber down over me and I catch it between crossed blades. He pushes until it slides to my hilts, just inches from my face. My arms are losing strength. My head hurts too much, and I'm losing blood. I have to end this, quickly.

Hartwell smiles and exhales hot air onto my face.

"This is it, Booker," he gloats. "You die here, since you were so eager for your trip to Hell."

"You're right," I admit with a nod, "this is the end."

I twist my parrying dagger, lock his fingers into his handguard, and wrench both weapons to my left. Hartwell shrieks as the saber is jerked from his grip and sent flying off into the empty plains. Hartwell, stunned, stumbles backwards and falls onto his tail. He kicks away as I thrust the tip of my sword towards him.

"You were so caught up in your anger that you threw everything you had at me," I tell him. "You wasted all of your strength and every weapon in blind fury. And now you're left with nothing—no guns, no swords, just and me and my blades.

Stand up!"

Hartwell begrudgingly complies, climbing unsteadily onto his hooves. His extends his arms out from his sides and stares me down. He expects me to run him through, all the way down to my cross guard. But I just frown, pitying him. Because I was there once too. Because I blamed myself for Ring's death, for the deaths of my parents. Because I learned my lesson too many sins, too many transgressions too late, only to realize I have nothing to show for my life except anger and resentment.

I lower my swords. My main-gauche is sheathed, but my small sword lingers, held aloft before my eyes. I read the words on the blade again and sigh. Hartwell drops his arms and stares with disbelief.

"When you blew apart my face high in the mountains, I thought I was dead. I almost bled out before a guide and survey crew found me. And when they were patching me up, I realized all the things I had done. It was stupid and selfish, the grief of a puppy, angry with the world," I say. "You killed Booker up on the mountain. You got what you wanted. Now go home."

"You faced no justice," he declares. "You escaped your fate up in the snow! I should've killed you or took you, manacled, to a noose! You didn't change. People like you *never* change! You just convince yourself you're reformed. And whether you strike me down or not, you will be hunted for the rest of your existence!"

"This isn't justice, Hartwell. This is revenge."

"What's the difference?"

We're silent as those words reverberate through my skull. One destroyed me. And it eats him, too.

I venture, "You were military police, weren't you? Not the kind that arrested drunks and perverts. You were of the kind that hunted down the real monsters."

His jaw and brow clench, confirming my suspicion.

"And you were a spy, reported right to Grant himself," he says. "I know everything, Booker. Your parents, your service, your robberies. You were a monster right from the cradle. How many have you killed? A dozen? Two? How many more will it take?"

Just the one, I think.

That thought makes me sigh, saddens me. He is right, unfortunately; this can only end one of two ways. And I suppose I have to make a choice. I turn and walk towards the back of the train.

"How far are we from the next station?" I ask.

"Ten miles, at least."

Metal crunches and clacks as Hartwell inches towards me. Even in total defeat, he refuses to accept it. I sigh and count the railroad ties rushing beneath the car, stretching out to infinity behind us. Hartwell is nearly on top of me when I resign myself to my choice.

"Then it'll be a long goddamn walk for you, won't it?"

I turn just as Hartwell raises a knife to stab me. I slice open his fingers and send the knife flying into the air. His watches it go with shock, and so doesn't see my left hook before it bashes his nose in. His body goes limp, and I catch him so he doesn't hit the ground head-first. I ease him to the roof and then roll him off the side into the grass.

He hits the ground and disappears into the distance. I holster that thin blade and cross my arms. This isn't the end, I don't think. But at least I know what I'm up against. Maybe Hartwell won't come around again. Maybe I've only strengthened his resolve. Even if it isn't him, it'll be someone else, a pup looking to prove himself; a desperate bounty hunter; another templar hoping to bring me to justice. There's always someone.

At least I've bought some time. I slip off the side off the train from the caboose balcony. It takes a half a day to walk to my house from the tracks. I know I can't stay there, but I always have enough to start over again. I recover my stash, pack up the things I feel like I need and can carry, and then lock all the doors.

When they come—and they will come—they'll find an empty house. I'll leave them nothing to go on and no indication to which way I'll travel. I think I'll head towards San Francisco. There are a lot of people there, easy to lose yourself in a crowd. I'll remember to always have my good eye open. Because the world may one day forgive your folly, it will never forget your face.

The Black Blade

Jaden Drackus

Of all the fighters assembled at the arena, only one held the attention of Marius Luciano: the lone jaguar leaning against the wall.

He stayed apart from the others, his eyes on the ground, giving Luciano the initial impression he was dozing. But his ears were twitching too frequently for that to be the case. Studying the jag, the wolf realized that his solitude wasn't the only unusual thing about him. His fur was dark— his spots all but disappeared, making him look solid black. He wore leather armor dyed in splotches of dark gray and black, and carried twin longswords on his hips. His gear stood out in a crowd of fighters in mail and plate armor with two-handers or bastard weapons. That fact, even more than his appearance or apparent lack of interest in the proceedings, kept the mercenary's attention on him. He sensed that even in an arena full of warriors, the jaguar was dangerous.

Luciano's eyes swept over the crowd—most of them mercenaries like himself, with a soldier or town guard mixed in. There was the eclectic mix of species one would expect from such a group: bears, wolves, cougars, hyenas, and a few other species. The wolf couldn't stop his tail from wagging: he was in the presence of the greatest fighters in the Empire—and he was counted among them. He still couldn't believe it.

Any further reflections were interrupted by the blare of trumpets. Luciano's eyes swept around the circular arena before being drawn to the viewing box that divided the seating in half. From the shadows of that box, a stag dressed in the scarlet and silver of the Staergrad city crest stepped to the rail. Behind him, a massive cougar in the chainmail and tabard of the city guard lurked. Strapped to his back was a broadsword, mostly obscured by the cougar's bulk, but something about the blade kept Luciano's attention until the stag began speaking.

"Hail, warriors! I am your host, Count Tavian of Staergrad." The count inclined his head. Some returned it, while Luciano and others put a fist to their left shoulder in salute.

"You have been summoned to take part in a great test of skill! Never before has the empire seen such a gathering of its greatest sword masters. I am humbled that all of you have accepted my invitation and graced my home with your presence."

The stag paused for a moment, as though he was expecting applause. He didn't get any, and Luciano thought he saw Tavian's ear twitch in annoyance as he continued.

"You have been called here for a great purpose! Over the coming days a tournament will be held to determine the greatest sword master in the Empire!"

This time there was some noise. Not the applause the count had doubtless hoped for, but a quiet murmur of assent.

"And for such a tournament, the rewards shall be great!" Tavian motioned the cougar forward.

The guard stepped to the rail and unstrapped the broadsword from his back and held it up. Luciano's eyes went wide as he studied the slice of night. The blade was an ebony metal that barely glinted in the sunlight. The sword's guard was also unusual, curving up in a half circle on each side of the blade. The grip was wrapped in black leather, and the hilt was capped by a strange purple gem. Something about the sword held the wolf's complete attention until the stag finally spoke again.

"This is Ashrune! This blade has decided the fate of kingdoms and turned the tides of wars! It has seen the paws of many great warriors," Tavian said as he gestured to the guard to lower the sword. Luciano's tail twitched in excitement as his gaze returned to the stag. "And it shall soon be in the paws of one of you."

Luciano barely heard the rest of the stag's speech. Ashrune. The wolf knew many tales of that blade. It was claimed that Ashrune had an enchantment that made the wielder invincible in battle, and it chose only the greatest fighters to wield it. The sword would often vanish for long periods of time, but always turned up at some pivotal moment. What would it be like to wield that blade? Luciano looked up from his thoughts to find the assembled crowd departing. The wolf shrugged and moved towards one of the exits.

"You should walk away now," a quiet voice said.

Luciano's ears swiveled and his head turned towards the voice. Most of the other fighters were filing out of the arena, nowhere near enough for even a feline to hear something said just above a whisper. It took him a moment to realize that the jaguar hadn't moved from the wall. He stood there, still, leaning against the stone, eyes on the ground. Luciano blinked, then snarled.

"So you'll have an easier time winning yourself?"

"The prize is a poisoned gift," the jaguar replied. "It's not worth it."

"Why do you even care?" Luciano snapped. "You don't favor two-handers."

That got the jaguar to lift his head and the wolf finally got a look at his face, which did nothing to change the wolf's opinion that he was dangerous. His nose was still healing from a slash and the side of his muzzle had a line of lighter fur over a scar. The eyes held Luciano the most—golden orbs that seemed to see right through him. There was ancient pain hidden in those eyes, but one thing was missing from them: fear. Despite being faced with a wolf in full armor with his hackles up, the jaguar wasn't worried. It was Luciano that took a step back as the knowledge that the jaguar could and had a plan to kill him dawned on the wolf. Finally the jaguar pushed himself upright.

"Just some advice," he said before turning away. "The sword is cursed. Think about that."

The jaguar left without another word, leaving Luciano to ponder his words.

Two days later, Shadow's whiskers twitched in annoyance as the jaguar waited for his second match of the tournament to begin. His first match had been uneventful, memorable mostly for passing the young wolf he'd had words with previously as he left the arena. It was a shame the mercenary hadn't headed his advice, but he wasn't the jaguar's concern; he was here on Imperial business.

Shadow was part of an elite group of Imperial operatives known as the Nightguard, here on assignment—which was his own damn fault. The emperor's interest in such a gathering of fighters ended with the knowledge that it was simply a tournament. Shadow had pointed out just how dangerous the prize was. That had gotten the emperor's attention; if the Master Assassin of the Nightguard—Shadow's formal and rarely-used title—thought something was dangerous, then it was. With Count Tavian still in the Imperial City to explain why he was gathering mercenaries, it was a simple matter to call the stag back and suggest that the Imperial Rangers needed representation in his tournament. Tavian fell over himself to correct this oversight, and had been more than willing to accept Shadow as a representative of the rangers. And so here the assassin was, dueling with the most dangerous fighters in the Empire.

The gate lifted, pulling him back to the present, and the assassin strode out of the shadows and into the midday sun. He reached the center of the circle and reached up his chest just under his throat to touch the locket under his armor. He mentally recited his promise to himself, and dropped his paw back to his side. Properly prepared, there was no way he would die today.

He crouched down in the sand just as the general hum of conversation from the crowd began to die down. Shadow looked up to see count stepping out to the rail of his viewing box. The stag smiled out at the audience and waited for the polite applause to end. He raised his paws in a gesture that took in the arena.

"Friends! Welcome to the next bout in this tournament! On

this day we have a special treat for you!"

Shadow remained crouched, but looked around as the crowd cheered. The crowd was the usual mix of deer, foxes, and weasels that one expected from this region, plus a mix of wolves and others that had come to watch the tournament. The count introduced him by his formal title of "Lord Tra'iskia", a high-ranking member of the Imperial Rangers. That was his official cover, since the Nightguard didn't exist, though some of the participants in the tournament that dwelt in the shadow world likely knew who he was. Tavian's grin turned devious. He put both his paws on the rail before speaking again.

"As you can see, our competitor favors using two blades once! With that in mind, let's see how he does against multiple opponents at once!"

Shadow's ears folded back as the crowd broke into a roar. *You know*, he thought up at the count. *Bastard*. For a heartbeat, he wondered who had told the stag. The answer came quickly at the trumpets played a fanfare.

He waited, his tail carving arcs in the sand behind him. The two gates on the wall under the count's box opened and four figures emerged: a male and female wolf, a cougar, and a wolverine. All were armed with bastard swords and the cougar had a main gauche. Shadow remained crouched as he watched the quartet maneuver around him. His eyes moved back and forth between his opponents.

The crowd had begun to cheer when the quartet emerged, but the level of noise dropped to a buzz as Shadow remained still. The jaguar waited as his opponents encircled him, all of them tense and waiting to see what he would do. They twirled their blades as the jaguar finally straightened up and put his paws on his blades. He nodded at the cougar, who seemed to be the leader.

"We have agreed to disarming," the cougar said in the language of Uverther. He growled the words, as if they were an insult. The crowd probably mostly spoke Imperial Common, so they took it as such.

"I agree," Shadow returned in the same language. "No need

to take lives."

The cougar nodded and raised his blade with a roar. Shadow waited. For a heartbeat, nothing happened.

The attack came from the sides, the two wolves lunging forward in tandem. Shadow danced backwards, then to the side as the wolverine slashed vertically at him. The jaguar let out a relieved sigh; the group was on the same page—this engagement was for show and not for blood. "Show" was outside his usual trade, but it was nothing he couldn't handle. The wolves lunged again, slashing at him. This time Shadow didn't just step back, he drew his blades. With a flash of steel, the jaguar parried the wolves' attacks, then went on the offensive himself.

He drove forward against the wolf to his right, then switched to the left wolf. He kept his blades close, using quick slashes to push her back enough that he had space to intercept and turn aside the wolverine's next attack. The crowd cheered as the jaguar danced between all three of his attackers at once. Behind the melee the cougar paced, watching for an opportunity. Back on the defensive, Shadow took a moment to assess the situation.

All of his opponents were good, the jaguar admitted. His speed advantage with his lighter blades was neutralized by the multiple well-trained adversaries. But while the odds weren't in the jaguar's favor, this was hardly the first time he had faced this kind of situation—usually with much higher stakes. He was formulating a plan when he noticed that the trio fighting him kept glancing back at the cougar, who had still not engaged.

So this is *a free-for-all.* The jaguar gave a tight smile as he parried the wolverine's slash and lunged at the wolves. He focused his attention on the one to his right, deflecting a chest-level slash and stepping toward his attacker. The wolf, no doubt expecting the jaguar to continue his pattern of giving ground, was caught completely off guard. His eyes went wide as the pommel of Shadow's right hand sword connected with the side of his head, sending him sprawling. The crowd cheered as jaguar moved away from his fallen opponent, making sure to kick the fallen blade away to ensure the wolf honored their agreement.

The other wolf lunged forward point-first, attempting to

skewer the jaguar. Shadow danced aside and sent her sprawling by sweeping his leg through hers. Again he made sure the blade was out of reach, in case the wolf reconsidered the agreement in a moment of frustration. He spun and got his blades up in time to meet the wolverine's attack. The smaller fighter swung his weapon in tight arcs, keeping the jaguar off balance. Shadow dodged and deflected the strikes, and was just about to take the offensive when the cougar finally joined the fray.

Shadow had no choice but to give ground against the onslaught. The feline was bigger than his other companions, and so had no issue using his larger blade in one paw. Combined with the speed of the dagger in his off paw, the jaguar had to focus all his attention on keeping the new pace. The cougar got his dagger inside Shadow's guard, nicking the jaguar's chest piece just under the shoulder.

Shadow hopped back, opening the separation between them to more than a blade length. The cougar didn't press his attack, but simply smiled. Behind him, the wolverine looked on in frustration and puzzlement. The jaguar's own eyes narrowed. That attack wasn't aimed to disarm. The rules had changed. His opponent nodded.

"I will make this fair," the cougar said. "Know that there is a bounty for whoever takes you out of the tournament. Double for your head."

Behind the cougar, the wolverine's eyes went wide. He looked back and forth between the two felines, then shook his head and tossed his blade to the sand. The wolves, who had begun to stand, shared a look and remained seated. Shadow made no verbal response to the cougar; he simply nodded to the wolverine and gestured his opponent forward. The cougar's roar as he lunged was drowned out by the applause of the crowd. That applause grew even louder a few heartbeats later as the cougar dropped to the ground, blood from a cut on his head staining the sand.

Shadow sheathed his blades and stepped over the prone figure, pausing to check him for signs of life. The cougar was still breathing. The jaguar made his way over to the wolverine, who was holding his paws out in a gesture of peace. Shadow passed him without saying a word, to the relief of the fighter and the disappointment of the bloodthirsty crowd.

With the finals of the tournament two days away, the *Foamin' Dragon* tavern was crowded. Most were spectators, but there were a good deal of competitors who had dropped out of the tournament already. They acted as a buffer, making sure that the four remaining competitors had peace as they ate or drank.

Luciano sat alone at a table near the bar. The wolf's ears swiveled, taking in the sounds of the crowd as he took another pull of his ale. His eyes swept over the tavern, picking out possible threats. He saw two more of the final four competitors—the only one missing seemed to be that jaguar, Tra'iska. Nero Cassius, famed soldier in the Imperial Legion, held court at the bar with a pack of fellow wolves. He had come to Luciano's table an hour and two pints before to tell the mercenary that he was looking forward to their bout. They'd shaken paws and agreed that the fight didn't have to be to the death, something Luciano had been eager to agree to in spite of how most of his bouts had ended. Cassius's exploits were part of the reason he'd become a mercenary in the first place, and he'd not been happy with the thought that he might have to kill his idol. The grizzled wolf had laughed at that and joked that while he was glad to have inspired such a talented fighter, he would have been more glad if Luciano hadn't had to choose to live by the sword. They parted company, leaving Luciano to his meal and drinks.

Across the room, the massive caribou that Luciano heard called Saunn lurked. His eyes flicked back and forth across the tavern, as if expecting a fight. Around him a small heard of tough-looking deer of all types hovered. The wolf snarled into his ale—something about the caribou rubbed him the wrong way.

"You didn't take my advice," a voice said from next to him.

He looked up in time to see Tra'iska sit down across from him with an ale in his paw. The jaguar took a long pull from his mug and studied the wolf. Luciano set his own down and returned the other's gaze, choosing to ignore the feline's violation of his privacy.

"I don't regret it," the mercenary replied as he crossed his arms across his chest.

"I suppose not," the jaguar said. "You've done well. But it doesn't change the prize."

"The prize is worth it," Luciano growled, his ears folding back. "And no lies about it will change that."

"I did not lie. The blade is cursed."

"Its history says otherwise."

"History is written by the winners. And they sweep many things under the table."

Tra'iska stood up and stepped away without saying another word. Luciano snorted and turned his attention back to his drink. He was just about to call for another when a shadow fell on the table. He looked up to see Saunn towering over him.

"Don't got to worry about that cat," the caribou sneered. "But ya shoulda taken his advice."

"And I suppose I should be worried about some blowhard moose?"

"Ya should," the other snorted. "No one has walked away from a match with me."

"And yet I'm not," Luciano said with a sneer.

"Keep telling yerself that," Saunn replied with a mirthless smile. "You'll learn if ya can get past Cassius."

The caribou turned and took a step away from the table. Luciano decided that he disliked Saunn enough to tell him the truth. The wolf set down his mug hard enough that the other paused.

"You won't get past the jag. He's beat better than you in pairs."

The caribou froze and stiffened. He slowly turned to face the wolf, his fist tightening into a ball. Then he lunged at the mercenary. Luciano braced himself to move, but the blow never came. He looked up to see Tra'iska clutching Saunn's wrist. The jaguar and the caribou locked eyes, and a mug came flying from the direction of the mercenary's confederates. The ranger dodged it, but it struck a patron behind him. The caribou swung at the jaguar, and the brawl was on.

The badger that had been struck by the errant throw lunged towards them, only to be intercepted by the tournament dropouts that were milling about. On Luciano's other side, Saunn's confederates charged to their leader's aid as Tra'iska ducked the swing and retaliated with a body blow. Luciano didn't see any more of the jaguar, he reacted—flipping the table over and lunging at the charging deer. All around him, he heard the crash of furniture hitting walls and floor and mugs shattering.

The wolf tackled a sika deer to the ground before jumping up and smashing a red stag in the muzzle. Two more deer joined the fray, sending Luciano sprawling. As he fell, he saw a server dash out the front door—presumably to fetch the guard. He couldn't worry about that, he kicked out at the hooves of his attackers, sending one to the floor beside him as he blocked the blows from the other. The attack only lasted a moment, as the deer was barreled over by another wolf. Luciano scrambled to his paws, kicking one of his attackers before ducking under a broken table leg. As he came back up, the wolf got a glimpse of Tra'iska tangling with three deer. He lunged at the fox that swung the leg, slamming the vixen against the bar. He grunted as a mug hit his shoulder, and he kicked back at the rat that had smashed it against him.

The din of the brawl was shattered by a long howl. The combatants with more sensitive hearing cried out and covered their ears. Luciano looked over to see Cassius lowering his muzzle and glaring at the combatants. They began disengaging, but a yowl of pain brought their heads around. Saunn was kneeling against the bar, his arm pinned to it by a dagger of a design that Luciano had never seen before. The second thought the wolf had was to wonder how the hell anyone had gotten a weapon in here. He'd been searched thoroughly before he'd entered the tavern, and was sure everyone else had as well.

The answer came as Tra'iska snatched the weapon and put the blade to the caribou's throat. Saunn didn't move, almost as if he couldn't. Luciano's muzzle dropped open as he saw the jaguar's right forearm glowing through his sleeve. The jaguar had a dagger bound to him. That was not a typical magic...

"Tra'iska!" Cassius shouted.

The jaguar stopped, leaving the blade pressed against Saunn's throat, but looked back at the legionnaire. His long tail flicked in agitation. The wolf gave him a warning look and shook his head. His ears folded back as he took a step forward.

"Not that way," Cassius said. "His Majesty wouldn't approve. Beat the fool on the sand. That is the way he'd want."

Tra'iska continued to look back, seeming to consider the wolf's words. For the first time, it dawned on Luciano that the ranger and the legionnaire knew each other. The mercenary's ears swiveled as he looked between the wolf and the jaguar. The jaguar nodded to his fellow soldier. The glow on his arm faded and the dagger vanished. Saunn sighed and began to relax, as if he'd just regained control of his body. Tra'iska wasn't done. The jaguar slammed the caribou's head into the bar.

The mercenary rebounded and fell to the floor, points on his rack cracking as they kept his head from smacking the wood of the floor. The jaguar was on him before he could recover. Saunn could only put his paw to his nose before his widened eyes met those of Tra'iska. The jag put a paw close to those eyes and let his claws extend. The caribou started shaking.

"Get out," the ranger whispered. "The wolf saved your life. Show up to the finals and I take it. Understood?"

The caribou nodded and took off as soon as the jaguar gave him space. He shot through the doors of the tavern like an arrow, holding his bloody snout. Cassius looked after him and sighed.

"Not exactly what I had in mind. But I guess congratulations on making it to the finals are in order."

"He may still try and collect the bounty," Tra'iska replied. He picked up a chair and set it back upright. "Lots of them have been that stupid."

Around them order was being restored. Most of those involved in the fight were filing out, limping and rubbing bruises. A few were imitating the jaguar and setting tables and chairs back upright. Luciano watched as the two soldiers continued talking.

"Why is there a bounty on you?"

"I know things."

"You know a lot of things you're not supposed to." The wolf let out a barking laugh. "What specifically?"

Tra'iska studied the wolf and dropped himself into the chair. His eyes flicked over to Luciano and then back to Cassius. His ears flicked, his tail twitched, and he licked his fangs in thought. Finally he sighed.

"Ashrune is dangerous. Neither of you want it."

The wolves looked at each other, puzzled and a little annoyed. Luciano sneered at the jaguar. Tra'iska made no response.

"You said that when we first met. Didn't dissuade me then. It will not now."

Cassius locked eyes with the jaguar. Tra'iska met his gaze without flinching. The contest continued for a long time before the wolf sniffed and looked down at the bar. Luciano let out the breath he hadn't realized he'd been holding.

"I believe you," the soldier said finally. "I wish you'd say plainly what the danger is. But you wouldn't be here if it wasn't true."

Tra'iska said nothing as he played with a piece of broken crockery on the bar. The only sounds in the room where the crackle of the fire and the quiet thump of the jaguar's tail on the floor. Cassius looked back at the jaguar, and then back at Luciano. He spun the fragment and stepped away.

"However, I too must continue. If this weapon is enough of a danger that you are here, it is a danger to the Empire. It is my duty to protect the Empire, no matter the cost to myself."

"The cost will be great," Tra'iska muttered as the wolf walked past him to depart.

Cassius paused, but said nothing for a long moment. Then his head turned to the jaguar. Tra'iska didn't meet the other's gaze, instead staring at Luciano.

"If that is true," Cassius whispered. "I place myself in your paws. I trust you to set things right."

With that, the wolf strode out of the tavern, leaving the ranger and the mercenary facing each other.

"Nothing you can say will dissuade me," Luciano growled.

"And I'd prefer not to kill you," the jaguar replied. He slapped his paws against his thighs and stood up. "Which leaves us at an impasse. I will see you then."

With that, he turned and headed to the door. He pushed it open when Luciano barked at him. He looked back at the wolf.

"That dagger," the mercenary licked his lips.

"Save your breath," the ranger sighed. "You don't want it bound to you. It nearly killed me."

Without another word he was out the doors and into the night, leaving Luciano alone with the thought.

As he stood in the competitors' entrance waiting for the gate to lift, it dawned on Shadow that he hated the Staergrad Arena. It was a crude imitation of the arena in the Imperial City, done in the local sandstone rather than the concrete of the capital's stadium. They had white-washed the stone to try and give it the same look— but with the paint flecking off, driving home to the assassin how crude it was. It was not a place he'd pick to die in. Of course, a member of the Nightguard wasn't often allowed the luxury of choosing the place of their death.

He closed his eyes and let his paw drift up to touch his locket. The locket contained a portrait of his fallen mate, Raj'arr—a fellow member of the Nightguard. Raj'arr had been a painter of considerable talent in addition to his skill as an assassin. But those skills hadn't been enough to protect him, and he died almost a year ago in Shadow's arms. The jaguar's fingers tightened against his armor, making a fist over the locket as he recited his promise to the dying Raj'arr. With that last bit of armor in place, the jaguar stepped up to the bars of the gate, ready for the battle he'd known was coming. He wondered what form it would take, and let his eyes drift to the other competitors to find an answer.

Cassius was still as he knelt behind his gate. He leaned on the traditional Imperial gladius, his nose pointed to the sand, his eyes closed, his muzzle moving in what Shadow guessed to be a prayer. Cassius finished and stood, straightening his Legion armor as he did so. He met Shadow's gaze and gave the Nightguard the Imperial salute before sheathing his blade. He spoke again, and this time Shadow saw the words: *By the grace of the gods, into your paws I place my fate.* The jaguar nodded and suppressed a shudder. He knew that line: the soldier's parting. Cassius expected Shadow to ensure he committed no dishonor. Whatever that took. The assassin turned his gaze to the final competitor.

Luciano—in full plate armor save for his head—was pacing behind his gate, ears swiveling and tail lashing. His eyes kept flicking back and forth between Shadow and Cassius. He finally stilled when he saw the jaguar's eyes on him. He glared at Shadow with his fangs bared. Shadow returned his gaze without flinching, and held it for a moment before deliberately turning his attention to his blades. He doubted the wolf actually thought his display would intimidate the jaguar. If he did, it was better to dissuade him of the notion now rather than embarrass him on the sand. Shadow looked up and saw the wolf persisting in the show. He sighed. So it was the young mercenary then. Not unexpected, but still a shame. Luciano saw the disappointment on his face and frowned, but any further interaction was forestalled by applause from the crowd.

Shadow's entrance was directly across from the Count's box, which gave him a full view of the stag as he raised a paw to acknowledge the crowd. The ovation went on for a few moments, and Shadow's attention drifted past Tavian to the cougar standing behind him. The cougar still had Ashrune, and was staring back at the jaguar with a smirk on his muzzle. Shadow kept his face neutral. It was almost time. His tail twitched behind him in anticipation, and a healthy amount of fear.

"My friends!" Tavian called out when the noise died down. "It has been a long journey, but today that journey comes to an end! For the past two weeks, the greatest sword masters in the Empire have displayed their skill for your enjoyment and the ultimate prize! Now, only three remain!"

The stag paused as the crowd cheered. Shadow looked up at them, but with the sun almost directly overhead they were just shadows. Even their scents were a confusing mishmash. The jaguar's attention returned to their host as Tavian shouted his name. The gate in front of him lifted, and he stepped out onto the arena sand. Cassius and Luciano waited out in the middle of the ring. The older wolf nodded at the feline, his ears rotating toward the count as he kept his eyes on the mercenary. Luciano was no longer pacing, but his hackles were up and his teeth were bared as he glared at his two opponents. Again, Shadow ignored the wolf and kept his eyes on the cougar behind Tavian.

"Easy, pup," Cassius soothed before he followed the assassin's lead. "This is sport. No need to get worked up."

"Today these remaining masters will demonstrate their skills at the highest level in three-way combat!" Tavian shouted. He paused for the applause from the crowd, and Shadow saw a smirk spread across the stag's muzzle. The jaguar's tail flicked as a bad feeling grew on him.

"The ultimate prize awaits! The legendary blade Ashrune! But with such a reward in reach, these competitors must risk all to claim the blade and the title of the greatest sword master in the Empire!"

Shadow felt the jolt of energy pass through him as his body prepared for action. According to Raj'arr, despite the jaguar feeling his whole body tense, the only movement at these times came from his whiskers and nose twitching. The assassin let out a hiss of warning. Cassius's ear swiveled, but the count cut off any response.

"And so! The final match of this tournament must be all or nothing! Our competitors will leave with the prize, or not at all. For this match is to the death!"

With that, the stag made a chopping motion with his paw. Over the roar of the crowd, a gong sounded. Cassius stared up at the count's booth, his ears back, his muzzle open as if he was about to protest. No words came.

Shadow was already moving, but the dagger the assassin

drew on instinct wasn't enough to stop the blow from the mercenary. It did turn the strike, so that it was the flat of the blade that connected rather than the edge. Cassius went sprawling to the sand. The jaguar lunged, flinging the dagger in his paw as he drew his own swords. Luciano hopped back, the dagger grazing his cheek. The wolf snarled at the assassin now standing guard over his fallen prey.

Shadow pointed his right blade at the mercenary, and a flash of orange light passed from hilt to tip. Luciano blinked—the wolf knew what it meant: Shadow was using enchanted blades. He shifted, his eyes locked on the jaguar as he processed this new information. But the wolf didn't back down. His hackles remained up and he bared his teeth again. His eyes remained locked on Shadow, and he followed as the jaguar took a step to his left—away from Cassius's prone body.

"I told you Ashrune was dangerous," Shadow said, risking a quick glance back at the fallen wolf. The sand moved in little waves in front of his muzzle. "Do you finally believe me?"

The only answer he got was a snarl as the crowd chanted for blood. Luciano's grip tightened on his sword, but still he hesitated. Shadow took another step to his left. Again the wolf followed. The jaguar smirked.

"Or do you really think that's your own voice in your head telling you to kill?"

Luciano blinked, then shook his head as if it pained him. The shouts from the crowd grew louder and more intense. Shadow looked up at them. He had to get the situation under control—now. He lowered his blade.

"I'm tired of this game!" he shouted. The crowd went dead silent and Luciano went still. "I've watched this one fight. You know as well as I that he can't beat me. Nor can you!"

A chuckle broke the silence. Up in the count's booth, the cougar advanced to the rail and grinned down at the combatants. Shadow glared up at him.

"This is between you and me. It always has been."

"You denied me," the cougar growled. "We would have been great together, assassin. But instead you keep those butter knives of yours."

"They brought me home more times than I can count," the jaguar returned. Behind him, Luciano stared at this strange debate.

The cougar vaulted the railing and landed on the sands in a crouch. Shadow brought his blades into a defensive stance as the cougar stood and advanced. The only sound was the *click* of the cougar's armor as he walked.

"They will fail you," the cougar said. "They don't even have names."

"They have not failed me."

"But others things have, perhaps. Where is that caracal partner of yours anyway? I've not seen him all tournament."

"I'm not playing your game any longer, Ashrune. You are coming with me." Shadow's paws tightened on his hilts at the mention of Ra'jarr.

"What?" Luciano barked.

"Oh, you're not playing my game any longer?" The cougar laughed as he drew the sword from his back. "After weeks of playing it, you're stopping now?"

Shadow snarled. "You would have run."

The cougar, formerly the captain of the Staergrad Guard— now nothing more than the tool of the blade he wielded, paused and returned the snarl. "I'm not running now."

"Prove it. You and me. No one else."

Ashrune cackled again. His gaze drifted past Shadow. "Do you hear that, pup? He wants to deny you your prize!"

"Don't listen," the jaguar called. "Ashrune only cares about is its own hunger—not you."

"I offer much to those that feed me well."

"At great cost."

"And still you hold back. Still keeping secrets, Nightguard. It matters not. I keep no secrets from my bearer."

Behind him, Shadow heard a yip of surprise at the mention of the Nightguard. Clearly Luciano had enough connections on the wrong side of the law to know the name. The tip of the jaguar's tail smacked the sand in agitation—it was time for action. In front of the jaguar, Ashrune pointed.

"You denied me, assassin, and now you'll lock me away. I will not surrender to you. So you, wolf. Aid me in killing this fool, and I will be yours. Together, we will become a legend."

No answer came, only a moment of silence. It went on just long enough for Shadow to glance up and see that those in the crowd were staring straight ahead, their eyes unfocused. He hissed as he dropped into a crouch—Ashrune had not been able to affect the minds of so many in their last encounter; the blade had fed too well during the tournament. The jaguar's body tensed, his tail stilled, his mind cleared. He waited for the sign that the battle was about to begin.

It came in a whisper of leather and a clink of steel. Shadow spun to parry the lunge from Luciano before whirling back to block the slash from Ashrune. The jaguar hopped back as he repelled the next set of attacks, pulling the contest away from Cassius. The noise of the crowd returned as Ashrune gave Shadow his entire focus. The assassin continued to give ground as his blades flashed to keep up with his opponents' attacks.

He growled as he parried a slash from Ashrune, tried to follow with a stab of his own, but was forced to intercept a cut at his hip from Luciano before blocking another attack from the cougar. Ashrune hadn't been this skilled in their last encounter; the soul-stealing blade had gained much in the intervening years. He deflected a vertical cut from the cougar and thrust forward, slashing the tabard before blocking the wolf's next assault. His mind whirled as he tried to come up with a plan.

It should have been simple: win the fight, killing his opponents if needed. But Ashrune's presence complicated things. The blade always had the ability to steal the soul of those it killed and influence its wielder, but now it seemed that proximity was enough to allow the blade to feed and control those around it. From his earlier encounter with Ashrune, Shadow knew that first part—but the sword's abilities had grown beyond what he had expected. At least now he understood why so many duels in the tournament had ended in death. So far, he'd been able to resist Ashrune's influence. Would he if Luciano's soul was given to the blade?

The wolf was good. It was no wonder the Emperor was interested in him. Given time and experience, he would easily become a great sword master—likely the best with a bastard sword once Cassius retired. But today, to Shadow's practiced eye, the flaws were evident: a parry that wasn't a crisp as it should be, an awkward shuffle to get his hind paws in the correct position for a slash, a half moment of hesitation when a strike was blocked as he planned his next move, a swish of his tail that indicated an attack. In time, these would go away—but today, Shadow could exploit them. Except he couldn't, because killing Luciano would feed his energy and knowledge straight to Ashrune.

Killing the cougar who wielded Ashrune would be a safer option, except for the possibility that the wolf would claim the blade. He snarled, blocking slashes from both his attackers as his mind raced. He was giving too much ground—soon he'd be backed against the arena wall, and when that happened the end was inevitable.

Shadow swore at himself, even as his blades kept dancing. The greatest member of the Nightguard, the Emperor's personal agent, the assassin with a plan for everything defeated because he had no plan. For a quarter of a heartbeat, he was almost glad Raj'arr wasn't here to see him reduced to this. He regretted the thought even as it formed.

You'll find a way, he heard his former mate's voice in his head. *You always do. That is why you are the best.*

The jaguar wasn't feeling like the best at the moment. He staggered back and only half-parried a strike from Luciano which forced his arm wide. The tip of the wolf's sword slid along the inside of right forearm, parting the leather thongs of his bracer and dropping the armor to the sand. The crowd roared as they sensed that first blood would soon be spilled. Shadow growled as his eye flicked to his now-bare, fur checking for damage. None that he could see, no marks beyond the brand of the Nightguard insignia…

His conscious thoughts ground to a halt, even as his arms

kept his blades moving on instinct. His brand. The one that bound the Shadowedge to him. The Shadowedge—a dagger with a very useful enchantment for an assassin.

And the situation he found himself in now.

A savage grin split the jaguar's muzzle. Ashrune didn't know about the Shadowedge; their pervious encounter had been before the dagger was bound to him. The cougar noticed the grin and disengaged. The entranced Luciano, his eyes slightly unfocused under the blade's influence, followed a heartbeat later. Shadow stared them down, working his blades through a series of spirals as he summoned their enchantments. One blade caught fire while the other frosted over.

"Finally decided to take this seriously?" Ashrune sneered. "I was beginning to wonder if you were going to actually put up a fight."

"Sorry to make you wait."

The jaguar lunged, driving the cougar back. The black feline kept the tawny cat on the defensive with rapid strikes that barely allowed Ashrune to keep up. The former guard captain snarled as he blocked the assassin's assault. The cougar's eyes darted over Shadow's shoulder, the only warning the jaguar had of Luciano returning to the fight. A smirk of triumph passed over Ashrune's muzzle as the assassin spun to face the wolf.

The smile likely died as Shadow risked a brief moment of imbalance to lash out with a kick that caught the cougar in the midsection and sent him stumbling back. The sound of air leaving Ashrune's lungs, followed by the clatter of armor, told Shadow that his foe was out of the fight for the moment.

A moment was all he needed.

Luciano was good, but Shadow was better. And the Nightguard had an advantage the wolf didn't have time to overcome: his enchanted swords. The mercenary was shaking his head, coming back to his senses as Ashrune's control slipped. He still slashed at the jaguar, but it was a weak attack that even off balance Shadow blocked cleanly with his offhand sword. Frost ran up the wolf's blade as it was deflected into a vertical guard.

A streak of orange scythed across the sword and the blade

parted. The crowd gasped in shock. Luciano was frozen for a pair of heartbeats, staring at the shard of his weapon. Shadow was on him before the wolf's eyes came returned to him.

The jaguar dropped his flame-enchanted sword, focusing his thoughts just enough to summon the Shadowedge. The brand glowed as the dagger appeared in his paw. Even as Luciano realized what had happened, Shadow was inside his guard and lunging for his throat. Even completely off guard, the wolf managed to dodge enough that the dagger strike only nicked his skin—but that was all the assassin wanted. Even as he passed, the mercenary went stiff as the dagger's enchantment paralyzed him.

Several feet away, Ashrune was collecting himself and was already to one knee. But even as the stunned Luciano crumpled to the sand, Shadow spun and flung the Shadowedge with practiced ease. The dagger flew past the cougar, grazing his cheek. His eyes went wide as his body went stiff and crumpled to the ground. The black blade clattered next to him, out of his paws. The crowd went silent.

Shadow straightened and blew out a deep breath as he surveyed the carnage. He retrieved and sheathed his swords before stepping over to Luciano. The wolf was still breathing. The jaguar sighed in relief before turning his attention to his true foe. The jaguar padded over to the fallen cougar and mentally prepared himself. He took one final breath and reached down, then took hold of Ashrune's hilt. The sword's mental voice was like a scream inside his head, but he smiled as he stood back up with the sword in his paw.

You're mine now, the jaguar hissed, his fangs bared as he dismissed the Shadowedge.

The blade made a last desperate assault to take over the assassin's mind. But with the price of surrender lying next to him, he would not give in. He twirled the black blade before sliding it into his belt. The sword's voice went silent. Next to him, the cougar shuddered and went still. There wasn't enough left of the captain's mind to keep him alive once the blade changed owners.

"What the hell took you so long?" a voice broke into the

silence. Shadow turned to find Cassius pushing himself off the sand. "I was thinking you were going keep at little game of yours all day."

"Sorry," the jaguar replied. "Took a bit to think of winning a sword fight with a knife."

"And only you could win a sword fight with a knife," the soldier chuckled. "You didn't kill the youngster, did you?"

"Paralysis," the assassin said. "Starting wearing off when I dismissed the dagger."

"Good." The wolf stood. Around them, the crowd began to chant for them to fight. Cassius looked up at them. "I guess we do still have to finish this."

He knelt down with his head down and his ears folded back in the traditional lupine gesture of submission. He held his blade out to Shadow and waited. Above them, the crowd continued chanting: some calling Cassius's name, others calling for the wolf's death. Shadow let them continue for a moment before he reached out and took the blade. He held the point against the wolf's neck for a heartbeat before he stepped back and offered Cassius the hilt.

"Always a flair for the dramatic," the soldier said with a laugh as he stood. He took the sword and sheathed it. "Well, the tournament is over and you're the victor. At the celebration, you can tell me what all the fuss was about."

"It will have to wait," Shadow replied. "Ashrune is too dangerous to leave in the open."

"So I suppose you're off right away. Well, I'll take care of the youngster and this lot. What are you going to do with that thing?"

Whatever it is, you know I'll get out of it. I always do.

You'll find that difficult this time, Shadow answered the blade. "Best you don't know."

"Very well."

Cassius offered his right paw. Shadow reached out and clasped the other's forearm. Without another word, the jaguar turned and strode into the shadows under the arena gate.

The Lord of Strange Deaths

Steve Cotterill

The picnic was laid out next to the river and the lords and ladies sat in the sunshine eating sandwiches and sipping lemonade. It was summer, and Augusta Chatnoir's set had fled the city in favour of the fresh countryside air. The Great Stink had engulfed London once again, despite Bazelgette's sewer system, and so they returned to their great houses and spent the summer months hobnobbing around each other's homes. It was an odd time, one where aristocrats arranged marriages and made connections.

Augusta sat at the edge of a blanket, her tail curled around her. Her whiskers twitched as she sipped her lemonade and absently straightened her hat, where it perched between her ears. She was bored, listening to the gossip, and found herself examining her claws as Jemima Polseand waxed lyrical about the dashing young drake she was going to marry. She waved her hand around to show off her engagement ring while the other ladies cooed over it, exclaiming how lucky she was.

Privately, Augusta wished she could do something else; even reading a book would be more fun than listening to wedding talk. Why did women go gaga over the things?

"My Hector hasn't got the ring yet, but we're going to be married next year," Lucinda Dogslip said, admiring the ring.

Augusta allowed herself a small smile; it was good to see Hector make a promising match. She was fond of the beagle but he was a hapless creature, stuck as a sub-lieutenant in the navy for most of his career. Lucinda would keep him on the straight and narrow.

Lucinda waved, suddenly. "Hector, over here, darling."

"Dear heart," he called, waving back as he emerged from the house. There was no denying he looked dashing in navy blue. He bowed and the ladies beamed up at him; even Augusta was impressed.

Sweeping in, Hector embraced Lucinda to whisper sweet nothings in her ear. The two were obviously smitten, but still, there was something about Hector's manner that gave Augusta pause. Something in his gaze seemed troubled.

Rising on a whim, she said, "I think I'm going to get some shade, ladies."

They looked up, almost as they'd forgotten she was there, and made the appropriate niceties when one of the host's family withdraws. Augusta knew she wouldn't be missed; her reputation as one of life's oddities had been established back at school. It was simply accepted she was going to be a little strange. Still, with a history that reached back to the Conquest in 1066, strangeness was expected, even encouraged.

Besides, this way Hector could unburden himself discreetly, which was probably the only reason he had for attending the party. The two were old friends, and her family had helped him out a few crises over the years. Perhaps once he was married, there would be fewer of those.

She reached the veranda and occupied a discreet, shady spot that had been a favourite of her great, great grandmother's when she had entertained her lovers. It didn't take Hector long to join her, swapping his cap from hand to hand. "Ah, Augusta, I'm glad I found you."

"I thought you might need a friendly ear," she replied with a glint in her eye.

He gave a half bark of agreement and shook his head, chagrined. "I don't mean to be beastly, but I was hoping you might help me out?"

"I rather thought you might need my help," she drawled. "You're like an open book."

He blushed, tail drooping. "Really, gosh. That's not good, is it?"

"It depends on your point of view. I imagine it's one of the reasons Lucinda adores you." She patted his arm, consolingly. "Let's see, if it were money, you'd go to Rafe because he has the Devil's own luck with the horses." Privately, she wondered if the old cat magic had rubbed off on her brother. He wasn't lucky exactly, but everyone else around him seemed to have the worst luck. That affected horse races, games of chance, and angry husbands who found him bedding their spouses. "If it was your health, you'd be in Harley Street seeing your quack." Glancing at him, she asked, "So what do you need my help with?"

He shifted on his feet. "Well, a few months ago I was transferred to Intelligence by the Sea Lords, working under First Lady Regina Diomedeidae."

"That seems like a unique position for you to be in— working in Intelligence, I mean."

"Steady on, I have got a brain in the old noggin, you know," he protested. "Besides, I was in charge of maps and reports. They didn't trust old Hector with anything sensitive." He looked down as soon as the words were out of his mouth.

"Except for one thing, something you've managed to lose," Augusta said, quietly. "What was it, some important orders?"

He shook his head and made a pretence of being fascinated by a plant, sniffing its yellow blooms. "No, no nothing like that. It was, ah, just a seal."

Her eyes widened. "A seal, presumably not the flippered kind."

"Ah, yes. Silly old Hector had it in his bag, you see, had to take it out of the office so the dear old albatross could affix it to some orders and then had to take it back to the office." His tail drooped as he spoke. "But, well, I've had some…" he coughed.

"I can imagine, so you stopped off to see your quack and left the bag with his secretary or forgot to take it with you?" She twirled her parasol, idly. "When you went back it had vanished, and you weren't sure if you'd had it when you left, but the underground company doesn't have it, nor does the cab company you used to travel from your chief's home to Harley Street. Ergo, someone took it, or you actually did leave it on the underground and it was stolen."

"Gosh, how do you work all that out?" Hector asked.

"You're a creature of habit, dear, it doesn't take much work to know you stick to the same routine. You always take a cab to see the grand old bird of Naval Intelligence, and you always travel by underground when you're in the heart of London. You also have a habit of leaving your bag, hat, or cane behind."

He coloured. "Ah, I see what you mean. I am a bit of a silly, aren't I?"

She kissed his cheek. "We wouldn't love you if you weren't, dear. Is there anything else you need to tell me?"

"I don't think so," he said. "Can you help? It would get me out of an awful pickle."

Squeezing his hand, she said, "I'll see what I can do."

"Thanks awfully!"

"Run along now, Lucinda will be missing you." She smiled, encouragingly. As he left, she let the smile dwindle away and she sighed, pressing a hand to her brow. The situation was typical Hector, if only it weren't a matter of national security. She hurried inside and found Rafe in the hall, bent over the telephone. "I have to go upstairs for a moment, can you cover with Mama?"

He raised an eyebrow, "Are you up to something, Sis?"

"I'm afraid so, the usual." All the Chatnoir children knew the family business. Every member of the clan had been part of it, going back generations. Only fusspots like Mama thought it odd for girls to take part; she worried about Augusta's future. As the sole daughter, she was to be protected, not allowed to face danger. For all Mama Chatnoir's own adventures as a girl, she had grown to be keenly aware of the role of women and had pushed for her daughter to be raised as a proper lady.

Fortunately, nobody else gave a fig about that and the girl had been tutored in cryptography, politics, and botany. By the age of ten she could identify poisons and the plants they came from, and identify a dozen sects, cults, and secret societies that threatened the Empire. Her Governesses were specially chosen for their skills, and the young Augusta learnt swordplay, archery, and shooting along with a number of hand to fighting hand skills. Her time at finishing school had been leavened with other lessons, and her first assignments for the Black Room, the spy ring the Chatnoir clan worked for. Now she was on call, like her seven siblings, for the good of Queen, Country, and Empire.

She slipped up to her room, ringing the bell to summon her maid, Molly, who had been with her ever since finishing school and knew everything. She had been vetted by the Room and quietly trained in weapons maintenance and other things maid schools unaccountably missed off their curricula.

As she waited, Augusta opened a secret cabinet in the wall and removed some small cases. Opening them, she drew out her weapons—a pair of Peacemakers from America, and her sword, a long slim blade forged by a master craftsman. She drew it and made some practice strokes, feeling the sword's balance.

Halfway through her tenth stroke, Molly arrived. She blanched and shut the door behind her. "Miss, what if Her Ladyship saw?"

Augusta shrugged. "We'd have to deal with it later. We're leaving tonight."

"Where are we going?" Molly asked, already moving into action.

"London." Augusta slid the sword back into its scabbard. "We'll need to see Drummond."

The tortoiseshell nodded, already packing. The case's false bottom was open, and she slipped the weapons inside. She placed clothes on top, working as quickly as she could.

"Thank you, dear. When you're done, call Drummond and tell him we need to meet." Augusta began to change, pulling on her travelling clothes.

"Yes, Miss," Molly said, bobbing a curtsey. "May I use the telephone in the Annexe, Miss?"

Augusta nodded. "Yes, once my brother's finished it with it. I swear he's calling his bookies again." Sweeping down to the parlour, she found Rafe and Miles enjoying the shade as they smoked cigarettes and read slim penny dreadfuls. Neither man was the sociable type, and it was rare to see them at home. Rafe spent almost all his time working for the Room in London, while Miles had enlisted in the army, putting his training to work teaching sappers in the Royal Engineers.

"I'm leaving," she said. "I have business in London."

"Oh?" Rafe raised an eyebrow. "What's pulled your tail, Augusta?

Briefly, she filled them in on Hector's problem, nodding sympathetically as they swore at the dog's idiocy.

Later, mounting her steam car, she glanced back and saw Rafe watching her leave, loitering on the porch, nonchalantly smoking a cigarette. He waved as she pulled away. She waved back and turned her face away. London, and work were waiting.

Dr Mallard's office was quiet. Augusta was the only patient, kept waiting by the koala receptionist as he spent more time reading the betting papers than paying attention to his work. Occasionally he looked over the paper, eyeing her. She sat, in her best Sunday suit, staring at her paws with an uncanny focus. An initial glance around the room had confirmed that Mallard was legitimate, for a quack anyway. There were framed certificates attesting to his credentials on the walls, and the place fairly oozed with the tranquillity of private medicine.

Not that there was really any other kind. Charity hospitals were few and far between, the services they offered basic in comparison to private clinics. Closing her eyes, she listened to the sound of vacuum tubes in the room beyond as Mallard worked on a patient.

A little while later a large ox woman emerged the room, leaning heavily on a crutch. Her foot, swaddled in bandages, protruded from her under crinoline. The doctor guided her out of his consulting room, hovering as she paid for the appointment. He smiled around his bill and ruffled his feathers, looking pleased with himself.

Alighting his gaze on her, he beckoned her. "Ah, Miss Chatnoir, would you care to step into my consulting room?" His tones were rich and with a rolling Scottish cadence.

She followed him, leaving her little case behind.

The consulting room was far more opulent than the waiting area, a mahogany desk nearly filling the back portion of the room. Mallard retreated behind it, seating himself in a leather chair. Once she was settled, in an equally grand chair, he leant forward.

"Now dear lady, what seems to be the problem?"

Augusta hesitated, looking down at her lap. She artfully twisted a ring on her finger, one that passed closely enough to be an engagement ring. "Well, it's just that I'm getting married soon, and I'm awfully worried."

"Why is that, my dear?" Mallard asked, smoothly. "Is there something that might impact on your nuptials?"

She forced herself to blush, "A friend of mine said her fiancé came to see you about his," she dropped her voice, "downstairs problem, and that you might be able to help me."

He smiled, consolingly. "I do specialise in matters of that nature, my dear. I would need to know more before I could guarantee my assistance, however."

Augusta let her hand tremble as she reached out to rest it on the desk. "Well, it's like this, Doctor. A few years ago I had an…error of judgement. My parents had arranged a marriage for me, to an American who seemed like a good-hearted, sincere man. He was beautiful, Doctor, and so smart. It was like talking to a genius." She dropped her gaze again, and with her free hand plucked her handkerchief from a pocket and dabbed at her eyes, to hide the lack of tears. "I was weak, Doctor. I let him bed me, and now I'm worried my new fiancée will notice on our wedding night."

He nodded, reaching out across the vast desk to pat her hand. "I see. Well, I don't think it's anything to worry about."

"You don't?" She lowered the handkerchief, widening her eyes. "But, but, what do you mean?" She shifted on the seat, feeling uncomfortable. She glanced out of the corner of her eye. A chair like this should be one of the most comfortable things to sit in, and yet it wasn't.

"Your situation is less rare than you'd think, and easier to fix too," he said. "A simple procedure should repair the…part in question, and your beau need never know." He removed his spectacles and cleaned them, vigorously.

Augusta thought he looked slightly flustered, for all his charm. As he busied himself with his glasses, she looked around the room. After a moment's scrutiny, she realised a lot of the opulence was flash, expensive coverings on cheap furniture. The whole office looked alarmingly temporary, as if Mallard could pack the enterprise up in a matter of hours and move, or just abandon it. Idly, she wondered how many offices he'd occupied over the years.

Another door led to what she assumed was the treatment room, and as there was no sign of Hector's attaché case, she threw herself back into her role. "Might, might, I see your facilities? One hears so many stories about how horrible these places can be, and it would set my mind at rest."

The doctor placed his glasses back on his beak and rose with a nod. "Well, of course. It's only natural to be a bit nervous, though I can assure you there's nothing to fear." He opened the door to the next room, revealing a white-washed room, with a single operating table in the centre and a series of machines—rented, she guessed—set around the outside. There was a small gallery on each side of the room, where people could watch the operations.

"You won't let anyone watch my operation will you, Doctor?" she asked, a little breathlessly, as if her first thought was her reputation.

There was no sign of Hector's bag.

As Mallard explained what would happen, taking pains to emphasise the cleanliness he practiced and that her privacy would be respected, she let the words wash over her, already thinking about where to search next. Unless Mallard had hidden it in a safe, the bag wasn't here.

Or perhaps that it was no longer here, she amended. Something like an attaché case was easy to lose, especially for Hector. During his time as a navigator, he'd lost the Isle of

Wight, and France. She supposed it was one of those things where he'd been promoted until he couldn't cause any more trouble. Which meant he'd probably be an admiral in five years if she could save him from the noose.

A clock sounded the hour and she started, checking her watch. "Oh my, I'm sorry, Doctor, I have to rush. I've got a dress fitting."

Retreating to the office and then waiting area, she swept out, her bag apparently forgotten. She shut the door and hurried down the stairs to the near-empty street. Placing a hand over her face to keep the stench out, she waited, but no one followed to return her bag.

As predicted, she thought.

Some quiet inquiries had confirmed Hector had been in possession of the bag up until this point. The doctor's office had been where the trail had gone cold. That meant nothing, of course, especially now she had seen what sort of characters the doctor and his assistant were.

"Did you find out anything, Miss?" Molly asked as Augusta met her in the tea room at the corner where she sat alone. It was a different world to the one the young noblewoman was used to. Oilskin cloth-covered tables and cast-iron chairs filled the cafe. Faded prints of seascapes and adverts for tea covered the walls.

"Nothing substantial. What did the General Medical Council say about Mallard?" Augusta sipped a cup of tea and helped herself to a slice of cake.

"He looks legitimate, no warnings about malpractice. As far as I can tell, he's never lost a patient, or stolen a body for vivisection."

Augusta eyed her. "Next you'll be telling me he wasn't a real student and never decorated a statue of Gladstone with a chamberpot."

Molly coughed and hid a smile. "I don't think the records have that information, Miss."

"Shame, they should." Swallowing a mouthful of cake, she added, "But then that wouldn't be held at the GMC, would it?"

"What did you find out?" Molly poured herself a cup and

sipped it sparingly.

"The whole thing smells of a flimflam," Augusta said after another bite of cake. "They're set up to vanish at a moment's notice if they have to, and the receptionist's more interested in *Bell's Life in London* and *Sporting Chronicle*. I'd wager the equipment there's all on loan, or worse, stolen."

Outside, the thick yellow fog began to rise, cloaking the street. The headlights of steam carriages began to appear, shining beams cutting through the pea-souper. They barely penetrated, but inside the tea room they could be seen, in the same way the heavy engines could be heard clanking as they drove the carriages. A siren sounded, blaring out over the streets.

A shop girl, a chubby hamster, coughed discreetly. "Please, Miss, we have to shut up early on account of the fog. When it's like this, we have to clear out."

"I didn't realise it was so bad here," Augusta said.

"Yes, Milady, there's a new law about it. Ma says one of the bigwigs finally saw what it was like here, when they're usually off in the country shooting and hunting instead of working." The girl blushed suddenly as if she realised she'd spoken out of turn.

Augusta smiled and pressed a five-pound note into the girl's hand. "Here take this for the tea and your time. You don't seem to have many patrons."

The girl glanced down, her eyes widening at the money. "Miss, you shouldn't."

"I should and have. You're obviously struggling, and I won't have you going out of business because of the vagaries of the season." It was obvious the cafe would be filled normally with middle-class ladies taking tea, but they would be at the seaside, or in the country now. "This time of year must be very hard for you."

Molly rose from the table and slung a waterproof cape over her shoulders. She held one out to Augusta and set cases containing respirators on the table. The London smog wasn't safe to breathe, but if they were to find out what Mallard was up to, they would have to brave it.

Mallard was easy to follow. He was swaddled in a large rubber coverall and gas mask that did nothing to hide his identity. He rode a large bicycle, turning east towards the slums and rookeries.

Augusta and Molly tracked him, always keeping him in sight but never getting close enough to be spotted. Their clothing was markedly anonymous' nobody looked twice at either of them as they walked the capital's streets. As the city grew rougher, they both slipped their hands into their pockets, readying their guns. The fog grew thicker and above their heads. They could sense, rather than see, the gangways and lines that connected the rookeries to each other. Augusta's neck hair prickled; something told her trouble was waiting for them.

As if on cue, a shot rang out from a walkway above. The women snatched their guns from their pockets and crouched. Augusta drew her blade, feeling a surge of comfort as it whispered out of its scabbard. There was something good about holding the sword in her hand. It nestled in her grip as if it was designed for her, rather than an heirloom from the family's spotty history of dangerous escapades and sudden betrayals.

Her ears turned, catching the sound of something landing in the street. Taking a careful sniff, she detected unwashed rubber and bodies beyond the respirator's range. Another sound of someone entering the street, this time heralded by shrieking hinges. Bulwarks fashioned out of the wreckage of walls jutted into the street, dividing it up into a killing ground. With the fog they stood a chance, but only because it might cloak them enough.

"What can you sense, Molly?" she hissed, peering up through the heavy rolling air.

"Do I have your attention?" A voice, laced with a Cockney accent, boomed over their heads before Molly could answer. There was something gruff in the voice, which made Augusta think of the old badger who had taught her to fight hand-to-hand. She peered up, trying to see through the fog.

"Get on with it," she called back, fighting the impulse to fire back. The way his voice had bounced off the walls had confused her; she wasn't sure where he was.

"This here is the local taxation department," he continued. "Hand over your valuables and we'll let you go. If not, well, let's say your families will have to start paying for your release, right lads?" There was a note of self-congratulation in his tone as if the speech had been the product of long hours of work.

Around them there were cheers, and mutters of "too right".

Augusta counted the voices—there were more than two. They were in for a more difficult fight than she'd hoped. The fog would cause enough problems, but all they could hope was that it would cause their attackers more problems than them.

"Molly, back to back," she instructed. "Do you have the Claws?"

"Yes, Miss," the servant said, fishing them out of a pocket. A set of five blades that strapped to the hand, the Tiger's Claws were an oddity looted from India by one of Augusta's uncles. They jutted over the knuckles, and were just the right size to fit a dainty hand like Molly's. Family legend said they had belonged to one of the infamous Tiger Queens that made so many of the young men in her set shiver in fear, and desire. Uncle Darius had wooed one of the fearsome breed and bedded her before bringing her into the Empire's fold, or so the story said.

Molly gave a practice swing with the Claws, cutting through the fog.

Augusta lifted her respirator and called up to the unseen leader. "If I were you, I would withdraw your men before someone gets hurt." She raised her blade to illustrate the point. "My companion and I are armed and dangerous. We won't hesitate to fight back."

"Oh you would, would you?" he shot back, the sneer obvious in his words. "Sounds like we've got a mouthy female, boys."

On cue, the figures—mangy-looking rats and dogs, for the most part—moved forward. Augusta fired, smiling with satisfaction as one dropped out of sight. Molly's gun barked repeatedly, spitting bullets through the fog. She ducked as a ruffian fired his own gun, blasting the street with something that sounded like an antique blunderbuss.

Then they were on the pair with cudgels and knives. Augusta thrust her pistol back in its pocket and got to work with the sword, grinning as she swung. The sword was her passion, the thing she excelled at. The cut and thrust, the lunge and parry, all of them sang in her blood. She caught the blade against a cudgel, and turned it aside to clatter to the floor before slashing her way across the footpad's front with a single stroke that ended his life. Turning on her heel, she parried a knife thrust and punched the wielder—a rat leering out of the confusion—in the face.

Beside her, Molly fought, alternating between her Peacemaker and the Claws. She raked the latter across a rabbit's face, tearing an eye from his head so hard he fainted. Her hand shook visibly as she pulled it away.

"It's all alright, Molly. We do this for Queen and Country," Augusta said, as if that was all that mattered. She thrust the sword through another man, twisting it so he slid down the blade and to the ground.

Above them a gun fired, but the shot went wild. Cursing, the gang's boss reloaded loudly.

Throwing a glance up to the gantries, Augusta saw him aim down into the street and ducked to the side, trying to draw the fight towards the wall nearest to the badger. Some of the thugs followed, and she twisted and turned to take care of them.

They fell, bleeding out into the gutter.

Their boss fired again and Molly screamed, falling into a heap in the middle of the street. Augusta hurried to her side, leaning down to lift her from the cobbles. Her maid dangled, limply, in the crook of her arm.

"Molly, are you still with me?" she shouted as she dragged her back towards the street's edge.

Above her there was the sound of the gun being reloaded and then, mercifully, a clicking sound as it jammed. "What on Earth?" the gang boss said, shaking the rifle. "Stupid thing, conking out on me now."

The cat sighed with relief and completed the retreat to the street's edge.

A narrow passage opened behind her and Augusta half carried, half dragged Molly down into it, setting her down. Groping around her body she found the bullet wound, making her aide scream as she probed it.

"Quiet now, Girl. I know you can manage. Bite this." She shoved a rubber bit under Molly's gas mask. As the girl obeyed, she renewed her examination of the wound. The bullet had punched straight through her rubber cover and the armoured corset she wore under her clothes and was caught in her chest. They would have to extract it, quickly. In better circumstances she would risk her rudimentary medical skills, but there was neither the time or the calm such an operation required.

That meant calling on Drummond's services sooner than planned. The bulldog had access to off-the-books doctors, as well as other things she would need.

The only problem was the price. His services didn't come cheap, and even with Room's generous stipend, the more she needed from him, the more it would hurt. She grimaced at the thought. If only he weren't the most dependable fence and information broker in London.

Dragging her mind back to the situation at hand, she cupped Molly's head. "I have to finish this, alright? Then we can go to Drummond and get you fixed up."

The maid nodded to show her understanding, and Augusta patted her shoulder before she rose and crept back to the street. Dimly, she saw a shape she could only assume was the gang boss standing in the middle of the street, glancing about. Now she could see his silhouette more clearly, see his muscular frame and the shape of his head.

He was definitely a badger.

"Damn it, why did you have to be Brock? Why couldn't you be something easy to kill like a rhino?" Badgers were notoriously tough. There were accounts of Scottish Badgers fighting off cavalry with nothing but a pitchfork or claymore in Medieval battles, and they had been some of the Duke of Wellington's finest troops, able to fire the heavy many-barrelled guns far more easily than anyone else.

None of which exactly filled her with confidence. Aiming the Peacemaker at his head, she cracked off a shot. The bullet spun from the barrel, slamming into the side of his head, and she moved. Running behind one of the bulwarks she fired again, this time tagging him in the chest. He jerked to one side, but didn't fall.

Instead he ran towards her, drawing a sabre from his belt. It swung down in an arc. She parried and shot at him again, from blank range.

The badger swung again and this time she ducked, letting the attack carry his weight forward. Augusta slashed the tip of her sword across his chest, scoring a thin line. She retreated a step.

"Why don't you give up? Most of your men are dead and I've no quarrel with you."

He snorted. "If word gets out that two people took us down, everyone will be trying it."

"So this is about your pride?" She thrust and he dodged to one side.

"No, it's about respect and survival. You people have no idea what it's like down here."

"You people?" She let him swing the sabre, ducking to let it go over her head and lunging to knick him the armpit.

"Toffs," he replied, pulling away. She could hear a hint of panting in his breathing. "I can hear it in your voice." His stance changed, protecting himself more.

"What about it?" she asked.

"Like I say." He paused for breath. "You got no clue about what it's like here. If we're defeated, then every chancer this side of Regent's Street will be trying to take over. It's bad enough with Micks, Haggis's and Frogs all over the place cutting into business, but the new gangs are brutal."

"Perhaps I can help you out there?" She lowered the blade, just enough to let him catch his breath. Catching a closer look at him, she realised he was older than she'd thought. Silver mixed with the black markings on his face.

"You? Help?" he laughed. "Do me a favour. When did a toff do a bloke like me any favours?"

"Let us go and I'll make sure nobody touches your turf."

He raised an eyebrow. "And if I don't agree?"

"You're tired, old, and struggling. There's nothing to stop me killing you." She made her voice as clear as she could. "I'm not a policeman and the law won't touch me. My kind, as you put it, are above the law." Stepping closer, she added, "I could blow this street to smithereens and nobody would do more than raise an eyebrow." It was true, though admittedly there'd be an inquest. Still, once the Room's name came up, the whole thing would be brushed under the rug and no more would be said. That was the sort of power the small organisation wielded. Heads of state had been assassinated, wars begun, and ships sunk on the order's command, and not even the Prime Minister knew about it. The Room's history was shrouded in secrecy, and there were rumours about the role it had played in Napoleon's defeat, as well as in the beginning of the French Revolution.

No matter how far the British Empire stretched across the world, sooner or later everything came back to France.

He hesitated, staring at her in disbelief. "Nobody has that sort of power."

Behind the respirator, her eyebrow rose. "Do they not? Let us go and you'll see how much influence I have."

"How do I know you'll keep your word?"

"I'm a creature of breeding. My word is my bond," she said.

"Yeah, that's what the Prime Minister said before he decided to crush the Unions," the badger said. "My dad died in the rioting."

Augusta grimaced. The Communard Riots had happened while she was a child, but their memory lingered on both sides of the class divide. Her own father had damned the Unionists, saying they were, "Damned delusional dunderheads led astray by that dunce, Marx," in a moment of rare alliteration. The legislation banning Unions, Combinations, and other forms of worker organisation was still law. Even cooperatives, which worked to provide cheap food for the poor, were illegal because they might prompt a revolutionary spirit in the workforce. The fact that across the channel, the French had never reinstated their monarchy even after Napoleon's defeat, was part of the antipathy the British felt towards such developments. Up and down the country one only needed to mention the Revolution to get relatives and friends hiding their silverware.

The badger lowered his blade. "Go."

She nodded and backed away, only sheathing her weapons when it was clear he meant to honour his word. Then she ran to Molly's side, scooping her up in her arms.

They set off in the direction of Drummond's gaff.

Drummond lived in what seemed like a small shop, close to the river front. It was his place of business and he never bothered to leave it. He also never locked the door; everybody knew that it would do more harm than good to rob the place, and the bulldog was owed too many favours for anyone to want to lose his business. Usually the shop was busy, even at night, but now it was empty with only a single light shining in the store front.

Augusta pushed the door open. "Drummond, where are you?" Molly clung to her, coughing behind the rubber mask. "We need medical assistance!"

The dog appeared, his tiny eyes open with alarm as he hurried forward. "God, woman, what have you done?"

Augusta laid Molly on the counter. "We met a group of thugs, and things didn't go well."

He eyed her, warily. "Which group?"

"How should I know? They were led by a badger."

Drummond nodded. "Them, I know. Shouldn't bring any trouble this way." He looked thoughtful and pulled the shop's blind anyway. He let out a long sigh and leaned against the door.

She pulled the respirator off and shook out her hair, staring at him. "Since when did you care about that sort of thing?"

He made no reply, busy examining Molly, stripping her mask and coverall with surprising care. He pulled a face when he saw the bullet wound. "Nutkin, get up here!" he bellowed into the back of the shop.

A red squirrel appeared, paling as she saw the body. "Let me get her downstairs and I'll see what I can do, Chief."

"There's a good girl." He patted her shoulder. "Hang on, Molly. We've got the best surgeon in the East End."

"How do you figure that?" Augusta asked.

"Well, she's not a laudanum addict, or on the gin," he said. "Most of the quacks around here can't examine a patient without thinking they've got an identical twin."

She nodded, sympathetically. "Speaking of quacks, we were tailing one. A Scottish duck by the name of Mallard. Do you know where he's likely to be going?"

Drummond poured a measure of scotch and pushed it across to her. "Mallard doesn't exactly narrow it down, Your Grace. There are thousands of ducks by that name in London. But," he paused, "I think I know your boy. He's got a feather in with the Chinese down in Limehouse, hangs around one of the opium dens that way."

"He didn't look like an addict," Augusta said. "Rather too fat and pleased with himself."

Drummond nodded. "That's the boy. I don't know that he smokes the stuff; something else seems to be going on."

She sipped the whiskey, enjoying the fiery feeling that tumbled down her throat. "You haven't had an attaché case in, have you? It would have the initials H.G.H engraved on a brass plate just above the clasp."

"Let me check," he said with a frown. Turning, he entered the storeroom behind the shop and Augusta heard him sorting through things. A moment later he returned with a case. "This is it."

"Is there anything inside?" she asked, knowing it would be empty.

"Nah, they never bring stuff like this in full. Why? What's this chap of yours lost?" Drummond gave her a quizzical look. "I assume it's the usual defence of the realm gubbins?"

She nodded. "Naval documents and an official seal."

"Blimey, what idiot managed to lose that?"

Augusta tapped her nose. "Ask me no questions, I'll tell you no lies."

Drummond looked quizzical. "It's like that, is it?"

She nodded and helped herself to another measure of whiskey. "I'm afraid so. It has to be kept quiet." Changing the subject, she pulled her Peacemaker. "Do you have any ammunition I can buy?"

"Oh, yes," he said, reaching under the counter for a box of bullets.

The opium den Dr Mallard frequented lay at the edge of Limehouse. Fashioned like a Chinese pagoda with a golden dragon rising over the top, it looked bright against the grim slums clustered around it. Tacky too, Augusta thought as she approached, with Drummond at her back. He'd insisted on coming with her, saying she needed someone to back her up.

She wasn't sure if he meant it, or if it was just another way of earning money.

They climbed up towards the entrance and the bouncers, big burly apes, were moving to intercept them. "No entry, members only," they shouted in broken English.

Smiling broadly, Augusta held out a hand. "I'd like to discuss joining."

The bouncers paused, looking at each other in confusion. No matter how she was dressed, there was no way Augusta looked like their usual sort of client. Their confusion grew as she eased the respirator up, revealing her sleek black fur and pointed pierced ears.

"May I speak to your maitre d?" She stepped forward, as if she would happily just bypass them completely.

"Our what?" one of them asked, scratching his head.

"She means your boss," Drummond put in. His hands were thrust deep into his pockets. "We want to talk to him about joining up."

"You Drummond, why you want join?" one of the apes asked. "You big cheese, boss says."

The dog puffed his chest out. "Well, laddie, that might be why I want to be part of your club. I hear you're moving upmarket."

The other ape frowned. "We are?"

Drummond patted his shoulder, patronisingly. "That's what I heard. Of course, your boss probably didn't bother to tell you. Now, why don't you run along and tell him two important people want to talk to him, eh?" He lit a cigar and indolently strolled up to the door, waiting as the apes ran to pass the message along.

"You didn't have to do that," Augusta said. "I could handle it by myself."

He blew a smoke ring. "Sure, I know that, but they weren't going to listen to you, were they? The shock of you being a woman was too much to handle from the start. Whatever came out of your mouth had to get past that to reach what passes for their brains." He lounged against the wall, puffing contentedly.

She bridled. How dare he? Didn't he realise she was capable of taking care of herself? She gritted her teeth. "Nonetheless, don't do it again."

He glanced at her good-humouredly and shrugged. "As you wish, boss." Absently, he fingered his revolver as he puffed on the cigar.

For long minutes they waited. Even after dark the city was noisy, the sounds of industry never ceasing. Automata worked the factories deep into the night. The workshop of the world never stopped churning out more goods to sell, more weapons to kill. That was how both Greater Prussia and the USA had been kept at bay, despite growing hostilities. It was louder here than in the west or north of the city. You could do almost anything and nobody would notice. Parliament chose to ignore the area as much as possible—there were no constituencies, no rotten boroughs to appease. It was a no man's land of factories and workshops where being a minute late for work could mean destitution, and where employers had few scruples about paying their staff in their own scrip, forcing them to shop at the company's shops. Some even had doctors on call so that illness would pay the employer, and Augusta had heard of one enterprising chap who had bought out a firm of undertakers so that even in death his employees paid him money.

Behind them, the opium den door opened, and a greasy young mouse stepped out, peering through spectacles so thick he might as well have been a mole. "Can I help you, Sir, Lady?"

"We want to join your membership list," Augusta said.

The mouse blinked, "I don't see how that could be a problem. We accept members of all creeds and breeds." He cast a withering look at the doormen and led them inside.

The smell of opium filled the air inside the building, but the lobby was free of dreamers. Instead, a group of young women, pretty foxes and cats dressed in long silk robes, loitered, guiding those who had come to chase the dragon deeper into the building. They brushed aside beaded curtains, revealing darker rooms which were lit only by what looked like candles.

"We strive to ensure our customers can relax in peace, offering the ultimate in discretion," the mouse intoned, leading the way up a broad set of stairs. On the landing above there were more doors leading off to more rooms, again lurking in darkness. The vapours of sickly sweet opium undulated from each room. Somewhere, someone plucked lazily at a sitar, filling the air with music so slow it was hard not to fall asleep listening to its strains.

"Who owns this place?" Augusta asked, looking around at the bright prints and the hanging lanterns.

"Nobody important, just a businessman," the mouse said, turning to her with a bright smile. "He is kind enough to offer succour for poor souls who need to escape from the world for a while. A few years ago this was a simple opium den, now he has transformed it into something else."

"Looks like a normal opium den to me," Drummond huffed.

"Ah, well that's because you're looking at the space for the dreamers," the maitre d returned, cheerfully. "If you'd like to follow me, I'll show you what else we offer." He beckoned them onwards, past more opium rooms and into the back of the building. Here, things changed. Bottles of alcohol appeared on tables—beers, gins and whiskies, even Spanish port, and the sound of faster music filtered through the walls. "My employer is keen to offer as many things as he can and so, while the other side of the building caters to those that chase the dragon, here there are more conventional pursuits." He smiled back at them and opened a door into a bar.

They threaded through the bar, passing between tables of deckhands, dockers, and dollymops who drank large tankards of porter. At the far end, there was a door labelled "Office", and the mouse unlocked it and led Augusta and Drummond inside. He seated himself behind a paper-covered desk as Augusta sat in one of the chairs in front of it and the bulldog leaned against the door.

The mouse barely had a chance to register something was wrong before Augusta had flicked her claws out and had them held to his throat. "Hands away from the desk," she snarled.

Obeying, the mouse squeaked, "Who are you, what do you want?" He blinked and then said, "There's no money here, you know?"

"We're not interested in money," Augusta said. "We want to know why Dr. Mallard comes here."

For a moment he froze, staring up at her, then he managed to stutter out, "Wh— Who? I don't believe I know the gentleman."

"Sure you don't, mate," Drummond drawled. He pulled his gun out and drew the hammer back slowly. Its click seemed to fill the room.

"You, you can't kill me, the shot will bring everyone running."

"Why do you assume they'll hear anything?" Augusta asked, playing along with Drummond. "We all know they'll just think it's a machine noise."

His eyes widened. "No, no they won't, they won't. The master will know what you're doing, he probably already does!" Throwing back his head, the mouse began to scream. "He won't be stopped, nothing can stop him. Not even the Black Room!"

Augusta plunged her claws into his throat, tearing it out. Blood spurted over the desk, covering the documents. He slumped forward and she cleaned her claws on his shirt sleeve, shaking them. They hurt where she had plunged them deep into his throat. Once, they might have been offensive weapons, but no cats she knew used them for that sort of thing, apart from Rafe, and he was a barbarian at times.

"That's torn it," Drummond said, easing off the door. "We'd better make this quick before anyone comes looking."

"I know, if he hadn't screamed..."

"Yeah, I know, the fact he named your lot didn't help either did it? I thought you were an official secret?" His tone was cagey. The fact he knew about the Room without being a member was enough to hang him. They had an uneasy truce over the matter, where they both pretended not to know what the other did.

"We are," she said, still staring at her claws. Rousing herself, she began to look through the desk drawers, revealing stationary and a set of keys, but little else. Drummond moved an indifferent watercolour on the wall to reveal a safe. Pulling out a set of cracksman's tools, he began to break it open.

Outside there was a sudden lull in the sound, and Augusta crept to the door, sword in hand, bracing for it to fly open and a hoard of goons to burst in. Her breath caught as someone passed close by and she raised her blade, only to hear them move away again. The piano picked up again, playing *Roll out the Barrel*, and the punters began to sing along.

Sighing, she eased away from the door.

There was a click, and Drummond sighed triumphantly as the safe door opened. "I thought they'd have something more sophisticated in place," he said. An instant later there was a hissing sound. The door swung open to reveal a brass cylinder, from which gas was escaping in white wisps.

Augusta's eyes widened. "Oh for the love of..." her voice faded as the world turned black.

She woke in a cold cellar, and it took a moment for her eyes to adjust to the darkness. A moment's investigation revealed that she had been disarmed, but not bound. Curious. She pushed herself up and patted the large lump beside her. Drummond. He was still asleep, snoring heavily and likely would be for some time. She shrugged and began to look around.

The room was full of packing crates and barrels, all of them unmarked but for a set of Chinese characters running vertically that were slightly raised, allowing her to trace their shapes.

Inwardly Augusta fumed; she had never learned to read any of the many Chinese dialects, and had no clue what they said. Except for the fearsome mark of a demonic mask that seemed to appear regularly. That couldn't be good.

Perhaps this affair involved the Lord of Strange Deaths her brothers always talked about. Except he was a myth, a fiction.

He didn't exist.

Further down, out of sight, she could hear someone shifting from foot to foot. She crawled out and peered. A stoat in a uniform was guarding them, clutching a rifle in his hands. Between him and them was a set of metal bars, with a door set into them.

"Bloody rat, putting me on guard duty. Just because someone lucked out on finding our lair," the stoat said to himself. "Like it's my fault Mortimer got himself killed. That's what you get for playing with cats."

Augusta rose to her feet. "Hey, you. Where are we?"

"Shut up," the stoat snapped back, spinning around to stare into the cellar, come prison. "You don't want to know where you are, or who's captured you."

"It sounds like you're not exactly happy about the situation," she said, and picked her way forward to him. Listening, she could hear the trickle of water. They were close to the river.

"Yeah, well, that don't matter, does it? I just does as I'm told." He eyed her. "Besides, why should I trust you? You killed Mortimer."

Brushing her hand over the bars, Augusta shrugged. "Was that his name? I didn't ask. It couldn't be helped, I'm afraid. He was screaming."

The stoat scowled. "You'll be screaming too, you bitch. I've seen what the boss does to the likes of you; it ain't pretty."

A groan behind her told Augusta that Drummond had woken. "Who hit me?" he growled. "When I get my hands on them, they'll wish they'd never been born." He shook his head and groaned. "Damn it, Augusta, why'd I agree to help you?"

She rolled her eyes. "For the money, Drummond, remember?"

He brightened at the thought and then frowned as he sniffed the air. "We're still near the river, underground though, and there's another river close by. The Fleet, maybe?" He crossed to the bars, feeling his way through the dark. "Oh, and stoat; I'd know that stink anywhere."

"Watch it, dog." The guard lowered his gun. "I won't hesitate to kill you."

"Give it up, sunshine, you're Lenny Potter out of the Potter Boys gang. Or at least you were, but you got taken over a few months ago, didn't you?" Drummond drawled. "Hoovered up by whoever's decided the East End needs to be run by one boss."

"You didn't tell me that was happening," Augusta protested. "The badger I spoke to seemed concerned about other gangs trying to take over."

"But he also mentioned a boss, right?" Drummond asked. "There are no other gangs, only the one run by the Lord of Strange Deaths. It's been hell for business, I can tell you." Pressing his face to the bars, he added, "I'm surprised you took his shilling, Lenny. Didn't he have your brother killed?"

The stoat looked abashed for a moment. "Why do you think I'm working for him, Mr. Drummond? I don't want to go the same way."

He shuffled on his feet, cocking his head to listen suddenly.

"What's going on?" Augusta asked, straining her own ears. There were footsteps approaching, a steady trudge of boots sounding as if they were splashing through water. Presently, a group of figures appeared, dressed in a dark-grey uniforms that only just showed up in the gloom. Drummond couldn't see a thing; only eyes attuned to the dark picked them out.

"He's ready for them," one of the newcomers—a brown bear who barely fit into his uniform—said.

"Right," Lenny said, unlocking the door. "What does he want me to do?"

"Boil your head," the bear said, pushing him away. "Right you, get out here." He beckoned to the prisoners and set his mouth into what might have been a smile if it weren't so terrifying. They shuffled out and looked at the others. Unlike their leader, they were a motley bunch of street toughs dressed up to look more menacing than they actually were. A few of them seemed almost nervous, and fingered their guns in a fashion that made Augusta glad they were on the other side. That way, at least, they were more likely to hurt their friends than her and Drummond.

They made their way through a series of tunnels which seemed to intersect with the underground river, parts of the sewers, and cellars. It was an entire complex tunnelled out below the city and reminded Augusta of the penny dreadfuls her brothers liked to bring home after their time in the city. In those, the villains always seemed to have the most improbable lairs and gadgets that put even what Britain's finest minds dreamt up in the shade. Of course, they had the advantage of being fiction, and the authors clearly didn't bother with what was actually possible most of the time. The labyrinth felt like it could have sprung directly from *The Terror of the Towers* or some such rubbish.

They were brought to a large, round chamber furnished with rich red velvets and golden curtains. Asian artifacts littered low tables and the walls were decorated with images of legendary creatures, like dragons and phoenixes and the strange hairless apes that vanished with the Flood. In the centre of the room, a figure sat on a large cushion. A large hat with a fringe of golden chains tumbling from the brim hid his face and he wore a golden robe.

"Sir." The bear saluted. A note of uncertainty entered his voice. "Presenting the prisoners as ordered, sir."

The figure nodded and made a small gesture with one hand.

The bear looked confused. "Sir, these people are dangerous. We have reason to believe they may work for your enemies. Are you sure—"

The figure cut him off, pointing to one of the others, a scrawny rat with gold rings in his ears. "Kill him." The voice was male, but contorted as if the figure was making an effort to disguise it.

Without a word, the rat drew his gun and fired. The bear tumbled to the floor. Turning, the rat ushered the other guards to carry the body out of the room, obviously now their captain. They slunk away, shutting the door behind them.

The figure waited until they were gone and rose, manipulating something to raise the lights as he did. "God, Sis, you gave me a fright." He removed his hat and blinked.

Augusta stared. "Rafe, what on earth are you doing here?"

He smiled and looked a little embarrassed. "Would you believe, my job?"

"The Room sent you to do this?" she demanded, looking around. "Did they also get you to decorate it like a brothel?"

"Hardly, old girl. No, they wanted a crime lord to deal with all the gangs, so they created one." Rafe walked over to a statue of Buddha and flipped the head back, jiggling a lever which opened a section of the wall to reveal a drinks cabinet. "What can I get you two?"

"Scotch," Drummond said, stirring himself. "I suppose you and I had better talk."

"We will." Rafe nodded, pouring a generous measure for the bulldog, followed by one for himself. "I have a slot free in a few weeks, once the war's started."

Augusta paused, turning from the print she was inspecting. "War? What are you talking about?" Suddenly, she sprang across the room. "Is this to do with Hector's valise?"

Her brother blinked. "Of course it is, what else could it be? Mallard took it because we needed to forge some documents. We're going to make it look as if French anarchists had launched an attack on London, then we'll use the forged documents to launch our own attack, and Bob's your uncle. Of course, most of my compatriots will die in the bombing of the East End but—" He shrugged. "I doubt anyone's going to miss them."

"And what about Hector?" Augusta asked after a moment. A sense of terror mingled with one of righteous indignation. How dare the Room do this? She knew what they were capable of, but to start a war and risk the life of a friend and loyal subject was beyond the pale. Besides that, how many lives would be lost in the bombing? It wasn't enough to say that it was acceptable because they were poor.

Rafe shrugged. "He'll hang. Let's be honest, the role of scapegoat fits him perfectly."

Shaking her head, Augusta said, "That's not acceptable. He's done nothing to deserve death."

"Of course he has," Rafe scoffed. "Has being part of the Room taught you nothing? Everyone is guilty of something." He took a long swallow of scotch. "We knew the clumsy ass would lose his bag on the way, so we stole it and appropriated the documents so that we could commandeer the Navy's new flying corp. Across the channel, well, we're not worrying about that. The attack will come from a secret airfield in Kent, but the pilot has been conditioned to only speak French and to swear by the writings of Marx." He smiled. "You see, it's a perfect storm. War will follow and we'll crush the Communards before their sickness spreads. Before you know it, we'll have added France and her colonies to the Empire. We'll dismantle the Arc de Triumph and bring it to London, brick by brick."

"You're mad," Augusta said. "I can't believe the Room would countenance this!"

"You know what they've done in the past," Rafe countered. "Nothing you can do will stop this. If it hadn't been for your stupidity in helping that stupid mutt, you wouldn't even be here. I tried to stop you coming here, but you weren't at the townhouse when I arrived." He loomed over her. "Go home, Augusta. Listen to Mama for once. You're not cut out for this life—get married and have a litter or five."

She took a breath. "How dare you, you utter cad." Her paw moved in a blur, striking him across the face. Turning, she snatched a sword from the wall. "If you're so good, then fight me, brother."

He laughed as he rubbed his cheek. "Why would I do that, Sis? I'll just end up hurting you, and then Mumsie will chew me out for not letting you be a girl." The humour in his eyes died. "Seriously, go home. Nothing you can do now will stop what's going to happen. Certainly killing me won't do anything." He drew himself up. "I don't see why you're being so stubborn. Can't you see this will be good for us?"

She placed the tip of the blade against his throat. "All I see is that you're following in the family tradition, and it's just going to ruin people like Drummond's lives. You can just swan off wherever you want, he has to live here." Pressing, she pricked a tiny spot of blood on his throat.

Rafe sighed. "You are impossible. Father should have beaten you more." He pushed her sword down. "Very well, since you're being so damn obstinate." Taking a sword down, he swung it in the air. "Take your mark, Augusta."

They took up places on each side of the room, blades extended. They tapped each other's swords as they began to circle, getting the measure of each other. Despite being siblings, they seldom duelled at home, and none of the Chatnoir clan had much of an idea of each others' skill with the blade.

Rafe feinted to one side and Augusta's blade met his. She disengaged and lunged, tapping his wrist. A scowl spread across his face.

"You're better than I thought you'd be, for a girl."

She laughed. "You'll have to do better than that, Brother." So saying, she whipped her blade across his front, missing his silk clothes by the merest whisper. "I had all that rot when I was growing up, and I know I'm at least as good as the other boys."

He knocked her blade away and slashed her sleeve with the tip of his own. "Is that right? I heard they landed you on the ground nine times out of ten."

"Typical men, lying to disguise their inferiority to a woman." She parried his next thrust and the next, letting him do the work for a while as she wondered if his scheme had ever made sense. Why take her bag if they were specifically after Hector's? It made no sense unless they were trying to make a distraction to hide the fact they only wanted the one bag. One theft was significant, many just meant you had a bag snatcher. The rest of the scheme barely added up either, but she had seen too many odd plans come out of the corridors of power to believe it was nonsense. Give the War Office a slice and they took the whole cake.

Idly, she lashed out with the blade, slashing his trousers, just to make him think she was paying attention as she considered the situation. He riposted, she parried and disengaged, stabbing the blade towards his shoulder, to be met by his parry.

The look on his face grew more serious as he realised how skilled she was. He moved his sword faster, harder, crashing it onto hers.

"I don't think your teachers would approve, Rafe," she commented as she stepped to one side to let his blade slide by. "By the way, your scheme makes no sense."

"What do you mean?" He frowned with concentration. "It makes perfect sense. I calculated every angle!"

"And yet, you have Mallard stealing people's bags when you only needed the one, why?" She cut his shirt open, revealing slightly paler fur on his chest. The family crest hung on a chain around his neck, and she took a vicious delight in slashing the chain, casting the crest across the room.

He hissed, suddenly, ears lying flat on his head. "I'm sick of this!" He swung with renewed vigour, closing in on her. The sword flashed, too fast for her to keep up all of a sudden.

"Does that mean you concede my point?" she needled. A glance at Drummond confirmed he'd decided to keep out of the fracas, preferring to watch and sip Rafe's Talisker.

Grunting, Rafe hammered blows on her, his eyes a blazing fury of green. His tail was puffed into a thick coil of fur. His whiskers bristled.

Retreating, she suddenly tripped on something. A queasy feeling spread through her, and she gasped as she felt something cold spread through her body. Wild magic, the family's secret weapon. How could he use it against his own blood?

She gaped up at him and felt his rapier stab the shoulder of her sword arm. Her blade tumbled from her grasp, clattering as it struck the stones. A look of triumph crossed Rafe's face and he raised the blade for a killing move.

"Don't," she howled.

"I have no choice. Don't worry, your body will be found among the other victims of the French attack. I'll make sure nobody asks why you were here. But then, you always were a wild child; nobody will be surprised by you turning up in

Limehouse." He stared down at her and she closed her eyes, unwilling to look at him for any longer. The cold feeling inside her twisted and she coughed, baring her teeth.

"You always did cheat, Rafe." Letting herself sag to the floor, she groped for the sword, hoping he was too caught up in his moment of triumph to notice. The hilt felt reassuring in her hand, solid, real. Not like the roiling chaos writhing inside her. "And you've always been a bastard with your gift."

He smiled, calming himself, and placed the tip of his sword against her throat. One thrust would kill her. "At least I have a gift, Augusta. All you have to look forward to is the grave."

She opened her eyes. "If you must kill me, then let me die on my feet."

"No, I don't think so. You side with trash, so you can die like them." He pressed harder, she felt the skin part, grimaced as pain spread across her throat. The cold feeling inside her twisted, evading her as she tried to coax it into her control. It was hard, but she had grown used to doing two things at once. It was the sort of lesson her governess' had delighted in teaching. So, while she gripped the sword, trying to ignore the pain in her throat, she reached for the cold sensation, the magic, and she drew it forth. Slowly, it eked into her control and she let it spill out.

The lights went out, plunging the room into complete darkness. At the same time, an electrical crack sounded and Rafe panicked.

"What's going on?" He lifted his blade from her throat and she swung, knocking it from his hand. A moment later she thrust up into his torso, stabbing up under his ribs and into his heart. She held the blade there until he toppled to the ground.

Augusta sat up, pressing her hand to her throat. "Thanks for the help, Drummond." The dog switched the lights on again, glancing at her with a raised eyebrow.

He helped her up and bandaged the wound.

"I suppose you want paying for this?" she asked.

He shook his head, "I'll just help myself to the drinks cabinet. The stuff in there would pay off most of the debt you owe."

That was something, at least. "Thank you." Looking down at Rafe she felt the first of many tears streak down her cheek. "What am I going to tell Mama?"

The Medjay's Son

Aneal Pothuluri

The young cheetah cub peered curiously at his father from the doorway. The elder warrior sat, sharpening a gleaming bronze khopesh. The ornate Egyptian sickle-sword had been passed down from father to son since the day it was forged, but it was more than a simple heirloom; it was a right of honor. The boy's father stopped his sharpening and held the sword up to the morning light, revealing a beautiful engraving on the blade. It read "Montu," the name given to the sword by his ancestors. An awestruck gasp escaped the child's lips as he admired the sword from afar, prompting the elder cheetah to turn his attention to the six-year-old cub.

"Aten?" the boy's father called. Knowing he was caught, he reluctantly stepped forward.

"Yes, Father?"

"What have I told you of spying?"

"I'm sorry, Father. I just wanted to see Montu." Aten pouted and hung his head low. His father gave a small chuckle, petting the boy's head.

"You need only ask, Aten. It will be yours one day." Aten smiled, his tail swaying eagerly at the thought. "Uncle Maat and I were planning on sparring. Would you like to observe, Little One?" his father asked with a smile.

"Can I really!" The little cub burst with excitement.

"Of course, my little warrior," the elder cheetah said, leading his son outside. Aten watched with bright, beaming eyes as his father trained. The sparring match lasted for what felt like hours in the young boy's mind, but in reality, it only took ten minutes before the boy's father managed to disarm and knock down his opponent. "Next time, Abasi," the zebra warrior said with a lighthearted smile.

"We shall see, Maat," the cheetah answered, helping his friend back up. Abasi had known the zebra since they were both Aten's age. They'd grown up together, trained together, fought side by side. Maat was like a brother to Abasi. The cub cheered loudly as the two warriors walked back towards the shade of the large palm tree the cub stood under.

"Enjoy the show, Little One?" Abasi asked with a chuckle before patting the boy on the head.

"Father, when will you teach me to fight?" the young cheetah asked, tugging at his father's arm.

"Soon, Aten. Very soon."

"Your boy will make a fine medjay, Abasi," Maat said, patting his friend on the shoulder.

"He is his father's child," spoke a radiant cheetah wrapped in fine white linen and colorful beaded jewelry. "Dinner is ready, My Love," the woman said, planting a kiss on Abasi's cheek before turning to Maat. "You will join us, won't you?"

"I do not wish to trouble you."

"Come, Friend, you must try my wife's bread. It is truly divine," Abasi insisted.

"Very well then. Thank you both." Maat smiled, following the cheetahs into their home.

Aten watched the adults intently as he gobbled up the soft bread his mother had baked. Uncle Maat was telling a story of how he and the boy's father had chased off a group of would-be robbers from desecrating a tomb outside the oasis. The cub soaked up every word with perked ears and bright eyes. Aten idolized his father. He could think of nothing more to strive for than to follow in his footsteps—to be a medjay, a protector of the pharaoh's lands and her people. To Aten, there was no greater honor.

The story was nearing its conclusion when a frantic lioness

barged into the home with a look of horror on her face.

"Medjay! A man has been killed in the marketplace!"

"What!" Abasi bolted up from where he sat.

"A group of men were arguing with one of the merchants—then one of them cut his throat!" the woman explained shakily. Aten watched as his father retrieved Montu from its case.

"Stay here and watch Aten, Nenet. We will return soon," Abasi said to his wife as he and Maat rushed out the door. But Aten was young and careless, and before his mother could stop him, he bolted after the two warriors. He'd never seen a real fight before, and he wasn't about to miss all the excitement. His mother chased after him, her voice full of fear and rage as he darted through the dust-covered streets, but unfortunately she wasn't quite fast enough, and soon her young cub was out of sight.

Even when deserted, the market remained alive with the smell of exotic spices and phantom scents of the merchants and customers who'd occupied the winding alleys and dusty paths mere moments ago. It would be easy for someone to lose their senses in such a place, but Aten was determined to follow his father and Uncle Maat's trail without distraction.

The boy hid behind one of the empty stalls to avoid detection as the scene unfolded. The lioness had told the truth; there was indeed a group of six men looting the empty stalls. Not far from them, a middle-aged goat lay slumped over a barrel of apricots, a crimson stream flowing from a large gash in his neck, tainting the sweet fruit beneath him.

"Stop! What is the meaning of this!" Abasi snarled, surveying the grisly scene before him. All the men stopped their pocketing, but only one of them answered the medjay. A white-scaled viper with a red scarab tattoo on his forehead stepped forward, blood still dripping from his dagger. He was young, only sixteen years of age, but he showed no fear of the older warriors before him.

"There is no need for hostility, Medjay. There is a reason for all of this," the viper spoke, giving the warriors a sharp-fanged grin.

"What reason have you for spilling the blood of an unarmed

man?" Maat questioned with narrowed eyes.

"It's very simple: this man offered me great disrespect. I had no other choice but to defend my dignity by silencing him," the viper answered plainly.

"How were you disrespected?" Abasi pressed further.

"I simply stated that his prices seemed unreasonable, and in response, he told me that I was a 'foolish boy' who knew nothing about quality and that I should come back when I wasn't so simple," the viper explained with disdain.

"That does that seem like a foolish response. But, if you're so sure this act was justified, then you should have no objections to standing before a judge and repeating what you've just told us."

"I'm afraid I cannot," the viper said as the other five grown men he was with flanked him on either side. "My friends and I are on a pilgrimage to the Shedet Oasis to pay tribute to Lord Sobek, and we can't be held up any longer."

"Lord Sobek will understand the reason for your delay. You have no other choice." Abasi tightened his grip on the khopesh in his hand.

"I believe I do." The viper's eyes were filled with anger as he gestured to the men at his side.

Aten's heart raced as he watched the men draw their weapons. Excitement and a tinge of concern both swam in his mind. His father and Maat were both great warriors, but they were outnumbered and the odds seemed against them. The cub's fears were lessened as he watched his father swiftly cut down one of the men as they charged him, but it seemed before the man could even hit the ground, three more were upon Abasi. Two of the men jabbed at him with spears, while one shot arrows from a distance. Abasi might have been overpowered, if not for Maat.

The zebra warrior hooked one of the spear wielder's legs with his own khopesh, tripping him up before thrusting the bronze sword deep into his chest as Abasi parried the other attacker's blows.

The cheetah's own attacks became more and more vicious as he brought down blow after blow, until finally his opponent's weapon splintered in two. Abasi buried his blade deep into the man's neck. Aside from the viper, who stayed out of the skirmish, opting to wait for the perfect opening, there were only two men remaining: a hulking brute of a hippopotamus wielding a hefty stone mace, and a short, twitchy hyena archer. While Maat busied himself with the hippopotamus, Abasi set his sights on the archer. The hyena's brow was dripping with sweat and his hands shook uncontrollably, throwing off his aim. Abasi easily dodged and blocked the arrows as he made his way to the hyena. The archer panicked, dropping his weapon and running.

Aten wasn't paying attention; he was too engrossed in Maat's battle with the hippo to notice the hyena running in his direction. Similarly, the fleeing archer did not notice the small boy crouching out of sight. He collided with the cub, sending both crashing into the sand. The cowardly hyena rubbed his shoulder with a groan before looking up to see Abasi still advancing toward him. His heart pounded in his chest as he saw the cold determination in the cheetah's eyes. That's when he noticed the whimpering cub next to him, and he did the only thing he could think of to save his hide: the coward grabbed Aten by the scruff of his neck, drawing a knife from his belt and holding it to the boy's throat.

"Stay back, or I'll kill this boy!" the hyena shouted shakily. Abasi stopped dead in his tracks, his eyes wide in shock and disbelief.

"Aten?" The boy cried out for his father in response, and in an instant, Abasi's confusion melted into a pure boiling rage. "You will put him down or I swear you will enter the afterlife in a hundred pieces!" the warrior snarled. "Put him down!" he repeated even louder.

Aten and the hyena were his sole focus. The rest of the world simply faded away, so he didn't notice the young viper behind him until he felt the serpent's dagger plunging deep into his back. Aten watched in horror as his father cried out, falling to his knees.

The cry was loud enough to distract Maat. The warrior froze for an instant, and the ferocious hippo took advantage of the moment, landing a powerful blow with his mace, knocking the zebra into a wall and causing him to lose consciousness. The viper loomed over Abasi, a satisfied grin blooming across his scaly maw as he ripped his dagger from the cheetah's back and slowly cut his throat. The hyena dropped Aten once the light left his father's eyes. The boy fell limp to the ground, tears flowing from his face as he dragged himself toward his father. The viper looked on with indifference before turning his gaze to the two remaining men in his company.

"Grab what you can carry on the journey; we're leaving."

"What about the boy?" the hippopotamus asked.

"We don't have time to deal with him; others will be here soon," the viper hissed, and with that, the men looted and then moved on, leaving Aten alone. The cub was silent now, his voice lost from sobbing. He lay there, squeezing his father's limp hand. The lively scents of the market slowly faded away until the only thing Aten could pick up was the sickening, metallic smell of his father's blood.

Fourteen years passed. Fourteen long, bitter years. Aten trained relentlessly in the art of combat, never forgetting those three faces responsible for the scars in his mind and the void left in his life. Once he'd learned all he could, he set out to do the thing he'd dreamt of ever since that awful day.

Lord Ra had just ferried the sun from the underworld, heralding the dawn. Aten, now a man in his own right, fastened the saddle on his camel, trying his best to keep the beast silent as he did so.

"Planning on leaving without a farewell?" his mother's voice rang out behind him. Aten stopped what he was doing and slowly turned around with a guilty frown and lowered ears.

"Mother…"

Nenet stared at her son. He had the look of a scolded child, but he was no child. Not any longer. "So, the time has come for you to leave me as well?" the old cheetah asked sorrowfully before wrapping her arms around her son.

"I'm… I'm so sorry, Mother," Aten said, softly returning the hug.

"I knew this day would come. I knew it the moment you started training with Maat."

"Father would want justice."

"Those men will get the fate they deserve when their hearts are weighed by Osiris," Nenet answered.

"And until that day they are free to ruin or end as many lives as they desire? I must go, Mother. It's the only way I can find peace."

Nenet sighed. She knew there was nothing she could say to stop him. This was his path, and she could not bar his way. "Very well. I understand. Come with me, then. I have a gift for you before you go."

Aten followed his mother. Age and loss had humbled her. She no longer decorated herself with fine jewelry and makeup, nor did she carry herself with the same grace and dignity she had in her youth. She'd tried her best to be strong for her son, but there were still many days Aten found her weeping in secret. Her anguish broke his heart. He felt responsible for her pain. After all, his father might still be with them now if Aten had just stayed home like he was told.

They walked in silence, and soon Aten realized where they were going. He knew the path well; he'd walked it many times before.

Abasi's tomb sat waiting for them. The monument was a modest one: a simple, sandstone hut, just spacious enough for his sarcophagus and a few visitors, but it stood as a testament to what Abasi meant to the people of Siwa. The most his family could afford was a pitiful hole in the ground, but out of the kindness of their hearts, the citizens of the village gave up their own hard-earned money to see a proper tomb built for the hero who spent his life keeping them safe. The two cheetahs entered and Nenet opened a case beside the sarcophagus. Aten's eyes went wide as he watched her retrieve his father's khopesh.

"Montu?" Aten whispered under his breath in disbelief.

"He would want you to have it," Nenet said, holding the elegant, bronze blade out to her son. Aten smiled, taking the sword in his hand. He felt his father's presence with every swing and thrust as he tested the blade in his hand. Maat had always lectured him about the weapon being an extension of the warrior, but those words never rang truer than with this sword. It guided him, empowered him, and made him feel like the great warrior he'd dreamt of being ever since he was a cub.

"How does it feel?" Nenet asked with a smile.

"I've never known, nor ever will know a better blade. Thank you, Mother."

"Good." Nenet's smile faded. "Then go do what must be done, but promise me you will return."

"I give you my word, Mother. You will see me again," Aten swore, sheathing his father's sword and planting a kiss on his mother's forehead. He let his hand rest on his father's sarcophagus, speaking his goodbyes to the fallen warrior and swearing to make him proud. Then he left the tomb and, for the first time in his life, he ventured out, leaving his oasis home behind. Nenet stayed with her husband, watching her son go, and once his silhouette disappeared over the dunes, she fell to her knees and wept.

"Mother Isis, I beg of you, keep my child safe. Sekhmet guide his blade and let justice be done, and Abasi, my love, watch over your child. He will need you now more than ever."

For over a year, Aten scoured Egypt. He traveled from wide stretching deserts to bustling cities and villages. He never wavered in his hunt, even when it seemed as though he'd be searching for a lifetime. He never lost his conviction.

Finally, he was rewarded for his efforts in the great city of Memphis. As he'd done countless times before, he questioned whomever he could about the three men he searched for. Most had nothing to offer. It seemed as though the city would end up another dead end like all the others, but then, to his surprise, he found what he was looking for.

"A white viper? Yes! Yes! I remember him!" an old beggar woman said to Aten with a scowl. "He came here years ago with the two other men you spoke of. I remember him because he took all the coins I'd gotten that day, then threatened me with a knife," the haggard rabbit explained.

"Do you know where he went from here?" Aten asked hopefully.

"No, but the hyena he came with decided to stay here in the city. He might know."

Aten's ears perked and his eyes narrowed at the revelation. "Where can I find him?"

Aten stood in front of the door to a small home. He'd dreamt of this moment for over a decade, and now he had the chance to make that dream a reality. He knocked hard on the thick, wooden door, and after a moment it creaked open. A frail, old hyena stood in the doorway. He squinted his eyes at the cheetah in confusion.

"May I help you?"

Aten stared down at the weathered old beast with contempt. "I've been searching for you for a very long time," Aten said coldly.

"What? Do I know you?" the hyena asked in confusion.

"You wouldn't remember me as I am now. But tell me, do you remember the little cub who's throat you threatened to slit?" Aten asked, a snarl slowly forming over his muzzle. "Do you remember the Medjay whose death you had a hand in?"

The hyena's eyes bulged and his jaw dropped as he staggered back, prompting Aten to step farther into the doorway. He was an imposing figure cloaked in the dark robes of a desert dweller, far from the young, frightened cub the old hyena had last seen him as. "Do you remember that day, Coward!" he spat. His hand gripped tightly around Montu's hilt. The hyena fell to his knees, weeping at the cheetah's feet.

"Please, gods, don't kill me! I beg of you!" the old man pleaded pitifully, his commotion sending three more hyenas rushing to the door.

"What's going on, Heru?" The old hyena's wife appeared, putting her arms around Heru in concern. Two other hyenas, no more than fifteen years of age, looked on in fear. Aten looked at the scene, remembering himself as a weeping cub beside his father's body. He would not, could not subject this man's children to that same trauma. There was no righteousness in that. His anger faded, and his snarl was replaced with a solemn frown.

"On your feet," the cheetah said, taking his hand off of his sword. "For years I thought about this day. How I'd make sure you never hurt anyone again, but now I can see you're already no harm to anyone. Osiris will judge you when the time comes, but you have nothing to fear from me."

Heru wiped tears from his face, thanking the cheetah profusely. "Your mercy knows no bounds. I am forever in your debt," Heru spoke, still groveling before Aten.

"You can repay me by telling me where I can find the viper and hippopotamus you were with that day," Aten said, helping the old man to his feet.

"The viper is called Serapis, and the hippo is Ubaid," Heru explained, his fur standing on end as he recited the names. "I haven't seen either of them in years, but if nothing has changed, I may still know where they both are."

Aten retrieved a map from his bag and held it out to the old man. "Can you show me?" That same pang of hope sparked within him as the man marked a barren location towards the west desert.

"Be warned, Medjay's Son. Those two will not repent as I have, and they will not be alone."

"I'm prepared for what may come," Aten answered plainly.

"Then good luck to you." Heru handed back the map before turning to the two young hyenas in the room. "Children, fetch the man some water for his journey."

"That is not necessary," objected Aten, but Heru would not hear it.

"It is the least I can do for you."

Aten took his offerings and traveled west toward the scorching desert. Heru and his family lingered in his mind. He never thought he would spare any of the men from that day. He knew it was the right choice, though. He wrapped his hand around the hilt of Abasi's sword and felt the old warrior at his side. It should have been him that taught Aten how to wield a sword. Aten felt that old, familiar ache in his heart, an ache that drove him forward to the last two men who would answer to him.

Aten traveled through the barren desert for a week until the blood in the air indicated he was on the right track. It wasn't long after that he saw the slaughtered horses and the dying jackal bleeding out beside them. Aten jumped off his camel and raced to the scene, kneeling down beside the dying man. Crimson blood seeped from a deep wound in the jackal's stomach.

"Be still," Aten said, retrieving the medical supplies he kept in his bag. He began dressing the wound in lint, animal grease, and honey, just as Maat had taught him. The jackal cried out in pain through it all. "What happened here?" Aten asked the poor man.

"We were returning home to Memphis," the jackal stated weakly between gasps of pain. "Bandits ambushed us. Killed our horses. They stabbed me and took them."

"Took who?" Aten questioned, his heart throbbing in his chest.

"M-my wife and daughter," the man answered, tears streaming from his foggy eyes. "You have to...have to help. Please help," the jackal pleaded, weakly gripping Aten's wrist. "Please save them...Medjay." With those words, the air left his lungs and his pained, pleading eyes rolled back into his head. Aten stared down pitifully at the body.

"May your journey be a safe one," Aten said, swallowing the lump in his throat. The man's words echoed in his head, making his blood run cold. A wife and a daughter. Another family, now fatherless. Another innocent man dead. Aten may have been wrong about Heru, but not the others. His icy blood turned to fire, thinking of all the evil that they had done, and all the evil they would do if not challenged. He wouldn't let that happen. They would answer for this and everything else.

The jackal had called Aten a medjay, a protector of the innocent and a punisher of the wicked, just like his father. And that's exactly what he would be. "I will see that your family is safe. You have my word," Aten said, scooping up the jackal's body and hoisting it up onto his camel. He couldn't just leave the body of the jackal. He would get a proper burial when his family was safe.

Aten rode forward till he found the area Heru had marked on his map. The bandits were hiding in an abandoned turquoise mine dug into the side of a towering sandstone cliff. Just outside the entrance stood a large, hulking hippopotamus. Ubaid had not aged nearly as harshly as Heru. His skin was wrinkled, but his shape remained just as imposing as it had all those years ago. The hippo watched, eyebrow raised as the cheetah approached.

"A wise man would turn around," Ubaid warned.

Aten said nothing. He simply dismounted his camel and stepped forward.

"Last warning, boy, you have no business here," Ubaid said, raising up his heavy stone mace and thick wooden shield.

"You're wrong. My business is standing right before me," Aten said, unsheathing his khopesh. A smile spread across Ubaid's large maw as the cheetah charged toward him. The older warrior blocked Aten's blows with his shield before sending the cheetah toppling down the sandy dunes with a powerful swing of his mace. Aten spat blood onto the baking sand as he pulled himself to his feet. Fire burned in his eyes as he ran back up to meet the giant. Bronze and stone clashed as the two traded blows.

Ubaid was the stronger warrior, but Aten's speed lent him the upper hand against the hippo. Aten was able to deliver multiple blows in the time it took the large hippo to raise his mace. Ubaid stood tall and immovable, absorbing the cheetah's frenzied attacks with his shield. He waited for Aten to tire, then he struck, staggering his opponent with a hard shield bash. Aten's senses returned just in time for him to evade a killing blow from Ubaid's mace. The two warriors circled each other, both anticipating the other's next move. Aten had to find a way past the hippo's defenses if he hoped to get any further.

Luckily, it seemed the gods had granted Aten their favor. Montu was more than a match for Ubaid's weathered shield.

The wood was splintering right above the center. It was just what he needed: a single weak point in the goliath's defenses.

Aten ended their cat-and-mouse game, charging once more at the brutish hippo. Ubaid raised his shield, once again anticipating another barrage of futile blows, yet Aten only delivered one a single powerful thrust that tore through the weakened wood and allowed the razor-sharp sword to pierce the stunned hippo's shoulder. He cried out in pain as Aten forced the blade in deeper before ripping it free.

Ubaid dropped the broken shield to the ground, blood trickling from the gaping wound in his shoulder. His face contorted into an expression of pain and primal rage. He swung his mace at the cheetah in a frantic daze. Aten dodged and parried the blows with newfound confidence. Ubaid was panicked, his movements becoming increasingly sloppy. The tide had turned.

Aten advanced on his wounded enemy. Ubaid was growing weaker by the moment. He needed to keep distance between himself and the cheetah, but he was making no progress head-on, so in one last desperate attempt, he brought his mace down hard at the cheetah's feet. Aten jumped to the side, just narrowly avoiding the powerful mace.

Now was his chance.

Aten swung with all his might into the hippo's unprotected mace-wielding arm. Bronze bit into muscle and flesh, and with a sickening crack, met bone. Ubaid wailed, dropping his weapon as Aten pried his blade from the hippopotamus's arm. Now was the time to deliver the killing blow.

With one swift cut, Aten opened the hippo's bloated belly, letting his insides spill onto the scorching sand.

Aten panted as his eyes fixed on Ubaid's carcass. He'd done it. He'd ended a life, a wicked and murderous life, but a life nonetheless. He felt different than he expected. He thought he'd feel a righteous sense of pride ridding the world of such a horrible man, but he didn't. Instead, a hundred different emotions and thoughts all grappled with each other for supremacy.

Aten tried his best to push the thoughts from his mind. Now was not the time. His only priorities were to get to the viper, avenge his father, and free the jackal's wife and child. He wiped the blood from his khopesh, thanking the gods for his victory and praying for protection. Then, he stepped into the mine.

Aten crept through the dimly lit tunnels until he reached the center of the mine. After all these years, Aten laid eyes on the ghostly-white serpent who took his father from him. He seethed with hatred at seeing that familiar fanged smile. The viper—Serapis—alongside an ox, boar, and crocodile stood appraising the bound jackal woman and her crying daughter.

Their words echoed through the chamber sickening Aten. "She'll make a fine whore, and someone is bound to want the child," Serapis spoke.

"How much do you think they'll fetch?" the boar asked eagerly.

"More than a fair price," the viper answered, his grin growing even wider. "We will take them to the dealer first thing at dawn."

"You will do no such thing," Aten said, stepping out of the shadows.

The viper's men drew their weapons, but Serapis himself simply stared in puzzled amusement at the sudden intrusion.

"A guest? Now how on earth did someone manage to get past Ubaid?" the white snake asked, cocking his head at the feline.

"Your brute is dead," Aten spat.

"Impressive. And just who are you?"

"I am Aten, son of the medjay Abasi of Siwa. Years ago I watched as you cut my father's throat. Now I've come to make you answer for it," Aten answered, drawing his father's blade.

Serapis roared with laughter at the cheetah's answer. "Is that what you've come here about, Aten of Siwa?" Serapis asked in a mocking tone. "I killed my own father. What makes you think I remember or care about killing yours?" the viper chuckled as Aten glared daggers. "Allow me to explain something to you: you're not the first person to come to me with a score to settle, and I promise, you won't be the last. Cut him down." And with that, the three men charged.

The ox, wildly swinging an ax, was the first to meet the feline warrior. He lacked skill. A simple parry was all it took to grant Aten the opening he needed. With a single chop, he brought his blade down into the side of the ox's neck. The boar and crocodile both handled themselves much better, attacking in unison with a spear and sword in hand. Aten didn't falter, however; he used the two warriors against each other, pushing the crocodile into the boar's spear before ending the swine himself with a shift chop through the top of his head.

"Well then, I suppose you're getting a chance to make your father proud," Serapis said, unsheathing a set of gleaming daggers, one in each hand, as well as a third gripped tightly by his flexible tail. He gave Aten one final grin dripping with malice and venom, then made his move. The cry of metal against metal rang out through the hollow mine as the two warriors fought. For a man who stayed back while others fought his battles for him, Serapis was exceptionally skilled. He struck with lightning-fast movements, taking advantage of all three blades to overwhelm the cheetah. He sliced Aten's clothing to ribbons, and left his body riddled with nicks and gashes. Pain seared through the young feline's body. His battle with Ubaid and the other guards had taken a toll on his abilities. Fatigue was slowly taking him. He fell to the ground as Serapis kneed his stomach.

This was it. After all his searching and the battles he'd fought to get here, he was going to be killed, just like his father before him. As he lay there waiting for the viper to end him, his eyes met the jackal woman. Her face was full of fear, and in her eyes was a pleading desperation, not just for her own sake, but that of her daughter as well.

It sparked something in Aten. Thoughts of his own mother and Maat flashed through his mind. His grip tightened on Montu, feeling his father's fire burning through him. He would not die this easily, not with so much at stake.

Serapis basked in the feeling of slowly breaking Aten. He was so confident, so sure the fight was won. He always liked to drag out the moment before ending a life. He slowly brought the dagger in his tail to Aten's throat, the same wicked grin on his face as the day he'd killed Abasi, but before he could slit the warrior's throat, Aten sprang into action, slicing nearly half of the viper's tail clean off. Serapis screamed in agony as blood gushed from his mangled stump of a tail, giving Aten enough time to spring to his feet.

His heart beat with newfound life as he cut into the snake's wrist, disarming him of another dagger. Desperation and fear crept over the viper as he found himself in the position he'd had Aten in only moments ago. He panicked, freezing as Aten wrenched the last dagger from his hand before thrusting his khopesh through Serapis's stomach. The white snake spat blood and fell to his knees as the blade slipped out, and with one final motion, Aten cleaved the serpent's head from his body. Time almost seemed to stand still.

Once the fight had ended, Aten almost felt like collapsing then and there, but he still had work to be done. He lumbered over to the two softly weeping captives, cutting their binds and helping them to their feet.

"Thank you," the mother jackal said, still wiping tears from her eyes.

"I just did as your husband asked of me."

"Is he…"

Aten lowered his head shamefully at the question. "I did what I could, but I am no healer. He…is gone now."

The woman choked back her grief as she scooped her daughter up, holding her tight. "I will take you both back to Memphis so he can be buried properly," Aten said in a low, sympathetic tone. The woman simply nodded.

Aten made good on his word. He brought the woman and her child back safely to the great city, and handed over her husband's body for funeral rites. Once he'd done all that, he could prepare to leave. His job was done now. Killing Serapis and his men did nothing to dull the pain and bitterness he felt, but he did find some solace knowing they would cause no more pain on this world. He clung to that fact, hoping it would be enough to bring him the peace he craved.

"Where will you go?" the jackal asked him as he mounted his camel.

"Home," Aten answered, looking to the horizon.

"We will not forget you, Aten of Siwa. May your journey be a safe one," she said. With those parting words, Aten began his journey. He felt a tinge of regret leaving the two alone, but they were home now, and home was where he must go. He'd made a promise to his mother; she still needed him, and beyond that, Aten didn't have much of a purpose anymore. He'd spent so much of his life brooding over revenge, but now what did he have?

He stared down at the sword at his waist. His hands almost instinctively grasped the handle. He felt that familiar guiding presence flowing through him once more, and as he unsheathed the blade, he saw not only his face reflected in the shimmering bronze, but also a warm, comforting face he hadn't seen since his childhood. As his father stared back at him in the reflection of Montu's blade, he knew what he would strive towards. He would follow in his father's footsteps and continue his legacy. He would protect his home and his people, just like his father would want. Maat was growing older. He'd spoken for a while of retiring, but Siwa would need another medjay, and that was exactly what Aten would become.

Nenet waited outside the village, as she had every day since her son had left. From dawn to dusk, she waited day after day, month after month, hoping beyond hope he would not be taken from her too. With every passing day her fears worsened, but she never stopped praying, and on one fateful day, as she waited in the sweltering heat, her prayers were answered. A dot appeared on the horizon, then it became a silhouette, and as the figure drew closer and his features became more visible, Nenet recognized the familiar, loving smile she'd longed for all this time. She dropped to her knees, and for the first time in fourteen years, she cried tears of joy; her son had finally come home.

Wren of the Foxes

James Stone

The wren shifted the baby he carried under his wing, away from the falling snowflakes, and looked up the hill. Smoke drifted over the ridge. He looked over his shoulder at the smoke rising behind him. He needed to get far, far away from what that was coming from, especially with a hurt wing and a baby to protect. The smoke ahead could be a danger as well, but he had to get somewhere safe, and it was worth the risk. He fluffed his feathers under his coat for warmth and continued up the hill to the ridgeline. He settled to the ground and peered down into the valley below, moving a wing to cover the child when he fussed. "Shhhh. Shhhhhh. Soon enough."

Nestled among the cedars in the valley were a number of sturdy houses. White smoke drifted upward from their chimneys, and Wren breathed a sigh of relief. The village was still here, and seemed safe for now, though Wren dreaded the reception that safety might bring. He stood and pushed the bracken aside and started his way down into the valley.

As Wren descended the hill, he smelled the homelike scents and tried to quiet his thoughts. Cedar smoke instead of charring flesh and singed fur. The hint of food cooking over those fires instead of cold seedcakes hastily stuffed into a sack. The musky aroma of foxes that reminded him… Wren clicked his beak.

He circled around the edges of the village to enter from the west. The snow was keeping the foxes indoors, but Wren didn't want to take any chances. The west side of the village was closest to Cotton's house.

Wren stepped up to the door and knocked. He listened for footsteps but didn't hear any, and looked around before knocking louder. This time he heard the soft footfalls of a kitsune that stopped on the other side of the door. "Who is it?"

"Cotton? It's me, Wren. Let me in, please."

The door opened to the ruddy face of a middle-aged kitsune. He looked Wren over and saw the baby, and his ears perked up as he burst into a big grin. "Wren! You brought my grandson for a visit!"

"Cotton, sir—"

"And where is Blossom? Where is my daughter?" the fox interrupted, leaning forward to stick his head out the door and look up and down the path.

"Cotton... She's gone."

"What do you mean? Where did she go?" he asked, still looking outside for her.

"Cotton, sir. She's gone to the west. I couldn't save her and the baby both," Wren said, clacking his beak and trying to keep from crying.

The fox pulled back inside and looked at Wren's face. His ears drooped and the grin faded to a frown. Wren reached his hurt wing up to the fox's shoulder to comfort him.

"Cotton. I'm so sorry."

"You're sure she's gone?"

"I'm sure. Let us in out of the cold and I'll tell you."

The fox looked back down at the baby and nodded, stepping back and opening the door wider. Wren stepped inside and handed his child to Cotton, and removed his overcoat. He sat down by the firepit as Cotton laid the baby down on his sleeping mat and fetched some cloth strips to start cleaning Wren's wounds.

Cotton tied the bandages tight around Wren's wing. "What happened? How did she die?"

"Eagle clan bandits set fire to the house," Wren said, looking at the floor. "They broke in while we were sleeping. Told me that I was 'complaining too much and hurting their business'.

Business! Waylaying travelers and bleeding farmers dry! I was able to get my shovel and fought them as best I could. I led them outside to get them away from Blossom, but I hadn't realized they set the thatching on fire at the rear."

Cotton had stopped fussing with the bandages and stood still, his rough hands clenching against the bird's hurt wing.

"She was brave, Cotton. She must have wrapped herself in one of the rugs to keep the flames away so she could get to our son in the side room." Wren had raised his head and was looking across the room past Cotton, replaying the events in his mind. "I guess the fire got too hot, and she couldn't get out. She managed to cut a hole in the side wall of the house and shoved him out through it. You should be proud." Wren paused a moment. "I heard her screams while those two eagles were laughing. It was terrible."

Warm drops of tears fell on his feathers like the beginning of a summer shower.

"I got to my feet and tried to run to the house, and the eagles held out their wings to stop me. I may not be the best swordsman, but for all I knew they had killed my entire family," Wren said, reaching his free wing up to comfort Cotton. "I got the shortsword from an eagle's sash. A quick thrust into his side and then a foot stomp and a slash across the other's throat. While they lay dying, I tried to put out the fire. It was too much. Too much."

Wren went silent and waited for the old kitsune to speak. The tears slowly ceased.

"Why couldn't you have left them alone, Wren?" he asked, looking down at Wren. "Why? They weren't any worse than the bandit clans that were here before them."

"Cotton… Father—"

"Don't call me that!"

Wren lowered his head more, bowing before his father-in-law's anger. "Fine, Cotton, but you were Blossom's father. As a father too, I wanted something better for our son. Something more than working the fields and meekly bowing to bandits who think he's an animal."

"You are an animal, Wren. Don't you think we had some wisdom to our meekness? Do you think we're stupid?" Cotton shouted, his ruddy hairless face becoming darker. "A high creature takes the needs of all into account! The eagles had no challenge here! Who can feel proud and strong when your opponents are foxes holding their tails between their legs and giving you the food from their pantries? They might have beat us once or twice. After that, they left us alone!"

Wren kept silent. The baby started to cry from the raised voices. Cotton crossed the room and picked him up, bouncing him in his arms and cooing. His tail flicked rapidly against his coat, showing he hadn't calmed in the slightest.

"You can stay here."

"Thank you, Cotton."

"I wasn't talking to you, Wren. My grandson can stay. You need to leave."

"But I'm his father!"

"Wren. I loved my daughter. I would have given the world to her with both hands, and when she said she was in love and wanted to marry you I consented, despite what you are."

"And what am I?"

"You're a typhoon, Wren. You do what you will do, and you wreck things. You're an animal who thinks he's a man. You took my daughter away because of your pride. I can't blame you for your nature, but I won't have you around. You know he'll be safer too if the eagles can't find you here."

Wren looked up at his father-in-law and son with his dark eyes glittering with tears. "Where will I go?"

"I don't know. Away. Go farm somewhere. Go join the Emperor's army if they'd have you. Find a sage and contemplate the mountain's essential spirit. Maybe that'll train this tempestuousness out of you." The frown on Cotton's face showed his opinion on that eventuality.

"Can I visit him?"

"I'm not a monster, Wren. Of course you can," the fox said, turning his back and carrying the baby into deeper into the house. He reached back and slid a screen between them. "Visit him when you are no longer an animal. Until then, stay away."

Wren sat by the table for a few moments, crying. Losing his love. Losing his child. Losing his family and all his connections to the world. It was too much. He put his head down and sobbed. The hilt of the dead eagle's sword poked into his belly. Wren sat up and gulped air, and pulled the sword from its sheath. He held it with his wings and set the edge to his throat. He sat there, breathing and trying to convince his arms to move and end his suffering. The edge of the blade tugged at his feathers and skin with every breath. With every beat of his heart.

Eventually he sighed, and lowered the sword. He slid it back into its sheath and got up. He stepped over to the fire and put on his overcoat, and then moved to the door. He stood there listening for Cotton and the baby, but heard nothing. Wren opened the door and stepped out into the cold night.

=

Years passed before Wren again saw the village of the foxes. It had spread to cover the valley floor, there were fewer cedars, and many of the buildings were larger than he remembered from his youth.

The gate to the village was more symbolism than substance, meant to keep evil spirits out. Still, two young farmers had noticed the armored visitor walking down the hillside and stood at the gate, blocking his path. They had wrapped their smocks up around their legs and tails to keep them from tripping if it came to a fight, and both carried long spears inexpertly. They were clearly more used to holding hoes than weapons.

"Who goes there?" the first called out when Wren stepped close enough for him to hear.

"Easy, friend," Wren said, holding his arms wide. "I'm Master Wren. I've come to see your headman."

The two foxes turned to look at each other and back at the bird. Wren could see how their eyes drifted from his beaked face and down to his sheathed sword thrust through his sash, then back to his beak. Their noses wrinkled in disdain. The obvious question was coming.

"How do we know?"

"Friend fox. I am clearly a wren. These are my wings. This is my armor," Wren gestured down his front with a feathery hand. "This is my crest. This is my sword."

"We see all that. You could be a bandit!" The kitsune stood a little taller and puffed out his chest to appear bigger, despite towering over the wren already. His tail wagged a little, even.

"Do bandits often come to your village in such a manner, walking calmly up to the gate?"

"It could be a trick. You could have killed this Wren and taken his armor!"

"Friend fox, I have no patience for this," Wren said, lowering his wings and striding forward at the pair. "If I were not Master Wren, and had killed him, do you think you would present any challenge? If you fear an attack from me, then take your initiative and attack me from behind. I seek only hospitality."

He walked between the bewildered foxes and headed deeper into the village. They looked at each other and at the retreating back of the bird. One looked back out of the village and up into the hills, peering as if to make out bandits lurking in the trees. He turned back to his fellow farmer and shrugged, motioning to him to fall in behind the wren.

The center of the village had a small square with a well, directly in front of a larger house. Wren strode up to the door and knocked. The door opened and a middle-aged fox stepped out, brushing his hands on his smock. His ruddy face was so familiar to Wren's memory that the bird did a double-take. "Cotton? Is that you?"

"What? No. I'm Cotton's son, Burlap. My father passed on several years ago. Who are you and what do you want?"

"I'm Master Wren. I am here to visit my son."

The fox's eyes widened and his ears went back. "I'm sorry, Lord Wren. I didn't recognize you," he exclaimed. He started to kneel down before Wren, but the bird made an exasperated click of his beak and reached out a wing to stop him.

"Master Wren. Not 'Lord'," the bird corrected. "You don't need to kneel."

Burlap stood back up and brushed his hands down his smock

again, his bushy tail twitching between his knees. "Would you like some tea, Lord—Master Wren?"

"Please. It has been a long trip."

"Of course, of course," Burlap said, stepping back and opening the door wider so Wren could enter. He looked at the pair from the gate standing in the square and glared at them. "What are you two doing still here? Go back to work!" he shouted, before turning and following Wren inside the house. He shut the door and busied himself heating water for tea, making more nervous glances at Wren. When it was ready, he motioned for Wren to sit down and he poured it into a cup.

"I'm sorry Lo—Master Wren. It's just regular tea. Not what I'm sure you get in the capital," Burlap said, standing beside the table and watching the bird expectantly.

Wren sighed and weighed the merits of trying to correct the nervous fox. He reached a wing over, picked up the cup, and took a sip. "It's fine, Burlap. It's good. Best tea I've had in weeks."

The fox smiled and his tail finally came out from between his legs. He set the teapot back near the stove and took a seat beside Wren at the table. His tail was wagging wildly behind his chair. "What can we do for you, Master Wren?"

Wren sipped his tea again. "Nothing more than telling me where my son is."

Burlap's tail stopped wagging though he continued smiling. "He's not here."

"What do you mean he's not here?"

"His house is away from town, down the valley a bit. Downstream as it were," Burlap said.

"Why doesn't he live in the village?"

Burlap's smile had faded and his tail curled under the chair. "We... We told him to leave."

Wren set his tea down and shifted in his chair. "You did what?"

The bird's tone hadn't changed but Burlap flinched as if Wren had shouted. "We told him to leave, Lord. Master. My father said he was here for protection from the eagles, but they haven't been seen around here for years and years. When father passed to the west, nobody wanted an an…"

"A what?" Wren asked, his dark eyes fixed on the fox's hairless face.

"An animal. Animal living with them. So we told him to leave. I mean, we weren't mean to him, Lord! We helped him build his hut!" Burlap's ears were back against his hair and his nervous grin was all pointy teeth.

"I see," Wren said. He stood up and Burlap flinched back. "Do you know why the eagles don't come around anymore, Burlap? Because I hunted them. To keep your village safe. To keep him safe. And what do you do? You repay my efforts by sending my son away to live alone?"

"He's not alone! He has a wife and a kid," Burlap practically squealed in fear.

"Enough. Where is his house?"

"Follow the stream down the valley, Lord. Not too far. We aren't monsters!"

Wren strode to the door and opened it, causing a couple of his feathers to float away in the gust. "Foxes keep telling me that. We're all monsters in our own ways. Try not to be one."

Wren did as the fox directed him, and followed the stream out of the village. The busy sounds of the kitsune faded away. The stream burbled as it ran over pebbles and rocks, and Wren tried to take in its tranquility to center himself as he walked.

Soon enough he came to a small hut. To the foxes' credit, it did appear well constructed. The field next to it was neat and tended. Wren puffed up a bit with pride at that while he walked up the path to the front door. The hut was made by the foxes, if he was to believe Burlap, but the field was surely tended by his son. He knocked on the simple plank door.

"Go away!"

"But you don't even know who I am or what I want!"

"Don't care. Only folk who matter to me are in here. You should leave."

"Please. Open the door. I've come a long way to see you."

"If I have to open the door it's going to go badly for you. Go away!"

"I do insist…"

Wren heard a bump inside the hut, and then quick footsteps across the floorboards. The door flew open and a walking stick swung at Wren's head. He took a step back and there was a sharp crack as his sheathed sword was in his hand, and blocking the blow. The wren inside the hut gasped in surprise, but it quickly cut off when Wren swept the legs out from under him and he landed on his back on the floor. A vixen was sitting at the table with a kit hiding behind her skirt. Wren chuckled.

"When is it going to go badly for me?"

"Owwwww. Guh, who are you?"

"That should be obvious. I'm Wren. Your father." Wren held his sheathed sword behind his back and reached his right wing down to help his son off the floor. The younger bird took his hand and got up, rubbing his back. "What should I call you?" Wren asked.

"Mud," the younger wren mumbled.

"What?" Wren asked, his eyebrows raised. "Your grandfather named you Mud?"

"Yes," Mud replied, looking at his feet. "My name's Mud. I don't think grandfather cared too much for me as a baby. My wife there is Fern, and my little daughter there is Birch." The kit made a squeak when Wren looked over at her and hid further behind her mother's chair.

"It's good to see you again…Mud. Here, let me take a look at you!"

Mud moved back across the room to his wife and daughter as his father's eyes followed him. Mud was clearly a wren, but clearly not just a wren. His fuzzy fox ears peeked up alongside his crest, and his eyes were fox's eyes: golden like an autumn sunset. His feathers were lighter brown, but unlike the kitsune he didn't have bare skin on his body or face.

"How have you been all these years?"

Mud looked back over at Wren. "Just great, Father. Best life an orphaned animal could ever have."

"Those are your grandfather's words, I'd say."

"No, Father. They aren't. It's the whole village!" Mud said, setting his chair back up and sitting down. "Bad enough that I'm an animal, but I'm a mix-breed too. I'm lucky that Fern took pity on me or I'd be out here alone."

Fern put her hands on her husband's shoulder and shook her head. "I didn't take pity on you. I think you're unique. All the other girls can have plain fox husbands and plain fox kids. I got my choice," she said, smiling. She looked over at Wren. "Would you like some refreshment, Father?"

"Thank you, Fern. That's very kind of you."

She rose and gestured to the chair she got up from, and went to the cupboard with Birch trailing along behind her. She returned and set a cup of water down in front of the bird with a little bow. Wren glanced at the cup and bowed back at her, then picked it up and took a sip.

"You know, Mud, there are places in the world where people are more like Fern. Places where people don't care if you are low or highborn, especially if you have valuable skills. You could come train with me."

"Is that the reason why you came back, Father?"

"Not entirely, Mud. I obeyed your grandfather's command until I felt I had satisfied both the conditions. His grandson is safe from the eagle clan bandits, and I am no longer an animal. I have at last tamed the tempest and am the quiet in the eye of the storm."

The younger wren looked at his father with his head tilted to one side.

"To put it plainly, I missed you, Mud. I never wanted to leave you. I did what I did to protect you, and for that I am sorry. I know I don't look it, but I'm old. Years training and fighting have worn me down. I've lost so much time. Time that we can never get back."

"Just pretend like you never left me behind?" Mud asked.

"Yes."

"And what then? Leave to train with you to be a warrior? I mean, who will watch the farm?"

"The farm is of no consequence," Wren said, reaching into a pouch on his belt and withdrawing three steel coins to set them on the table. Fern gasped. "Keep it. Sell it. Let it fall into ruin. Fern could go live with her parents while we are away—"

The younger bird sat up straight in his chair again. "What? Fern couldn't come with me?"

"Of course not. The frontier forts are no place for a kind vixen and your child."

"I won't do it."

"It's your legacy! I've been protecting this valley for years, and I won't always be around."

"Father. Wren. I don't care. Why would I do anything for the foxes? Aside from Fern and her family, the only one who ever cared for me at all was grandfather, and he's gone. Find someone else," he growled.

Mud got up and stormed out of the hut. Wren looked over at Fern. "Can you talk some sense into him?" he asked.

"I'll talk to him, but because he's my husband—not to do your bidding...Father. I don't want him to leave."

"You understand what my presence means for the valley?"

"I do, Father. We know how it used to be."

"Fern, every day I wake up with stiff joints. I keep feeling now that I have finished my work that death is walking beside me. When I am gone, if there is no one to replace me, the valley will be as before. All of my work lost in the dusty wind. The emperor is more concerned with the capital and the frontier. This valley ravaged by bandit clans means little when he worries about holding the empire together. There's nobody else I would trust with this task. He says he doesn't care about the valley, but you know that he does."

Fern closed her eyes and nodded. She stood and smoothed her skirts with a hand, and followed her husband outside, leaving Wren alone with little Birch. She stood, peeking around the chair that her mother been sitting in, and she had her tail in her hand and was chewing on the tip.

"You're a big girl, Birch. How old are you?"

She left her tail tip held between her lips and held up two

hands to show six fingers. Her kitsune heritage was more clear—
smaller feathers on her face and a smaller beak than Mud or
Wren had. Her grandfather studied her with his dark eyes.

"Do you want to come out from behind the chair and let
your grandfather take a look at you?"

The kit shook her head and hid further behind the chair, and
glanced toward the door at the raised voices outside. Wren
picked up his cup to sip, forgetting that it was water and not the
expected tea. He could hear Mud and Fern talking outside but
couldn't make out what they were saying. Mud's voice loud and
upset. Fern's voice quiet and persuasive. He sat back in his chair
and closed his eyes to seek his center.

He must have fallen asleep because he awoke to Mud and
Fern coming back into the hut. The vixen laid a hand on the
younger bird's shoulder for a moment, then gathered her
daughter and left the hut again.

"I don't want to leave...but I will, Father. Not for you or for
the village, but for her and Birch, and her family."

=

In the morning, Wren took his leave of the couple for a few
hours so they could say their goodbyes. He walked up to the
village and purchased supplies. The foxes were glad to see his
coins. Inside the village, the economy was purely barter. With the
peace that came from Wren's efforts with the army, travelers
visited and had items to trade that couldn't be purchased with a
spare rooster or from helping to harvest the onions.

Wren returned to the hut around midday. Mud and Fern and
Birch were waiting outside. Mud had put together a pack with
clothes and some food.

They walked back through the village and the kitsunes would
peer out their doors as they passed. When they caught Wren's
eye, they would give a nod or a nervous bow. When Mud caught
their eyes, their reaction was usually shaking their heads.

Wren and Mud walked through the gate of the village and up
into the hills.

When they reached the ridge, Mud stopped and looked back
down into the valley. He raised his wing to shield his eyes and

peered downstream.

"They'll be ok. She has her family," Wren said.

"I hope. I didn't like the village, but it's hard to leave it behind."

"It was for me as well, when I was young," Wren said.

"When grandfather sent you away?"

"No. Before that, when I met your mother and we wed. The kitsune didn't accept me either. I was different and, in my ignorance, I thought that made me better. I thought they were jealous."

"Did they push you away too?"

"No. They did not. They were content to have me and your mother in the village, except for Cotton. That was unbearable to me, so we left. If I hadn't been as I was, there would have been others around to help when your mother was killed."

They arrived at the frontier after three weeks on the roads. Wren located the nearest fort and went to talk to the commander while Mud stood around in the courtyard, waiting. A group of the emperor's soldiers stood nearby, whispering and joking while they looked him over.

"Hey little bird. What you doing way out here?" one lion asked. "You and that other little bird here to sing for us?"

Mud clenched his beak shut and tried to ignore the soldier.

"Oh, so you're quiet? Not going to sing?"

"No. I'm not."

"You here to join the army then, little bird? Wait, you're not quite a bird, are you? Hey! Look at his ears!"

"Stop it."

"What was that? Did you hear that? A little bird tweeted at us!" he said, turning back to his fellows. "A little half-breed soldier? Why don't you show us how you fight," the lion said, and pushed Mud over backwards into the dirt. "Oh, sorry about that, little bird. I don't know my own strength. Let me help you up."

The lion bent over and reached out a burly paw. Mud reached up and took a hold, and the lion yanked him up and flung him at the two other soldiers. They caught him and held him while the lion walked over.

"What's going on here?" Wren asked.

"Oh look! The other little bird. You come to show us how to fight as well?"

"You three could use a lesson."

The soldier strode over and loomed over the old bird. He turned back to his fellows and shrugged, and then without any warning he turned back to Wren and carried through with a punch that would have spun Wren's head around. Instead, it swung through the air over the wren's crest as he ducked, and there was a loud crack as Wren's scabbard slapped against the back of the lion's knees while he fell over backwards on the ground.

The wren stood from his crouch and, with a melodic cry, he planted a foot on the lion's belly and used a flap of his wings to launch himself into the air towards the soldiers holding his son. The two howled when Wren's sheathed sword slapped against their outer shoulders. They released Mud and he was able to lurch forward out of the way. Wren planted another quick step on their shoulders to continue his leap, and landed behind them with his wings spread wide to soften his landing. He stood and turned to look at the soldiers. "Lesson one: never be over-sure of your control of a situation."

The two dogs turned around, rubbing their shoulders. They both growled and stepped towards Wren, trying to get their paws on him. Each reach or swipe brought about a trilling chirp followed by a crack of the scabbard and a howl or a yelp. The dogs backed off, licking their stinging paws. "You don't fight fair!" they accused.

"Lesson two: a fight is never fair or unfair. War is the application of the minimal effort needed to achieve victory."

The lion's voice came from behind the two other soldiers. "This doesn't look like a victory to me, you damned bird." The dogs looked back over their shoulders and stepped back, revealing the lion holding Mud with his armored arm wrapped around the young bird's arms and torso, and with his knife drawn and laid against Mud's throat. Mud's ears were back and Wren could see his tail quivering between his legs.

"Lesson three: pride and needless escalation of force has doomed many endeavors," Wren said, standing straighter. "You don't want to do this. All you've suffered so far is hurt pride, if bullying a weaker foe counts as pride. If I need to draw my sword, your pride will be the least of your losses."

"Hah. I'll cut your son's throat right here if I want," the lion bragged. The two dogs were backing further away and shaking their heads. His arm muscles tensed under his fur and Mud whined as the knife started to move.

Everyone in the courtyard seemed frozen in the moment. There was a puff of wind when Wren spread his arms and launched himself into the air. Beautiful, complex birdsong filled the courtyard and Wren's blade gleamed in his hand. His leap was carrying him over the lion and his captive son, returning him to the spot where the fight started. The lion looked up, his muzzle opening in surprise, as Wren passed overhead. Wren landed, pivoted, and slid his sword deftly into the back of the lion's skull. The tip emerged from his gaping maw, still pointed upwards. The master withdrew his blade and swept it down, flicking the dead lion's blood onto the dirt.

Mud felt the lion go limp, and there was a rattling sigh as he collapsed to the ground.

Wren closed his eyes and trilled again. "Lesson four: a drawn sword enacts a terrible price," he said. He crouched down and closed the lion's eyes, then he tugged his prayer beads from his sash.

The two dogs fled.

"You...killed him?" Mud asked. He was backing away in the other direction from the red pool forming on the ground under the lion's skull.

Wren's eyes were still closed as he prayed along the string of beads in his hand.

"Do you kill many men?"

Wren sighed and opened his eyes to look at his son. "Too many. Not enough, sometimes."

=

That evening the fort commander, Brand, invited them to dinner. He seemed unperturbed with Wren's actions from earlier.

"Justified, as my sentries described it. If those other two haven't fled into the uplands already, I can make sure they're thrashed. I don't want my soldiers acting like animals."

Wren sipped water from his cup. "They're poor students if they didn't learn from earlier."

"In any case, I apologize. I know you can handle yourself, Wren, but them roughing up your son is another matter," the ox said, turning to Mud. "You ok, boy?"

"I'm fine, and I'm not a boy. I'm thirty-six," Wren said, keeping his eyes on his plate where he pushed his vegetables around with his fork.

"Oh, no offense intended. I wish I had been able to grow to such an age farming and not caring about war and bullies."

"Why couldn't you?"

"Slaves kept for frontline fighting only think about three things: war, food, and when the whip is going to come."

Mud shut his mouth, blushing from embarrassment, and kept pushing his vegetables around.

Wren nodded, his dark eyes flicking from his son to the commander. "Slavers?"

The commander grunted and held out an arm covered with the strange swirling tattoos that the slavers used to mark their property. "That's right. I got away one night during a storm. Fled right into the hands of His Imperial Majesty's army recruiters. I was half-starved, and getting a hot meal for killing without being whipped didn't seem so hard a bargain. And as you can see, I've come a long way."

"You have indeed, Commander Brand. Thank you for your hospitality. Mud and I have been on the road a long time and, while we aren't starving slaves, a hot meal helps a lot to refresh us as well," Wren said, stabbing a carrot and nibbling at it.

"You're quite welcome, Master Wren."

"Are you still fine with us training here? You agreed to it, I know, but that was before I lightened your command by a soldier."

Brand paused with his mouth full of braised greens. "Of course, Wren," he said, swallowing. "Between you and me, he wasn't much of a soldier. Not like what I hear about that bunch that were with you."

"They were a good troupe, indeed," Wren said, leaning back in his chair and brushing his crest back with a wing.

"I don't know what treasure you were guarding in that valley for the emperor, but that campaign sure made waves. You broke the back of the eagle clan over that entire region."

Mud looked up at the mention of the valley and saw his father frown and sit back straight at the table.

"I merely did what was needed."

"Oh, of course! Of course, Master Wren. Still made an amazing tale. Now, you might be on the out with the court and the emperor, but your name means something out here with the real soldiers. They shouldn't hold it against you. War is a bad business. Innocents are sometimes caught in the way."

Wren's frown deepened and he clacked his beak.

"You are too kind, Commander," Wren said, pushing his chair back. "If you will excuse us, Mud and I have an early start tomorrow. Thank you for the dinner and the conversation."

Wren motioned with a wing for Mud to follow him. Mud looked at his half-eaten plate and sighed, then stood and led the way out the door while the commander stood and bowed to Wren.

"No! It's sweep left, sweep left, overhand, then crouch!" Wren said, swinging his scabbard against Mud's side. "You aren't concentrating!"

Mud winced and rubbed his ribs. "I am! I'm trying, Father!"

"Try harder!"

"How can I try harder? We've trained what, ten or twelve hours a day? For a month? That's more work than I ever did with grandfather or on the farm!"

Wren closed his eyes and took a breath, seeking his center.

"We don't have much time, Mud. You have to get better."

Mud picked up a cloth and mopped the sweat from his feathery face. "Has this worked for your other students?"

"You're my first student."

"Really?"

"Yes. I'm Swordmaster Wren. Not Swordteacher Wren," he said, and chuckled a little when his son smiled at the phrasing. "When I was learning the art, I was on the eleventh form by this point. You're on the second form, and still don't have it down."

"I'm not you!"

Wren shook his head. "No, you aren't. I had hoped that my skill was something that passed down to you. You're the only one I would trust to learn my fighting technique. We will just have to keep going," he said, raising his sheathed sword again.

Mud's ears drooped against his head. "Isn't there another way?"

"No. It's too dangerous."

"Which is it, Father: no other way, or only a dangerous way?"

"Forget it. Raise your sword."

Mud kept his arms as his sides, though now his ears were back up and his tail was swishing. "No. You keep saying we are short on time, even though you won't tell me why, and we both agree I'm terrible. Will whatever it is help me improve in time?"

"Yes. It could also kill you, or me, or both of us. Where will the valley be then? You think the emperor will come back without me to steer him?"

Mud stepped closer to his father and lowered his voice. "That's what Commander Brand was talking about, isn't it? You weren't guarding treasure. You were guarding the valley of the foxes."

"No, Mud. I was guarding you."

Mud's ears went back and he nodded.

"Your grandfather protected you by sending me away, and I protected you by convincing the emperor that there were a succession of conflicts brewing on the frontier that required his army, led by me, to mobilize. Those conflicts just happened to require the army to march near the valley."

Wren slid his sword back through his sash. "And through the eagle clan camps."

"We didn't know," Mud said, walking closer and putting his hand on Wren's sword arm. "Grandfather said that the eagles stopped coming because the kitsune didn't challenge them, and that proved he was right to send you away. To be honest, I thought you didn't care about me."

"Well, now you know. I loved your mother very much. I would have done anything for her, and it's the same for you, Mud. If nothing else, if I die tomorrow, this time with you has been wonderful."

Mud's lip quivered and he started to cry, and pulled Wren into a hug. Wren circled his son with his wings and held him while he cried, making soft trills.

When the tears had subsided, Mud stepped back from the hug. He wiped his eyes with his sleeve.

"We need to do whatever we can to make me a swordmaster, Father."

Wren clacked his beak. "I said it is too dangerous."

"So? I love Birch and Fern, and like you I don't want anything to happen to them. I want to protect them, and follow in your footsteps, Father."

Wren saw something different in his son. He had a light in his eyes. He stood a little straighter, like a weight was removed from his back.

"I know, Mud. Alright. Let's get a good rest tonight. We will leave in the morning."

Mud was awakened by the brush of dark feathers across his arm. The sky was just turning light, and he could just make out his father wrapped in his cloak with his pack over his shoulder.

"Come on. Gather your things, Mud. We have a long way to go."

Mud knuckled the sleep out of his eyes, and sat up in his bed.

"How should I dress?"

Wren gestured down his body with a wing. "Cold weather. We're going into the mountains."

Mud shivered a bit at the thought of snowy mountains and got up. He wrapped his smock close to his body and belted it, and set the cloak that his father had bought back at the valley on his shoulders. He stuffed the rest of his belongings into his bag. He turned, and his father was standing with something behind his back.

"I have something for you, Mud," Wren said. He brought his wings around to his front and held out a sheathed sword.

"A present?"

"No. This is no gift. A responsibility. A burden. A terrible price, sometimes."

"I understand, Father," Mud said, taking the sword from Wren. He ran his hands up and down the scabbard. It was clean and unmarked. "This isn't from here?"

"No. I had it made when I resolved to visit you, in the hope that you would carry on my legacy. Normally, I'd give you my sword, but for this journey we might both need to be armed."

Mud admired the blade, bright steel like his father's, with an egg in a nest engraved near the pommel. He looked up. "Are the mountains dangerous?"

"Mud, everything is dangerous. I am dangerous. Burlap is dangerous. You survive by accepting that truth and acting to minimize the dangers you can control."

The young bird swung the sword a few times through the air in front of him and slipped its scabbard through his sash as his father did. "I'm ready."

The pair said their goodbyes to the commander and set off through the gate. They headed up into the hills that made up the line of the frontier of the empire. As they trekked higher, the leaves on the trees started to change. Mud looked around as they walked, marveling at the colors. "I didn't know trees did this, Father. The cedars in the valley never changed from green," he said, glancing at his father who was stooped over looking at a trio of stacked rocks. "What are you doing?"

"See these? They mark the old caravan route."

"Caravan to where? Who'd build a caravan route on the frontier?"

"Mud, I know they say that the empire is eternal, but it isn't. There were civilizations before it, and there will be ones after it. This road, such as it is, should lead to our destination: the ancient bazaar city of Path."

Mud started to say that he hadn't ever heard of Path, but his father was already working his way along the decrepit road toward the next marker of stacked stones.

They continued on that way for a week or two, while the leaves turned deeper and deeper reds and the weather chilled. Wren showed Mud how to make simple meals from the wild herbs and a root that grew here and there along the road. When it got dark, they would stop for fear of missing the markers or stepping wrong on a stone and tripping.

Some nights Wren would tell Mud about his mother. How she and Wren first met. How she introduced the wren to her father, and then showed her spirit defending him when Cotton wanted her to find a husband of her kind. How they would lie under the stars at night while Wren was building their home once they left the valley. Mud would fall asleep thinking of a fox he never knew and wondering if she was anything like Birch.

One night he asked how she died, and when Wren told him, he lay on his cloak and cried while the old bird stroked his head with a feathery hand. "It's alright, Mud. They paid that debt thirtyfold," he said. Wren lay down with his back to Mud, and the young bird thought he heard his father quietly crying too as he drifted off.

A few more days of walking brought them to their destination. The two birds came over a rise to see a broad, low mesa in the distance capped with a sprawling ruined city. Wren pointed out the ancient roads that stretched out from the city's seven entrances. The air was dry, and only scrubby vegetation grew around the approaches to Path, so as they approached, the wind whipped around them and left them feeling raw and exposed.

The city entrance had no gate or barrier. The tops of the walls were wind-worn smooth. Dust had piled up in the corners and along the walls, along with the red leaves from the trees back on the ridge. Wren had slid his sword out of his sash quietly, and was cautiously checking alleys and doorways while they walked deeper in.

The center of Path was a grand, open marketspace that in its day must have held a thousand people. Now it held only two. The wind howled through fallen timber stalls and awnings. Wren walked into the center, with Mud following along behind, and stood, turning his head to look at each of the entrances.

"What is it?" Mud asked, shouting to be heard over the wind.

Wren jumped and turned, and made a downward motion with his feathery hand that held his sword. Mud covered his mouth and crouched down. He looked around at the forgotten bazaar and joined his father in nervously glancing from entrance to entrance.

A shadow appeared at one of them, and when Wren pointed it out, Mud drew his sword out of his sash as well. The shadow was coming towards them there in the center. As it got closer, Mud could see it was some kind of inky-feathered bird. It was probably just a trick of the wind, but Mud thought a cloud of dust and leaves swirled around the figure's feet while he crossed the pavement and stopped before them.

"What do you seek in this, my ancient realm?" the dark bird asked in a croaking voice.

Wren knelt and touched his forehead to the dusty ground. "Ancient Master. We seek knowledge. My son—"

"Needs to speak for himself," the bird said, interrupting.

Mud moved over next to his father and touched his own head to the ground. "A-Aancient Master. I seek knowledge. I need to learn to fight with the sword."

"Why do you seek this?"

"To carry on my father's legacy. To protect those who cannot or will not fight. For my wife and daughter."

"Your father's legacy, hmm?" the dark bird mused. "What legacy is that?"

"A village in a valley kept safe from harm for thirty-six years."

The dark bird made a strange coughing sound that echoed

off the bazaar walls, despite the howling wind.

"Yes, yes. How many in that village kept safe, two-hundred? Tell me, boy. When was the last time you saw an eagle?"

"Please, Master. Don't do this," Wren said.

"Be quiet, Wren," the ancient master said. "Let your boy answer."

"Ancient Master, the eagles haven't come raiding in probably twenty years."

"Yes, your father saw an end to that. Surely you have seen other eagles, though? No?"

Mud tried to remember seeing any eagles passing through the valley and couldn't. "No, Ancient Master, but the valley is isolated…"

The dark bird leaned closer. "You have seen none because none still live."

Mud glanced over at his father, still with his forehead on the stones. "Yes, Ancient Master. He said he killed all their warriors."

"No, boy. He killed them all. Thousands gone. All dead. There are no eagles anymore," the master said, turning his head toward Wren. "Tell him, Wren. The last eagle mother and child. Tell him what dreaded fighters they were, Wren. Tell him when you murdered them."

Wren was trembling, the first time Mud had ever seen him afraid.

"Master. I…"

"Tell him!" the dark bird thundered. "Tell him or I will kill you both and leave your bones here to turn to dust!"

Wren's tears made little circles on the dusty stones. "One week before I arrived back in the valley to find my son, Ancient Master."

The dark bird stood up again. "Is that the legacy you want to carry on, little bird? He used my teachings to keep you safe by murdering an entire race. Even though the court and the emperor eventually cast him out, he kept on carrying out his vengeance on beings who never heard even a whisper in passing of a vixen who burned to death, and her farmer husband. He thought that I, out here in my dusty tomb, couldn't possibly find out."

Mud had stood up and was backing away, his mouth hanging open in shock.

"Please, Master. Don't do this. He's the only thing I have left!"

"It's already done, Wren. See how he recoils from you now that he knows the price of his safety?"

Wren looked over at Mud. The younger bird was shaking his head and had backed up against a ruined stall. "Wren, how could you?"

"I'm sorry. I did it for you and your mother, Son."

"Don't call me that. I'm not your son," Mud said, dropping his sword to the stones with a clatter.

Wren howled and hit his clenched fist on the ground. His bright blade swept out of the scabbard and along the ground at the ankles of the ancient master. Mid-swing he stopped, as though his sword had hit stone. The raven coughed again and, through the swirling dust and leaves, Wren saw the raven's booted foot resting on top of the blade. The ancient master swept his wings down, giving him lift to kick Wren in the beak and send him flying thirty feet across the square to crash into a wall. Wren didn't move, and Mud took a step in the direction of his father only to find a smoking red blade barring his path.

"The gods have a unique punishment for those who cause so many to die, Mud. You're standing in the middle of mine," the ancient master croaked. "I could have saved my people. Steered them away from the wars that they waged. I told myself that I would step in when they went too far, but before I knew it, that moment had passed.

"This city wasn't always like this. A thousand years ago it was a garden. The gods cursed it and me. Winds came and blew the soil away. My people died and turned to dust, and the winds blew them away too. I expected to die as well, but I alone lived.

"When your father came to me, he woke me from my slumber deep beneath this city, and pled for the knowledge of invincible sword-mastery. He pled for his murdered wife's sake and to protect his infant son."

Mud moved toward Wren again, and the blade rose to rest against his throat.

"I gave him that which he sought, hoping that he might free me from the curse. He hasn't, and now he's doomed himself and you as well."

Mud backed up. "What do you mean?"

"I can't let either of you leave. I must keep this curse contained here. With you two dead, perhaps my legacy will really be forgotten. I'm sorry, little bird. The gods won't mind another two deaths against my soul."

The raven's blade, like that of the lion's back at the fortress, started to tug at the skin of his neck. He closed his eyes and made his choice. His father couldn't save him now. If he was ever going to see Fern again, he needed to fight. He moved his blade just enough and drove it into the old raven's thigh. The ancient master cawed and flinched, nicking Mud's neck, and backed away.

Beautiful birdsong filled the ruin. The ancient master cried out and spun away, bleeding now from a gash in his arm as well. Wren stood, blood dripping from his beak, his stained sword naked in his hand.

The red leaves around the raven's feet swirled, and Wren shifted his stance as the ancient master slid across the stones between them. The old raven's dark blade flicked and darted, sometimes blocked by a sweep of Wren's sword, but often finding a gap and wounding the smaller bird. Wren's attacks now seemed ineffective against the ancient master's skill.

Wren kept backing away, trilling and singing. Sweeping his feet against the Ancient Master's legs. Thrusting with his wings to get some height before slashing at the old raven's eyes. Bleeding from dozens of cuts. Mud had backed out of range of the ancient master, and Wren retreated before the raven's onslaught to widen that range. He failed to see a wall hidden in the dust, and stumbled backwards to the stones.

The old raven launched into the air with a croak, and his booted foot landed on Wren's sword. It had fallen across a paver, and the force of the Ancient Master's landing snapped the blade as easily, as if it were a dry twig. The ancient master loomed over Wren and thrust his red sword into Wren's chest.

Birdsong that wasn't his own swelled in the bazaar and the old raven lurched forward, crying out. Mud was on the ancient master's back, and his blade emerged from the old raven's chest. The ancient master coughed blood and slumped against Wren, feeling like nothing more than a bundle of bones wrapped in old rags. Mud pulled the body of the raven off of Wren, and started ripping strips from his cloak to try and stop Wren's bleeding.

"Mud. I'm sorry."

"Shhh, don't speak. Save your strength."

"I just got lost. I loved your mother so much. Hated the eagles. So much. I wish…had more time. Wish I…wasn't…monster, Mud."

Mud bound his father's wounds as fast as he could, but the older wren had got quiet. Mud couldn't see him breathing anymore. The blood from his cuts slowed to a trickle, and Mud knew he was gone. The young bird sat down on the ground, clasped his father's sword hand, and cried.

Fern was mending one of Birch's dresses at her father's house in the village when a shadow crossed her lap. She looked up to see her husband standing at the edge of the porch. She jumped up and hugged him, and felt his wings wrap around her in return.

"Where's Wren, Mud?"

"He's gone, Fern," he said, reaching up to wipe his eyes.

"I'm sorry, Mud. He was a good man. Did you learn what you needed, Mud?" she asked.

He held her closer. "Not quite a good man, and I'm not quite a swordmaster. Someday I may be. For now, it's enough to be here, and be a husband and a father."

"What about the bandits?"

Mud pulled back and held up his father's gift in its scabbard.

"If they ever come back, I'll show them what a wren can do."

Arisen

Chris Williams

"Shay, hit him with fire!"

"On it!"

Shay, ears flicking as he recalled the proper words, cried out the arcane tongue of spell-casting, fingers aimed at the relentless horde of undead foes. Lysander ducked out of the way as the spell blasts flew out of the tiger's paws, pelting three of the wraiths with licking blue flames. Two of them crumbled into dust instantly. The third remained upright, though staggering, and lurched forward, flinging a bolt of green energy that smacked into the mage, silencing him.

Not good.

Lysander thrust his blade in the path of the wraith, which had advanced towards the relatively helpless, and now mute, spellcaster. The blade flashed, slicing deep into the wraith's emaciated chest. It screamed and collapsed to the floor, moving no more. Lysander had just enough time to search the body before it crumbled into dust. Not much there, of course. A couple of gems and a single finger bone with an iridescent sheen. Creatures of habit, the wraiths were, and not especially intelligent.

"Are you all right?"

Cyrus and three of the other Heroes of Mistvale—Lysander hated the pretentiousness of calling themselves that, but the majority had decided—had filed into the chamber. Cyrus, every bit the stereotype of his pack-oriented species, glanced at each warrior in turn as he made a bee-line for Shay who stood glowering, arms folded, tail lashing, muzzle clamped shut.

"By the force of nature, I remove your curse," Cyrus intoned, placing a glowing paw above Shay's chest. After a moment, the glow ceased. Shay's white paw crackled with energy as he regarded his claws. His orange bengal brother, Jace, stood silently close by, warhammer in hand, ready for action.

"Thanks. Now, let's go get Necros before he does...uh..."

"Whatever he seeks shall serve no good," Cyrus finished, his tail lashing. His armor glinted in the beams of moonlight that managed to enter through the cracks in the dilapidated walls as he moved closer to Lysander.

"Ready to go?"

Lysander swallowed and nodded, mentally cataloging the wounds he'd taken so far. Minor as they were, they could become a disadvantage later. He depended on the healers, but if they were silenced, or incapacitated, he could drop quickly.

After a deep breath, the black fox settled himself. He wasn't facing the evil alone. Cyrus, his mentor, would be beside him. Shay, the elementalist, stood ready to rain fire down on the undead from a safe spot, and his beast of a brother would be right there to keep him safe. Shay could cover their retreat with a fire wall if necessary. Then there was Fellwyn, a mouse cleric of the deep forest. She kept the group healed quite well. The archer, Faythe, could take out a zombie's eye-socket from a hundred yards.

Lysander smiled at the memory of when Faythe, a fellow fox, albeit one of the Northwinds, with glowing fur-stripes along her muzzle and cheeks, had met him and promptly used him to steady her aim and finish off a rampaging troll across a field.

Jace, a large-framed orange Bengal, carried a massive hammer and shield. Once he planted his paws, he was unmoving. He tended to stay quiet.

And of course there was Cyrus, the lupine paladin and Lysander's mentor in the fighting arts. It was Cyrus who rescued him from the band of wild gnolls that had captured him, who'd taught him to fight. Watching the wolf enter battle, single of purpose and with a focus more honed than even the fine edge of his runic blade, filled Lysander with a great sense of righteous purpose. With Cyrus leading them, the adventurers could overcome any foe.

Lysander allowed himself a moment to take in Cyrus in full armor. The wolf stood a foot taller than he did, with great broad shoulders. His muzzle had begun to show a frosty tinge of silver around his nose and whiskers, and the tips of his ears had also begun to show some age. His mentor, friend, and life's partner, Cyrus looked like a radiant warrior angel to Lysander. When this was over, he was going to give his wolf a shoulder rub and a nice stiff drink.

"Let us ascend," Cyrus said, with a smile flashed at Lysander. "Necros will face our justice. We fight for the light!" the wolf shouted, extending his paw. The others all placed their paws on his, Lysander placing his atop them all.

"For the light!"

The stairs led upward to a wide, expansive chamber, lined back to front with columns. On a raised dais, within a glowing circle of protection, stood the party's quarry, muttering words of arcane power over an altar draped with a crimson cloth.

"Necros, prepare to end this unnatural existence!" Cyrus shouted, pointing across the chamber at the lich.

Horrible, decayed flesh hanging from his muzzle, Necros ignored the pronouncement of the warrior of light, continuing to speak. Finally, his voice rose in thunderous command with the final words of the ceremony.

Ritual complete.

"Rise, my dark minions! Rise! *Rise!* Rise and destroy these fools!" the lich cried. He raised his putrefied arms in a gesture of terrible command.

From the shadows in the corners of the chamber, the barest hints of movement flickered in the fox's awareness. Lysander held his bastard sword at the ready, his shield raised. The sound of something skulking reached the fox's ears.

"On your guard!" he called out. From those shadows

emerged shambling, skinless creatures, snapping oversized teeth in impossibly large jaws. They lurched forward quickly, claws raised. There were at least six of them in the light, but Lysander could see more lurking in the shadows, waiting, watching.

Cyrus raised his sword and swung, slicing into the creature closest to him. It screeched at him and staggered but remained upright. Slime dripped off of its exposed muscles. Lysander could see now that not only did the creatures lack any kind of skin or fur, but their eyes were hollow sockets.

Lysander swung his sword at the recovered creature. It swatted his sword away with not a bit of damage to its foot-long claws. Two of the other creatures began to flank the group. Faythe began flinging arrows at the creatures. As the first two bounced off harmlessly, she snarled some manner of swear in her native tongue, and then whispered something over her quiver, setting her arrows aglow. When next she fired, the arrow penetrated, staggering, but again not stopping two more of the monstrosities.

Lysander swung again at the nearest creature. This time his blade found its mark, tearing a gash in the creature's arm. It shrieked and swung its claws at him, ripping through his chest armor and scraping at the fur beneath. Another swing of the claws got around his sword and raked his right arm. The pain grew excruciating, and he could feel the flow of blood from both wounds as a spreading warmth. This was bad.

The monster received a glowing warhammer to its shoulder, shattering bones with a wet crunch and sending it, unmoving, to the floor. Jace had moved in, shield raised to block the blows of the monsters nearest him. The dead monster crumbled into ash.

Fellwyn raised her paws and spoke her prayers, and Lysander could feel his wounds closing. He wasn't fully healed—his arm remained stiff—but wouldn't bleed out anytime soon.

"Watch our flanks, Fellwyn and Shay!" Cyrus called. Lysander turned to see that more of the abominations had risen and gotten around the forward defenders.

Fellwyn moved left, and Shay right, each whispering prayers to their respective forces and extending arms. The creatures hissed and backed away, moving around to the front of the group again. Lysander took a few steps back, hoping to create more space in which to fight. Shay and Fellwyn moved as well. Faythe continued launching arrows over the group's heads

"Having trouble, *heroes?*" Necros laughed. "I haven't even joined the fray yet and you're already struggling."

Lysander, having managed to finally fell one of the creatures, looked and saw Cyrus, still forward of the battle lines. He was moving faster than Lysander had seen a swordsman move in his entire life. Three of the creatures had surrounded him in front, striking out with each of their claws. Cyrus's enchanted armor held, repelling the assaults. Cyrus himself turned and spun, sword raised, blocking blow after blow and lashing out with his own flurry of attacks. One creature backed away, seeking to come at him from another angle.

"Cyrus—" Lysander started to warn him, but a pair of glowing arrows from Faythe's bow dropped the assailant.

"Thanks, Faythe!" he called. Lysander stepped forward to help drive Necros's creations back.

Cyrus's blades flashed in the stream of moonlight pouring in through the cracks in the crumbling stone of the tower walls. He spun in unceasing curved blows, driving the snapping abominations away in a whirl of steel and blood.

"*Yes! Go, Cyrus!*" Lysander cheered.

"Face me, Lich!" Cyrus called, "If you're not afraid!"

"Afraid? Of a mere mortal?" the lich rasped in hideous laughter. "Not a chance in the nine blazes. Come to me then, if you would face me!"

"Cyrus, don't! He's too strong for you," Faythe shouted, flinging another volley of arrows at the masses of decaying flesh and teeth swarming from the shadows.

"I curse you with Paralysis!" shouted the lich from his protected dais, firing a blast from his fingertips that landed squarely on Lysander's chest. He felt his body tighten, his muscles seizing and unmovable even as his mind screamed commands at them.

That's when everything really went to hell. Three more

creatures shambled forward, raising the total of foes to nine plus the lich himself.

Cyrus, realizing what had happened, took a few heavy swings, driving his attackers back, attempting to get to Lysander, who could only watch helplessly.

Another incantation, another paralysis curse, and Cyrus stood facing Lysander, his eyes wide with worry. Those eyes, moist and unblinking in fear, pierced into the fox's soul as the creatures surrounded Cyrus and began to cut into him with their claws.

Faythe continued firing arrows, but in tight quarters her shots were not so strong—she had to be careful, Lysander realized, not to hit Cyrus or himself.

Shay stepped forward, paws raised and arms outstretched, tail lashing, towards the undead creatures.

"By my command, undead be gone!"

The creatures turned to face him, as if pushed by an unseen bubble.

"Be silent!" the lich shouted from his dais, raising his grey, desiccated arms towards Shay who, for the second time today, had his speech taken. He continued to hold his arms outstretched, never breaking his line of sight to the undead creatures. Necros's rotting muzzle cracked a twisted grin. "Fall into the depths of slumber."

Fucking great. Sleep and silence. Get us the hell out of here or we're going to wipe.

The undead, now free of Shay's command, skittered forward, surrounding Cyrus once more.

"By Lilana's Grace, I dispel your curse."

Fellwyn had moved in behind Lysander. Once more, he could move.

"I'm out of arrows," Faythe shouted, "and they're flanking us!"

"Get them off Cyrus and let's fall back," Lysander shouted, his tail lashing furiously as he strode forward, blade flashing. Cyrus's attackers peeled off to attack, leaving the wolf torn and bloodied on the ground. One of the creatures dropped to the ground under the fox's assault. The other two attacked in unison. Lysander's focus narrowed to the creatures and their massive claws. He could hear other sounds of battle, spells and prayers being flung back and forth. He was dimly aware of being forced backward as he blocked strike after strike.

When a new third creature joined in, he was blocking two out of three strikes, but feeling something resembling a dull pain each time one got around his blade and into the weak joints of his half plate armor. He could taste iron, and he was wobbling rather than backing away smoothly.

"—to get out"

"But Cyrus—"

"Leave—"

Lysander's focus widened again at the snippets of words, and he became suddenly aware that he had backed into the rest of the party at the stairs.

The rest of the party, except for one. Cyrus lay unmoving where he had been paralyzed, and where he had fallen.

Fellwyn held the creatures back, with some great effort. Shay worked his mouth, trying desperately to speak an incantation, but though the paralysis had clearly been lifted, the silence spell had not. Faythe had slung her bow over her back and drawn twin silver daggers. They'd cause some hurt to the undead, but not nearly enough in these numbers.

"We can't leave Cyrus!" Lysander cried, sidling closer to the group.

"We can't get near him," Faythe said, pointing.

Three more creatures had emerged from the shadows and were tearing at the wolf.

"He'll have to resurrect," Fellwyn said. "It's either we leave him or we all die. We're no good to anyone dead. Especially not if Necros manages to raise us and put us into his service.

If he res's, he might not come back.

"Go on, *heroes*, run away with your tails between your legs," Necros laughed.

"You come out from behind your cowardly little circle of power and we'll see who runs away!"

"You aren't worth my time, fox. The only one of you who might have been is lying bleeding at my feet. Aren't you going to try and rescue him? He's right there! Surely you won't abandon your best friend and mentor, will you?"

Lysander's fur bristled and he strode forward, hacking at the undead from just outside their reach. His swings were wild, doing little if any damage, and he knew it, but the fury filled him from ears to tail tip.

Paws grabbed at him pulling him back.

"Stop—" He swung again. "By the gods, *stop!*" Faythe shouted in his ear, dragging him back to the group.

"I won't leave him!"

Shay, from a leather pouch carried at his side, produced a palm-sized, five-pointed crystal and held it out. Faythe, struggling to hold Lysander back from the fray, reached out with one paw and touched the stone. Shay extended a paw and placed it on Fellwyn's shoulder.

Transport 3

"NO!" Lysander shouted

Transport 2

"Let me go! I won't leave Cyrus behind!"

Transport 1

"CYRUS!"

Everything faded from view, as Necros laughed his horrible laugh.

"Thank you, NPCs," the group called in unison back into the converted barn which housed the majority of the indoor adventure modules. 'Cyrus', sprung to his feet as Jake—or 'Lysander' as he tried to consistently think of himself during the weekend—waited, leaning against the wood of the doorway. The others lingered in a clump outside. Faythe's player, Sandra, had pulled out her phone and was muttering about the incompetence of her coworkers.

"Man, you guys are getting too good." Tom grinned at the motley group of people with grey and green makeup smeared through their fur. "I'm actually breaking a sweat in these fights now. Cyrus isn't going to be happy when he res's." He earned a few laughs and congratulatory taps on the shoulder with the NPCs's red boffers—the padded, duct-tape covered PVC pipes that served as safe weapons for the game. Jake noted the warmth in the wolf's smile and grinned a little himself, in spite of just how shitty that module had just gone.

Necros grinned beneath the full-head latex appliance he wore. The effect was almost as chilling as when he was in character. Beneath it, Phil the pine marten was a warm, if unassuming, accountant. The fox found himself jealous of the marten's flexibility, both literally and figuratively, as he played various villains and antagonists. He was tough to fight because he was so slinky and pliant, a fact which was always in the back of Jake's head no matter how hard he tried not to metagame.

"You guys should get back to the tavern," Phil said, locking eyes for a moment with Jake. "We've got to take Cyrus to Monster Camp so he can res."

Jake's ears twitched in mild irritation. He'd wanted to post-mortem with his wolf out of game, if for no other reason than to apologize for things happening as they had, and to give his boyfriend a kiss. He was more frustrated with the others who had made such a dick decision to leave someone behind. Cyrus, as a character, was loyal and had been a true companion to the player group since there *was* a player group. He was also the strongest fighter. He swung ten silver damage per sword strike with that runic blade of his, which was enough to hit most undead creatures and do some serious hurting. Beyond just his stat card, though, Cyrus—or rather, Tom—fought with a swift and ferocious fervor. He never swung hard enough with the padded boffers to actually hurt anyone, but he moved fast enough that he was tough to block and tougher to hit.

"I'll see you guys back at the tavern," the wolf said, waving. Jake nodded and slunk out to join the others on their walk back.

Fellwyn, whose player-name Jake hadn't learned yet, walked in sulking silence, mirroring Jake's own feelings. Johnathan, who played Shay the elementalist, picked at his claws and prattled on about what a rough fight it had been and how he already had strategies in mind to come back and take out the lich. Scott, the orange bengal tiger who played Jace, the stoic brother to the sarcastic and mouthy Shay, was busy with one of the NPCs reliving some moment from the fight and laughing loudly enough to be heard three counties away.

Jake tuned out Johnathan's jabbering, focusing on the memory of the last few minutes of the battle. In his head he'd been counting down the time until the paralysis effect wore off of Cyrus. It couldn't have been much longer, though admittedly he had been trying to fight off the onslaught of whatever those undead things were supposed to be. Jake forced his imagination to re-create them as something new, looking past the smeared, hastily applied makeup and foam-and-duct-tape-covered PVC into the threat presented.

The group arrived at the tavern building, sticking for the moment to the ring of cheap, battery-powered rope lights where Cyrus would resurrect as soon as he was done with the event staff.

"I think we need to rethink how we fight these fights," Jake said, breaking his silence. The others turned to him, still out of game for the moment.

"If we do, we'll decide that in-game and in character," Sandra said, sharply. "In the meantime, we should get back to it."

"In a minute," Johnathan said. "We just got our asses kicked. I think it might be ok if we just chilled a minute before we gate back in. Give Tom a chance to get up here for his res."

"Yeah. I'm wiped. And if we go back in game right this second, Lysander is going to be eight kinds of pissed off at you guys. I need to rest for a bit before we dive into that shark tank," Jake said, scratching at his ear. His tail lashed back and forth, while the vision of Lysander and Cyrus jointly running their blades through Necros and ending his threat once and for all played through the fox's head.

"Ok, you guys can wait if you want. I'm going to go ahead and head back into the tavern and start prepping arrows. That takes some in-game time. Especially since I'm going to be making a batch tailored to undead."

Jake nodded, and the others mumbled agreement.

"Transport 3. Transport 2. Transport 1," Sandra rapid-fired, and then she was gone and Faythe had returned, striding off towards the tavern, no longer seeing Jake or the others.

After a few minutes, Tom appeared at the bottom of the little hill where the resurrection circle lay and walked up to meet the group. Jake's ears folded back when he saw the look on the wolf's face.

"I just came to tell you guys, from staff. I perm'd. Cyrus is dead and gone," he sighed.

"What?" Johnathan yelped—uncharacteristically for a tiger. "Oh man that fucking sucks! I'm so sorry."

Jake stared blankly. To have a permanent death happen mid-event was always a kick to the groin. Doubly so when it was one of your best players.

"Do you have someone else ready to go?"

"It's going to take some time to do. I'm going to NPC shift for the rest of this event and get the new character set up after," Tom said. "Not ideal, but I need time to decide if I want to stick with tank or if I want to go nuke or something else this time."

The dejection in Tom's voice sank Jake's heart deep. Cyrus was a long-running character. All the players knew death could happen, but this felt to Jake just as rough as if someone he actually knew had died. The character implications sent a chill down his spine. Beyond just that, Jake knew exactly what Cyrus meant to Tom as a whole. The fox would have to take especially good care of his wolf in the coming week.

"That means that Lysander is the best fighter we've got now," Jake said, incredulity lingering on each word. "That's not a good sign. Especially not if we're going up against Necros again, with those creatures of his."

"Lysander will do fine, babe," Tom said. "You're a good player. You need to work on your weak-side blocks, but you did a lot of good in that fight. If the paralysis hadn't gotten you on a lucky shot, it wouldn't have gone down the way it did."

"I tried to dodge that damn packet too, but like they say in cartoons, I zigged when I should have zagged."

If Jake was good at anything, dodging the thrown cloth packets of bird seed that represented spells was one of them. This time though, he'd dodged right into the paralysis curse. It was his fault and only his fault.

"All right, I gotta get back to Monster Camp. I'll take it easy on you guys as much as is fair if I come out as a crunchy."

Jake, Johnathan, and 'Fellwyn' all nodded. Then the four of them came together in a tight hug.

When it was over, and Tom had disappeared over to the staff building, the group prepared themselves and stepped back into game.

The circle of standing stones where those who were killed resurrected if they were strong enough of spirit gave off a faint white glow from a series of ancient runes carved into the timeless megaliths. No one now living knew what the markings meant, other than that this was a place of rebirth. Cyrus, had he been killed, should have returned here. But after an hour of waiting, he had not appeared.

"Do you think he's still alive, then?" Lysander asked Shay, ears pricked. Jace stood off to one side, silent as usual, looking lost in thought. The orange tiger was taller than his brother Shay, more imposing, but not so magically inclined. He tended to remain quiet during discussions of the spirit or of magic.

"Shay?"

"Let me try and get a read. I can usually tell if someone's still alive through the circle, even if I can't tell much else."

The white tiger knelt down, his claws crackling with energy as he touched the nearest stone. He remained silent for several minutes. Lysander's tail lashed, and he could feel the fur on his neck standing up. A spirit read never took this long.

"Anything?"

Shay squeezed his eyes shut, his ears folded back in an expression that looked like pain.

"I can't sense any life in him, but I can't get a read on his spirit at all either. It's like he's—"

"What?"

"Like he's gone on."

Every muscle in Lysander's body tensed at once and his eyes flooded. The blurry black and white shape of the tiger rose up in front of him.

Shay started to say something, but the fox turned away and wiped the tears out of his eyes long enough to find the path to the tavern and to set off down it.

How dare they? This had all been their fault. They'd forced him to leave Cyrus to his fate! He could have gotten to him. If they'd just backed him up, he'd have been able to drag Cyrus out of the pile of piranha-like undead. They'd left him to die to save their own skins, and they'd forced Lysander into their panicked flight.

The moment they reached the tavern, Lysander felt the pain and rage boil over within him. The hole where Cyrus had been in his heart felt like it had been hollowed out by acid. He rounded on his compatriots, fighting the urge to start swinging his blade.

It was not easy.

"I hope you're all pleased. Cowards."

He turned his back once more on the stunned group, tromped up the uneven wooden steps to the back door of the tavern, and slipped inside.

Inside, he grabbed a stick of dried meat from the communal basket and gnawed at it, pointedly ignoring Faythe sitting quietly in the corner making a new batch of arrows. The salt and savory flavors of the meat smoothed the roughest edges of his rage. As the anger faded into the background, the sense of loss and sorrow, that hollow place inside where his friend had once been, rose up to cling to his heart. It felt like the sludge left behind when a gelatinous cube was killed had crawled from the depths and wrapped itself around his lungs. Breathing became a forced act, conscious and deliberate.

In it flowed, like water being sucked through thick cloth, and out again, leaving within him the feeling of hollowness and void.

Shay was the first to approach. The massive tiger turned one of the creaking wooden chairs around and straddled it, arms folded, staring Lysander down. The fox did not offer a reaction.

"I'm gonna let what you said go, Lysander, because I know how close you and Cyrus were. The others, well, that's up to them."

"Ask me if I care what any of you think of me," Lysander sneered, not meeting Shay's gaze.

Shay's lips curled back, and he bared his teeth with a snarl. Pryde, the chocolate-furred hound, sat upright in the chair in the corner he'd been napping in, his fingers crackling with energy as he surveyed the scene.

"Gods damn it, you will listen to me and you listen good!" the tiger shouted as he slammed a massive fist on the table.

Holy shit, Johnathan!

Lysander's ears pinned back and he winced at the aggression, the sudden realization of what he had said and what he was doing causing his cheeks and ears to burn.

"You don't have to like us. You don't have to accept our reasons for what happened. But you're alive now thanks to us. If we could've gotten to Cyrus, we would have. But there was no way it was going to happen and you know that. The needs of the many—"

"I swear to the fates if you say 'outweigh the needs of the few or the one', I won't be responsible for what happens."

The words came out with less humor than might normally be present, but Shay seemed to get the idea. He relaxed a bit in his chair, and his teeth were once again, mostly hidden by his lips.

"Fine. But if we didn't get as many of us out of there, Necros could just crush the world at a whim , and there'd be no one left to stop him. Like Cyrus always said," the tiger said, his striped tail lashing behind him, "we have to stand together. I know you loved him. Love him. But we have to press on. He wouldn't want us to waste our time grieving."

"Yeah... Yeah, you're right, but if I'm the strongest fighter we have, we're in trouble."

"We've got your back. That is, if you've got ours. Comrades?" Shay asked, extending his giant paw.

Lysander wanted to shove that hand away, shout more, tell

the tiger than he didn't need his syrupy sentimentality. But as he looked into Shay's eyes, seeing there a wash of concern, compassion, and steely determination, that bitterness shrank back to something more manageable.

"Friends," Lysander responded, clasping it and rising from the chair. It wasn't their fault, he repeated to himself. It was on him. He hadn't been fast enough, and it had cost Cyrus his life.

"All right everybody, he's calmed down now. You can come in and we can start making plans!" Shay shouted.

As the evening wore on, Lysander's unease grew. Necros was out there somewhere, plotting, planning. He had to know where the adventurers were based. They made no secret of defending this town in their quest against the darkness, after all. The number of times that the group had to fight back evil on their very doorstep was almost beyond counting.

Townsfolk had come in and out, taking small groups of the adventurers to help them with this or that problem. Lysander, though, remained behind, mulling over plans in his mind. His ears twitched in thought. The lich's tower could not have been his primary headquarters.

Intimidating as it was, it was just too small to make an effective main fortress. Likely he was using it to establish a foothold on this continent, and to field-test his walking piranhas. The test, Lysander thought bitterly, had been a rousing success from Necros's point of view.

"Lysander," Faythe called from the doorway. "We've got a problem."

"Big problem!" Shay added, staring out the window. "We got undead swarming out there."

Lysander jumped out of his chair and rushed to the window. His heart jumped into his throat. He'd expected it, but even so, the shock of the writhing mass of rotted flesh and fur outside set his hackles on end.

"Where are the others?" Faythe asked as she readied her bow.

"Still off with that unicorn guy who needed help clearing out his barn of the giant spiders."

Lovely.

Lysander and Shay stepped out onto the porch, the greying wood creaking beneath their feet. Faythe took up a position to the left of the steps, along the railing, and Shay took the right, leaving Lysander to hold the center. Beyond the steps—at a safe, yet menacing distance—a group of eight undead, some zombies, some skeletons, and a couple of wraiths, stood, leering at the tavern. To their rear, a massive, armored shape loomed, arms folded, its face veiled in the shadow of a hooded cloak. His armor, black and constructed of hundreds of small metal scales, glinted in the lamplight streaming from the tavern. At his side, he carried a longsword, charred and blackened. Black steel vambraces, pauldrons, and greaves rounded out the terrifying ensemble. Beneath the hood, lights glowed an eerie blue where the figure's eyes should have been.

"What do you want here?"

"We have come to give you notice, *heroes*, the shape boomed. "Our master will no longer tolerate your presence within his domains. He has generously granted you one night to set your affairs in order. After that, the consequences shall be...dire."

"Your master was too afraid to come himself?" Lysander needled. If he could keep the figure talking, the others might return in time to put an end to this on a more even footing.

The figure laughed.

"You are too far beneath my master's dignity for him to come in person. He is a very busy creature. Ruling the world is not easy."

"He does not rule the world, yet!" Shay snarled. Lysander took note of the glow of aura around his fingers. He was ready with spells should it come to a fight.

"It is only a matter of time."

Lysander drew his sword with a low growl. He would *not* allow that.

"I have only come here as a courtesy, my young fox. I should caution you not to overplay your incredibly weak hand."

"Fight me, if you think I'm so weak!"

"Lysander, don't," Faythe said, grabbing him by the upper arm, holding him back.

"Would that please you, fox? To know just how outclassed you are? The best among you could not defeat my master. Cyrus's pale imitation will fare no better against me."

"You mean against the pale imitation of Necros?" Lysander needled. Shay had grabbed him by the opposite arm to prevent him pulling free.

"Come down then, little one, and I will show you the error of having an overinflated ego. You two," the figure said, pointing at Faythe and Shay. "My minions will remain at a respectful distance, and will not interfere in combat. I shall expect the same courtesy from you."

Faythe opened her muzzle to shoot off a response. Lysander caught her with his gaze and gave a tiny shake of the head. She stopped.

"I can take him. And if I can't, you guys can hold them off until the others get back. I'm still strong of spirit. I'm not likely to pass on if I die here."

"What if you're wrong, Lys? What if you die too and we don't have a fighter? There's not much that's going to hold back Necros without some muscle. I'm tough, but I can't hold a blade worth a damn, you know that," Shay grumbled. "And Jace back there is a behemoth but he's slow."

"If it will assuage your fears, my dear adventurers," the shape boomed, "I will allow you healing spells. Once he has fallen the duel is finished, and we shall depart until tomorrow, when your eviction takes effect. He need not offer me such quarter. Defeat for me means destruction. Does that satisfy you?"

"Guys, let me do this," the fox pleaded, then added as a whisper, "it'll buy us time."

Faythe sneered but said nothing beyond giving him a curt nod. Shay nodded his assent. Lysander stepped down onto the grass, sword raised.

"Whom shall I say am I dueling," Lysander asked. "I would know the name of the one I'm about to defeat."

The shape let out a rasping noise that Lysander came to

realize was laughter. "'Shade' will do, for now."

'Shade' stepped forward, through the line of his undead soldiers. True to his word, the swarm of minions stepped back, leaving the battleground well clear. Shade took his place opposite Lysander, and flipped his cloak out of the way before offering the fox a formal bow, though he never took his eyes off Lysander. Lysander, after a moment, lowered his blade and bowed in return, also keeping his eyes up.

Shade drew out that charred sword from where it hung at his side and held it *en garde*.

"Let us begin."

Lysander kept his distance, circling the creature, who turned to keep the fox square in his field of vision.

He had to remember what Cyrus had shown him. Swift attacks, but always with one eye to defense. An overextended attack would leave one dispatched in the span of a heartbeat. Turtling behind one's defenses, whatever they were, only delayed the inevitable, like a besieged army with no relief on the way.

He raised his blade in a swift motion, but rather than strike forward, spun clockwise in a full circle, bringing the blade not down in an overhand strike, but up from below, striking at Shade's ribs.

The creature, with preternatural speed, brought his smoking sword into a perfect gull-wing parry. The force of it shoved Lysander's own sword away. Shade swung in retaliation, catching Lysander across the chest.

Ten magic. What in the hell is this thing?

Lysander staggered, but kept himself upright. His armor bore a jagged, smoldering scar across the torso. Shade did not immediately press his advantage.

"So you see, little one? You're no match for me. My master would find you comically unchallenging. I make my offer one final time. Leave, and you may go in peace beyond Necros's borders, until such time as Necros fully controls this world. Better to live a while than to die here, now, is it not?"

Lysander coughed and put a paw on the damage to his armor. Another few strikes like that and he'd have no protection left. Should he walk away? Could he? The others would insist on fighting.

Cyrus would be disappointed in him.

That did it. He snarled and swung. Overhead, left, right overhead. Each blow, deftly parried by the undead monstrosity before him, enraged him further. He unleashed another series of strikes, forcing the creature to take steps backwards even if he did not feel the sword's sting directly. The clash of blades rung in Lysander's ears with each strike.

Panting, he feinted another overhead attack, but whipped his blade over the parry, driving for the creature's shoulder and, finally, struck his foe.

The sword hilt vibrated with the force as Shade's pauldron cracked under the ferocity of the strike.

"Ah. Not bad after all, little fox. Maybe there's hope for you yet," Shade laughed beneath his hood.

The shadow swung a flurry of blows: overhand, side, side, overhand, thrust. He flowed from one attack to another seamlessly, catching each attack of Lysander's with his own perfect parry, and countering with a strike of his own. Lysander twisted and jumped, dodged, and threw his blade in the path of the assault. His lungs screamed as he sucked in air, trying his best to remain at the ready. The pain in his side dug deep, like a serrated dagger made of flames. He couldn't keep up this pace.

The flurry of blows continued. Lysander staggered backwards under the force of the undead's strikes until one slipped beneath his sword arm, knocking his blade out of the way. Before he could back away and reset, Shade's charred blade tore through Lysander's chest armor. He could feel, despite the blade's burnt quality, a coldness spreading from where it pierced.

Shade wrenched the embedded blade free of the fox's chest. Lysander dropped to a knee, seeing the ground spatter with his own blood.

"This battle is over," Shade thundered, no longer giving the fallen fox any attention whatsoever. "Heal him, and make your peace with whatever powers you follow. By tomorrow you will be gone or you will face my master's wrath."

Lysander's face and ears grew hot with shame, and he did not look up.

"Before I depart, a gift for you, little fox."

Lysander heard the clattering of a blade on the ground. He was dimly aware of the tingling that came with being close to a gate spell being cast. Before he could think much about it, a warm ray of light surrounded him, suffusing him with healing energies. The gaping hole where the sword had pierced him now sealed, the fox pushed himself to his feet. Shay stood close by, arms folded.

"That could've gone better," he grumbled.

"Yeah."

"That was ridiculously stupid of you, you know."

"I know."

He did know. Of course he knew. He was not Cyrus and would never be. He could not turn and strike and whirl in a cyclone of blows and not just get cut down on the spot. Cyrus had tried to teach him the fundamentals of that, using a clock as a reference point and the hours as his cardinal directions, but it just wouldn't take.

Aggressive, yet methodical, Shade had sought out the perfect openings. He'd been patient. Worst of all, and the thing that set Lysander's ears ablaze with embarrassment again, was that he'd given the fox every opportunity to get out of the duel.

"So what's that he left there?"

Lysander blinked, his ears twitching curiously. On the ground a few feet away, where moments ago the figure of Shade had stood over him, lay the creature's charred blade. Long, sturdy steel, etched with a runic script to give it enchantment. Flames, of some sort, had smoked the steel black, partially hiding the marks. The hilt bore red padding and a silver wire wrapping. At the end of the pommel, a blue gem—

Oh, you're kidding...

"Well, let's get going, fox. We've got to talk this through with the others. Figure out if we're going to let some tin can full of worms push us out of town, or if we're going to get smart, and find a way to turn this around on Necros and screw up his plans but good."

"Are you sure it's safe to bring that in here?" Fellwyn asked, staring wide-eyed at the black sword.

"As safe as anything," Shay rumbled. "It's been in here a thousand times before."

"Is it really his?" Faythe asked, raising her paw and scraping a claw along one of the blackened runes. "Not just a forgery or a magic copy?"

"Shay did a read-object spell on it. It's Cyrus's sword all right."

"Okay, that's creepy," she said, loading a batch of arrows into a belt carrier to protect the arrowheads. "Why would that creature leave you with Cyrus's sword?"

"To mock me," Lysander replied.

But was it really? Necros was sadistic, but it felt like a huge waste of time. Same with him giving them an ultimatum and time to leave. Necros wanted them dead or subservient. They weren't going to be the latter. He had to know that. So then why toy with them?

"Necros already had enough time to mock us during the fight. This was something else," Fellwyn said. Her mouse tail twitched and her brow furrowed in thought. Did you see his fighting style?"

"Yes. I was taken apart by it, as you may recall."

"I wasn't talking to you. The rest of you. Didn't you notice that he seemed familiar? It was Cyrus's fighting style."

Lysander sputtered.

"Do you think he had time to raise Cyrus?" Shay asked. "It's usually a pretty complicated ritual to make a greater undead like that, and if you leave any of the personality around, it can come back and bite you in the tail."

"This Shade creature wasn't Cyrus," Lysander countered, trying to keep his teeth from baring. The fox did not want to get into a snarling fight in the middle of the tavern.

"Maybe not, but it could be partly him. We don't know what the full extent of Necros's powers are," said Faythe. "*If*, for the sake of argument, it was Cyrus, then it would make sense for the fighting style to be the same."

"It's. Not. Cyrus." Lysander gritted his teeth, his ears pinned back and his fur raised.

"Well, whether it is or not, you better be ready to fight like you're fighting him, because we're probably not taking him down without you." Shay folded his striped arms.

Lysander stood and sent Shade's sword clattering across the table.

"Then you're all dead,- because I'm not even close to good enough. I wasn't fit to polish Cyrus's boots, let alone use his sword in battle and win!"

The fox wiped at the tears welling up unbidden in his eyes and turned away, pushing through the tavern door and out into the gathering night, tuning out the shouts of his friends begging him to come back, and luckily managing to accidentally dodge some spell or another that was tossed his way. Probably a pin or imprisoning spell to keep him from getting away. They weren't going to be lucky enough to catch him this time. He may be broken, but he was still a fox: fast, agile, and cunning.

Being faster than the majority of the other adventurers had its advantages, and Lysander was away from them, in a shaded woodland clearing at a safe distance, before they had a chance to see which way he'd vanished.

"Okay," he mumbled to himself, wiping away the tears that he could no longer fight back. "What would Cyrus want me to do?"

Without realizing what he was doing, he had drawn his sword from its sheath at his side and adopted stance one of the first set.

Cyrus always said that first principles were the key to everything; they were the key to focus, to control, and to victory. Lysander tried to remember what control even felt like. He'd known, before earlier tonight. Necros had cracked that illusion. Shade had shattered it utterly.

The fox held his sword with the guard at chest level, pointing the blade straight up into the sky, and the edge centered in his vision. His feet tensed at shoulder width apart, legs like coiled springs waiting to leap.

One.

Using his tail for counterbalance, he lunged forward on his right paw, raising his sword above his head and striking downward with it, bringing it to a halt where it might strike an enemy's head just as his step touched ground.

Two.

An overhead block.

Three.

Swinging the blade out and away from the body on his right side, tip down and arm extended like the broken wing of a gull.

Four.

As he continued moving through the forms, he did feel all of the cacophony of his thoughts falling into order. Extraneous, unrelated fancies drifted away. It was as if a flooding river had returned to its natural banks, flowing evenly through the twists and turns of its bed.

"You look like a fox on a mission," rattled a high, raspy, amused-sounding voice from behind him. Lysander spun, blade at the ready.

The sight before him made him instantly lower it. An old wolf in tattered grey robes and a wide, floppy hat leaned on a walking stick. The grey fur around his nose and eyes had started to become more silver, with a tinge of white, than the rest. The corners of his eyes crinkled in amusement.

"You could say that," Lysander replied. "Is there something I can help you with, good sir?"

The wolf grinned. "Oh no, no, just passing through, really, and saw you looking all serious and grim and practicing your sword-waving. I couldn't resist saying hello!"

"Sword-waving?" Lysander felt the heat rise to his cheeks and ears. Was it only sword-waving to this wandering wolf?

"Well, you're waving your sword around like a fool," he said. "So if you're going to play the role of a fool, you'd be better off learning to swallow it. It's more impressive."

"With all respect, sir," Lysander began, mustering all the

politeness he was capable of at this moment, "I doubt you're much a master in the ways of combat."

The wolf grinned. "I'm sure I wouldn't stand up to a powerful and precise warrior like yourself. Would you care to test that theory?"

The fox blinked. Was he serious? The guy might have been some sort of alchemist or sorcerer, but he certainly was no fighter.

"Here, allow me," the wolf said, and reached up and snapped a branch from a tree by the edge of the clearing. "Shall we begin?"

"I'll hurt you!"

"If that's what happens, so be it," said the old wolf, tossing his staff to the side and raising the stick into an en garde position.

"I don't think this is such a good id—"

THWACK!

Pain radiated out from the fox's shoulder where the wolf had struck with the broken branch.

"Ow, hey, what the—"

WHAP!

His other shoulder was struck. The whipping action of the tree stung even worse.

"Stop that!"

The wolf remained silent and swung the branch overhead. Lysander tried to move his sword into position to block, but too slow, and took the hit square to the head. He staggered, putting a hand between his ears where the makeshift weapon had struck, feeling the tickle of a droplet of liquid. Looking at his paw, the stick had actually drawn blood. Not much blood, just a tiny bit, but the sight of it elicited a low growl, filling the fox with frustrated fury.

He lashed out, striking for the old wolf. The wolf stood as still as anything Lysander had ever seen, moving only his wrist at the last second and perfectly parrying the blow, whipping the branch around and delivering another strike to the fox's head.

"Would you *cut it out*," shouted Lysander, rubbing at the second sore spot on his head.

"Because the forces of darkness will certainly stop fighting at their best if you ask them nicely, won't they, cub?" The wolf chuckled. "Really, you're holding back too much. They're not going to fight fairly or honorably, and neither should you feel you must."

Lysander, panting from the exertion and rubbing at the sore spot on his head, scoffed.

"If we don't fight with our principles, victory is meaningless."

The wolf's face took on a glowering demeanor.

"Meaningless? How many will suffer under the reign of someone like Necros? How many will die? How much suffering will you allow for the sake of your vaunted principles, cub?"

Lysander opened his mouth to answer, and caught a tree branch to the face. He staggered and raised his sword once more, but another thwack of the tree branch knocked him back off balance.

"Either you learn to fight with everything you have, or you and all your friends, and the whole world are going to die!" the wolf snarled.

The swirl of all of the fox's feelings of uselessness, inadequacy, and—worst of all—the responsibility for Cyrus's death began to spark and burn within Lysander's chest. His eyes watered, and he blinked back the tears. He could feel the blood drain from his knuckles as he squeezed the hilt of his sword.

"Coward."

Lysander's vision, blurred with tears, now tinged with red at the insult. He swung his blade full force at the wolf, aiming the edge to strike at the base of the old man's neck.

The wolf parried once more with a flick of the wrist.

"One!"

Lysander moved the blade to a vertical defensive block, without processing the verbal order he'd just been given.

"Two!"

Once again, Lysander let muscle memory guide his blade, this time mirroring the first block on the opposite side of his body.

The wolf called out three and four, eliciting proper responses from Lysander, before he was able to put together in his thinking mind what was actually happening.

"Five!"

Lysander reversed his overhead block as the stick swung.

"Six!"

From overhead, a quick pull down to the shoulder.

"Seven!"

This one was a parry in front, weapons crossing in a V shape. Useful, the fox remembered from Cyrus's training, for preventing a strike at the legs or upwards towards the nether or torso.

"Eight!"

Eight? There was no eighth—Lysander inverted his wrist in time to catch the strike. Same attack, but from the opposite direction.

"So, you see? You do know what you're doing after all," the wolf said, chuckling as he lowered the branch. "Now. Strike me down in return."

"You're not armed!"

"Am I not? Does the blood on your forehead and muzzle not mean anything, cub?" The wolf's eyes stared him down, unblinking. Even past the amusement that crinkled the corners of the old man's eyes, there was a steel determination that remained unbroken.

"Very well," he said, dropping the branch to the ground and reaching into his cloak. From somewhere within, he pulled forth a simple longsword, and raised it. "Now you have no choice, cub. Kill me or you run the risk of dying yourself."

Lysander blinked, his ears flicking. "You're going to put yourself through all this to kill me?"

"Maybe I will, and maybe I won't, but you're going to have to fight like I will kill you. Because if you don't, you're definitely going to end up dead one way or another."

Lysander's tail lashed. The wolf stood stock still.

What would Cyrus do?

No. That was a bullshit question. Cyrus was Cyrus, and

Lysander was Lysander. Cyrus would have done anything necessary to stop evil and to protect the innocent. Even if this old wolf were the most innocent being, the fox had the moral imperative to protect himself, those he loved, and the world as a whole.

The wolf was right. There could be no more waffling, no more self-doubt or fear. Either Lysander and the others would stand together and face down the evil, or they would die. Either way, they had to make their final stand before the foe. Flashbacks to Cyrus teaching the young fox the basics of swordsmanship rose up in Lysander's mind. Cyrus had been a two-handed swordsman. Foundationally, that's what he had taught to Lysander. The fox had picked up a shield and begun using a single-handed blade much later.

"Well?"

Lysander raised his blade, and placed his left paw on the hilt, below the right. He felt the memory of Cyrus's paws guiding him. He felt *right*.

"Come on then."

Lysander struck faster than he had ever moved in his life. Blades clashed as each strike was deftly parried, but something was different this time. The wolf stepped backward at each block, trying to put distance between himself and Lysander.

The fox feinted an overhand strike, which the old man predictably moved his sword to parry. Once the blade was in motion, Lysander whipped his own around and under, halting the edge just shy of the wolf's throat.

"Good, lad. Very good. You're finally fighting like it means something," the wolf said, lowering his sword to his side before dropping it to the ground with a thunk.

"All right, now that that's over with, you can start by telling me your name."

"You can call me Aetius, if you like," the wolf said, smiling.

"That's not your actual name, is it?" Lysander asked, feeling the weariness of the fight creeping up on him.

"We are who we say we are, cub. I think you have more pressing questions than what word I choose to call myself this week, don't you?"

The fox stifled an exasperated growl. "Okay then. Let's get to the heart of it. What was this all about, *Aetius*? Wandering sword masters don't just turn up in the woods right when you need them."

"No, we certainly don't. But I'm not the sword master here, my dear cub," the wolf chuckled, that same amusement crinkling the corners of his eyes. "You are."

From the folds of his cloak, the wolf produced a small medallion of hammered copper and offered it to Lysander. Etched into it was the icon of a sword surrounded by flame.

"This is—"

"Our order felt that the situation with Cyrus required a bit more direct intervention. You, as the closest thing to an heir that our comrade possesses, needed to be tested. You had to prove yourself worthy of continuing the fight in his name. And to do that, I felt you needed more direct prodding than we normally engage in."

Lysander sheathed his sword at his side and stared at the medallion. Cyrus had always been secretive about the Order of the Flame. That Lysander knew their name at all was something of an oddity.

"Now, understand this. Normally the masters of the order don't act directly, so don't expect it in the future, but you're going to have to take on Shade as well as those minions of Necros's that nearly killed you all before. No matter what else happens, it is imperative that Shade be destroyed. The medallion will give you some help in that direction, but use it wisely, and use it discreetly." The wolf nodded solemnly.

"Do you accept this great 'honor' which I have bestowed upon you?" he asked in a voice that betrayed a dripping irony.

"If there were any other option, no. But it must be done, and so I shall do it."

The wolf bowed. "Then go with the strength of your pack. Do not hesitate and do not falter. The fate of our world rests with you and your friends."

A crack resounded from the woods behind Lysander,

followed by a shout.

"Fox, where in the nine blazes are you?" came the booming bass of Shay. Lysander turned to look.

"Here, old friend!" he shouted.

When he turned back to say a farewell to the old wolf, he encountered only a gentle breeze blowing fallen leaves across the clearing.

"What're you doin' out here? We've got stuff to take care of! The others sent me out since you might actually listen to me, if nothing else."

Lysander fingered the medallion that he'd slipped into his belt pouch.

"I needed to work through some things. Meditate on what has to be done."

"You look like you got into a fight with a rosebush. You wanna talk about that?"

"Thorns and brambles, Shay. Nothing worth your time. But I think I've worked through the worst of this. Let's get back to the tavern; we need to formulate a strategy. We're going to Necros's lair, we're going to destroy those abominations he's constructed, and we're going to put a stop to his plans."

Speaking the words, Lysander felt determination and strength well up inside him. Purpose and resolve narrowed his focus to a single set of tasks. Destroy the creatures that had killed Cyrus, return Shade to the dust he'd come from, and stop Necros once and for all.

"That's the Lysander I know," Shay rumbled. "Now let's get back."

Out of game, Jake smiled as he left the staff building and headed back to the tavern, where the other players waited, in character, for their best fighter, Lysander, to reappear, so that they could take the chance at mopping the floor with Shade and Necros once and for all.

The outcome certainly wasn't assured, but that didn't matter. Either this was going to be the biggest heroic moment for the adventurers, or it was going to go down in LARP history as one of the all-time great lost causes. Either way, Lysander's encounter with the master of the Order had given Jake a real case of the grins, which he tried to stifle.

Jake had to go away now, and Lysander had to be here. Lysander certainly wasn't going to be grinning about anything.

As he approached the tavern, he stopped, letting the character's personality settle back in over his own, before stepping back into the world of the game.

Lysander stood at a cleared away section of the tavern, one of its long tables arrayed at the center before him. To one side, Faythe continued preparing arrows, but her ears were raised and pointed in his direction. Shay stood to one side at the end of the table, his massive feline arms folded across his chest. His tail twitched and lashed, betraying the nervous excitement he no doubt felt. Jace kept vigil from the corner.

"We know from before that those minions crawl out of the shadows surrounding Necros's chamber. Shay, you had a plan for that?"

"Course I do. Fellwyn and I go in right behind you," he said, nodding to the quiet hound sitting glowering in the corner. "Once you get Shade out into the room, and before that worm-eaten old bastard knows what hit him, we surround the chamber with a wall of spirit flame. It only lasts for five minutes per cast, but if she and I stagger it, we can keep the ring up a long time. I can cast it three times a day, and she can cast it twice. So I'll go first, and she'll follow, and we'll alternate."

Faythe continued sharpening arrowheads and fitting them into the masterwork shafts she had produced. She spoke firmly but without breaking attention from her task. "Jace and I will pick off the critters that crawl through the fire and aren't wiped out by it. Probably not going to get a shot at Necros himself, and you'll be fighting Shade if all goes according to this half-baked plan of yours."

Jace nodded silently from the corner.

"You have a better plan?"

"Nope. I love this plan. I'm excited to be a part of it. Just because it's half-baked doesn't mean it's not the best we have. I'm behind you."

"I'll keep the undead wards and healing spells going as best I can, but you'd better bring every healing item you've got: potions, crystals, anything. I'm one mouse and I'm not going to be able to keep up when the fur starts flying," Fellwyn added. Lysander hadn't paid much attention to her before, but right now she seemed much older than she usually did. The fox wondered if she'd had any rest.

The heroes spent another few minutes discussing strategy, and dividing tasks amongst themselves and the other adventurers who were newer residents of the town, deciding that the less experienced among them should set up a rear guard action to evacuate civilians if things went sour and the assault team couldn't make it back. Lysander cursed himself that he hadn't yet learned the names of the new arrivals, but resolved to do so before this was all over.

Lysander's tail lashed nervously as he stared through the tavern's windows to the west. The sun had all but disappeared below the treelike on the horizon. Soon it would be do or die time. He gripped Cyrus's sword by the hilt. The feeling of Cyrus's paws guiding his own into proper position during his training returned. Those big appendages covered the fox's own, their warmth a comfort as much as the wolf's closeness behind him as he guided him into position, walking him through each parry and each strike until they became second nature.

The tavern door opened, allowing a hunched, raggedly dressed old mustelid to step inside. Lysander screwed up his nose against the pungent scent of the creature.

Fortunately the weasel was only inside for a few moments, speaking with Jace in hushed tones that even the fox's ears couldn't pick words out of. He passed something to the tiger, and slipped back out the door, leaving behind only a whiff of his musk. Lysander released the breath he didn't know he had been holding.

"We've got intel, people," Jace rumbled. "There's a weakness in Necros's patrols. The Thieves' Guild is going to send us a scout to guide us there with as little disturbance as possible."

Jace glanced up at Lysander. "Unless of course you'd rather just break down the front door?"

Lysander's ears twitched with the heat of embarrassment, but nobody laughed. Jace's stony exterior cracked only a little, as he gave the fox a subtle wink.

"How long?"

"We need to leave here within the hour."

Lysander nodded, gripping the hilt of Cyrus's blade firmly, feeling the comfort of its weight at his side. It weighed no more than his own sword, but its heft radiated with desire for revenge—no. Justice.

"Let's get ready and move."

The Thieves' Guild scout hushed the assembled heroes with a raised fist. The group crouched, ears and eyes open for passing undead patrols. The scent of decay permeated everything in the vicinity of Necros's tower, but the thicker, sweeter stench growing stronger along the path perpendicular to where the party now hid was unmistakable.

The groaning of a pair of zombie canids, now more skeletal than flesh, echoed in the foggy night air. They passed a lighting-shattered oak tree and shambled onward down the path, oblivious to the heroes. Lysander let out a breath he hadn't realized he'd been holding. The weight of Cyrus's runic blade hung comfortably at Lysander's side. He'd foregone his shield this time; Cyrus's sword was a zweihander for the smaller fox. He felt, deep in the marrow of his bones, that a shield would make no difference in the coming fight. His swordsmanship, his connection with Cyrus, and his determination would carry the day, or the Heroes of Mistvale—and all the world—would be dead anyway.

"We move when the next patrol has passed," whispered the guild scout. He wore all black, concealing his fur and features beneath a ninja-style mask, and a sleeve that contained his tail. His shape was feliform, but that's all Lysander could tell, and he wouldn't pry. The Thieves' Guild kept its secrets close, and their usefulness at infiltration and espionage meant that he wanted to stay on their good side.

Faythe fidgeted. The glow from her facial markings remained faint but flickered a little.

"What's wrong?" Lysander whispered to her, leaning close and pricking an ear.

"This feels wrong. A handful of patrols, and only the weakest-looking of old rotgut's troops? It's a trap."

"Of course it's a trap. He can't expect us to just run away and cower. He knows it's better to wrap us up and take care of us before we can cause him more heartburn. That's why he sent Shade. And that's why we're going to give him exactly what he wants."

"For the record, I don't like it either," Shay rumbled—even at a whisper the tiger's voice could not be mistaken for another's. "But we're committed now. It's all or nothing.

"All of you be silent," Jace hissed.

The scent of the patrols grew strong again. This time, a group of three less-decayed zombies shuffled along the path. Every member of the party once again held their breath. Lysander shut his eyes, forcing the scent out of his nose. His eyes snapped open again as he shifted his weight, and a crack resounded from the twig he hadn't known was there.

Way to be a walking cliché.

He stiffened, willing his body to be like the stone. One of the zombies stopped in its shuffle and raised its decaying nose into the air, sniffing in the direction of the shattered tree. If it raised the alarm, this fight was going to turn ugly fast. There just weren't enough of them to fight the battle of a whole army.

After an eternity of absolute stillness, Lysander watched the undead canid turn and follow his patrol, having satisfied itself that nothing was amiss down the dark path. He dared not speak again until the guild scout turned to face the party.

"Quickly. The lower entrance to the tower through the cracks in the rock face is unguarded. You may surprise the lich and his servants while they are unprepared," the feline said, rising and slipping across the path where moments before the patrols had crossed. Lysander bolted across next, keeping in single file with the scout. The others soon followed, and as the trees across the path gave way to a clearing, they found themselves at the foot of the once-abandoned tower that the lich had taken for his sanctum. The tower's foundation rested on a rocky mount, with sharp, eroded fins jutting outward, perpendicular to the base like the great toes of some tremendous, clawed foot paw. Between two of the 'toes', the scout beckoned the group.

"Inside, this way, quickly," the scout whispered. "Two minutes until the next patrol will come into view."

Lysander ducked between the rocks and found, as he stepped out of view of the clearing, that there was a narrow cave entrance hidden by the shape of the mount. Not quite large enough for a deliberate doorway, it nonetheless ought to fit all of the group. Even Jace would make it through if he turned sideways.

"Through this cave you will find a set of unfinished stairs leading into the cellar, and from there you can fight your way up to the lich's chambers," the scout said as the last of the party squeezed inside.

"What about you? Aren't you coming?"

"No. But very soon there will be a lovely distraction. We were able to reach some of the people of the hills. Despite their...shall we say 'uncouth' nature, their superstitions and taboos against the undead will ensure that they assault this place from the front. The lich's main force will be preoccupied with the frontal assault and leave him a little less protected. Now, pardon me, I must send the signal to our agents with the hill tribes to begin."

The scout took a look in both directions, slipping back through the trees just ahead of the next patrol.

Lysander pushed deeper into the cave to get away from the entrance, and to allow his eyes to adjust to the darkness. The dripping of water broke the silence.

"Let's move, guys."

The cave floor leveled out, and in the dim glow of the meager magical light sources that Shay and Jace had conjured, the cave's thick columnar supports, worn away by time and erosion, reached up to the low ceiling. Combat here would be disastrous. Lysander held his tongue, listening to the soft, wet padding of feet and the dripping of water. The party moved as silently as possible deep into the gloomy dark.

After a few minutes the cavern floor began to slope upward, and in one corner, a half-hewn set of steps led up toward a dim light. The cellar that the guild scout had mentioned, it had to be! Lysander put a finger to his lips and then pointed upward, drawing Cyrus's sword. The runes hidden beneath the scorching and blackening of the metal glowed dimly.

This is it, 'Lysander.' You know what you're going to find up here. You know you have to play this right. Plot team's not going to protect you. So take everything Tom taught you, and everything that Cyrus taught Lysander, and use it. The world is at stake here.

He placed his foot on the first step, feeling the pounding of his heart as he ascended.

To his surprise, the cellar he emerged into sat unguarded and empty. In the almost absent light, rows of experimentation tables lay empty, covered in blood or some other substance, their tools discarded. Lysander signaled the others to join him so that he could get the additional illumination.

"By the fates," Shay whispered as his light fell across the walls. Lysander clamped a paw over his muzzle to avoid making a sound.

Adhered to the rough stones of the wall hung bulging, round, fluid-filled sacs, their edges secured to the wall by a crusty, crystalline substance. Within the sacs, something stirred, twitching and turning over themselves.

"Is that..." Lysander began, approaching one of the tumescent pouches.

The creature inside turned again, its face squeezing and stretching the translucent film that held the sac together. For just a moment, as it stretched, he saw what was in them: more of Necros's walking piranha undead.

"They are smaller than the others," Jace said, staring into another sac. "Not fully formed.

"I say we destroy them now," Fellwyn said, shuddering as

one of the creatures churned in its artificial womb.

"I disagree. If we do that, there's every chance that we'll get swarmed by whatever's waiting for us upstairs. We'll blow the element of surprise entirely," Shay said, folding his massive arms.

"Lys," Faythe said, "you're in charge. What do you think?"

All eyes turned to watch Lysander, and he wished in that moment he could hide away from their gaze.

Both were good ideas. Who was he to make decisions? He was just a protege, a student.

No. He couldn't think like that. A decision had to be made, and he was the one leading this assault. Cyrus would think through the options, but Cyrus also wouldn't hesitate. Lysander grimaced.

"Destroy them now. Necros knows we're coming; that's why the patrols were so light. He wanted us to get in here. He wants us to go down for good."

The fox raised Cyrus's runic blade, and with both paws, stabbed it forward into the nearest abomination. The hiss of liquid followed as it poured out onto the floor. The sickly green fluid mixed with a black ichor oozing out of the now unmoving creature that had been gestating.

The stench became overwhelming to Lysander, who had to cover his vulpine nose to try and blunt the worst of it.

Shay, Jace, Fellwyn, and Faythe all made their next attacks on the sacs until, at the end, none of the piranha larvae were left behind. No noise came from up the stairs at the end of the room.

Way too quiet.

"Let's get up there, and get this over with," Lysander said, grimly. Together, the adventurers progressed upward, into the antechamber they had so recently stood inside, planning their first assault.

Two rotting canid guardians stood unmoving at either side of the double doors into the great hall. Lysander climbed stairs at one end of the long, narrow chamber, though the undead did not see him at first. By the time they did, he had closed half the distance to them. Shay's magic held them in place as Lysander swung Cyrus's sword. One, two, and the creatures' heads were off, their bodies slumped on the mildewed remnant of carpeting that had once been elegant.

The fox faced the double doors, looked to make certain that the others were behind him. When each had joined him and nodded, he raised his foot and kicked the doors in.

Braziers of black flame now surrounded the great hall, casting flickering, dim shadows where it had been wholly dark before. Tapestries had been hung from the ceiling bearing Necros's dark sigil. The dais where Necros had stood during the last battle sat empty, save for a plinth, atop which a great, dark, crystalline orb hovered, glowing red and purple. On the ground level, a black-armored figure stood with its back to the adventurers, its hooded head bowed.

"Like we discussed!" Lysander shouted, "Go!"

The Heroes of Mistvale filed into the room, taking up combat positions. The walls between the lit braziers swarmed and swirled with the flesh of the piranha undead, which began to stir and stagger forth.

Shay called forth his words of power and a wall of bright blue flame erupted from nothing, extending outward in a circle until it had surrounded the adventurers and put itself between the undead and them.

"Spirit flame," came the deep voice of Shade. Despite its volume and the resonance of it rumbling in Lysander's chest, its tone was such that he could have spoken it from a foot away, softly. "I am impressed. But you'll find that my master's servants are not so easily stopped." He still had not turned to face them.

Lysander glanced to either side. The piranhas had broken away from the walls and approached the barrier of fire. One reached its twisted claws into the fire and drew them back, blackened and smoking but still moving. It took one step, then another, into the fire. The sound of its flesh beginning to roast was the squeal of steam escaping. But in spite of it, it pushed against, into, and through the fire, staggering out the other side charred but whole.

"Faythe!" Lysander shouted, but she had already released an

arrow. It sailed overhead and pierced through the piranha's chest, not slowed by passing through flesh and bone, and shattered into glowing shards against the floor. The creature staggered and lurched, but remained upright, dragging itself towards the group.

More of them began to burn themselves in the spirit fire to move inward. One or two dropped lifeless to the ground, and were incinerated.

"It's hurting them! Pick off the stragglers," Lysander commanded. The words gave him confidence. They could do this.

Faythe's bow twanged as she fired arrows into the burning piranha-creatures, dropping them to the ground. Two more of the creatures dropped, unharmed, from the ceiling, past the ring of fire, but Jace cleaved the first of them before it could take a step towards Lysander.

"Face me now, Shade. You're going down this time!"

"Am I?"

The shape drew itself up to its full height and turned to face the fox. The light of the spirit fire lit up the shadows within his hood. Lysander's heart sank into his stomach and his eyes stung.

Inside the hood, torn and scarred, was what remained of Cyrus's once-handsome face. The fur and skin on one side of the wolf's muzzle had been ripped, leaving his teeth on that side permanently exposed, like some sort of cockeyed rictus grin.

"What's the matter, my love?" the creature asked in a tone of unmistakable mockery. "Don't you find me dashing anymore?"

He reached up and pulled the hood back, exposing the newly-created undead features it had hidden: bloodstained grey fur, fresh but unbleeding wounds, and eyes that, instead of Cyrus's pure white, were a solid, irisless black.

"You're not Cyrus. Cyrus would never become what you are."

"The power of Necros is strong, my fox. It was a...difficult process for sure, but I am now as you see me before you. Why don't you give up and come join us? We can have immortality and be together always. Perhaps in time we can even supplant the lich, you and I."

The orb, hovering over its plinth, pulsed with its violet and crimson light. "Shade" had already beaten Lysander once. Maybe it was inevitable. If he surrendered and let himself be taken, he would at least be with Cyrus again...

The fox shook his head and blinked. His thoughts ran slow and thick, as if his brain had been wrapped in damp cotton. He flicked his ears, trying to focus.

"What about the others?" he managed to ask. His head hurt. Somewhere behind him he could hear voices shouting...what? His name? He couldn't make it out.

"They can come too. The master does not seek disunity and revenge. He only wishes to unite the world under his benevolent rule." Cyrus's voice was sibilant, and poured over the fox like honey.

Close behind him he heard words being spoken and felt a surge of energy enter through the center of his back. He caught the last part of a phrase:

"—awaken!"

The fog that had enveloped his thoughts dissipated. He blinked, feeling the sudden absence of the pain and slowness of thought he'd just moments before been mired in.

"You back with us, buddy?" Shay asked in his ear.

Lysander glanced at him. "Thank you. Yes, I'm feeling much better."

"You can't hold out forever, love. Why don't you just give in? With or without magic, you're going to lose this battle," the wolf-thing sneered.

"Join you? Cyrus would never ask me to surrender to Necros's rule just to make myself feel better. You're not Cyrus. You're what's left of him, warped and twisted to try and control me, but you're not him. And it's time I put you down so he can rest in peace."

Lysander raised Cyrus's runic blade into a ready stance. The markings glowed brightly beneath the scorching of the metal.

"Very well. If that is what you wish. I will offer no quarter a second time, little fox. And there will be no help for you!"

Shade drew his own sword from its sheath at his side and raised a paw. In an instant, a wall of orange flame erupted from the floor, catching Shay, who was still close behind Lysander, in the paws and face, sending him sprawling backwards to the floor. Lysander turned just enough to get a view out of the corner of his eye to see the others had closed ranks around the downed tiger. Faythe and Jace fought off the piranhas while Fellwyn knelt and applied her healing magic.

He was cut off here, alone with the specter of his mentor, his lover. His friend.

He raised his sword, focusing fully on Shade, who stood opposite, fully mirroring the fox's stance.

"One last chance. Surrender, and we will make your release quick and painless."

Shade laughed and, in a whirl, closed the distance between them in two giant strides, spinning around and bringing his blade down full force at Lysander's head.

Lysander swung Cyrus's sword to meet the incoming strike. This time his arms and shoulders stung with the force of the blow, but his parry did not waver. He could feel the innate power within the blade seeking its release, and the ties to its former master who stood so close.

Lysander would not remain on the defensive this time. Instead he ducked under the wolf's raised arms. Remembering the clock and how it related to each attack and defense, just as Cyrus had once taught him, it was his turn to spin. The runic blade whirled and slammed its edge into Shade's cloak, and into the armor beneath it. A flurry of sparks erupted from where the metal of the scales found themselves struck, cleaved off, or suddenly bent. Part of the cloak dropped away.

Shade's balance, thrown off by the force of his own attack immediately followed by the fox's strike, gave way. He clattered to the floor on his hands and knees, inches from his wall of flame.

He chuckled as he heaved his way back up onto his feet and turned to face Lysander, who had backed off. Rushing for a death blow was what got you killed. Cyrus had told tale after tale of the arrogance of knights thinking they would end a fight in a single blow, raising their sword high overhead, only to be caught in the gut with a hidden blade strike.

"You've gotten better, fox," the undead wolf snarled.

"I had a good teacher."

Shade reached a clawed paw up and tore the clasp of his cloak free, letting the remnant fall away.

His black eyes widened, suddenly, looking not at Lysander, but instead just over his head, behind him.

At the orb.

He put a paw on his head, wobbling unsteadily, and staggering a step or two. His sword swung down limply, clattering and scraping along the ground. Lysander watched, keeping his position and his distance.

Shade looked up, paw still clutching his head in pain. His eyes, before deep pools of black, had lightened. White now asserted itself in the center, pushing back the blackness.

"L–Lysander?"

"Cyrus?"

The voice, before deep and rich and sinister, had softened. It was ragged, and barely above a whisper, but it was Cyrus's voice, without question.

"It hurts," the wolf whispered. "I can feel him...inside."

"Tell me what to do, Cyrus. I'll do it, just tell me!" The fox's chest tightened, and he had to fight the urge to rush to the wolf. Not here; it was too dangerous.

"You have to destr—" Cyrus cut himself off with a wail that became a snarl of rage and torment as his undead body spasmed. His grip on his sword never wavered, clattering and scraping along the stones of the floor. He came dangerously close to the fire wall where he would have immolated himself. Beyond, Faythe and Jace and the revived Shay fought wave after wave of incoming piranhas, aided by Fellwyn's repulsion spells driving them back into the flames.

"I have to destroy what? Tell me what to do!"

"You've got to destroy me, of course, my love."

The sinister bass of Shade had returned, his black gaze once again meeting Lysander's before he charged forward, whirling with his blades like a cyclone of death. This time, Lysander did not try to stand his ground. Holding an untenable position wasn't going to work. Naturally spry, the fox ducked and twisted out of the way of the swirl of blows, swinging and landing his own only once and only glancing off of the undamaged front of Shade's scale mail.

"Come on, Cyrus, you fought him before. Keep fighting! Come back to us!"

"Cyrus is gone, love. I'm Shade now. I serve Necros the Undying, and willingly or not, soon so shall you!"

Their blades clashed again. Shade's larger, stronger form twisted the locked blades into a lever, forcing Lysander to bend farther and farther in order to hold his position. In moments he would be overcome, fall to the ground. If he was lucky he could scramble out of the way, but he was in serious trouble.

Inside his shirt, beneath the armor he wore, he felt heat begin to glow. The warmth of enchantment, of magic, flooded through him. Time itself slowed in his awareness. He could see the heat rippling in the wall of fire, each strand of fur left on Cyrus's head moving independently. The medallion that Aetius had given to him began to burn. The sensation of unbridled power journeyed from the fox's chest to his arms, and up into his head. It filled him, top to bottom, from ears to tail tip. Cyrus's runic blade began to glow with an aura surrounding the whole of the blade. This was what Aetius had meant by direct intervention.

Lysander became kinesthetically aware of just how overextended the wolf was. Dropping one foot behind, he released the pressure he'd been holding Shade's sword away with and stepped sideways, once more throwing the wolf off balance and sending him forward. Lysander swung the runic blade again and landed the blow in the same place as before, this time cutting into flesh and bone beneath the damaged armor.

The undead wolf yelped and howled with pain, dropping to his knees at the foot of the plinth, below the pulsing orb. He flopped over onto his damaged back, leaning against the plinth for support. His legs sprawled at odd angles to his body and did not move. His damaged muzzle bore a twisted grin on its unharmed side. Black fluid oozed from the corners of Shade's jaw.

"I see you've met Aetius," he coughed. "Of course the old man wouldn't leave things be. Do it then. Put an end to me, and live forever with the guilt that you were the one who destroyed your own teacher. Your friend. Your partner." He laughed, rasping, a sound like tar being gargled.

Lysander's chest hurt, and his eyes stung. Had it really come to this? Could he?

What would Cyrus have done?

He would have done what he had to do. That was the answer. That was the answer that Lysander had avoided since their first retreat from this place, and from the battle where Cyrus had been lost. Cyrus had done then what he had to do in order to protect the others. To protect Lysander.

The fox no longer attempted to hold back his tears as he raised the blade once more. The runes glowed brightly now, and the aura surrounding the blade warmed the very air around it.

"I love you, Cyrus," Lysander whispered.

The blade came down with a crash.

The orb, now split in two, ceased to glow, and fell to the stone floor, shattering into thousands of tiny shards.

Lysander dropped the sword to the floor where it clattered, forgotten. The fire wall died down, allowing Shay and the others to approach as well.

The fox knelt by the remains of his love, leaned in and kissed his lifeless muzzle, and began to weep.

Within the bounds of the Circle, first the outline, and then the features of Cyrus appeared, his body the same glowing blue as the circle's energy. Fellwyn knelt at the circle's edge, directing her magic to power the summoning. Cyrus wouldn't be able to stay long, Lysander knew, but long enough. He had to be here for this.

"Lysander," Cyrus said. His voice sounded hollow and faded

in and out as if it were being blown on an inconstant wind. "Fellwyn, Shay, Faythe, and of course Jace. I've come to say goodbye."

"Hey, buddy. Good to see you one more time," Shay said, giving the wolf's spirit an affirming nod. Jace stood close to him, a silent guardian.

"I'm sorry to have to see you all like this, but I'm glad I'm able to be here, and to tell you all farewell in person. Though I will no longer sit at your tables, laugh with you, or fight with you, know that I am proud of all of you. Especially you, Lysander. Without your courage, I could never have been freed."

Faythe sniffled.

"Your battles are not over. I know that Necros fled, and that he will be seeking a way to improve his new creations. He remains a threat, but you, all of you, together, whether new adventurers or long-time friends, will prevail if you stand together."

Lysander struggled not to cry, but Cyrus looked to him, placing a translucent paw on the fox's cheek. "Don't grieve for me, love. You carry my sword and you carry my memory with you. I'm never gone as long as you fight for what is right and remember fondly our time together. Pass on what I taught you, and pass on what you have learned for yourself." The wolf's white eyes stared deep into Lysander's. Many a time he had thought he could lose himself in those eyes. "I will always love you."

"I love you too, Cyrus," Lysander wept.

"In the end, you all have the strength within yourselves to prevail. Not just the power of magic or the skill with a blade or bow. You have the power of friendship. Your bond will hold you to the quest and to each other."

Cyrus's image flickered, the details of his outline becoming softer and less distinct.

"My time seems to be coming to an end. I am sorry I will not be there in person to see your triumph, but I will be with you in spirit."

Lysander drew his sword, Cyrus's old runic blade, raising it vertically, the flat side towards his face and the cross guard at eye level. The archaic duelist's salute that Cyrus had taught him felt right.

The others all made similar gestures of honor and of farewell, each maintaining their composure as best they could

Cyrus gave a wag of his fluffy lupine tail, and raised his paw in benediction and in goodbye as his spirit faded away entirely. The circle's glow returned to its low, nearly imperceptible dimness.

"That was the most intense thing I've ever had to do," Jake said as he loaded his costume gear into the trunk of his car. His armor now safely tucked away, he felt strange in cargo shorts and an anime con t-shirt. Tom grinned. There were still remnants of makeup and spirit gum in his fur from the undead makeup.

"You played it beautifully, hon. Seriously it was all I could do not to break down crying the whole time you were talking." Tom leaned in and kissed Jake's forehead.

"If you *ever* make me cry that much in a game again, I'm going to hit you with an actual stick, and not one covered in foam!" Sandra said, glaring playfully at the couple. She now wore a tank top with a faded band logo and black slacks. Flecks of blue paint remained on her muzzle where Faythe's markings had been.

"Hey, it wasn't my fault!" Jake said. "I wasn't the one who set the whole thing in motion. Blame Plot!"

"Johnathan says he's going to be scarred for weeks after this. Shay is already apparently making plans to dump all of his hoarded treasure into an armed expedition across the ocean to go take out the source of Necros's power or whatever. I don't even know. He goes overboard—no pun intended." The vixen chuckled. "But seriously though, that was awesome. I really appreciate you guys playing it so hardcore."

Jake's ears warmed. He never knew how to respond to compliments like that. "I just did what had to be done, you know?"

"Well, you came through with flying colors as far as I'm concerned," Tom said, draping an arm over Jake's shoulders.

"What's that line again? 'When I left, I was but a student. Now I'm the master'? Kinda fits Lysander now, doesn't it?"

"Don't do that. I don't like being looked to as the leader."

"Well tough shit, my dude! Looks like everybody's gonna take their marching orders from the sword-fighting fox now. I think Faythe is going to start calling you *Master* Lysander just to needle you a little more," Sandra said, laughing. "Ok, I gotta get going. I'll see you guys in a few months. You've got my number and I'm on three different messengers, and seriously if you don't keep in touch I'm going to drop you on your head."

With that, the vixen trotted off towards a scuffed up but serviceable hatchback parked nearby, started it, and drove slowly away up the gravel and dirt road leading away from the camp.

"Want to say any more goodbyes before we get going, hon?" Tom asked, looking down at Jake. Jake grinned up at his wolf.

"I think I'm done with goodbyes for the weekend, honestly. But a few 'see-you-later's would be okay."

"Fair enough... *Master* Lysander."

Jake glared at the wolf, then leaned in and kissed him. "Don't make a habit of that. We'll see how bad things get in October." Together, the two of them headed for the tavern building to say their last see-you-laters.

Bios

ALLISON is a Vietnamese-American writer based in Texas. She has anthro fiction published in ROAR, Zooscape, Infurno, Arcana—Tarot, Symbol of a Nation, Difursity, and Wolf Warriors. Some of her non-anthro fiction are featured on Tor.com and Locus recommended reading lists. When she isn't writing about dysfunctional families, talking animals, and cultures real and imagined, she's studying medicine and caring for axolotls: her favorite critters and the closest thing she has to Pokemon. You can find a list of her published short fiction here: https://allisonthai.wordpress.com/short-fiction.

KIRISIS "KC" ALPINUS is a passionate and deeply sensitive writer who can usually be found with her nose buried in a book. Her works have appeared in *Inhuman Acts, Bleak Horizons, ROAR Volume 9, Give Yourself a Hand*, and several more. When she's not writing, she's usually working on ignoring her growing army of miniature figures that need to be painted or growing her "To Be Read" pile. Oh, she also is a political science graduate student who studies conspiracy theories and social media's effect on voters. If given a choice on what type of animal she could be, it would be a hard pick between a dragon and a dhole. Find her at @Darheddol or @Swirlytales on Twitter.

Originally from Great Britain, **BILLY** now lives in Washington State, where he enjoys hiking, playing guitar, working towards obtaining a pilot's license and fursuiting when not writing. His work has also been published in anthologies such as 7 Deadly Sins, Wolf Tails and FANG Volume 8.

STEVE COTTERILL lives in the UK, and has had stories published in various online magazines, as well as in anthologies. They have self-published a novel, A Strange and Sudden Fury, and Forest Brides a collection of stories. A gamer, history and folklore enthusiast, they have an MA in Creative Writing from Birmingham City University and currently live with their partner, and two lovely, if silly, pets.

DANIEL is a Pennsylvania-based writer of historical fiction, noir, and fantasy. His works have also appeared in anthologies such as 'Wolf Warriors V' and 'Even Furries Hate Nazis.' His first novel, 'Aces High,' is on shelves now. Follow him at http://www.twitter.com/Greyhound1211 for all his latest musings.

ROYCE "SIR TALEN" DAY is the fifty-something author of the popular *Red Vixen Adventures* sci-fi romance novellas. Day also created the dystopian *For Your Safety* science-fiction series, and his short stories have appeared in Armoured Fox Press' collections *Purrfect Tails, This Book is Cursed,* and in Furplanet's *The Reclamation Project: Year One.*

If you wish to purchase his works, they can be found at Amazon.com.

Alternatively, you can support him at Patreon: https://www.patreon.com/RoyceDay or Ko-fi: https://ko-fi.com/royceday.

NIGHTEYES DAYSPRING is a known troublemaker who is rumored to have a penchant for coffee and an interest in dead, ancient civilizations. He has been actively writing furry fiction since 2010, and his stories have appeared on *The Voice of Dog* podcast and various anthologies including *Heat, Fang,* and *Werewolves Versus Fascism.* He also co-edited *Dissident Signals,* an anthology of dystopian furry literature. Currently, NightEyes resides in Florida with his boyfriend, where in his spare time he masquerades as an IT professional. For updates on his writing, visit nighteyes-dayspring.com, and for day-to-day nonsense, follow @wolfwithcoffee on twitter.

JADEN DRACKUS, or Jay Dee is a dragnox from Maryland. He has been writing furry stories since 2010 and writing for publication since 2016. A historian by training, he was inspired in his youth by science fiction and fantasy, and now tends to write in those genres and historical fiction primarily. Jay Dee lives with his boyfriend. When not writing he plays video and card games, builds plastic models, and reads. He is an alumnus of the Regional Anthropomorphic Writers Retreat. His current project is his first novel that brings his favorite sport of stock car racing into a furry world.

His stories can be seen in Foxers or Beariefs also from Armoured Fox. Shadow has appeared in The Infurno from TH Bound Tales, Fang 10 and the upcoming Fang 11 from FurPlanet. Jay Dee can also be found on FurAffinity and SoFurry as JadenDrackus. His silly observations on life can be seen on Twitter: @JadenDrackus.

TONY GREYFOX has been writing science fiction and fantasy for longer than he likes to admit. His works, ranging from dieselpunk to near future SF to slice of life, have appeared in a number of anthologies. He lives outside Vancouver, B.C. with a fascinating cast of characters, a corgi and way too many trailing plot lines.

THURSTON HOWL is an erotic horror writer and an HIV rights activist. Their book *Blood Criminals* was nominated by POZ Magazine as Book of the Year 2020. They live with their husband Weasel and their dog Temerita.

FRANCES PAULI writes anthropomorphic and speculative fiction. She is the author of the Serpentia and Hybrid Nation series along with numerous furry short stories.

Her books have won 2 Leo awards, 2 Coyotl awards, and her book, *Disbanded*, was nominated for an Ursa Major. She lives in Washington State with a menagerie of pets and far too many houseplants. You can find all her work and a few freebies on her website: francespauli.com.

ANEAL POTHULURI is an aspiring author living in Austin, Texas with his family and two dogs. He is an avid animal lover, and considers writing stories with anthropomorphic characters to be his passion. He is honored to have his short story, "The Medjay's Son" to be his first published piece of furry fiction included in *A Swordmaster's Tale*.

Aneal has a love for storytelling and has dabbled in all types of genres, including fantasy, historical fiction, romance, and horror. While not furry in nature, two of his short stories "The Scarecrow's Hat" and "Whispers From the Void" have also been published in the anthology *Wicked Writing, Volume 1,* edited by Megan J. Meehan. He looks forward to crafting more tales for your enjoyment for many years to come.

JAMES PRATT has been writing horror, fantasy, and sci-fi short stories as a hobby for over ten years. His stories have appeared in a number of anthologies including *Urban Temples of Cthulhu, Dark Hall Press Cosmic Horror Anthology, Sunny with a Chance of Zombies, Corporate Cthulhu, How the West Was Weird Vol. 3,* and *These Vampires Don't Sparkle.*

JAMES STONE is the pen name of Syr Otter. He discovered his love of furries in 2001, and first tried his hand at writing stories in furry worlds in 2011. His previous works are "Blink" in *Bleak Horizons* from Fur Planet and "Cat Problems" in *Dread* by Weasel Press. He can be found as @jamesstoneraven on Twitter.

CHRIS "SPARF" WILLIAMS is a writer, actor, retro-gamer, and sometimes podcaster, hailing from the Washington D.C. metro area, where he lives with his husband and any pets which may have found their way into his life. He has been editor of *FANG* vols. 10 and 11 from FurPlanet, and has had stories published through multiple furry publishers. He was the 2019 Coyotl Award winner for his story "Pack" in that year's *New Tibet* anthology *Patterns in Frost* from Sofawolf Press. In his spare time he helps administer the organization responsible for the Regional Anthropomorphic Writers Retreat (RAWR), a residential writing workshop focused on furry work. When he's not staring at words on a screen, he sometimes disappears into the woods to hit his friends with foam-covered sticks.

Manufactured by Amazon.ca
Acheson, AB

13374531R00214